DANCER IN THE BULLPEN

BY

CHANA SHINEGBA

© 2024 copyright Jaded Ibis Press

First Edition. All rights reserved.

Printed in the USA. No part of this book may be used or reproduced in any manner without written permission from the publisher, except in the case of brief quotations embodied in critical articles or reviews. For information, please email: info@jadedibispress.com.

ISBN: 978-1-938841-27-9

Cover and interior book design: Nicole Roberts
Cover art illustrator: Mariona Lloreta

This book is also available in electronic book format.

Shinegba, Chana

Dancer in the Bullpen / Shinegba

PROLOGUE

Selah

At first glance, there was nothing special about it; just another summer Monday in 1975, the sun rising with no red carpet, hidden in the haze of Brooklyn's clouds. It was early morning, and the streets were anorexic. I imagined school children sleeping in, next to disarmed clocks, as I watched first-shift workers hustle to punch in. The city felt indifferent, exhausted yet hesitantly open, as if daring for a miracle. The chalk-matted sky muted fluorescent graffiti on the cracked concrete canvases whizzing by. I could smell my favorite challah bread baking behind rolled-up security gates. Delivery trucks idled, sighing pipe smoke curbside, as rows of brownstones turned into one long brick wall, preventing the trucks from getting in, or maybe us from getting out.

"Hey baby, don't worry, aight? He just laid back like his papi. If I were him, I wouldn't want to come out either." Your father's right hand was sandwiched between my sweaty palm and ripe belly. I was riding shotgun in his black Cadillac Deville and usually would scold him for navigating with only one hand on the wheel, but this morning I had hoped his touch would ignite some movement from you. For the last several days, you hadn't danced in my womb like usual and I was worried. Though Dr. Edelman dismissed my concern, it had been three weeks since you were due to make your grand entrance, so it was time to give you a much-needed push.

Without taking my eyes off the street theater, I engaged your father with some agitation. "I don't know why you keep saying 'he.' Our baby's a girl. I've seen her in my dreams, Mike, and even your daddy saw a vision of pigtails and pink lace trimming when he touched me last week. Did you see his face? That was real, Selah. My daddy sees Jesus at his dinner table every Sabbath ... and actually speaks to him. Are you really taking his superpowers seriously?" I looked at your father, and he could see that my smile had jumped out the window a block back, so he softened his tone a bit.

"A girl, huh? Ok, what we gonna name her?"

"Well ... I like Nicole."

"Hmm, Nicole. That's cool," Mike said. "But will she reach her goal and be a queen in control with a name like Nicole?" Your father straightened his posture and gripped the steering wheel tight, impressed by his own wordplay.

"Oh, you a poet now?" I shot back, unable to muffle my laughter at his amateur rhyming.

"If I am, it's 'cause of you, baby. I be checking out those poetry books of yours. All I'm sayin' is, this world's fate depends on strong Black women like you, resilient and beautiful." Your father pulled his hand from my belly and gently caressed my face, eyes still on the road. "Our daughter could be anything—an activist, a world-traveling performer, spreading love to the hopeless. So, if it's ok with you, I'm gonna think of another name."

I easily submitted, because I didn't have the energy to focus on anything other than bringing you into this world without too many bruises.

***

I don't remember many of the characteristics of the hospital I spent the next two days in. It seems irrelevant now. But I do remember everything was white and quiet, except for the loud shrill noise of a mother and child bouncing off the walls like they were in a ping-pong competition.

Dr. Edelman said if you didn't take a turn, he would have to cut me open in the morning and go in and get you. You still hadn't shifted your legs or wiggled your toes from the nest of my flesh, and I had been in my hospital bed for ten hours, drip needle stuck in arm, waiting impatiently for you to make your reveal.

"Mommy, sing to me."

I was frightened at first, gripping my belly in a protective hold. Though the voice was clearly feminine and angelic, I looked at your father, who was peacefully sleeping next to me in the recliner chair, limbs awkwardly hanging over the armrests and foot extension.

"Mike, did you say something?" I frantically whispered. But his silence just stared back at me. I pulled myself up and my eyes quickly cased the room, the only parts of me dilated. All I could see was an empty bed adjacent, waiting for the next expectant mother. The walls were coated with years of dried condensation, envious of the window's view of the full moon as it brushed shoulders with Crown Heights high-rises. I wondered where the werewolves were, and then, if I was losing it.

"Mommy, sing to me."

Time glitched my mouth ajar, until I finally took a chance, hoping not to be discovered by reality. I quietly asked you: "What should I sing?"

"Who's singing?" *Your father lazily woke from his stupor, catching the tail end as usual. He wiped drool from his goatee, stomach loudly grumbling like clockwork. It was easier to redirect.*

"I'm ok, just going a little stir-crazy. Nothing yet, still waiting on her."

Mike grabbed my hand. "Baby, sometimes these things take time. We been waiting on her for almost three years now—prayers, body prep, temperature checks, and down-to-the-minute wild position screwin'. She's coming ... but just taking her time, ok?"

"Ok," *I said, trying to mute my anxiety.*

"So listen, baby." *Mike leaned in close, whispering.* "You still got some of that leftover jerk in the fridge?"

Ridiculous. I knew your father would be hungry. I packed him some snacks for this very reason, but of course, he ate them as soon as we arrived at the hospital.

"Yes, but you need to hurry and eat fast. Nothing is certain," *I warned, already regretting the words coming out of my mouth.*

"I'll be fast, baby, I promise. It's all gravy. And I know she ain't makin' any moves without her papi. Come on now, girl," *he bragged, right before open-mouth kissing my closed lips. Your father was a lot to handle, but undoubtedly a charmer. It was difficult to reject that wide smile and seductive tone, even when he was spitting nonsense.*

He hurried out the door, leaving a trail of blown kisses, and now you and I were alone.

We were both still at first. I was waiting for you to ask me again. But when you didn't, I drummed up some courage, dropped my head down, and explained myself. "First of all, I can't sing. That's why me and your dad played jazz records and let Nina Simone serenade you all these months. Is there something you wanna hear?" You responded with silence. I couldn't tell if you were sleeping, angry, or had just lost interest. "Ok, love, fine. Mommy will sing to you."

And so I did—an off-key original. "Baby Poo, Baby Poo, Baby Poo, I love you. Baby Poo, Baby Poo, Baby Poo, I love you."

I knew it was a silly song, but it made me calm. I began to feel your weight again, the heat from your skin, your limbs stretching, like a dancer in the bullpen before a big performance. So I sang it again, and again, and again. And like magic, there they were, the heels of your feet pushing up against my stomach, gurgling your liquid air.

"Ok there, girl, slow down!" I screamed. Rebellious, you flexed and pointed your toes, practicing pirouettes on my organs, using my voice as your orchestra. I immediately stopped singing, replacing its rhythm with deep methodical breathing. But it was as if I was opening my mouth wider and belting out louder, because you just kept dancing, leaping down into my pelvis, singing like a mermaid under the sea ... and then, splash! You broke my water.

"Ahhh!" I screeched. This time, the attending nurse came in. I think she was not only new to the hospital but new to the profession itself.

"Mrs. Abadie, you ok?"

What a silly question, I thought, sitting in your ocean, unable to close the curtain of transparency on my face.

"Ok, let me get the doctor," she corrected herself, hearing my thoughts clearly.

As the nurse rushed out the door, a blue hummingbird appeared outside my window, tapping methodically on the glass, like it was trying to send me a message but I couldn't understand it.

"Hey little one, what are you doing here?" I asked. It didn't feel strange talking to a bird, after I had just been speaking to you. The bird stopped tapping like it was going to respond, and for a moment I waited for an answer, until you stretched your limbs again, making me wince and scream out in pain. "Ahhh!"

The bird started tapping the window again. But this time in a rapid frantic rhythm, fluttering its wings, like it wanted to fly, but couldn't—or wouldn't. It was as if you two were talking to each other.

"Oh, look at what we have here," Dr. Edelman said as he walked into my room with a big smile. His bifocals hung on to the top of his nose as he put on medical gloves and lifted the hem of my hospital gown. I nervously chuckled at the thought of them falling on the edge of my vulva, magnifying his view. Dr. Edelman and the nurse shot each other looks sharing telepathic concern. Ok, so maybe I was flirting with delirium, but I could finally feel you, and my emotions were overzealous, trapped in a tight room, bumping into each other. Someone might have thought I was drugged, but no, a natural birth was always the plan ... to feel every part of you enter this world through me.

Suddenly, I thought about the hummingbird and whipped my head in the direction of the window. It must have gotten quiet when the doctor entered my room, because there the bird was, just sitting on the ledge, its beautiful ocean-hued wings glowing under the moon's light. It looked at me, and then flew away.

"Well, this is it," Dr. Edelman concluded, looking back up at my face. "Your baby is ready." I refocused my attention to the challenge in front of me, and I was petrified.

"*Asshole.*"

"*Come again?*" Dr. Edelman responded, perplexed. *I didn't realize I was insulting your father out loud.*

"*Can someone please call my husband to tell him that I'm having his baby now?*"

"*Yes ma'am,*" the nurse answered.

"*Thank you,*" I responded softly, realizing this privileged southern belle might be my only partner in this thing, so it made sense to be a bit more friendly.

"*No problem, Mrs. Abadie.*" The nurse left as I was being wheeled into the delivery room. It felt like you were clutching and squeezing my uterus with your small hands every five minutes, reminding me that you were anxious for a new view. In my peripheral, a post-delivery table was all prepped for you with tools and accompaniments, and the light above prevented me from making out the faces in the distance between my knees. I saw the nurse appear next to me on my left side, one hand in mine, elevated and close to my shoulder, while the other was supporting my back as I tucked my chin down to my chest.

"*Deep breaths, now. I'm right here,*" the nurse whispered.

"*Ok, on a count of three,*" Dr. Edelman commanded. "*… 1,2,3, push!*" It was 10:02 p.m. My contractions were on top of each other, and you had finally submitted to leaving the old stage. No more dancing, just the tingling of your head in my opening.

"*Ok, Mrs. Abadie, your baby is almost here now,*" the nurse assured, words stretched wide in her country drawl as she continued making eye contact with Dr. Edelman.

"*I think this one is it*" the doctor said. "*Again, on a count of three … 1,2,3, push!*"

"*Ahhh!*" I screamed, giving it all I had, feeling you enter the world. It was 10:12 p.m.

"You did it!" the nurse exclaimed, almost laughing with happiness, but mostly in awe. "You have a beautiful baby girl."

"Yes, my princess," I softly responded, shaking with fatigue, my adrenaline masking the pain. But then my heart stopped with the silence. "Why isn't she crying?"

I desperately asked anyone who could answer. But no one did.

I was flat on my back now, attempting to lift my head to see what Dr. Edelman and his team were doing on that table with you, but I was now a solid ton of concrete, throbbing from the pressure of pushing. The nurse left my side and walked over to you, assuring me it would be ok, but not looking confident. Still nothing, just some loud suctioning sounds and mumbling. I was terrified at the thought of your death, but Mike had convinced me a long time ago that miracles didn't die.

"Baby Poo, Baby Poo, Baby Poo, I love you." Through my tears and with a trembling voice, I sang your song.

After the second round, I heard you let out the most clamorous cry, and Dr. Edelman exclaimed "There you are, baby girl!" while his medical team clapped with relief.

Perfectly swaddled, the nurse finally placed you in my arms. And at that very moment, time halted, and you began to glow. A warm honey-gold illuminated from your skin out into the waiting room, forcing the other physicians and nursing staff to take a step back, yet unable to turn their heads away. This organic light guided your father to our side, without him even realizing it.

"Oh my god, baby, I'm so sorry! There was a fucking accident around the corner. Was something wrong? They took forever letting me back here. Damn baby, I'm sorry!"

"Mike, Mike, shhh. Come here and meet your daughter."

Your father could barely catch his breath when he came over and looked at your delicate face. The room's overhead gleam was dull now, yet his eyes were squinting from the brightness of your light. They welled up with tears from the pressure of his love and relief. "My god, Selah, she is you."

"No, she is us."

"What do you think changed her mind?" your father asked, looking like Vietnam and civil unrest had never happened. He had not a care in the world, bouncing you in his arms while pacing the room.

"I don't know for sure, but maybe because I sang to her?"

"Ahhh, so you were talking to her when I was sleeping earlier, hmmm?"

"Ok, yes I was. People say you supposed to talk to your baby, so it's normal," I said, though I didn't tell your dad I was certain you were talking to me too.

"There was this hummingbird at the window right before it was time for me to push," I continued, still amazed at the experience. "It was so strange, because it was too late at night for birds to be perched up on window ledges. And it just kept tapping on the glass, like it was trying to communicate something."

"Wow baby, that's weird. You sure it wasn't just Mama's gas?" your daddy asked you with a self-amused laugh.

I couldn't help but laugh too, but it still was baffling.

"Babe, what's a hummingbird doing up so high?" Mike asked. "Don't they fly low to the ground ... you know, close to the flowers and shit?"

"Mike, watch your mouth! And actually, they fly pretty high. Just not in the middle of the night like this ... unless they're migrating." I let out a long sigh. I was too tired to contemplate further.

Suddenly your father stopped pacing, pulled away from your gaze, looked at me, and backtracked to the previous topic. "Selah, I'm sorry I left you. I didn't think she would come so soon."

Of course, I forgave your father. It was difficult to stay angry while watching him fall in love with you.

"So, you sang to her and then what?" he asked.

"Mike, it was like I was a snake charmer. She was grooving and even singing to the sound of my voice."

"Oh yeah, a little Jo Baker, huh?"

"Yeah, but then she scared me. She wouldn't breathe. Like she wasn't ready, or maybe testing me to see if I was."

Your father came over and sat on the edge of the bed, gently giving you back to me. He leaned in, and kissed me again with an open mouth. But this time, mine was too. After coming up for air, he said, "You can't rush magic, baby," and then we both kissed the top of your head. The warmth of our bodies intensified your glow and the heat rose to the ceiling, painting the gray maize-gold.

The nurse returned, smiling at the vision of you. "Do you two have a name for her yet?"

Without hesitation, your father responded, "Yes. We'll call her Nina Josephine Abadie."

CHAPTER ONE

"Remember, we didn't see Chad today, baby." This is Selah's third attempt to convince Nina's fragile mind of her false truth, riding up an elevator that can easily carry a herd of elephants. Maybe it just seems massive in contrast to Nina's four-year-old body.

"Yes Mommy," whispers Nina with her usual soft, submissive voice. She holds Selah's hand tightly just in case the elevator drops suddenly, like in her nightmares. Watching the floor numbers quickly climb to the top of their Brooklyn high-rise apartment, Nina keeps repeating Selah's words in her mind. *We didn't see Chad today, we didn't see Chad today.*

Nina is afraid of making a mistake, like when an adult asks her to spell her name. She wants to be a good girl for her mother, but is distracted by the pink tights violently itching her inner thighs. Her ballerina bag suddenly feels heavy, weighing down her right shoulder even though the only items in it are her ballerina shoes.

Selah is also nervous—but more so—stunning. Mile-high legs that stop at the top of Nina's bun, milk chocolate skin, lean but voluptuous curves in all the right places. A full mouth, sad-but-kind eyes, and a soft dark-brown cotton afro. She mimics an *Ebony* model and Nina is her fair-skinned sprouting replica.

Chad is Selah's coworker, and he's a hungry butterfly. He often finds Selah's scent, follows, and eagerly flutters behind her. Though he'll never have the opportunity to taste her nectar, he appreciates every moment he engages in conversation with the most beautiful woman he has ever known. Selah never asks him to hang out but allows him to self-invite, not just because she feels sorry for him but because he's funny and she enjoys the attention. However, earlier today, Chad didn't just want to be near Selah, he needed help. He'd been afraid of getting fired and only trusted Selah to give him the best advice.

Nina doesn't understand why her mother is so concerned about not telling Sam they saw Chad.

He's a friend, like Sam. What's wrong with everyone being friends? Sam doesn't even live with them. He has his own house with his own family in it, but Nina sometimes wakes up with him there, unknowingly beating her to the bathroom, making her hold her pee like when on long road trips.

As Selah opens the apartment door, she takes a deep breath in, and Nina watches her closely, waiting for her chest to exhale. Still, it doesn't happen, or maybe Nina is distracted by Sam's jovial singing. He belts out the lyrics to "I Will Survive," as he sways his hips in the foyer to the melodic groove of the sweet-voiced songstress, like he's the opening act for an Earth, Wind & Fire concert.

Sam has a wide smile, perfect white teeth, and smooth, almost purple-dark skin that looks like he just rubbed himself down with coconut oil. The chain of his gold lion medallion twinkles every time he makes the slightest movement. His face is cleanly shaven, and his hair is cut so low it blends in with the shade of his skin, almost making him appear bald. Nina always feels he could wear a pants size larger and a shirt size smaller. He exudes a deep tone when he speaks, slow and rhythmic, patient and calculating, like he's marinating on every thought before he voices it. He's charming, kind to Nina, and always looks like he won the lottery when laying eyes on Selah—even if she's only absent for a few hours.

"Hey sweeties!" Sam boisterously greets.

"Hi Sam!" Nina reciprocates with the same energy, running to hug him.

"How was your day?"

"Good, baby," Selah blurts out, hoping to halt any chance of a mishap. Sam met Chad a couple of times. Once outside Selah's office, the other time coincidentally at a local coffee shop Selah and Chad were dining at. Sam disapproves of their friendship because he knows Chad wants more.

"How was ballet, Nina?" Sam interjects, giving Selah the "let her talk" side-eye.

"Good," Nina whispers, pulling back from his embrace, head down, scratching the back of her left knee with short-cut nails but finding no relief.

"It's pretty late. What did you two do afterward?"

Nina shoots Selah a glance but receives no buoy, and answers in a way she predicts isn't quick enough. "We got cheeseburgers."

"Oh yummy, you guys forgot to bring me one," Sam accuses jokingly. Relentless, he continues the interrogation, kneeling and finding eye contact with Nina. "Where did you go after you ate those delicious cheeseburgers?" Sam's hands are gently clasped to both of Nina's upper arms, as if he is preventing a fall, even without unstable ground.

"We went to the park," Nina responds with a slight smile in her voice, unable to completely reject the recollection of unexpected fun.

Sam's expression plummets, giving Nina a cold blank stare like he's searching for his own response elsewhere. And then, like the flip of a light switch, he gives her the biggest smile she has ever seen and lets out a hearty chuckle. Nina feels anxious and nauseous from the roller coaster of emotions. "Well, well, what a day, ladies!" Standing up slowly, Sam now seems content and relaxed. "Come here and give me some sugah, woman," he demands, reaching his hand out to Selah, who is still standing by the apartment's front door. Selah struts over, carrying her signature seductive grin, and allows Sam to swoop her into his arms for a warm embrace and a heavy kiss on her mouth.

Selah uncomfortably pulls away and looks down at Nina. "Come on, baby, let's get you out of those itchy tights," she says, cheeks flushed.

As Nina follows Selah to the back, the living room décor is screaming her name for another playdate. Nina has taken many rides on the maroon vinyl couch, pretending she is playing captain on a spaceship, or nestling herself in the round orange beanbag chair in the corner. The white wooden end tables displaying matching fluorescent green lamps are her cafeteria and medical stations. And, of course, there is the magic mirrored coffee table. When she requests at least three wishes from her reflection, one of them is always granted—if she says it loud enough.

"Not now. I have to change my clothes first," Nina whispers to her playmates.

Selah glances back at Nina, smiling. "You talking to yourself again, princess?" Nina doesn't respond, and instead lets the bright yellow-and-blue beaded curtain hit her in the face as she passes through the doorway to the back rooms, happily knowing she'll return to her own world soon. Nina doesn't like discussing her private world with her mother because the more she knows, the more opportunity Selah has to take it away if she doesn't like it or thinks it's dangerous. Nina was born seeing life in magic form, so she is protective of it.

All of Nina's clean clothes are in Selah's room, some in a tall woven basket between piles of old college textbooks and battered notebooks on the floor. The others are nicely folded in military-styled rows trying to stay uniform on the king-size waterbed. Selah helps Nina change into her favorite pink and white sweatsuit before she rushes back to her rainbow room to see if Sam will play with her. He always has an exciting story or a new adventure he takes Nina on, like when he let her sit on his lap and steer the wheel of his sports car when he was driving. Nina felt like such a big girl, unlike with her mom sometimes, who never lets her do anything grown-up like that.

Sam is sitting on the vinyl spaceship watching the news, something about an actor running for president. Nina is beside him on the couch, not daring to speak, as he seems focused on the television screen. Selah comes from the bedroom with another clothes basket. "I'm gonna throw these in the washer machine. Be back in a minute. Nina, be a good girl."

As soon as the apartment door closes, Sam turns to look at Nina. "Hey sweetie. Tell me again what you did after ballet class today?"

Nina's body tenses up, and she suddenly has to pee. But she remembers what Selah said. *We didn't see Chad today; we didn't see Chad today.* "We went to get cheeseburgers and then went to the park," she whispers, again with her head down.

"Oh yeah, that's right," Sam responds. "The park must have been fun. Did you go on the slide?"

"Yes."

"And then what?"

"And then Chad pushed me on the swings." Nina immediately knows she's made a mistake and is terrified. "No, wait, I mean, Mommy pushed me." Tears well up in her eyes, and she feels like she has to vomit.

Sam's face remains gentle when he says, "It's ok, Nina. I'm not mad you saw Chad. You're a good girl for telling the truth."

Even though Sam doesn't seem mad, Nina's sure her mom will be. *Maybe Mommy will be ok. Sam seems ok.*

Selah walks back into the apartment with an empty basket and sees Nina and Sam playing spaceship adventure. She barely reaches the edge of the rainbow room when Sam stands up, staring at Selah with an evil, menacing look. Nina has never seen a look like this outside of the television screen before. Selah looks at his face, drops the basket, and yells at Nina to go to her room, but she doesn't listen.

Sam walks up slowly to Selah and slaps her face so hard she falls to the ground. "Oh, so you saw Chad today?" he asks in his usually deep and methodical tone, but this time, he sounds like a treacherous monster from Nina's storybooks.

Nina is balled up on the spaceship crying, begging Sam. "Please don't hurt my mommy. I'm sorry!" But Sam ignores her plea and keeps kicking Selah as she's lying face down, gripping her fingers into the long strands of the golden rug, unable to hold on each time his foot hits her legs, thighs, and waist.

"Please, please stop. I'm sorry. I won't see him again," Selah desperately promises.

"What did I tell you? Huh?" Another kick. And then another kick. And then another kick.

Nina feels she has to do something to save her mommy, even through her sobs. She has to be brave; she is the captain of her ship. Sam towers over Selah, unaware that Nina has balanced herself on the edge of the spaceship's arm, waiting for the right moment. She jumps on the monster's back, gripping his neck, fingers entangled in his medallion. Unbalanced, he begins to stagger, clumsily turning in circles to loosen Nina's grip. It's just enough time for Selah to rise up as Sam finally swings Nina off him, into the captain's beanbag chair that saves her. Selah begins to back up, avoiding Sam's bloodshot eyes, carefully maneuvering closer to Nina.

"Where you think you goin', bitch?" Sam's agitation is unwavering, but he's out of breath from the strain of his assault. Nina extends her frail arms and grips each side of her captain's chair, trying hard to ignore the sudden cramping in her legs.

"Ouch," Nina winces, closing her eyes and dropping her head back, enduring the sharp stabs in the back of her calves. She is scared and confused. What's happening to her body?

"Nina?" Selah questions, afraid to discover what's happening.

Nina doesn't hear her mother. She's micro-focused on fighting the piercing pain, so she can be ready for the monster's next move. She straightens her posture, scooting up straight in the chair, eyes locked on Sam. Her vision is blurred by the mysterious dust finding its way into the pockets of her eyelids. Nina feels her body temperature skyrocket and is certain that she's melting, like soft ice cream left out under the hot sun, but her body is dry. Her eyes are watering, desperately trying to flush the dirty invasion.

Am I turning into an alien? What's wrong with me? I can't move, I can't see. A second feels like an hour, and Nina only has the strength to dig her fingers deeper into the edges of her captain's chair.

"Don't think you gonna be saved by your dramatic daughter. She just faking," Sam accuses, noticing Nina's body tremble, yet dismissing any reason to be a human.

"Oh god, Nina baby, you're shaking—your eyes! Mommy is so sorry, princess. Are you ok?" Selah is crying with despair as she takes the final steps toward Nina; without hesitation, Sam lunges for the mother and daughter duo, but trips over the laundry basket, disoriented. He can't find his balance and falls, ass first, into the magic mirrored coffee table. It shatters, and Nina is immediately released from her trance.

"Sam!" Selah screams. This time, Nina chooses not to move or say a word; she just wipes her wet eyes and continues to stare at the monster, embracing a new sense of relief as her body temperature suddenly drops back down to normal and the pain in her legs disappears.

Sam attempts to get up but his legs buckle, plopping back down into the jagged shards, punishing him again. Selah calls 911 but she doesn't come to his rescue.

"Selah! Help me, baby," Sam begs, with only a hint of guilt. Selah ignores him, and lets him sit in his pool of karma.

Nina refuses to move or be held by Selah. She's feeling safe and comforted by her captain's chair. She taps her fingers to the song of the ambulance sirens, and watches Sam's blood, mixed with his cowardly tears, drip onto the golden rug. Nina has never seen a red so bright before, not on television, in her art books, or even in her active fantasy world. And though it should be horrifying, instead it's the most beautiful color she has ever seen. Like she's the one who created it. And now it's her favorite.

CHAPTER TWO

It's as if Sam never existed. His clothes and the lingering stench of musk cologne are nowhere to be found, and the flesh-shattered mirrored table is replaced by a mahogany tree trunk with stunted legs. Not a word is spoken of Sam's disappearance, and Selah promises herself not to expose Nina to any frivolous or questionable suitors again. But Nina sometimes wakes up in cold sweats, after battling memories of the living room warzone and glass weaponry that saved them from evil. If a door closes too hard, or a voice rises too high, the rumbling of fear dances in her belly. The weight of Selah and Mike's broken promise a couple of years ago is already a lot for Nina to carry. It isn't easy being navigated back and forth between her mother and father, struggling with why two people who say they love her more than anything can't seem to save enough for each other.

"But you and Daddy are supposed to live happily ever after," Nina expresses one day while on the way to meet her dad.

Selah is at a loss for words when Nina asks about why Daddy doesn't live with them, but she musters up the truth as she knows it. "Sometimes things just don't work out, baby. Your daddy and I love each other but not in the same way anymore."

Nina doesn't believe her. Her mom still displays the pictures of herself in the white princess dress in the pretty church castle, just like in the story books where all of them are still happy together. Nina is sure Mommy and Daddy just made a mistake and don't know how to fix it. She wants them to be a complete family again so she won't ever have to miss either of them.

Selah and Mike fell in love at college. They were two of the few African Americans admitted to one of the most prestigious Ivy League institutions on the Northeastern side. Though Selah was a fiery, outspoken girl from the rural South, and Mike a laid-back New York City boy, their love for the literary and dramatic arts brought them together through their study of English and Theater. Nothing much prepared them for the incomparable bond they created through their fight for civil rights and social justice on campus—the walkouts, the sit-ins, the advocacy. And nothing much prepared them for the stress of being Black in America outside of the college space, in a flawed world without faux protective walls.

Their relationship was rocky, but laced with a layer of hope when they agreed to try for a baby, or some may say that Selah desperately wanted a child and Mike agreed to it. He thought he was willing to do anything it took to make Selah happy, and after a grueling fertility journey, they were blessed with the beauty Selah had dreamed about. Nina's light kept Selah and Mike's love warm for a couple of years, until the strain simmering on the back burner moved to the front and began to boil at high speed. Nothing was enough for the both of them, and finally, Mike took the lead in separating their paths, without hostility and without a fight.

Selah and Mike now live a neighborhood away from each other. Nina spends every other weekend with Mike, which usually becomes every other weekend at his parents' brownstone, where Nina gets an authentic home-cooked Caribbean meal and perfectly braided cornrows from the hands of Grandma Rosa. She is the only person on Mike's side of the family who can manage Nina's small head of unusually long, thick hair. "We have to tame this mane so everyone will know you come from a good family," Grandma Rosa explains to Nina while conquering her tangles.

Shortly after Nina was born, Grandma Rosa wanted to clip a clothespin on her nose to thin it out, for the same reason the wild locks had to be restricted. But Selah refused to let that happen. "I know you mean well, but your granddaughter has your son's nose—wide and beautiful. We don't need to whiten it," Selah said.

The one thing Grandma Rosa refuses to alter is her traditional cooking. Curry chicken, rice and peas, fried plantains, and cow's tongue with a bit of yellow mustard. She chops up her staple supper in just the right-size pieces for Nina to devour each visit. "Slow down, bella, before you choke," she warns, amused at how quickly Nina abandons the plastic baby fork and digs her chubby fingers deep into the rice, clutching chunks of chicken gold, happily licking all the gravy residue clean from her palms.

What Nina never looks forward to is bath time with Grandma Rosa's long sharp fingernails. "She's always scratching me, Daddy. Like she's washing my butt with dog's teeth," Nina complains. "I'm a big girl now. I can wash my own butt!"

"I think she wants to make sure you get the hard-to-reach spots," Mike defends. "But I'll talk to her and see if there can be a compromise."

Nina has no gripes about Grandpa, despite the rumblings from cousins that he may have owned his own people in a past life because he's so mean. Nina doesn't experience any friction and enjoys his quiet coddling. He isn't the most emotionally expressive man, similar to her father, but he shows up to every one of Nina's ballet recitals with Grandma Rosa. "How does someone so small move so big?" he asks as Nina puts the audience in a trance, as usual. Though Nina is one of the middle grandchildren, she feels the warmth of being the favorite. Selah agrees, believing it's partly to do with Mike also being the special middle child—the most intellectual and fairest of the three siblings, which seems important to Grandpa.

Scooting back from the kitchen table after a gluttonous Sunday dinner, with a Santa gut hiding his worn leather belt, Grandpa taps his right knee and says, "Doll, come talk to your grandpa a minute, and let me tell you a story." Sometimes that story is something he's shared the last time Nina was perched on his lap. Often it is a brand-new fable, but it always involves mangoes and rainbows, kings, queens, and Maroon warriors from his Caribbean homeland of Jamaica, or his brave survival fighting for America in the Second World War. Nina adores Grandpa's stories because he takes her to a place that resembles her mind, and he talks funny, singing his words and sometimes adding a "*cha*" at the end of a sentence when excited. Selah explains to Nina that Grandpa's unique way of speaking is called an accent, a reminder of where he comes from, and Nina can't wait to explore there.

Despite the "no fun on Sabbath" house rules, the discipline and structure of Grandma Rosa and Grandpa's home is a warm place Nina feels safe in, and she loves them for it. But it's Uncle John who is Nina's favorite person. He's incredibly tall, lean, and good-looking despite his chronic acne and awkward mannerisms. Uncle John is kind, quiet, and the youngest of Grandpa and Grandma's three sons at age nineteen. Nina is happy he's still living at home with them, making him consistently available for Nina's entertainment during her visits.

"Do you go to school, Uncle John?" Nina asks.

"No, not anymore, lil' one. I just finished high school and have a job now," he responds, putting *The Catcher in the Rye* spreadeagled on the plastic-covered couch so he doesn't lose his page.

"Oh, then why you reading?' Nina questions.

"Because reading is fun, you learn something new each time you read something, and you should learn something new every day."

"Why?" Nina asks, still intrigued and not satisfied.

"Because the more you learn, the smarter you are, and then it's harder for people to trick you and tell you lies."

"I can't read so good yet," Nina confesses with her head down.

"That's ok. You will soon," Uncle John responds gently, now looking Nina directly in the eyes.

"I can't write so good," Nina presses on, attempting to convince Uncle John of her shortcomings.

"You know, they say kids who are slow like turtles have so much in their brain that it takes a little longer for what they know to come out. It's ok. Soon, you'll be reading and writing like you dance."

Nina smiles wide, basking in the warmth of Uncle John's comfort, and says, "Ok, can you read to me?"

And so begins a tradition of Nina and Uncle John reading to each other each time they're together. Dr. Seuss to Shel Silverstein to Maya Angelou. Fairytales, tragedies, newspapers, books of haiku poetry. Even the Bible is explored, to avoid any backlash from the elders for participating in non-Sabbath activities. Not being able to watch television has its benefits.

***

Selah and Nina don't attend church regularly. Still, Selah makes sure her daughter has a beautiful dress, fancy lace tights, and perfectly polished church shoes in every weekend bag she carries anywhere, especially when going to her grandparents' house. It's been ingrained in Nina's head that God is the one who makes all things and all people. He loves and protects everyone … even the bad ones. Nina says grace before meals and her prayers before bed, but she's never actually seen God or felt him. Mike tells Nina that God don't make no junk, but Nina isn't so convinced after the bloody Sam incident.

Nina doesn't like how strict and boring church is, and Grandpa and Grandma Rosa are faithful parishioners. She can't wear her pink bubblegum lip gloss or sparkling fluffy earrings Selah won for her at the city fair. Everyone is forced to be silent and only speak when reading big words from the Bible, which Grandma Rosa describes as the most important book in the world. It seems no different than the others Uncle John reads to Nina, just more people and stories in it. There's also a leader who stands at the front of the church and tells people what to do—when to talk, sing, stand, and sit. There's music, but it's mostly read from another book that Nina is intimidated by. The songs sound like the poetry Selah reads to her, with a funny-sounding piano in the background. Grandpa and Grandma Rosa's church is not like Grandma Daisy's: the one Nina attends when visiting Selah's side of the family. The people there seem to have more fun, jumping around and screaming and singing with big drums and guitars.

"Hey, flip that frown upside down. This will be different. Your Grandma Rosa is singing this morning. Have you heard her sing?" Uncle John asks discretely.

"I dunno," Nina says, forgetting to whisper. She's distracted by the regret of not sneaking her cherished Barbie doll into the church with its pink princess purse.

"Well, you're in for a treat, lil' one," Uncle John assures with pride. It's rare that he smiles when speaking, so Nina pays attention.

"Why is she singing a song today?" Nina probes.

"Someone who has been worshipping in this church for a long time has passed away, gone to Heaven, and Grandma Rosa is honoring him."

"That's nice of her," Nina says, genuinely looking forward to seeing Grandma Rosa, who came to church early to practice before the rest of the family arrived.

After twenty minutes of standing up, reading, sitting down, and listening, Nina can't take it anymore. She leans in toward Uncle John and asks with a big sigh, "When she gonna sing?"

Uncle John can't hide his amusement and says, "There she is, look!"

Grandma Rosa slowly stands up from the left side of the front pew and walks up to the center podium. No one can keep their eyes off her. Her black Cuban mane is swept up in a disciplined bun, complimenting her mournful ensemble—an onyx silk dress with an accordion-style turtleneck that drops and stops just past the knee, accented by modest black heels. Even without her usual matte burgundy lipstick or pearl barrettes, Grandma Rosa sparkles like a magical diamond. Her deep dark-brown eyes find Nina in the congregation, and then she parts her lips and begins to belt "Amazing Grace" in an operatic soprano.

The first note rides on a feverish gust of wind, circling Nina's delicate body, landing deep in both eardrums. The second note rises high and freezes, carving rows of goosebumps onto the skin at the back of her neck. The stained-glass windows begin to shake, forcing the glass to pop out of their frames. Nina grabs Uncle John's hand, but he doesn't seem to notice. The walls of the church dance with an intense rhythm before violently collapsing around them, miraculously not striking anyone.

"Uncle!" Nina screams, but he doesn't hear her. "Grandpa!"

Nina leans over her deaf uncle, attempting to capture Grandpa's attention. Nina suspects he must hear what she hears, see what she sees, 'cause he knows God pretty good. But he seems to be deaf too.

The roof lifts and rotates up like a flying saucer, melting into the sun, which is high-noon blinding, so Nina can't question it—ask why this is happening. The earth is quaking, and her teeth clank together like cowbells. With great physical strength, she turns her head back to Grandma Rosa, and submits to the pull of the spirit the Bible talks about. No one is jumping up and down or clapping their hands, but God is here. And for the first time, Nina sees him.

"Do you see him, Uncle John?" Nina whispers this time, hoping to get a reaction.

"Who?" Uncle John whispers back, confused.

He hears me, Nina thinks, feeling validated but nervous to speak her truth now. She wants to tell him that God is standing right next to Grandma Rosa with one hand on her shoulder, while the other is bracing the back of her neck. And that he's just like Daddy when he and Nina are waiting for the green light at the street corner, keeping her safe.

"God is standing beside Grandma," Nina whispers to Uncle John. "You have to see him, Uncle. Do you?"

Uncle John is learning fast about Nina's visions and how important they are to her. "Yes, I do, lil' one," he reassures. Even though he doesn't really see him, he does see Nina.

Nina walks out of the church that God shook down hand-in-hand with Grandma Rosa and Uncle John, making them carry her weight so she can swing her legs off the curb toward Grandpa's car.

"Did you like church today, bella?" asks Grandma Rosa.

"Yes," Nina replies without hesitation, looking up at her and smiling warmly. Nina is continuously in awe of how pretty her grandma is despite her age. And now, to hear her sing! It's as if she's God's favorite. "Grandma, you sang so nice."

"Thank you, sweet child," Grandma Rosa responds, squeezing her hand gently.

"Did you feel him next to you?" Nina asks.

Grandma Rosa glances at Uncle John, who smiles and looks down at Nina, allowing his mother to answer. "Who?"

"God," Nina responds nonchalantly.

"Oh, well, yes, of course. I always feel God next to me. Actually, I feel him all around me, inside me, all of the time."

"Really?" Nina is amazed. "You feel him right now?" She crawls into the back seat of Grandpa's car.

"Yes," Grandma Rosa responds with pride.

"Your grandma is an angel on Earth, like you, doll," Grandpa says as he starts the engine.

Nina is impressed with Grandma Rosa's connection with God, even though she didn't say she saw him—only felt him. Nina wonders if that matters. What she does know, is Grandma Rosa is special, and God loves her.

✳✳✳

"Hey, baby girl!" Selah yells as she opens her apartment door wide to greet her greatest gift.

"Hi Mommy!" Nina swoons, running into Selah's arms.

"Did you have fun with Daddy this weekend?"

"Yup," Nina responds, looking down at her feet because she hasn't seen him much the last couple of days, but she doesn't want to tell, get her daddy in trouble, and have him be mad at her. Nina considers Mike perfect, even when he's wrong—which Selah rarely is. Nina knows her daddy loves her, but he doesn't say it often like her mom does. It's as if Selah is on a mission to tattoo her love on Nina's heart and mind, but Mike is not really sure how to apply the glue, and that makes Nina insecure, more insecure than she already is about him leaving her. She tries to be a good girl for him, so she'll be worthy of being stuck too.

"She spent a lot of time with my parents and John this time, 'cause I had some important last-minute errands to run," Mike admits. Selah rolls her eyes and continues to engage Nina enthusiastically.

"Want to take a ride with your mama?"

"Yes! Where we going?" Nina questions with excitement.

"It's a surprise!"

"Aight, baby girl, your papi will see you next time. Maybe we'll plan a trip of our own soon," Mike reassures, bending down to hug and kiss Nina, attempting to suppress his guilt. Nina lets her daddy hold on a little longer than usual before darting to her room to drop her bags and find a suitable princess dress in her closet for the special outing with her mommy.

Selah softens. "Thanks Mike. She seems happy. Give your family my love, ok?"

"Yes, of course," Mike responds, slowly turning to walk out the front door. He stops and turns around, not realizing Selah is right on his back. Their closeness makes his blood temperature rise. "So, um, Nina saw her grandmother sing for the first time yesterday at church," he shares proudly.

"Oh yeah? That's nice. That must've been powerful for her to see. I know Mama Rosa has an incredible voice," Selah says, looking up at Mike with warmth in her eyes. "Do you still sing to Nina? She must know you have the same voice."

"Come on now, I don't have the same voice, woman. But thank you," Mike responds softly. Trying to keep the conversation flowing, Mike continues. "You still thinking about moving for school and putting Nina in that Quaker school?"

"Yes, we're still moving. We'll work out a plan, Mike, don't worry."

Mike isn't worried about Selah taking care of Nina. He just already misses them. He loves how brilliant and beautiful Selah is without effort. He tries not to stare at her curvaceous hips peeking out of her micro jean shorts, or the contrast of her smooth brown skin against her white t-shirt, but he can't resist commenting. "What you got on?"

Selah looks down at her shorts and chuckles. "What you mean? I look fine."

"Nah, I mean your perfume. What's that? It smells good."

"Oh yeah, it's Charlie by … Revlon. I think you bought it years ago, so thanks," Selah responds flatly, all of a sudden annoyed that Mike is flirting, when he's the one who wanted the divorce. Her mood drops back to a cold temperature.

"Mommy! Can you help me put my dress on?" Nina pleads from her room.

"Ok Sel, I'll see you soon," Mike murmurs as he retreats out the door.

***

Nina loves car rides with her mom, as they're rare. Most of the time, Selah keeps her cocoa-brown Corvette covered on the street and walks most places with Nina in the city.

The car was a steal. Her boss at the Jewish deli she side-hustles at gave it to her as a gift before moving to Europe. "A girl who's about to save the world shouldn't deal with the burden of transportation," he said.

Nina knows how much her mom loves the car. The only time Selah's loyalty to it was doubted was when Nina fell off a family friend's bunkbed. The friend's kid had given up the top bunk a few nights for Nina, and it was the only night

DANCER IN THE BULLPEN

Selah forgot to tuck the quilt deep under the mattress, so as to keep Nina's wildly restless body from plummeting—which was exactly what happened. Instead of taking the most efficient method to the hospital, Selah swung Nina over her shoulder—open chin wound and cracked teeth in tow—and sprinted a full mile for medical attention. Nina has always wondered why her mother didn't trust her car that night. *Maybe her love was faster.*

"Mommy, why we always walk when you have a car?" Nina asks.

"It's cheaper, and that's how you get to see life," Selah teaches. But on this day, a splurge is in motion.

Selah straps Nina in on the passenger-side first. The seat belt, which should strap a chest, grips Nina's neck so tight she can barely move it to look up and out of Selah's driver-side window—the only way she can watch the tops of buildings whiz by. Selah skips around the back of the car and jumps in, immediately flipping off her white platform heels and tossing them on the floor in front of Nina's dangling feet, which are strapped in Minnie Mouse sandals.

Nina giggles. "Mommy, you like my dress?" Her dress is Pepto-Bismol pink and way too big. It has so many ruffles and sequins it's hard to tell if there is a specific pattern.

"Yes, you look like a beautiful princess!" Selah confirms.

"Where we going?" Nina asks, even though she already knows. They're headed to get ice cream like they always do on special happy days, and her mouth is already watering.

"It's a surprise!" Selah exclaims, using her fingertips to shift gears, coming to a red light on the parkway. Nina can't stop giggling because her mother always tells her about the surprise before the surprise, but she plays the game anyway.

"Hey goddess, goddamn—you fine!"

33

Nina almost jumps out her seat when she hears the strange man's voice yelling at Selah from the passenger side of a white, dented van with pictures of paint buckets all over it. Selah looks at Nina. "It's ok, baby," she assures.

"Hey goddess!" The strange man repeats. "Wanna race?"

"Who am I racin'? 'Cause you in the passenger seat!" Selah yells back fearlessly, partly flirting but mostly daring.

The driver, looking like the strange man's twin, leans over with slight hesitation, body language lacking confidence. "I'll race you."

"Oh yeah? You sure?" Selah teases.

The driver doesn't like the questioning. "Girl, you should just call me God. I'm the best. I. will. Smoke you."

"Ok, bet," Selah says with a wide grin, unfazed. "I'll show him God," she mumbles to herself.

"What you say, Mommy?" asks Nina. But Selah doesn't respond. She's already in a winner's trance.

The light turns green, and cars are approaching from behind, but Selah couldn't care less. "On a count of three," she instructs. Both men let out a dark-rooted laugh, underestimating Selah, which she is accustomed to. She looks over at Nina, smiles, and instructs. "Hold on tight, baby!"

Selah counts down. 1 ... 2 ... 3! *Screech*! Eight tires grind hard on the pavement, and Nina is silent, clutching her seatbelt, watching her mother deliriously laugh at the men in the white van who look like they're about to win. She's riding so close; Nina can see the torn red console lining inside the van. Selah presses down harder on the pedal and grips the steering wheel tight. Nina's head is stuck to the back of her seat from the pressure of Selah's speed. She quickly leaves the men in the dust, slowing down only to the yellow light's warning.

"Mommy?" Nina whines with fear as Selah comes dangerously close to the car in front of her, abruptly stopping right before tapping the bumper.

"Ha! Suckas!" Selah yells, looking back at the losers with pure delight. She turns back around and tilts her head back, forcing out a deep exhale, finally looking over at Nina's worried little face. "It's ok, baby. We're alright," she announces, but Nina is still trying to find her courage. "Oh, come on, princess, wasn't that fun?" Selah is high on adrenaline, satisfied that the white van didn't dare pull up next to her again.

"Kinda," Nina responds, hesitant to tell Selah she hates when her mom drives too fast. She's simultaneously happy they're still alive and also scared: feelings she will soon get used to.

"Mommy?"

"Yeah?" Selah responds half-heartedly, a bit distracted. She's forgotten which ice cream shop they're headed to.

"Why that man call you a goddess?"

"Goddess?" Selah hasn't even noticed. Men call her all kinds of names all the time. "Oh, he just thinks I'm pretty, baby."

"He said he's God 'cause he thinks he's pretty too?" Nina questions.

"Yeah, and fast, which he's neither," Selah explains, laughing at her own response. But then she realizes the conversation is a bit inappropriate for mother and daughter.

"You said you were gonna show him God, Mommy. Did you? I didn't see him like I saw God at Grandma Rosa's church. Is it the same one?"

"You saw God at Grandma Rosa's church?" Selah asks, pulling into the ice cream shop parking lot. She parks the car and turns to Nina to give her full attention.

"Yeah, when Grandma Rosa sang. I saw God standing next to her, and he made the church shake and go crazy. It was kinda scary, but I liked it," Nina responds.

Selah now remembers Mike mentioning her daughter hearing Grandma Rosa for the first time. She struggles to hold back tears. "That's beautiful, Nina."

Selah means it, even though she's worried about the distance between her daughter's grandiose fantasy world and reality. "And no, baby, that's a different God. The only one you should care about." Selah kisses the top of Nina's head and asks softly, "Now, who wants chocolate?"

CHAPTER THREE

"The problem is your baby is too cute and happy," Rachael warns. Rachael is a self-identified hippie raised by conservative parents from Vermont, just one state above. She's also getting a PhD like Selah and is happy she answered her ad for a roommate. Rachael originally hesitated when Selah mentioned having a small kid, but it's working out since Selah doesn't mind sharing the larger bedroom with Nina and taking on the larger portion of the rent.

"You're right," Selah replies. She approaches Nina, who's standing in front of the bed waiting patiently for directions. "Ok baby, we gonna have to dress you up a little differently this time."

Selah is anxious, rummaging through Nina's dresser drawer, feverishly searching for clothes less than royal. She was denied food stamps last month, so she thinks bringing Nina to the office this time will soften hearts and uncap authorization pens.

"Mommy, these clothes look old," Nina announces with a scrunched-up nose.

"I know, baby. But we need to play a little dress-up game today."

"Oh. So, I'm not a princess?" Nina questions with disappointment.

"No sweetie. Well, you're always Mommy's princess. But today, you're going to be like Cinderella before the ball, a bit tired and hungry," Selah explains to the innocent and naive version of herself.

"You not gonna make my hair like Princess Leia?" More disappointment stains Nina's face. On the first day of kindergarten at her new Quaker school earlier in the year, Selah convinced Nina that the thick buns on each side of her head were how princess warriors wear their hair. And Nina was not a Black version of Princess Leia—she was the original—so there was no reason to be afraid. Nina feels like this is the same kind of day.

"Not today, baby. In fact, let's take out these braids." Selah runs her thick fingers through Nina's released waves, forcing them unkempt. She helps her into worn, burgundy corduroy pants that expose her bare little knobby knees, and an army-green turtleneck that has lost its elasticity. Nina doesn't like her new look but is excited to play this game with her idol.

The social security office is packed with a rainbow of black and brown bodies, all different shades and sizes. Proud, defeated fathers' eyes are weighed to the floor as their spirits, bigger than the limits of the room, graze the ceiling. Small, scared babies cling tightly to mamas' thighs. On one hand, Selah is hesitant to go through with this, as she thinks there are

DANCER IN THE BULLPEN

families more deserving of help. But she accepts that her plight to provide Nina with a good life requires this.

"Fuck it, the government owes us," Selah justifies under her breath.

"Next! Come on, come on. How can I help you?" The impatient social services worker has an unrecognizable accent but a familiar comb-over. Despite youthful and chiseled European features, he wears fatigue as if he's also two shifts past oppression.

Nina holds her mother's hand tightly, sometimes releasing it just a little to let the slippery sweat in between their palms cool. She stretches her neck up in an attempt to see what's past the chewing gum stuck underneath the dirty white countertop, but all she sees is a forest of trees growing from the worker's nostrils, and hears him going back and forth with Selah about student loans, pay by the hour, big numbers, and percentages—whatever that all means.

What's an asset? I'll have to ask Mom later.

"Please," Selah pleads. "That land in Georgia is not really mine, and there's no value in it. Listen, I filled out these forms honestly. I'm just trying to be better for her," she continues, frantically pointing down at her daughter, keeping her eyes on the man who makes all the difference. The worker leans over the counter and looks down at Nina, who immediately drops her mouth into a quivering pout, letting out a dramatically distressed moan. Selah swiftly turns her head down to Nina with surprise, and does her best to suppress a smile.

"Mister, I'm so tired and hungry ... and sad," Nina says, exuding great despair.

Selah's eyes widen, silently telling Nina, *That's too much, stop.*

39

Now the worker is concerned. "When is the last time this child has eaten?"

"Oh no, sir, she's eating," Selah chuckles nervously. "Breakfast was light just because we were rushing to get here. Don't worry, I'm making do, but I do need this help," she quickly explains, scared this white man will shift focus and plot to take her baby away.

The worker lets out a long sigh, keeping his eyes on Nina's melancholy face. "Jesus, fine. I'll be right back," he says, while walking into a back office with no windows. He returns and begins initialing papers without a word or expression to match. With aggressive movement, he stamps the last page. "You're welcome …. Next!"

The two walk out onto the hot gray pavement, passing a long line of more brown bodies. "Mommy, I did good, right? It worked!" Nina exclaims.

"Yes princess. It worked perfectly. You were great."

Nina is relieved and happy her mother is pleased. She feels valued and longs to find opportunities to make her proud.

"Now, remember we're ok," explains Selah. "Even if this game didn't work, and Mommy only has a quarter to her name, I can always take care of you. I just want a little help so we can save and be better. We deserve the help, ok?"

"Ok Mommy. So does this mean I can get a bike now?"

"Not yet, baby. But we can get a Christmas tree. How's that sound?"

"Yay!" Nina is thrilled, skipping down the street. "Can we get lots of sparkly ornaments with angels and candy canes?"

"How about we get one special sparkling ornament but lots of delicious buttery popcorn and sweet cranberries to wrap around it, so we can have fun eating them later?"

"Yeah, yummy!" Nina loves the idea. "Mommy, when can we play this game again? It's fun!"

"Oh, baby, hopefully this will be the last time," Selah responds, as she straps Nina in the passenger seat of her illegally parked Corvette, hidden four blocks from the social security office.

***

One benefit of Selah choosing to return to New England to further her education is that Nina gets to see Grandma Daisy often. Selah describes her mother as an icon, a trailblazer; a beautiful and demure woman whose strength is undeniable, who broke barriers as one of the first Black chief physicians in her city. But Nina simply knows her as Grandma Daisy, the woman who puts just enough molasses on her homemade biscuits, sprinkles the perfect amount of secret seasoning in her country-fried chicken batter, and makes the best collard greens after blessing the stove all day—no matter the season. Selah gets her spirit from her mother, even though Selah says Nina gets hers from Grandma Daisy as well.

"You're such a little Grandma Daisy, Nina," Selah blurts out on random occasions, like when Nina requests to drink her juice from a crystal glass or is caught giggling and gossiping with Grandma Daisy at the corner of the dinner table. "You're witty, sweet, and sensitive. You don't see it now, baby. But one day, you will," she assures, chuckling over the resemblance.

Every morning is the same at Grandma Daisy's house.

"You wash your hands?" Grandma Daisy asks, without pausing from conducting the orchestra of aromas and flavors.

Nina's response is the scurry of her feet to the bathroom sink, washing her little hands with the speed of light. She walks back into the kitchen quickly and sits at the table, waiting for approval.

Grandma Daisy puts her metal spoon down, wipes her hands on her apron, and walks over to Nina, who's swinging her legs back and forth under the kitchen table in anticipation of some good eats. "Let me see those hands. Are you sure they're clean?" she asks, holding Nina's hands in hers, inspecting every inch, bringing them to her mouth and kissing them vigorously.

Nina laughs with Grandma Daisy, always surprised at her silliness. *The kitchen with her is better than any movie.* Grandma Daisy shares rich and colorful memories about her journeys to Africa, her philanthropic efforts and lives she's saved. She particularly enjoys talking about her life on the southern plantation as a kid, the danger of getting spit on by white boys driving by as she walked several miles to school, and the teachers who broke the rules and let her learn more than what was required of a Black girl.

"My grandfather was favored by the plantation owner and was given a house and some land as a reward for picking the most cotton the fastest. We grew everything, from sweet potatoes to okra. I didn't feel poor until your grandad and I moved up north, despite us having jobs that many Black folks didn't have. People think it's better for us here, but in a way it's harder, because of the walls that are built to keep us from the good things we need to survive and thrive." Grandma Daisy has no hesitation in sharing her life and perspective with such a young mind. She knows Nina is smarter than some adults and refuses to sugarcoat anything for her firstborn granddaughter.

Nina wonders if the reason why Grandad is so scary is because the walls blocking him are too high to climb. The energy changes when he shuffles into the kitchen, like his feet are weighed down by discouragement. Grandad is enormous compared to little Nina—tall and wide with a big belly, evidence that he approves of Grandma Daisy's cooking. When Nina looks at Grandad, she sees a big old polar bear, an animal Selah has read to Nina about. You know it can be dangerous, but because it's so big, you foolishly think you can outrun it.

"Hi Grandad," Nina says, watching him drop in the chair next to her, as if he's already tired from the day that hasn't started yet.

"Morning," Grandad mumbles, barely looking at Nina, but watching Grandma Daisy place a plate of hot food in front of him. Most mornings, Grandad is quiet and disengaged. But sometimes he spills his agitation onto the table.

"You couldn't tell me the food was ready, Daisy?" Grandad asks, revving up his anger.

"I knew you would smell it, like you always do, and come to the kitchen when it was ready, like you always do," Grandma Daisy fearlessly shoots back.

The polar bear jumps out of his chair and elevates on his hind legs, now ten feet tall, hissing and growling. Grandma Daisy doesn't move when he charges at her, or when he halts right before he reaches her petite body, chomping his teeth on her personal space. She re-grips her metal spoon in a lunged fencing position, daring the bear to attack, as her granddaughter keeps still and watches, gripping the arms of the kitchen chair and gritting her teeth through the sharp pains in her calves.

Grandma Daisy snaps Nina out of her trance. "Nina. Go wash your hands, then get dressed for church," she calmly instructs, keeping eyes on her opponent.

Nina is scared for Grandma Daisy, but does as she's told, walking quickly to the bathroom and closing and locking the door, so the polar bear won't catch her scent. She pulls the footstool back out from under the sink, stepping up on it to gain easier access to the faucet handles. She feels her body temperature rise, cups the cold water in her trembling hands, and splashes it on her face, like her mother does when the air conditioning breaks in their apartment. Nina looks at herself in the mirror. *What is wrong with me? Why am I hot again, like when the monster was trying to hurt Mommy?* She starts to wash her hands with cold water, hoping it will cool her off, wondering if her spaceship is still nearby.

"Woman! Don't you talk back to me like that!"

Nina can hear the polar bear's roar through the pipes but keeps massaging the bar of soap between her hands, trying hard to keep them steady, and ignoring the faint ache in the back of her left calf.

Meanwhile in the kitchen, Grandma Daisy holds her ground. "Sit down and eat your grits, Joseph," she demands, with a resilient courage that disarms Nina's grandad.

"What? You don't tell me what to do, either!"

"You want coffee?" Grandma Daisy ignores the frigid air in the room, pretending she's questioning the charming husband she once married, and pours hot black liquid into a big white cup. The hungry polar bear turns around and shuffles back to his chair, grumbling.

Grandma Daisy brings Grandad his cup of coffee in one hand, cradling the metal spoon handle in the other, just in case another act of foolishness occurs. Grandad doesn't look up and shovels the combination of grits and pride into his mouth in silence.

Nina jumps down from the bathroom footstool and dries her hands on the only hand towels she's allowed to use—

not the fancy ones Grandma Daisy embroidered pink flowers on. "Those are for stranger guests. We don't want them getting their germs on us," Grandma Daisy had once said.

Nina slowly opens the bathroom door, startled by the gust of warm air coming through the cracked kitchen window. Her body is cool now and it's lost the shakes and aches, but she is unsure what's caused the sudden change. While walking to the grandkids' bedroom, Nina pauses in front of the kitchen's open doorway and sees the polar bear has been defeated. Grandma Daisy is washing her strong metal spoon in the sink, humming a hymn Nina doesn't recognize.

"What you staring at, child? Go on now, put on that pretty dress your mama sent with you. I'll be coming to fetch you soon."

Again Nina obeys her grandma, but this time with no fear, knowing there is nothing to worry about. It's clear that Grandma Daisy has battled scarier things than a tired ol' polar bear. *If Mommy is right, and I'm just like Grandma Daisy, maybe I can be strong like her too one day,* Nina wonders, as she rolls her pink bubblegum gloss over her lips.

***

Nina enjoys collegiate life with Selah, especially when her classmates crowd their small living room for homework, debate, and discussion after class, sometimes into the late hours of the night. Nina sits still and watches the pressure of hot voices rise before erupting like a volcano. If she moves too much, Selah's temperature plummets, making her notice that her daughter is still awake.

"Nina baby, go to bed."

"Ok Mommy."

But Nina doesn't move, knowing her mother is easily distracted. She instead flips through the pages of *Rapunzel*, reading the pictures. She never wants to leave Selah's side, even in the middle of the night when she wets the bed they share. She'd rather tread in a lake of her own fluid than trigger her mother to relocate her to the dry loveseat.

Selah mirrors Nina's adoration and need for closeness. Friends joke that Selah has a permanent dent in her right hip from carrying Nina as a baby. For more reasons than she'll ever share, she doesn't trust most people with Nina. It's obvious that Nina is the most important person to her, which creates an impenetrable armor of protection, along with Nina's self-pressure to be worthy of it.

Some would think Nina is also a student in the Ivy League school, often attending Selah's classes—including intimate lecture circles. Selah instructs her daughter to be patient and sit quietly next to her. Nina mostly complies, except for the days the King of Boring visits, like on the day when the professor provides insight on what will be on the next exam.

"Nina, you can't yawn so loud when the professor is talking. And licking that dirty quarter and sticking it on your forehead really gets Mommy in trouble," Selah complains as she strides long and fast over the street's cobblestone, forcing Nina to shift into a full run rather than walk home.

"I'm sorry, Mommy," Nina apologizes, out of breath, trying to keep up with Selah's pace. "But King Boring came and told me to have fun, or he would take me to his cave where kids can never have fun or smile and be happy."

Selah sighs, reluctant to engage about this cave, but she's anxious to understand her daughter's overactive mind. "Have you ever been?" she asks with hesitation, grabbing Nina's hand as they stride across the street to their apartment.

"Yes, but he lets me out when I promise to laugh and make your friends in class laugh," Nina explains.

"Have you ever seen anyone else in the cave?"

"Yes, sometimes, my friend."

Selah gently pulls Nina's hand down to sit them together on the stoop, since it's such a beautiful day. "And do I know her? Is she from school?"

"No Mommy, she lives with us, but you just can't see her," Nina explains nonchalantly.

"And you're the only one who can see her."

"Yes, but the only thing is …" Nina hesitates, looking down at her shoes.

"What, baby?" Selah asks, happy her daughter is opening up a bit about her secret world.

"I can't really see her too good," Nina admits.

"You can't really see her *well*," Selah corrects.

"Well."

Selah continues to probe. "What do you mean?"

"I can't see her face or her body," Nina shares, trying to trust her mom a little with her world. "I don't know why. She is kinda like a cloud who talks. I ask her to fix it, but she doesn't answer me. She only talks and plays when she wants to."

Selah accepts this explanation, just as the pediatrician suggested at Nina's last checkup.

"As you know, Nina takes her time with all milestones, but once she embraces it, she overachieves, speeding past expectations. I wouldn't worry too much about her vibrant imagination. I'm sure the theatrical visions will pass soon. Just continue to listen to her stories and normalize your response," the doctor had directed.

"And it's ok that she flies to outer space and has full conversations with a cloud, and hallucinates church collapsing because the singing was so loud?" Selah had asked.

"It'll be ok, Ms. Abadie. Nina has a creative and descriptive outlook on the world and her experience with it. Find ways to channel that energy into an activity. You mentioned her dancing back in Brooklyn. Have you continued her classes here?"

"Yes, and she's quite the ballerina. I'm thinking of introducing her to tap too. She seems happiest when dancing."

"That's wonderful. I think that's a great outlet. However, I do believe she is experiencing a bit of separation anxiety. How often does Nina see her father?"

"Often," Selah had quickly defended. "Well, not once a week like she used to. She sees him once or twice a month. It's difficult now that we don't live in the same state."

Switching back to Nina's delusions, Selah made herself clear. "I need you to know that Nina has been traveling to different places in her fantasy world since she began putting words together." Before Nina's pediatrician could open his mouth to respond, Selah submitted, "But alright, I'll wait it out and observe."

✳✳✳

Nina is smart, but school is a challenge for her, despite being poetically gifted. Her kindergarten teacher often overlooks her because she's quiet and compliant: except for the day she writes a haiku when assigned to describe the sky.

DANCER IN THE BULLPEN

Big birds and sun dance
The clouds and rain yell faster
The sky is happy

"Oh my goodness, baby, this is so beautiful!" Selah swoons when Nina brings her work home after the first week of school. "You wrote this haiku all by yourself, princess?" Though Selah has an entire bookcase dedicated to poetry, including Japanese haikus, she can't understand how someone who struggles with reading and handwriting gets this structured expression.

"Yes Mommy. Don't you remember? You taught me. Just write the words you say to the beat of a drum. Five beats, break. Seven beats, break. Five beats again, break. Like when we dance!" Selah looks at her special gift of a daughter and is amazed at how sweet and brilliant she is.

School is not often blue skies and happy times, like when Nina steals Tommy's brand-new red lunchbox the second week of kindergarten. She doesn't take it because she's envious, but to punish him for calling her brown skin dirty. She doesn't tell Selah and takes her punishment in silence. Being misunderstood has its benefits; the fewer real-life friends Nina has, the more available she is for dance practice, learning how to read, and having adventures with the friend no one can see.

Nina's real-life friend Francesca is the only student who looks like her, but unlike Nina, she doesn't keep quiet. Francesca talks back to the teacher, her mother, and even the dogs walking by with their owners. Her mother is also a part of Selah's collegiate living-room circle, but speaks with a sharp tongue like her daughter.

"Why do you have those scratches on your cheeks? And why do you wear those funny clothes?" Francesca asks Mr.

Abu, a friend visiting her mother for dinner. Nina is invited to stay for dinner too, but hesitates to join in the inappropriate interrogation. Francesca is confident in her movement, so Nina feels pressured to laugh in unison with her. Mr. Abu warns the girls not to make fun of what is not understood, but Francesca presses on until her mother snatches her arm and drags her into the back bedroom like a rag doll. As the dance of crying screams bounce their way down the hall, Nina tries to ignore Mr. Abu's stare. She is sitting in the oversized recliner opposite him, attempting to summon King Boring, thinking his cave must be better than this scary silence.

"Don't be a follower," Mr. Abu finally says, before crossing his legs and taking a big sip of the hot herbal tea Francesca's mother has made. He's sitting on the couch across from Nina, yet his powerful energy is brewing in her chest.

"Are you a king?" Nina asks, ignoring the instruction.

"Yes, I am."

"Do you have a queen?"

"Yes, and one prince and princess back home in Ghana, Africa." Mr. Abu smiles, enjoying Nina's colorful curiosity.

"I am a princess too, but I live here in America with my mom. She's a queen, but she doesn't have a king anymore. She needs a new one."

"The only way to become a queen is to be kind and brave," Mr. Abu advises, revisiting his original point as he slowly gets up to leave. "Tell Ms. Goodwin I will talk to her tomorrow," he says softly. "And you, little princess. Be kind and be brave. Don't follow evil witches."

Mr. Abu smiles, showing his white gapped teeth, and walks out the door with an empty stomach. Nina stands on her tippy toes to lock the top lock of the door as taught by Selah, which her mother describes as a "future habit." Francesca and her mother come out from the back room as if a war beat them both.

"Where did Mr. Abu go, Nina?" Francesca's mother asks, panicked.

"He left, Ms. Goodwin," Nina responds respectfully.

What does she want with someone else's king?

"Go to the bathroom! The both of you!" Francesca's mom pops, oozing anger from all crevices, not because Mr. Abu is offended but because she neglected him to discipline her daughter. Nina and Francesca do as they're told and get their throats choked with soapy washcloths. Francesca's screams find their way through the saturated fibers, but Nina doesn't bother. She keeps quiet and wonders if Mr. Abu went and got a hamburger, and if he knows she's sorry for acting like an evil witch.

Selah doesn't take the news of Nina's mouth cleanse lightly, though no conversation is had. Plans for future dinner visits at Francesca's home are canceled, though there is always an open invitation for second chances in Selah's home, where she can control the environment.

Nina doesn't mind what some may consider overprotection. It's a perfect trade for the indulgence of art her mother exposes her to.

"Everyone is a princess at the ballet," Selah whispers, as Nina watches every extended limb and graceful leap from *The Nutcracker* dancers, with her mouth open and eyes fixed. It's one thing to see the ballet on television, but quite another experience to see it live and in-person.

"I will be great like that someday, Mommy."

"You're great now, and you can be whoever you want to be, baby," Selah assures her daughter.

There's rarely a day off that passes where Selah isn't taking Nina to the library to check out a challenging number of books for the week's exploration. There's rarely a museum exhibit not visited within the first week of opening, a perfect setting for the "What does that image mean?" game. The same imagination Selah fears is the same imagination she has helped to feed, and Nina digests the nutrition with ease.

Lately, however, Nina has been spending more time with Rachael on the weekends. This is mostly because Selah is working overtime for Nina's added tap class; the other times she's entertaining a new beau she met down south visiting a friend. Selah has been guarded since the turbulence of Sam.

"David is different. I think I'm going to introduce him to Nina. What do ya think?"

Rachael absorbs the glare of Selah's glow. "I think this type of happiness should be shared with our little nugget, of course," she responds.

"I agree," Selah cosigns with confidence. Rachael has become an important part of their lives, so her opinion is valued. "I will take it slow. I mean, I think Mike is dating again too, so whatever. It'll be fine." Rachael gives her side-eye and laughs when she denies there are any leftover feelings for Mike.

Selah takes her time facilitating David and Nina's interaction. A few visits to the neighborhood ice cream parlor, an excursion to the kids' theater, and a casual dinner at the apartment help them get to know each other. It's obvious Nina likes him because she's talking a mile a minute, even inviting her invisible friend out of hiding to join. David speaks to the friend like he can see her, despite her lack of response. Nina is now certain he has special powers.

But it's not until David babysits Nina one afternoon that she confirms he's a true wizard. David is what Uncle John describes as "country." He does everything slowly—from walking to talking—stretching his words long and wide, always an easy-going energy. He's light-skinned like Mike, but shorter and wears blue jeans and a plaid shirt most days. He doesn't attend an Ivy League school, but he graduated from a historically Black one, and Nina is already fascinated by how easy it is for him to play with numbers. He loves numbers so much he teaches other people how to play with them too.

David happily agrees to escort Nina to her favorite park. They begin their journey on the cobblestone walkway, as Nina has done many times in the past with her mother.

"Nina, your mom tells me you like poetry. That you've even written a haiku. Can you tell me about it?"

"Um, the teacher told us we needed to tell her what we did in the summer. And we could tell her by drawing a picture or just talking about it," Nina explains. "But I wanted to write about it 'cause I can't draw so good … I mean, *well*. And I don't like standing in the front of the class talking."

"How did you know about haikus, though? That's a very specific kind of poetry. I know because my niece is a writer, like you," David shares with pride.

"Oh, I'm not a writer. I'm just a kid," Nina says with a serious face. "But my mommy has lots of those books from Japan. And she reads them to me and makes me practice reading them to her."

"That's nice, Nina."

"Can we play a game?" Nina asks, refocusing on her mission for the day.

"Sure, what's the game?"

"Can we pretend I'm blind and you're my guide?" Nina asks with excitement.

"Why do you want to pretend you can't see?"

"'Cause I wanna know what it feels like to be blind," Nina responds, as if the answer was obvious.

"Ok, but is there a specific reason why you want to know how it feels to be blind? Do you have a friend at school who is blind?"

"No, but if I'm gonna be a queen one day, I gotta know how people feel so I can help them."

"Ahhh, ok, that makes sense. Learning how to be empathetic is important if you want to rule the world one day."

"Empa-whuh?" Nina questions, perplexed.

"Yes, empathetic," David repeats, excited to provide a teaching moment. "It means just what you said, understanding how someone else feels, like putting yourself in their shoes."

"But what if my feet don't fit their shoes?" Nina questions innocently.

"Um, yes, well, good point. Ok, let me lead you, blind girl," David teases. He can't remember his nieces this age being so inquisitive and self-aware, but it's been awhile since he's been around children.

Nina is thrilled that David is enthusiastic. Selah doesn't usually have time to play these types of games, but Nina thinks her mom is just too scared that someone could get hurt. David successfully leads Nina slowly toward the park's edge, guiding her a little to the left and a little to the right. "Step up. Now step down," he instructs.

Nina diligently follows directions until she throws David a curveball. "Ok, now close your eyes too! I know you have special powers."

"Oh sweetie, I don't know if that's a good idea. My powers aren't that special," David warns, nervous at the idea of double vulnerability in these lily-white streets.

"Yes, you can do it! We can use our powers. It's ok," Nina assures.

David looks around as if he's trying to assess the life-threatening obstacles. "Alright, fine. Let's both close our eyes."

Holding hands again, they both slowly take a step forward. What sounds like a kid laughing on a ten-speed bike crosses their path so close the gust of wind forces their eyes open.

"No peeking!" Nina giggles through her demand.

"Me? What about you, young lady? How can you see me if your eyes are closed?"

They try again, and this time there's no peeking. The swings are about a hundred feet away, and a handful of families in the distance are watching their irresponsible joy.

One step, two steps, three.

Nina can hear the blades of grass chattering around her ankles, and feels the vibration of the jungle gym's rooted metal withstand the pressure of a dozen little bodies trusting it—running and jumping, swinging high to kiss the sky and thanking it for the bright warm sun.

Four steps, five steps, six.

Nina and David stride in unison, being led by their other strengthened senses.

Bystanders don't question their blind emulation. They simply stay out of the way, hoping nothing crazy is about to go down. The two reach the swings successfully with only a few stares on their backs.

"Mr. David, we made it!" Nina brags. "You can open your eyes now."

David slowly opens his eyes, surprised that they're standing at their destination with no damage.

"See, I told you. You have special powers like me."

"I see!" says David. It's obvious to the both of them that they're going to get along great. "How high you want me to push you on the swing?"

"All the way," Nina responds.

***

Selah is not wrong. Mike's also dating again, though his journey gets off to a rocky start.

"Ok baby, so her name is Veronica. She's a radio personality, and her job is super fun! I think you'll like her," Mike explains as he sprays way too much Obsession by Calvin Klein around his collar. Nina starts to cough, watching her father nervously and repetitively tuck his shirt in and out of his straight-leg trousers, making his six-foot-three frame skyrocket to seven feet. Nina has never seen her father take so much time and effort to prepare for anything, and she's jealous that this Veronica person is receiving such intense consideration. Nina is afraid that Veronica must be queenworthy and that her mother doesn't have a chance to get her king back.

"Daddy, what's a radio personality?"

"It's someone who has an on-air position on the radio, like the people you hear Mommy and me listening to in the car.

DANCER IN THE BULLPEN

Sometimes they introduce songs or go back and forth talking to their coworkers about interesting topics," Mike explains.

"Oh. Which one does she do?"

"She reports the weather."

"Oh, that's nice," Nina responds flatly. She knows no one is a better queen than her mother, especially a radio person who tells people when it's going to rain. But Grandma Rosa says Nina is a big girl now. She's almost in first grade and is old enough to recognize that her daddy needs to be happy too.

Nina and Mike are sitting at a swanky overpriced restaurant in SoHo that neither one of them can afford—no matter the amount in Mike's account or Nina's half-empty piggy bank. They wait twenty minutes, which Mike calls being fashionably late, before Veronica walks in.

Veronica looks exactly like one of Nina's Barbie dolls, except her skin is brown, and her boobs and booty are much bigger. She's pretty like Selah, but Nina wonders if she just came from performing on stage like Nina does at the city's holiday shows, because she's wearing many bright colors on her face. Selah says that heavy makeup is necessary so you can be seen clearly under bright lights, or if you're just ugly. Veronica's body is painted in a candy-apple red dress with red six-inch heels to match.

Nina leans in and whispers to her father. "Daddy, you sure she knows the weather? She looks like one of those girls Mommy says walk up and down the street looking for tricks or treats. Wait, I think she just said tricks."

"Shhh, Nina. Smile and be nice."

Nina watches brown Barbie set fire to every table she passes and witnesses her father melt. Mike can't suppress his signature *mmmph* sound, the one that he belts from deep within his belly when a beautiful woman graces his presence. Nina can already predict which women are *mmmph*worthy, and clearly, this Barbie receives a loud one.

Veronica quickens her pace when she sees Mike rise from the chair to greet her, and embraces him like it's been years since they last connected. "Hey, Big Daddy. So good to see you!" she swoons.

Nina doesn't understand why she's calling her daddy, "Daddy." *Don't she got a daddy?*

Veronica looks down as if she has just realized Nina's presence. "Oh my god, Hiiii Nina! I've heard so much about you, darling. I got you something."

Before Nina can be "nice," Veronica digs deep into her oversized Louis Vuitton bag and pulls out a small, battered teddy bear, as if suddenly his freedom is warranted. It's evident this bear has been through a lot and isn't new. Nina tries to hide her disgust as Veronica hands it to her across the high-end candle votives. *Maybe if I push the bear down into the fire, he can die right here and go to Heaven, which Grandma Daisy says is a better place anyway.* Nina can't avoid Mike's stare any longer, and notices the rising concern wrinkling his forehead. "Thank you," she musters, head down and holding her belly, hoping no one else hears it growling.

"Nina, your dad tells me you're quite the little dancer, yeah?"

"Yes, I love to dance," Nina shares, thinking Selah would be annoyed if she responds with a "Yeah." *A yeah sounds like you don't care enough to speak correctly*, Nina's mom always says.

Unable to take her eyes off Mike, Veronica continues, "What kind of dance do you take?"

DANCER IN THE BULLPEN

"I take ballet and tap. I want to take jazz too, but my mommy is worried it'll be too much because my schoolwork gonna get harder soon." Nina knows the brown Barbie isn't listening, just talking to seem interested, so Mike will be happy. *Everyone wants Daddy happy. But Mommy is better than her. He needs to find someone like Mommy.*

"Well, your mom is right. School does get harder, but there's always time to play, right honey?" says Veronica. Mike looks a little uncomfortable as he watches Nina's eyes scrunch up like they do when she doesn't trust someone. Veronica continues, noticing nothing but herself now. "Well, I don't know if your dad has told you yet, but we're thinking about taking a trip to Hawaii! I'm not sure if your mom will let your dad take you so far. I know she's super protective of you. But if she does and you have a passport, then maybe you can come with us, yeah?"

Nina feels the fire that was all around them, now in the pit of her stomach. But it's burning her insides, making her want to scream out in pain. "My mommy will let me go anywhere with Daddy, just not strangers. And you're a stranger," Nina reminds the brown Barbie. "And … you don't need a passport to go to Hawaii," she says with a daggering force, which even Mike has never seen from her.

Again, Nina is disgusted, but Veronica is too self-absorbed to notice her rage. "Oh, right, of course. All these islands we have sometimes confuses me," she admits, attempting to mask her embarrassment.

Nina doesn't waver. "I don't want to go to Hawaii. My Uncle John says it's far. And even though my mommy says we should visit every state in America one day, I think I want to skip the far ones."

"Maybe you'll change your mind one day, baby," Mike chimes in. "Life is sometimes unplanned and takes you to unexpected places."

"Wait, Hawaii isn't a state, love. It's an island," Veronica interrupts.

Nina shoots Mike a look and he drops his head, admitting guilt, the guilt of bringing this Barbie to her, who is not queenworthy after all.

"Hawaii is a state," Nina corrects. "My uncle taught me, so I know it's right."

"I don't think so, sweetie," Veronica persists.

"Yes it is!" Nina is angry, and she feels the tears welling up in her eyes. She doesn't want to cry and put out the fire. She wants this dumb Barbie to burn in her flames.

"Actually babe, Hawaii is a state," Mike confirms, coming to the defense of his furious daughter.

Dinner is cut short. Veronica goes home alone, and Mike allows Nina to throw away the raggedy teddy bear, apologizing for the tough time.

"Daddy, how come she don't know all the states when she a weather girl? How come nobody knows she's dumb? I feel like they gonna find out on the radio faster 'cause people listening won't be able to see her. Is it because she's pretty that nobody cares?" Nina has so many questions and concerns.

"I don't know, baby," Mike admits. He's exhausted and disappointed that this introduction was a failure.

"Is it more important to be pretty than smart?"

"No! Of course not. Being smart is most important."

"Then how come everyone was extra nice to her and gave her everything she wanted, even though she said dumb things, even you, Daddy?" Nina is still upset.

"You're right, baby. Sometimes we're all guilty of looking at only the surface, being lazy with our discovery of people. I'm glad you came to dinner with your papi. You reminded me of what's important."

"So, she's not going to be your new queen?"

"No, princess. My queen needs to know all the fifty states, like you," Mike responds with a wink. "And my favorite girl must agree she's queenworthy," he promises.

Nina tries to believe him.

CHAPTER FOUR

Nina insists she wears her wide-rimmed yellow Easter hat for the wedding. It matches the yellow flower-girl dress and white lace ankle socks with yellow bumblebees on the edges. Nina is adamant that this is the least her mom can do for her, since Selah's making her wear white, patent leather church shoes, despite Nina's desire to go barefoot.

"It's the country, Mom. Everyone goes barefoot."

"Not today, princess. And are you sure you want to wear a big hat like me? No one will see your pretty face."

"If YOU are wearing a hat, I want to wear one too."

"Understood," Selah submits, trying to ensure her only child doesn't feel misplaced. "Who's my favorite girl, no matter what?" she asks with a smile.

"I am," Nina answers softly.

"Who?"

"I am!" Nina yells, borrowing her mom's confidence.

"Good girl," Selah responds with satisfaction.

The wedding has a beautiful, farm country flair. The ceremony takes place in the rural Maryland backyard of David's parents' place, between the chicken coop and fishpond. Nina's new grandpa brings out the family rifle and shoots a snake out of the tree before it lands on the priest's head. David's mother may have lost her hearing, but it's clear she's thrilled her youngest son has found love. Nina can't remember everyone's names and faces at the wedding, but they all seem to love her and Selah. David's family is quadruple the size of Selah's family and friends, but it doesn't matter. The only person anyone can see is Selah. She is perfection in a sheer purple-and-gold wrap dress and a floppy violet sunhat. Francesca is in attendance with her parents (and she is already plotting ways to sneak a rabbit out of its cage) but Nina wants no part of it. She's not interested in a side of soap with her slice of wedding cake later.

All the festivities are a success, and the revised happy family returns to their new home in Baltimore to pack Nina up for her summer trip to see Mike and the rest of his family up north. Tomorrow will be the first time Nina travels on a plane alone, but she is almost seven now and ready to get her first set of pilot wings.

***

Mike meets Nina at the arrival gate, and he looks pretty much the same, plus a few extra pounds. This has been the longest they've gone without seeing each other—almost four months. "Jump in, big girl," Mike says. He still has the black Caddy and still opens the door for his little girl, regal style. "Look at you! You must have grown a couple of inches since I've last seen you." He gleams.

"How's your girlfriend, Daddy?" Nina asks, trying to quiet her rumbling belly as she straps herself in. She can't help but associate food with her dad's new girlfriend. When Nina met Ms. Dionne for the first time, the woman made all of Nina's favorites—including the best lasagna she had ever had, though she would never tell her mom that. Dionne is a great cook, an all-around domestic goddess, and brilliant. She's what Nina calls a numbers wizard, like both her dads. In fact, Mike and Dionne are both bosses in the same company, just different departments.

"Dionne is good," says Mike. "Actually, she's more than that; she's great! So, um, we'll be getting married next summer. I hope you're ready to be a flower girl again." He hasn't started the car yet. His left leg bounces rapidly like he's trying to get a bee off his pant leg. "Dionne is going to talk to you, of course. But I thought it would be nice if you and I have a father-daughter chat now before we see her in a few days."

"Oh, you're getting married, too? That's nice." Nina tries to be happy for her dad, but is worried there will be even less time for her now that he has someone always around.

"Don't worry, princess, you're still my favorite girl," Mike promises in a comforting tone. He can see Nina's little brain working overtime as she pretends to watch the cars whiz by.

"Ok Daddy, I'm happy you're happy."

"How about you, baby? You happy? You still like David?"

Yes, he's nice to Mom … and me," Nina assures. Sometimes she thinks her father secretly wants her not to like David, but then again, that would be mean.

"Ok baby, I'm going to drop you off so you can play with Grandpa and Grandma Rosa. Maybe if your Uncle John comes out of his room, you can play with him too. I have a few errands to run, but I'll be back around dinner time, and then later I have a surprise for you."

"Yay! I love surprises! But Daddy, I don't really play anymore. I'ma be in the second grade soon."

Mike chuckles. "I'm so sorry, princess. I stand corrected. But you still hang out, right?"

"Yes duh, Daddy, I hang out," said Nina, reciprocating his laughter.

***

Uncle John is in his room, just as Mike predicted, which is like an apartment and includes a private bathroom and kitchenette area. Grandpa and Grandma Rosa's home is a beautiful brownstone with three separate apartment-style rental spaces like the one Uncle John calls home. It's nice that as a young man, he has his privacy. But Nina worries he gets lonely up there by himself. She never sees him with any friends or girlfriends—no one. He always says that he's friends with his books. And his music.

"Uncle John, it's me, Nina."

"Come on in, little one." Uncle John is sitting at his desk watching a small black-and-white television Nina didn't know he had.

Nina immediately giggles and asks, "Why are you watching that little TV when Grandpa has a big one downstairs?"

"It'll be the Sabbath in a few minutes, and I don't want any trouble. But you shouldn't follow in your bad uncle's footsteps," Uncle John teases. But there's something a little different about him that Nina picks up on.

"Are you ok, Uncle John? You not feeling good?"

Uncle John looks up from the television and smiles gently. "You're an intuitive little thing, aren't you? I'm just a bit tired. Nothing to worry about."

Nina is not worried because Uncle John always tells the truth. She jumps on his vintage couch, crosses her legs, and closes her eyes in meditation mode, something she learned from Rachel. She lets the blend of mothballs and spring air freshener invade her nose.

"What about you? Are you ok?" Uncle John shifts the conversation, disrupting Nina's tranquility. "I heard your mama got married, and something about a new doggie?"

"Yes, David is Mommy's new king. Mister is my doggie."

"Mister?" Uncle John questions, perplexed.

"Yes, we got him from Great Grandad's house in North Carolina, 'cause nobody wanted him. He looks like Benji ... you know, from the movie. He don't got no parents or a name, and it's kinda too late to give him a real one. I think he just needs to feel special, so I call him Mister, like what Mommy and Daddy tell me to call a grownup or someone important. My doggie Mister is important."

"Nina, I think you meant to say, he *doesn't* have any parents."

"Yes. He doesn't have any parents," Nina corrects herself, letting her uncle mold her speech just like her mama does.

"You know that's a bit silly though, sweetie. It's never too late to name a pet. And to call him Mister just seems incomplete."

Nina's face drops. "I like the name Mister."

Uncle John sees she is attached to the name, feels bad, and shifts the conversation once again. "Ok, Mister's mama. Well, I know your seventh birthday is still a few weeks away, but now that you're getting older and aren't going to be able to visit your favorite uncle so much, I thought I'd give you a gift early. And since the number seven is your favorite number, I thought this year you need a special gift."

Nina loves gifts, so she watches Uncle John open his desk's top drawer. He pulls out a black velvet box and places it in her hand. "You always talk about loving your birthstone, the ruby," he says. "But I've never seen you with one. So, I saved a little and got you this."

Nina's heart is racing as she opens the box. Uncle John is not lying. Nestled regally in the ivory velvet bed lays a bright ruby ring with two tiny diamonds on each side. "Uncle! Wow, is that real?!"

"Yes, so you can't lose it. Wear it on special occasions, like when you see Grandma Rosa sing or visit the church of your Grandma Daisy. Whenever you get scared or something, wear it."

Nina hugs Uncle John and holds on tight with tears in her eyes. She didn't realize how hungry she was for some extra attention until now. She releases her grip and begins to run down the stairs, yelling back: "I'm going to go show this to Grandma Rosa and Grandpa! Thank you, Uncle John, this is the best gift ever!"

Mike is blinded by the sparkle of Nina's new ruby when he walks in the door of Grandma Rosa and Grandpa's house, way past dinner time. Nina has her right hand raised high as if it's perched on a pedestal in an exclusive jewelry store.

DANCER IN THE BULLPEN

"Daddy, you see the pretty ring Uncle John gave me?"

"Oh wow! That's super sparkly and fancy, young lady! A ruby for a ruby. Uncle John must think you're pretty special," Mike says, gently bringing Nina's hand down to kiss it.

"She deserves it," Uncle John responds softly, putting the newspaper down to witness the joy at the front door. Nina gleams and regally paces the room, feeling like a true princess.

"Well, I'm hoping you'll like the special gift I have for you too," Mike announces, interrupting Nina's rhythm.

"My surprise, daddy?" Nina stops twirling and gives Mike her undivided attention.

"Yes!" Mike sits down on the couch opposite Uncle John. "Who wants to go to Disney World with their old papi?"

"Oh my gosh, me! Will we get to see Cinderella and Snow White and the Seven Dwarfs?" Nina asks, exuding excitement.

"We sure will!" Mike assures, pleased that Nina is happy.

She jumps on her dad's lap and gives him a big hug. "Thanks Daddy! When we goin'?"

"We leave tomorrow, so you need to get some good sleep tonight. We have an early flight."

Nina quickly jumps off her dad's lap and gives Uncle John a goodnight hug before finding her other elders to do the same. Nina complies with ease because the reward is so great. She stops herself in her tracks and looks at her father with great concern. "Wait, Daddy! Does Mommy know I'm going? Did she say it's ok? 'Cause you know Mommy doesn't really like me going anywhere too far without her."

Mike chuckles at Nina's check-in, and says, "Um, I'm also your parent. My authorization is enough."

"Oh. So she don't know I'm going?" Nina asks, with even greater concern.

"No baby, of course she knows you're going, and is ok with it."

Uncle John turns down the edge of his newspaper and smirks at his big brother, knowing that Mike had to plead for months to get Selah to agree to Disney World without her. Mike returns Uncle John's expression with an eye roll.

"Oh ok, good," Nina says, and runs to the guest room to fall asleep fast, so tomorrow arrives early.

✱✱✱

First day of the trip to the most magical place on earth, and the weather man predicts it will rain every day.

"It's ok, princess. This is Florida. It never rains long. So, there'll be plenty of sun for us these next few days, I'm sure of it," Mike says, hoping he's not lying. Father and daughter are sitting at the kitchenette table of a modest hotel room near the amusement park, eating the greasy but delicious hot breakfast being offered in the lobby.

"Ok. Daddy, can we get the princess plastic raincoat dresses?" Nina asks, crunching on her favorite crispy bacon.

"You mean the ponchos?" Mike corrects, before taking a big sip of his hot coffee.

"Yes, those!"

"Of course, let's leave soon and gets those in the lobby before we head out. I see the clouds coming in."

As expected, it's pouring rain when Mike and Nina step out of the hotel. They both pull the plastic hoods of their ponchos up, securely protecting their heads from the buckets of water being dumped on them.

"Are you sure you still want to walk?" Mike asks Nina, concerned that they'll be two wet noodles before even making it to the park for the inside activities.

"I don't wanna walk. I want to run and dance there, Daddy!"

Before Mike can protest, Nina has already darted ahead of him, taking wide leaps down the concrete path to her real-life fantasy world. Her poncho hood loses its grip and drops back behind her head, allowing the rain to saturate her thick, full mane. Nina embraces her baptism and free-style dances on the nautical path. She sees the castle in the distance and quickens her pace, widening her jumps, until the ground below her can't maintain the power of her limbs and—*Crash!*—Nina's summer sandals hydroplane and she tumbles forward, using her knees as human brakes, scraping the top layer of skin from both knees— especially the left one—which gushes blood from deep within her flesh. Nina lets out an agonized wail, shifting her body to a sitting position and holding the most damaged wound with both hands, watching blood fight with the rain and win.

"Daddy!" Nina screams, panicked and engulfed in pain. "Daddy, help me!" But her father isn't there. Her eyes dart behind her, in front of her, on both sides of the street. No sign of him. Instead, she sees a gigantic weeping willow tree in the distance, close to the hotel a couple of blocks back. Its highest arched branches are a mile taller than the hotel's roof, and it has two trunks that serve as legs, slowly walking through quicksand toward Nina. Incoherent mumbles are coming from its core, and Nina is afraid.

"Daddy!" she screams again. "Where are you?" Tears are now dancing with the rain on her face. Nina feels completely abandoned and terrified that her father is no longer there and will never return. The weeping willow is moving so slowly—it's barely moving in place—as Nina's knees throb, streams of blood running down both legs.

Nina prays for the first time away from her bed or dining room table. "God, please find my daddy! I will do anything, and won't be bad ever again," she promises, before vomiting her anxiety of being fatherless all over the front of her poncho. It feels like it has been several hours now, as she continues to sit there sobbing with no sign from her father.

"Are you ok, hun?" a passerby asks with guarded concern.

Despite Nina's panic, she still remembers not to engage strangers. "I'm ok, my daddy is coming," she responds, even though she is starting to believe that he is not.

The weepy willow finally approaches, blocking some of the rain with its green hefty body, still mumbling.

"What you say?" Nina asks, squinting up at its lazy branches.

"Nina, you're ok," the willow says with clarity.

"Daddy?"

"Yes princess," Mike responds as he bends down to see how bad her legs are. "You're going to be ok, baby, but we may have to skip the park today. I'm going to need to carry you back to the hotel and fix you up," he calmly explains.

"Ok," Nina responds through the tears, accepting defeat. She can see how bad it is.

Back at the hotel, Mike picks up some rubbing alcohol, abrasion ointment, and bandages from the hotel's convenience store, and administers amateur medical care on his daughter once they return to their room.

"Daddy, are you sure I don't need to go to the hospital? I think Mommy would take me to the hospital."

"No baby. It's ok. I just have to clean it really well, let it breathe a bit, then put this medicine on it and one of these big bandages here. You'll be good as new, ready to start a new day tomorrow."

Nina is not so sure. She still remembers falling off the bunk bed when she was little and her mother hearing her impact, even though Nina was sleeping two floors up. She flew downstairs and ran with her to the hospital so fast, Nina barely remembers the pain.

"Daddy, where were you when I fell? I was yelling your name."

Mike is applying the ointment on Nina's knees carefully, sensitive to Nina's grimacing. "I was coming, princess. You took off so fast, it took me some time to get to you."

"You didn't run for me?"

"What you mean, baby? Run? On the wet concrete like you did? No, I was walking carefully, to make sure I got to you in one piece, so I could help you like I am now."

"Ohhhh, so you *are* the big droopy tree."

"What?" Mike asks, scared to get the answer.

"Never mind," Nina says, remembering her parents don't understand stuff.

Nina has two big white bandages on each of her little brown knees. She looks at herself through the hotel floor-length mirror, and can't help but think about how disappointed her mom would be if she saw her now—hair unkempt, swollen red eyes and matching knees. Nina attempts to enjoy the rest of the trip with the Disney royal family, but she is anxious about life outside of the kingdom.

***

Nina steps off the plane escorted by the flight attendant, looking for her mother's beautiful face in the crowd. Watching Selah's face light up at the sight of her daughter, and then darken with devastation once she sees her knees, is incredibly stressful for Nina. No matter how many times she explains what happened, Selah struggles to accept it.

"Mike, what the fuck were you thinkin'?! You put my baby on a plane with two tore up knees! She's gonna be left with two disgusting scars on her beautiful legs. She's a girl for God's sake! And why you ain't tell me when this happened? See, this is why she don't need to go nowhere with you or nobody fuckin' else! I can't believe this shit! That's it, I mean it. She's not going anywhere else with you!"

Nina watches her mother assault the kitchen phone, screaming at her father, almost pulling the cord out of the wall a few times, then slamming the phone down so hard the base cracks. She has heard her mother curse before, but never this many times using such improper grammar. Selah is the most articulate human Nina's ever known, but she's amazed at how quickly her mother can switch to an uneducated Black girl with no etiquette.

Before Nina's heart can slow back to normal speed after witnessing such intense rage, Selah completely shifts her demeanor. "Nina, I'm sorry baby. Mommy is just a little mad at your daddy for not doing the smart thing in Disney World. Everything is going to be ok. Cocoa butter will keep your knees from scarring, it's ok."

"Mom, don't be mad at Daddy. He did the best he could. You can still let me go on trips with him," Nina says as she hugs her mom.

"We'll see," Selah says, hugging Nina tightly. "I just need you safe all the time."

CHAPTER FIVE

Mister lets himself out the back iron gate when no one is watching, so when a strange station wagon speeds through the alleyway, no one sees him. When Nina hears the wheels screech, followed by a high-pitched whine, she knows something terrible has happened. She looks out the window with her heart in her throat.

"Mister!" Nina screams. She drops her glass of apple juice onto the floor, ignoring its shatter, and runs barefoot out to the back of the house. "Oh no, Mister!" Nina pees on herself a little because she's so scared her best friend is dead. The little mutt is lying on the ground but is still breathing.

"Wait Nina!" Selah demands from behind. She doesn't want her daughter to be traumatized by a worst-case scenario, but Nina is already there, watching Mister miraculously get up and limp over to her.

I'm ok, Mom, Mister says.

"Are you sure?" Nina asks, relieved she doesn't have to figure out how to survive without the one soul that gets her, besides Uncle John.

I mean, barely. This jerk comes out of nowhere, almost kills me, and doesn't even stop to see if I'm ok. Can you believe that shit? Mister is more angry than hurt.

"I'm sorry, Mister, I didn't see it. How are you walking?"

Well, the tire wasn't all the way on top of me, maybe 'cause it wasn't going so fast. I still think I could use a doctor, though.

"Don't worry, my mom is here. She'll take you. And I'm coming too," Nina assures him.

"Nina! Please. Stop talking at the dog, damnit!" Selah interjects with agitation. "We have no time for make-believe. Let me get Mister in the house and call the animal hospital. I don't see any bleeding, but there could be some internal problems."

"Mister was talking to me, Mom! I can't just ignore him," Nina shoots back defensively, angry her mother continues to get in the way. Selah ignores her reasoning and gently carries Mister back inside.

The house is beautiful, with three floors of chestnut wood encased by red clay brick. If there weren't any black iron bars on all the windows, Nina might have had a chance to feel free here. Almost a year ago, when Selah and David moved in, the realtor told them it would be foolish to carpet the floors, but Nina misses the warmth of her toes in plush fabric back in the apartment where Rachael still lives. There is a reservoir across the street, but Nina thinks it's pointless if you can't swim in it. David picked this house because it's the best one on the block, but Selah didn't feel great about moving into a home next to an alley, which is only magnified by this morning's incident.

Nina and Selah impatiently sit in the veterinarian's waiting room, hoping for the best. Nina looks up at Selah, hesitant to speak, concerned her mother is still mad at her for talking to Mister, knowing that Selah can't hear him like her. Selah returns the stare with the same sentiment and simply takes Nina's hand into hers, like she always does when words aren't needed to say *I'm sorry.*

As usual, Nina's thoughts shift with every mental wave that hits the shore. "Mom, when does David come back from his work thing?"

"It's just a quick work retreat. He'll be back tomorrow, baby."

"Do you like driving so far for your job?"

"No, not really. But it's a great job for us, and renting a house this size closer to D.C. gets pricey."

"But the dance school here doesn't have room for me in the classes I want to take. And Mister already got hit by a car. My room has a hole by the window, and there's a lot of creeper crawlers up there."

"Ok Nina, so what you want me to do?" Selah is spent from listening to the issues she's just too fatigued to complain about.

Nina takes a deep breath in and takes a risk. "I don't like it here, Mommy. Do you?"

Selah looks at Nina directly in the eyes, then looks away toward the receptionist as if the old lady has the answer she's looking for.

"Mom?"

"No, I don't," Selah finally admits. Tears well up in her eyes, and she squeezes Nina's hand. "I'm ok, baby, it's just been a long week. But I know you aren't happy here. I can tell. I'll talk to David when he returns, and we'll work it out, alright?"

"Ok," Nina says with a smile.

"Mrs. Abadie?" The receptionist calls out.

"Mom, she got your new name wrong. It's Dr. Chase now," Nina whispers proudly as they both walk up to the counter.

"It's ok. I don't need to be called 'Doctor' here, baby." Selah doesn't have the strength to explain that she hyphenated her last name because she's published with Mike's last name.

The veterinarian reports that Mister has no internal injuries, excluding some minor bruising. "It's pretty much a miracle that a station wagon didn't do more damage to your dog. I want you to give him these meds twice-daily for five days, and monitor him for any unusual behavior."

"Thank you," Nina and Selah respond in unison.

"You have a strong little doggie there," the vet says.

Mister gets a delicious steak treat with dinner and sleeps in Nina's bed. She is surprised her invisible friend didn't come out to see what all the commotion was today. The moon is unusually bright, which brings clarity to Nina's poetic thoughts. The imprisoned windows are less troublesome. Maybe it's because the light is ready to lead her to a new place.

✳✳✳

"Don't be afraid. You're not in trouble, Nina. I'm not going to call your parents. I just want to chat with you a bit if that's ok."

"Ok," Nina responds simply, afraid nonetheless.

Principal Baker is the first African American (well, Canadian) of her kind at Key Lake Elementary School, which is nestled in a quiet, predominantly white Jewish suburb, five minutes away from the only high rise that invades the cookie-cutter single-family homes. She is slightly over six feet tall, with striking dark brown features and a '70s beehive hairstyle that elevates her dramatic presence. Nina finds her intimidating yet incredibly interesting, always anticipating the unique way she pronounces certain words. Mike says it's because the Canadian government is so nonviolent, they had to make at least their language crooked and flawed—whatever that means.

"Nina, Mrs. Anderson mentioned your challenge with completing yesterday's assignment regarding careers of interest. Do you know what assignment I'm referring to?" Ms. Baker probes.

"Yes. She asked us to write about what we wanted to be when we grow up, or what type of jobs we would like," Nina responds with a shaky tone.

"Excellent. And what did you write about?"

"Well, I see the paper right there," Nina says, pointing at Principal Baker's desk. She continues anyway, as it's obvious the principal is looking for more from her. "I wrote about how I want to be a queen and a wife when I grow up. Is there something wrong with that?"

"No, of course not, Nina. It's just that you didn't mention anything else. Don't you agree it's smart to strive to be a queen, wife, and also something that contributes to society?"

"Being a wife is the best thing to be. It's the most important thing. Just 'cause we don't care about queens in America, I still want to be one. Queens do good stuff. They give back to their family, friends, and even strangers. And we get kings who love and take care of us."

Principal Baker is almost speechless until she finds an angle. "So, I take it your mother is a queen, yes?"

"Yes," Nina answers suspiciously, feeling the urge to pee knocking on her pelvic floor.

"And doesn't she have a career?"

Nina sees what Principal Baker is getting at, and she doesn't like it. "Yes," she confirms reluctantly.

"So, I'm thinking that in third grade, like you, your mom thought a little bit about what she wanted to be when she grew up."

"I understand," Nina responds with defeat, wondering how much trouble she would get into if she pees in Principal Baker's fancy leather chair.

"Nina, listen. This paper was incredibly well written. You made me even want to be a queen." Principal Baker snickers, but Nina is not amused.

"I understand you're a gifted writer," Principal Baker continues, "and I hear how articulate you are. Have you thought about being a journalist? Maybe you could write for a newspaper or even be a news reporter on radio or television. You have a great look for it. I bet the camera would love you."

"Ok, so do you want me to rewrite it?" Nina asks, thinking cameras only love models, and if she wanted to be a model, she would just ask her mom to take her to Sears and be one of those girls on their posters. *Or maybe I should train to be a weather girl like Daddy's ex-girlfriend—hypnotize a whole room with my looks, but not know Hawaii is a state. I'm sure Grandma Daisy would be soooo proud.*

"That would be great, Nina. Maybe you can finish your queen story for extra credit—like a fantasy piece."

But it's not fantasy. You're the only one who lives in a fake place.

***

Nina doesn't know why Selah keeps buying these overalls with the difficult clasps. They're almost impossible to get off, especially when in a hurry to pee. Nina would've relieved herself at school, but then she would've missed the bus, forced to walk twenty minutes rather than ride the incomparable five. Regardless, it's not looking so good for her. She reaches her apartment building lobby, legs shaking from the energy it takes to hold her bladder. Only one elevator is working, and it's lit brightly on the eighteenth floor. Nina lives on the twentieth, right under the penthouse, and would give anything to fly right now.

3 … 2 … 1 … *ping!*

The elevator is finally on the lobby level, and Nina quickly jumps in, feverishly hitting the "Door Close" button repeatedly while her legs dance like a grasshopper on hot coals. *Come on, hold it, hold it.* The elevator climbs to 14 … 15 … 16. *Oh my god, please hold it.*

It's ok, let go. You're almost home, please don't hurt yourself, Nina's invisible friend whispers in her ear.

"No, I can hold it!"

Nina can't see her friend's hand, but feels little fingers gripping her shoulder as they repeat, *It's ok, let go.*

As Nina reaches the nineteenth floor, she surrenders to her invisible friend's direction and relaxes every muscle, letting the warmth of her urine run down both legs, soothing her anxiety. She wipes the cocktail of sweat and tears off her face before taking the rainbow-colored key string off her neck to open her apartment door. So as not to slosh her pee-soaked sneakers into the foyer, she takes them off at the welcome mat, knowing she will return later with a trash bag.

Nina takes comfort in the fact that she has her usual three hours of freedom before David and Selah come home from work. But Mister can't hold his pee long enough for Nina to clean up hers. She's forced to put her dirty body in some clean clothes and take the little guy out for a walk. The evidence of Nina's accident is still puddled on the only elevator functioning, but Nina ignores it as Mister struggles some, pacing, sniffing, immediately recognizing its source.

"Shhh, Mister. Don't tell," Nina instructs her companion, who's not so talkative today.

18 … 17 … 16 … *ping!*

"Shoot!" Nina huffs. "Mister, don't tell," she warns again, partly threatening him this time.

Mister glares up at Nina and says, *I won't, Mom, dang.*

Nina looks down at Mister warmly and responds, "Ok, ok, sorry, love you," happy he finally said something. The elevator doors seem to open slower than usual, but it's just James. James from fourth grade, but who should be in fifth grade, or so they say.

"Not because he's dumb, Mom," Nina once explained to Selah. "I think it's 'cause he and his mom were homeless for awhile or something. I think she's kinda mean to him, though."

"If they were homeless, sweetie, she could just be sad and not mean to be angry at him, She could really just be angry at life." Selah doesn't know that James' mom beats him or that Nina knows because he told her teary-eyed in this same elevator just a few weeks ago. It must have been too difficult to hide his

DANCER IN THE BULLPEN

pain anymore, though he made Nina promise not to tell, or his mom would kill him. And Nina doesn't want him dead. In fact, because she knows his secret, she feels a need to protect him.

"Hey," James says.

Nina responds with the same energy. "Hey."

It's not like Nina and James have deep conversations, but they both don't have many friends. They seem to be the only Black kids at Key Lake who live in this overwhelming high-rise apartment building, though it's much better than the house with the bars she and her family left behind.

"Did Mister do that?" James asks, looking at the puddle Mister is still sniffing.

Saying yes would be the easiest and best answer to give, yet Nina can't play her sweet magic doggie like that. "Mister knows how to hold his pee. It must have been another dog or some little kid," Nina white-lies. "Did your mama do that?" she says, nodding toward James' black eye and busted lip.

"She lost her job yesterday. Shit is just hard," James justifies, speaking like a man who's lived far too long.

"What happens when the world burns down or something? What'll she do then?"

"I don't know, hopefully not pee in the elevator," James responds with a smirk, attempting to soften the dark mood while calling Nina out. "Want any salt and vinegar chips?" He knows Nina loves them from when he watched her eat an entire bag for breakfast at the bus stop.

"Nah, I'm good," Nina lies. She just doesn't want James to smell the pee at her doorstep when he brings them to her.

Though Nina hates boys, she still likes any attention from them and longs to get close enough to inspect and understand them. Not so much with James, though. He's easy to

85

read. Other kids from school think he likes Nina more than as friends. But Nina can't imagine that being possible. She doesn't feel pretty with her knobby knees, double layer of shark teeth in her mouth, and the doo-doo braids that Selah forces her to wear. Because Selah never buys enough barrettes to put on the end of Nina's pigtails, Nina has to braid the ends super tight and stick them back up in the middle of the weaved braids, which makes them look like pieces of crap hanging from either side of her head. *What boy thinks that's cute?*

When Nina and Mister get back to the apartment, she runs a warm bath for herself as Selah taught her, not too hot and not too high. *Because even adults drown in bathtubs if not careful,* Selah always says.

Now that Nina is clean, she bags the saturated clothes along with the welcome mat, and throws them down the trash receptacle in the hallway. "All the evidence is gone. Thanks for not helping," she says to her invisible friend, thinking how they're conveniently hiding once again.

I'm sorry. It looks like you fixed everything. I didn't want to get in the way.

"How are you in the way? I can't even see you," Nina complains.

I dunno, says the faceless voice. *What you think your mama gonna say when there's no welcome mat to wipe her feet on?*

"I hope she doesn't notice. But if she does, I'm just gonna have to say I don't know what happened to it. I mean, someone could have stolen it. That's possible."

You don't think she'll understand you couldn't hold your pee? It was an accident.

Nina is standing in the apartment foyer, looking as though she is talking to herself. Though Nina's friend carries a soft tone, it's her confidence that is loud and fills the whole room.

"You told me to pee. I could've held it, but you kept telling me to pee," Nina says, a bit annoyed.

You were in pain. It didn't make sense to hold it and have it hurt you. Better to just let go and clean up later.

Nina understands the point, but still wishes she could've been stronger.

There is homework to be done, specifically the revised career essay, but *He-Man* is coming on, so maybe it can wait a little longer. Nina is not allowed to use the stove when no one is home, so she makes a peanut butter and jelly sandwich and eats it with plain ridged potato chips. She loves the contrast between sweet and salty. It seems wrong, but the union tastes perfect.

Cartoons last longer than expected, and the evening news is already gearing up. "Shoot!" Nina panics. She's not watching the time. She turns off the television and takes a few cubes of ice, and wraps them in a cold washcloth before wiping down the top of the television tube. For a moment, she worries the ice is melting too fast, but she's careful not to electrocute herself.

This is new. David is running late, and Selah's keys jingle at the front door.

"Hey baby!" Selah yells down the hall, summoning Nina out of her room, who's diligently doing homework.

Nina comes to the living room and witnesses Selah massage the top of the chilly tube.

"You watch television today?" Selah asks with a stone-cold face.

Nina contemplates doing something different by actually telling the truth, facing the immediate consequence, and taking the burn to move on faster. But she doesn't. "No," she lies, immediately feeling the urge to pee.

"Nina, come here and touch the top of this thing!" Selah is furious for catching her in a lie. "This TV is cold, Nina. I know you feel that. There's no reason for this thing to be so cold unless you made it that way, covering your tracks," she says with the force of a hippo's bite.

Nina's guilt pushes her head down, but she feels little remorse, resentful that her mother has the audacity to come home early and disrupt her latch-key routine.

"No TV for a week, young lady," Selah reprimands. "And just because David and I aren't here, don't think we won't know what you're up to."

"Ok Mom." Nina withdraws and heads back to her bedroom.

"Wait Nina. Come back here. Principal Baker called me this afternoon," Selah shares in a concerned tone.

"Who's the liar now?" Nina mumbles. "*I'm not going to call your parents. Whatever.*"

"What did you say?"

"Yeah Mom, I know. I'm rewriting the essay to talk about how I want to be a journalist."

"'Yeah'?" Selah corrects.

"'Yes,' I mean."

"Nina baby, nobody is mad about that. But it's never too early to start thinking about your future. It's important to think about what type of work you'll want to do, which determines the types of colleges you'll need to explore to get there. It's 1983, and you're a Black girl. You must work extra hard to compete with those white girls in your school who don't have to worry about the same things you do."

"I know, Mom, ok? I got it." Nina submits.

"Alright, well, I know you're mad at me, but still come here and give me a hug," Selah demands. Nina walks over to her mother and lets Selah feed off her warmth, though Nina feels cold inside—like the top of the television tube.

***

Nina's week of punishment turns into three days when Selah finds a dance school ten minutes away from the apartment. It has plenty of availability and desire for a dancer as talented as Nina to bless the team. Before school supplies are even bought, she is enrolled in ballet, tap, and jazz classes. The only rule is that dance doesn't interfere with school. Little does Selah know that Nina's struggle with school is unavoidable.

Classes are Friday evenings for jazz and Saturday mornings for ballet and tap. Dedicating half the weekend to something Nina loves is barely a sacrifice to her; Selah never allows her to go to any kids' sleepovers anyway. Selah doesn't trust anyone she doesn't know, even if she's met them and they seem fine. "You can never be too careful," she warns.

Nina's friends are always invited to come to their apartment, *But who's going to say yes, when I never come to theirs?* she questions silently.

The good news is there aren't too many bullies at Key Lake, though there aren't many welcoming kids either. Lalita is Nina's only classmate who takes the time to engage and even offers help with math, a subject Nina struggles with the most. In return, Nina simply listens and is available. It appears Lalita has some stories to tell but not too many people to tell them to. Nina doesn't spend the night, but she sometimes has dinner with Lalita and her family the evenings both Selah and David work late. Their house is regally immaculate. Nina takes short excursions to India by way of heavy pastels and primary colors on the walls, beaded elephant statues, lively incense, and the rich aroma of red curry.

"Oh dear, how magnificent is that ruby you're wearing? Is that your mother's?" Lalita's mom asks.

"No ma'am. My Uncle John gave it to me as a birthday present. My birthday is in July, so it's my birthstone," Nina responds proudly.

"Oh, well, be careful. That's a fancy ring."

"Yes, my uncle tells me to be careful too. He says I'm supposed to wear it when I need to feel strong or on special occasions, and I feel they both happen a lot," Nina explains. "My grandpa died right after my uncle gave it to me. So, I started wearing it a lot after that."

"Oh sweetie, I'm sorry. I love rubies. They're special to me too," Lalita's mother says lovingly, clutching the bottom of the ruby-and-gold necklace hanging from her own neck.

"Let's go to my room," Lalita suggests, attempting to shift the mood for Nina.

"Coming here is like reading one of my favorite books," Nina admits.

Lalita smiles and says, "Maybe one day you'll write one."

Nina follows Lalita to her room and is greeted with towers of notebooks piled high on each corner of the room. "Sheesh, Lalita! What are these?"

"Oh, just my thoughts," Lalita says, blushing. No one other than family comes into her room, but when Nina spoke about writing in her head one night, Lalita felt she was worthy enough to see her method of managing thoughts.

"Is this like a diary?" Nina asks, while flipping through a notebook at the top of one of the mountains of words.

"No, just my thoughts. More like a journal, I guess," Lalita explains, hovering behind her, excited to see what she is seeing. "Sometimes what I write about is real, and sometimes it's real mixed in with some white lies."

"Oh, I get it. Not really the truth, but there's some truth in there somewhere," Nina says, turning around and attempting to see through Lalita's sea-green eyes.

"Yes, I think," Lalita says, giggling with Nina.

"You should stop trying to keep everything you write in your head and put it on paper. You never know what it can be." Lalita steps in closer to Nina, until they share the same breathing space. Nina feels her skin tingle, and is tempted to brush away the loose strand of hair stuck on Lalita's mouth.

"You're so beautiful—I mean, smart." Nina corrects herself, now blushing a pink rose. "These are good."

"I hear the doorbell," she continues. "David must be here. I'm gonna go. See you at school. But thanks. This was cool, you know?" She rambles nervously as she sprints, then hesitates, then sprints again out the door, leaving Lalita alone in her room, also feeling unavoidably smitten, ready to write another entry.

***

It has been a season and a few days, and the number of blisters on Nina's feet is competing with the number of journals building in her closet. She has followed Lalita's lead, and has begun writing her thoughts by way of poetry and short stories, even between ballet and tap classes. It's becoming almost as natural as breathing, unlike third-grade classes at school. Nina is getting through them, even though the content sounds like static and reads like a blurred abstract design, similar to her invisible friend's face and body: cloudy and confusing. But one thing is clear to her, no future kings live in elementary school. They're too busy tugging on her hair and flicking her pencils on the floor.

"Boys are stupid, Uncle John. They sometimes hit me and talk too much about dumb stuff."

Uncle John laughs out loud. "I know, little one," he admits. "They don't get much better when they're older, so try to forgive them now for their future stupidity."

Nina twirls the telephone cord around her finger, contemplating telling Uncle John about Lalita. She thinks he may understand how she feels about this amazing girl, but she's afraid that God will hear her and punish her sin by taking Lalita away. Nina can't forget the consistent messaging of Grandma Rosa's church leaders: it's against God's law for a girl to love a girl, or a boy to love a boy in the romantic way. If someone has these feelings, they must deny them and ask God for forgiveness. Nina doesn't want to be a bad girl and break any laws, but she doesn't want to stop feeling the indescribable warmth she has for Lalita. She ignores her need to confess and decides to wait, and tell Uncle John another day.

"Mister is good, and I'm in *The Nutcracker*, so maybe you can come see me perform," says Nina, redirecting her focus. "It's been a long time since you've seen me dance. I think it was with Grandpa."

"I know, princess. I'll try. I know you'll be wonderful. Make sure your dad takes lots of pictures. Speaking of dads, how's your other dad?"

"He's good. He drops me off and picks me up from dance class and Lalita's house, and he makes yummy grilled cheese."

"Well, what's better than that?" Uncle John teases. "And your new second mom? How are you two?"

"Good. She's teaching me how to be a lady, like how to eat right at a fancy restaurant and how to talk to people properly," Nina says with a curtsy, as if Uncle John can see her through the phone.

"Interesting. And you like all that fancy stuff?"

"Yes! Especially the part where she makes what she calls 'cocktail parties.' She brings out the fancy pretty plates and glasses and sets them on the table like in my fairytale books. She knows how to be a true queen."

"Wow, that's awesome. How's your ruby? You still love it?" Uncle John asks, massaging his forehead, trying to suppress a migraine he often gets but doesn't share with anyone.

"Yes Uncle, I love it," Nina says, anxiously rubbing her ringless finger. She is afraid to tell Uncle John she's not quite sure where it is at the moment. It's not lost, exactly. She knows it's in her room; she just needs to look harder. *There's no need to alarm him over the phone. It's not like I lied. I just didn't quite tell the truth.* "I miss you, Uncle."

"I miss you too, little one. Don't worry, I'll see you soon. Keep writing in your journal, and know you can call me anytime. I love you. Now go learn something."

"I love you too. Bye!" Nina hangs up the phone and attempts to pull the rock out from inside her chest. She must find her ruby ring before she sees Uncle John, or before she gets scared again.

***

It's Christmas week, and the air is filled with toasty firewood and pumpkin spice. Almost every window of the high-rise apartment building is decorated with Christmas lights, menorahs, and snowmen stickers.

"Wow David! Even Jesus will be happy with our tree," Nina jokes.

"Nina! That's not funny," Selah says, laughing. "I really do need to get all of us in church."

"No more cranberries and popcorn on the fake table tree," David says proudly. "Not that the tree from the past wasn't beautiful, but look at this!" He holds the tree straight up in the corner of the living room as Selah brings the tree stand and skirt, so the pine needles won't get lost in the plush cream rug.

"The top of the tree is scraping the ceiling, Dave," Selah points out, bursting the bubble a little.

"It's ok. We'll just clip that down a bit. No worries, baby!" And so he does, and for the first time, Nina has a big full sparkling tree decorated with glittery stars, colorful balls, icicles, and candy canes. Selah's new director position at the local hospital is paying off, and financial stress is dissipating.

"This is perfect," Nina swoons as she picks up Mister and hugs him tight. "Now all I need is a baby sister," she announces, looking at Selah's flat belly.

There have been rumors spreading that Santa Claus doesn't exist, but Nina still puts out two chocolate chip cookies, a glass of milk, and a note of gratitude for the jolly fat man.

This year, Nina drinks too much eggnog before bed and gets up in the middle of the night to relieve herself. And down the hall, in the living room, there they are—the faux Santa and Mrs. Claus putting up the Barbie dream house Nina asked for in her prayers.

David is on the floor upside down, screwing a couple of living room walls together, while Selah is placing miniature plants and end tables in their place. Nina thinks about blowing their cover, calling them out. *But what good would that do? No need to make them feel bad when they're the real magic.*

The next day, Nina pretends she's surprised that Santa miraculously knew what she wanted for Christmas and was happy to eat the cookies left on the coffee table. Selah makes her usual holiday feast, yet they still go to the house of David's family in the country, to eat a winter barbecue and avoid pig feet juice stains on their festive ensembles.

Mike and Dionne are on their own this year, but have Nina next Christmas. Mike and Selah worked out an arrangement for equal visitations every other major holiday, which means he submitted to her demands. All Nina wants is for everyone to have holiday together.

Back home from all the gluttony and celebration, Nina is in her room, looking for the missing ruby once again. She can hear the phone ring in the kitchen and wonders who could be calling this late. David is already passed out in their bedroom from a little too much whiskey, and she hears her mother talking to someone but can't make out the words. It feels like it's been hours. Nina decides to turn off the lights, lie back on the bed, and let the neon stars tell her a story to lull her to sleep.

As soon as sleep comes, Selah yells "Nina!" down the hall, but then decides to walk back to her room and be gentler in waking her. Nina is already sitting up in bed because she can sense something is terribly wrong.

"Mom?"

"Hey baby, I have some hard news," Selah warns. Her eyes are swollen and bloodshot, like someone pounded on them with a hammer. "I want you to know it's going to be ok."

"Mom, please, what is it?" Nina pleads.

"Baby, your Uncle John has passed away. We're still trying to find out what happened. But it seems like he went to sleep last night and never woke up. Grandma Rosa found him in a peaceful state after he didn't come down for breakfast this morning."

Nina's heart stops, and she immediately goes deaf. A colossal tsunami begins pushing against her bedroom window, looking for any vulnerable opening to break through and drown them.

"Nina? Baby?" Selah leans in and touches Nina's shoulder, looking for some type of reaction. "I think he's been hiding a sadness for a while now, and then it intensified when your Grandpa transitioned," she explains, hoping to convince Nina there is nothing anyone could do.

"I have to find his ring before the storm gets us," Nina finally announces through her dazed panic. She feels as if someone has broken her in half, letting her bleed out.

"Baby, don't worry about that now. Come, let me hold you," Selah says, but Nina can't hear her. She begins to ransack her bedroom, uncontrollably crying, inevitably waking David up.

"Nina, baby, please stop!" Selah begs, crying with her.

"I have to find his ring! Please help me before the water comes in! I'm supposed to wear it when I'm scared!" Nina screams, trapped in a tornado of despair, twirling around and around, watching the pressure from the water outside split the top of her bedroom window.

David is in Nina's doorway, trying to catch his bearings. "Is everything ok?"

"We're ok, David," Selah says, knowing that Nina only needs her mama right now.

Nina's room is a whirlwind of chaos, but the grief is unwavering among it. She drops on the bed, exhausted, going limp and letting her mom attempt to absorb the pain. Her head is heavy on Selah's lap. "Mom, we have to go. We gonna drown when the water comes in."

"Baby, there's no water," Selah whispers, petrified that Nina is having a breakdown. She looks up at David. "Should I call a doctor?"

David motions his hand downward like he's fanning the despair. "No Selah. Let's assess in the morning. We don't want to go down that route unless we have to."

"You're right," Selah agrees. "I'm going to sleep with her tonight." Nina is already passed out from emotional fatigue, but Selah doesn't leave her alone. She gets under the covers with her and stays until the tsunami dries out.

A week later, Nina still hasn't found the ring. And she doesn't go to Uncle John's funeral, like she didn't go to Grandpa's funeral a few months earlier. The decision is made that she's too young. *How can I be old enough for pain but too young to say goodbye?*

✳✳✳

Summer. It takes longer to return this year. Nina believes that God kept some extra warmth in Heaven for Uncle

John. Nina weathers the cold mostly at home, in her bed and under the covers, still in shock from the death of her uncle, asking Selah to cancel several of her dance commitments. And Selah does this until she's worried that Nina will spiral into a dark emotional state.

So she forces Nina out of bed, reminding her that that isolation may have been why Uncle John got lost in sadness. *But he had me,* Nina thinks. *I guess I just wasn't enough.*

"Nina, promise me you'll get outside often while you're away and enjoy the fresh air in those lungs. I promise it's healing," Selah pleads.

Nina doesn't want to go outside. She wants to see Uncle John and only think of him. At twenty-three, he must be one of the youngest adults in Heaven. "I just hope you're not lonely," Nina whispers quietly from her bed, tucked in comfortably with Mister. She wonders if Uncle John hears her somehow, and if she'll feel closer to him when she's in the airplane heading to Mike and Dionne.

Nina glances over at her purple suitcase in the corner by the door. She's afraid of flying, but mostly anxious about the hours leading up to the flight, as she always has to mentally prepare for the usual routine. Wake up early and ignore Selah's demand for her to be ready on time. Wait for Selah at the front door, anxious her flight will be missed. Feel Selah push her out the door and listen to her stress about being late, blaming her life, Mike, and sometimes Nina if she's less than on point. Nina will barely make her flight, but the stewardess will feel bad that she is sweating and shaking from the adrenaline, and give her a Shirley Temple right away. After the proper altitude is reached, Nina will be invited to the cockpit to be impressed by the pilots. She'll just want another set of gold plastic wings to add to her growing collection, but she'll smile and gasp like she's in awe.

"Nina! Let's go, get up! You have literally eighteen minutes to be by the door!"

You heard the lady. Time to get up, Mister says. *But can you walk me real quick before you go? David doesn't wait long enough for me to do some good poop business.*

With leash in hand, Nina hugs Mister and kisses him on his wet nose. "I'm going to miss you the most. But I'll only be gone for a month. I'll be back before my birthday," she promises.

Thirty-five minutes later, Selah jumps in the Corvette, throws her platform sandals on the passenger seat floor as usual, pulls out of the handicapped parking space, and looks over at Nina riding shotgun, now smiling, as if they both just dodged bullets. "We're on the way, baby! See, we're all good!"

Nina is tall enough to see above the door handle now, but has a hard time seeing past the stress her mother's rushed movements create for them both. She sees a boy walking across the parking lot in front of the car, and it looks like James. Nina rolls down her window and yells out, "James!" He looks up from under his hoodie, wearing fresh black-and-blue blotches on his cheeks and neck, much worse than when in the elevator with her the last time. Nina almost breaks her neck backward not to lose James' sad stare.

"Nina, get your head back in the car, girl! What are you looking at?" Selah questions with intense concern.

"It was James. Didn't you see him?"

"No. Why? What's wrong?" Selah probes, making a sharp, fast turn outside of the complex.

"I don't know, Mom. He doesn't look so good." Nina is tempted to tell Selah about the pain being inflicted upon him regularly, but what if his mother is faster than Nina's? And she kills him before Selah can save him?

"Nina, are you ok? What's going on with you?"

"Nuthin Mom, I'm just going to miss you."

"Awww sweetie, Mommy always misses you. Don't worry. You'll have fun up there with your dad and Dionne. I think you'll be traveling to see your other uncle and aunt and cousins for a bit and then go to some type of fun camp your dad and Dionne found for your last two weeks there." Selah doesn't realize she said "other" uncle, but Nina notices and tilts her head up, pretending to scratch her neck, making it easier to fight back the tears.

***

Mike is thrilled to have his daughter with him, and Dionne pulls out the red carpet for Nina when she arrives. It is no different from Christmas, spring break, or any random long weekend. Dionne reminds Nina of Principal Baker, but Dionne doesn't pronounce her words as funnily. She's tall, dark brown, and exudes an energy that demands a high level of attention. She dresses elegantly, even on the weekend when there's nowhere to go. There's always something in the oven or on the stove, or a colorful cocktail ready to be shaken—even if it's virgin for Nina. She has a high-level position at her job, like Mike, but doesn't talk about it. Clearly, she knows being a wife is the most important job you can have. It's evident that Dionne is a queen, and Nina wants to be just like her. She's already taught Nina proper dining etiquette, how to properly speak to elders, and even to your peers when wanting to be the better person. She describes it as "taking the high road."

"Always dress as if the most important person will see you," she teaches Nina. "A lady should always present herself as such, and good things will come to her." And Nina believes her. After all, Dionne convinced Mike to choose her.

Dionne and Mike have left the big city and moved to a beautiful big house, across the Hudson in an upper middle-class white suburb. They enjoy all things privileged. There are no kids on the block close to Nina's age or her culture, so she stays close to her journal, telling her dad it's something for school so he won't get curious. However, Mike doesn't get overly curious about most things. He's the most comfortable on the three-piece sectional with the oversized recliner, falling asleep to the sounds of the referee whistle, a newspaper resting on his chest.

Maybe because it's been longer than usual since Mike has last seen Nina, but he's a bit more inquisitive about her recent activities. "So, how's school?"

Nina is sitting cross-legged like she used to when meditating with Uncle John. But instead of having her eyes closed and taking in deep breaths, she's flipping through the piles of *Jet* magazine that live on the coffee table. Nina's only interest is the Beauty of the Week in each issue, and she compares each woman to herself. Most of them look like her, light-skinned with long hair. Some of them say they like to hike, read books, or dance, which is great because Nina does too. None of them have crooked teeth or bony legs though. Nina realizes she has a long way to go to get the curvy figures they have. But she is confident that if she continues to eat her vegetables, she will one day be voluptuous and queenworthy. Someone who has earned some king saying "Mmmph" when she glides by.

"Nina, are you listening to me?"

"Yes, sorry, Daddy. I mean, school is over for now. But it was alright. My grades could have been a little better," Nina admits.

"I know, your mother told me. It's not that you're doing terribly. We just know you could be doing better. We know it's been a tough time, you know, with recent sadness. But we can't let you fall behind. We're thinking about getting you some extra help this next fourth-grade year and limiting some of your distractions," Mike says, doing his best to be stern and authoritative like Selah.

Nina drops her legs down onto the floor, threatening to stand up. "I don't need extra help. I'll try harder. And I'm not distracted," she states with a ragged edge to her tone, as she continues to flip through the abundance of *Jet* magazines. She understands the only "distraction" open for discussion is her dancing, and she'll do anything to prevent that from being taken away.

"Nina, your mother, and I are not looking to chokehold you here, but we want to make sure you are starting off on the right foot with your education, so you can be competitive once you get to high school. How about you choose just one dance class and not all three?"

"No!" Nina yells, dropping her feet to the floor and letting the *Jet* beauties drop face down, suffocating into the family room rug. She realizes she has gone overboard with her volume by the look on Mike's face, and implements a lesson taught by her stepmother, who's in the kitchen baking Nina's favorite chocolate cake as dinner's dessert.

"I'm sorry, Daddy. I shouldn't have raised my voice. You're right. Extra help will be great. If I can show you and mom that my grades have gotten better in the first part of fourth grade, can you please not take any of my dance classes away from me?"

Dionne stops icing the cake and glances over at Nina with pride.

Mike softens and says, "Thank you, princess. I'm sure you'll be on the honor roll in no time."

"Hey you two," Dionne interrupts as she's whipping cake batter. "Y'all mind going to the store and getting me some more butter?" She does need more butter, but not until tomorrow. She just feels father and daughter need some alone time.

"Sure," Mike responds, looking at Nina. "You wanna take a ride with your papi?"

"Ok," Nina simply answers, missing her mom despite the fact Selah was the one who most likely set up this conversation.

Nina rides in her usual shotgun position, looking out the window, watching the cows eating grass pass by, listening to the music of awkward silence. She is conflicted. On the one hand, she wants her father to be less aloof, be sterner, set boundaries, and match Selah's loving, overbearing rhythm. But when he randomly tries to emulate her, Nina becomes resentful. She wants him to simply accept and embrace her and mean it. Either way, she wants him to commit to something.

They arrive at the grocery store, which Mike clearly doesn't visit often.

"Dad, I found the butter," says Nina.

"Good girl. Now let's get outta here."

Mike and Nina find the shortest checkout line, which is still long because it's Saturday. Mike proceeds to share with Nina their plans for the next few weeks, but suddenly is distracted by a gorgeous *Jet* beauty look-alike right behind them in aisle two. She's perfect.

"Mmmph. Mmmph." Mike bellows.

Nina's eyes are now pacing steady with her father's, running up and down the beauty's body. The woman is unaware of her onlookers, instead focused on the variety of cheeses to choose from. *How long it take for her to get like that? Maybe she was just born that way.*

Nina looks down past her own flat chest, to her skinny legs with scarred knees and big feet. *What if this is all I got?* she asks herself silently, confident that this grocery store beauty doesn't have overlapping shark teeth in *her* mouth. She refocuses on the hourglass figure just a few shopping carts away, wishing to get closer to see if she's even real.

Nina looks back into her father's eyes to see if he's forgotten her, or the wife who's been in the kitchen all day for him. She finds it annoying that he sometimes can't remember a conversation they had hours ago, but he'll most likely remember the color of this beauty's dress next week. Mike feels the heat of Nina's stare, pulls his eyes away from his vice, and laughs in a guilty-yet-unapologetic way. She gives her father no grace. "Dang Daddy. Can you NOT do that? I'm right here."

"Ok, ok. Sorry princess, I'll be cool," Mike whispers, embarrassed that his daughter saw him hypnotized yet again.

"Hey sweetie, your shoe is untied," the beauty announces to Nina with a big smile. Nina quickly drops down and ties her shoe, worried that the woman overhead their lust and envy.

Nina can't resist. She walks over to the beauty. "Hi. Sorry, um, can I ask you a question?"

"Yeah?" the woman responds reluctantly.

DANCER IN THE BULLPEN

"Did you ever have knife teeth or crooked knees when you were a kid?"

The beauty looks down at her exquisitely sculpted legs, and then back at Nina, perplexed. "Not that I can remember. Why?"

Nina's courage is short-lived. She suddenly feels silly and discouraged that this woman doesn't understand her need to one day be just as magnetic as her. *I bet she's just another Veronica anyway.*

"Hey sweetie, you ok?" the beauty asks, a little concerned.

"Yeah, no, never mind. Thanks for telling me about my shoe," Nina mumbles as she walks back to Mike's side, who is finally checking out the butter.

"Hey kiddo, what was that about?"

Nina doesn't feel like explaining that she hates him right now, and that she's trying to find the fastest way to be queen-worthy like Selah and Dionne. All she wants is chocolate, which comforts her during times she feels lonely, even though Dionne says it's a devil dressed in angel clothing, tricking kids to get fat and tired. But Nina thinks it can't be that bad; Dionne bakes chocolate cake all the time.

"Daddy, can I have some chocolate?" Nina asks with undetected anger.

"Sure baby. But just don't eat it before dinner," Mike says, glancing over Nina's head for one more Beauty of the Week peek. Nina rolls her eyes, grabs the butter, and stomps ahead of her father out the store. She's already in the car with a mouthful of chocolate when Mike slow motions into the driver seat. He ignores Nina's defiance and rolls down the windows, pumping up the volume on the radio. Hall & Oates' "I Can't

Go for That" is blaring out the speakers and Mike starts singing while he drives, playfully pulling on Nina's arm, trying to make her smile. "These white boys can wail!" he exclaims.

Nina can't keep her lips pursed, and begins laughing and rocking to the beat with Mike. Her dad has an incredible voice and charm to match. His singing voice is just like Grandma Rosa's—he just uses his differently. They pull up to the house driveway after stretching their lungs to three hit songs, and Nina almost forgets about the betrayal at the Shop Rite.

***

Nina's *other* uncle's house is big and old and sits close to a New England port. So most of the time, it's cold and windy. It's filled with Nina's aunt and eight cousins. It's like the Old Woman Who Lived in a Shoe rhyme, but Nina's aunt also has a husband. Nina has been told that a few of her cousins are adopted, but no one talks about which ones because it doesn't matter.

Nina can only remember visiting Mike's older brother and his family one other time. She remembers Aunt Jackie putting way too much milk in her eggs, but knitting the best sweaters. This visit is bittersweet, as it's the first time they've all been together since Grandpa and Uncle John passed away. It is nice that Grandma Rosa can make the trip. Everyone is grateful for her health and mobility. And, of course, her rice and peas and plantains.

"Let's toast!" Uncle Bobby says. "Here's to Dad for some of us, and Grandpa to many of us. Let him rest in peace and honor. And to my brother John, who blessed us with his warm and joyful spirit. May we never forget his love and wisdom at his young age. Does anyone want to say anything?"

DANCER IN THE BULLPEN

Everyone looks at Nina, knowing she was the closest to Uncle John, though not the most talkative. To the family's surprise, she scoots her chair back from the dining room table and slowly rises. Mike holds her hand, which pushes tears through her floodgates. Through sobs, she attempts to catch her breath.

"Take your time, sweetie. It's ok," Uncle Bobby says.

Uncle John was my best friend. He helped me learn how to read, write, and say big words. He taught me about music, strange food, and bullfighting in Spain—all kinds of things. He was not always happy, I think, but I don't know why. He was nice enough to give me a ruby ring for my birthday, but I didn't take care of it and lost it, even though I promised I wouldn't. And then he died. He probably died because I killed him by losing something so special. I miss him and just want to see him and talk to him. I'm really sad and don't know how to make it better. I'd rather him be here than all of you.

"Nina, you want to say something?" Mike asks, knowing that sometimes she gets lost in her own head.

Nina snaps out of it and looks around the dining room, realizing she has only shared her feelings silently. "I'm sorry, no, I have nuthin to say. Well … yes, I guess. Cheers to family." She holds up her sparkling apple cider, smirking at her own impression of Dionne, attempting to distract herself from the pain.

Nina looks at her stepmom, who supportively returns the sentiment. "Cheers to family indeed, Nina."

Just above her head in the shadow, Nina swears she sees a familiar body. "Uncle John?" The dark figure slowly retreats from behind Dionne into the back wall. "Uncle John?" she calls out again.

Nina's cousins look confused. They don't understand what's happening.

"Hey princess, it's ok," Mike says. "Why don't I take you upstairs to rest a bit? I think you're just tired."

Nina effortlessly submits. "Ok Daddy."

Am I going crazy?

Nina tries to believe she didn't really see Uncle John, but her gut tells her differently. Mike suggests she distract herself from the past and spend some time with one of her middle cousins, Lexa, who's already in sixth grade. She seems nice enough, showing Nina around her small town where no Black people exist. Everywhere they visit—the corner market, barber shop, pier, music store—are all places where the cute white boys Lexa crushes on hang out. Nina doesn't mind white boys; there are plenty in her school and the neighborhood she lives in. She just thinks it's weird to see no Black people at all. Nina begins to realize Lexa is not so much interested in showing her the cool places of her town, but rather saying that she did while executing her own mission. What Lexa doesn't consider is that all the neighborhood boys will be fascinated by a new exotic beauty in town, one who smiles with each word and dances with each stride. Lexa has been their only muse in this nothing-much of a town for a while now, until her vibrant new visitor arrives.

Lexa may be self-absorbed, but the two good things about her is that she hates the milky eggs her mother makes too, and she toasts the best-tasting bagels, spreading half with butter and the other half with peanut butter. They eat them in her room so the other cousins don't see and try to take the limited inventory. Lexa's room is a preteen haven. Colorful pastel paper covers the walls, a perfect template for all her Michael J. Fox and Ricky Schroeder posters. She has a closet filled with denim and neon t-shirts that are muted by a long white dresser with fun glittery makeup and lots of jewelry. Tons of draped necklaces, faux diamond rings, and one special gold bracelet with little hearts engraved all around it, given to her by one of the boys she crushes on. "This is my favorite," Lexa chimes in. "Maybe one day a boy will give you one." She doesn't care if that happens, but doesn't know that Nina doesn't care either.

Days with Lexa are bearable, even fun sometimes. But the nights are brutal. Nina thinks the night sky must have some type of evil gas that gets into Lexa's lungs and nose cavity, poisoning her brain.

"Have you ever been squished like a pancake?" Lexa asks Nina, right when she's settling comfortably in the bed with her. Nina is fine with sleeping on the floor, but there aren't enough blankets. So the adults say they must share.

"No, I haven't been squished like a pancake, and I don't want to," Nina responds, feeling her bladder weaken and nausea brewing in the pit of her stomach.

"Well, you're gonna tonight," Lexa says in the pitch-dark room, her tone matching.

She begins to take all her strong body weight and squish Nina's frail frame up against the wall. When Nina tries to push back, Lexa smashes her into the cold wall even harder. Nina begins to cry, and Lexa warns her not to wake up the adults, or she'll hurt her more the next day. Nina feels hopeless so she stops fighting. Her spaceship is in another galaxy, and her invisible friend must not be able to find her here in this strange house. The abuse seems to last all night. Lexa's strength is infinite.

"Please stop," Nina whimpers. Just when she thinks Lexa has relaxed her muscles, and she can now escape, she executes the painful press again. For a split second, Nina thinks her calves are cramping again, and her skin is warming, but she can't tell if it's coming from herself or the effect of Lexa's wrath. Her eyes begin to burn, as if the mysterious dust has returned and made its way into her pool of tears, but she is unsure. There is no Uncle John to protect her, or her ruby ring or Grandma Daisy's metal spoon to make her brave.

"You can't be a baby if you want to have boys like you," Lexa warns. Nina is too tired to question why her cousin would want to hurt her like this, especially after seeing her so sad yesterday. But she has a suspicion that maybe Lexa's mad the boys *do* like her. Each of the three nights in that room is humiliating, making the days a performance upon the corrupt stage Lexa has built.

Returning to Mike and Dionne's is sweeter than usual because of the turmoil at the Old Woman in the Shoe house. Nina has no interest in summer camp, but she makes the best of the next two weeks to appease all her parents. Swimming, field games, and local hikes are fun, but it's the writing workshop and art activities that lift Nina's spirits. She brings home many paintings and poems of evil witches and beautiful fairies, playing on the contrast of good and evil, joy and sadness, truth and lies. Mike and Dionne may not understand Nina's creations, but they make sure to frame them and hang them on their walls with pride, reminding them of her when she returns home.

＊＊＊

Nina is surprised to see David with her mom at the airport. Usually, it's only Selah who waits at the gate with a big cheesy smile. Now, there are two big cheesy smiles gleaming at Nina, and she feels loved.

DANCER IN THE BULLPEN

"Hi guys! Why are you both here?" Nina asks with a big smile of her own.

"What? I can't come and greet my amazing daughter too?" David asks.

Nina likes that David considers her simply his daughter, not what some of her mean classmates call a "hand-me-down" version. "Of course," she confirms, hugging David tightly and looking at her glowing mother over his shoulder.

"Come here, princess! We've missed you so much," Selah confesses as Nina rushes over to her and jumps into her arms.

Walking to the car, Nina glances over at Selah and feels like something is different. Her face is a bit fuller; her sweater is clinging to her stomach more so than usual. "Mommy," she whispers up to Selah, not wanting David to hear her observation.

"Yes baby?" Selah drops her head down to accept the privacy request.

"You got kinda fat while I was gone. Are you ok?"

Selah lets out a roaring laugh and announces loudly for anyone to hear. "Nina, you think your mama been eating too many cookies?"

"Mommy, shhh. Why you so loud?"

"David, tell Nina why I'm lookin' a little plump," Selah teases, rubbing her expanding belly.

"We're having a baby!" David announces with great excitement.

"Oh my goodness, Mommy, really?" Nina needs to make sure one of her dreams has actually come true.

"Yes princess. This surprised me and David too, but it's a blessing. You're going to be a big sister!"

"Yay! I'm having a sister!" Nina exclaims, skipping high, reaching for the sky in front of them both.

"Woah, slow your roll, baby girl," warns Selah. "We're not sure of the sex yet. I'll find out next visit."

"It doesn't matter, Mom. I know she's a girl! I prayed for one like you prayed for me, so she'll be a girl!"

"I'm going with Nina's prediction, honey," David chimes in. "She seems to have a sense of these things." He gives Nina a wink that channels their comradery.

"Well, whether it's a girl or a boy, I know you'll be a great big sister, Nina," says Selah. "And how do you think Mister will adjust to a new little creature running around the house?" she continues to tease. Clearly, she's is in a happy, fun-loving mood.

"It's ok, I'll have a talk with him," Nina assures.

Selah and David lock eyes over Nina's head and recognize their girl is definitely back home.

***

It has only been a couple of weeks since Nina's been home from Mike and Dionne's house, and already she has improved her math scores with the summer tutor Selah hired to help bring her *C*-level grades to *B*'s before the new school year starts. Though Nina has been heavily active in dance classes and recitals, she has reduced some of the journaling to keep herself academically focused, and to keep her parents' claws away from her number one outlet. It has been grueling for her, and she prays that no one figures out that she's doing more memory work than actual problem solving, and barely sleeping many nights. She's trying harder, and her teachers seem to value that enough to raise her grades and keep Selah out of their offices.

DANCER IN THE BULLPEN

Nina has been such a good girl that for her birthday, Selah suggests throwing a party. *But who's Mom going to allow over? The classmates she don't like?* Nina thinks. The only friends she has, besides those who live too far to come, are Lalita, James, and Mister.

"Those are the only people you want at your party?" Selah questions.

"Yes Mom. Those are the only ones, and of course you and David."

"Ok, well let's make some cute invitations," Selah suggests, trying to get Nina in the party mode.

"No Mom. You don't need to, I got it! You have a baby to feed." Nina watches her mother eat a bowl of spaghetti piled high, looking like she is going to pop any minute.

"Shhh girl. This baby is hungry!" Selah laughs, throwing a napkin at her daughter.

It isn't too difficult to get Lalita to Nina's birthday party; Selah and David just have to promise her parents not to have any pork served at the party. James is a bit more challenging. He doesn't like parties because he doesn't like to be seen. However, he loves good food. So, the description of Selah's famous spicy honey-barbecue wings and homemade potato salad gets his mouth quickly watering, though he has a concern that Nina knew would come up.

"I remember you saying your mom notices everything. I mean, do you think she'll notice the old bruises on my face? I can't really see them now, can you?" James asks sheepishly.

"Yes, she's kinda nosy, but she won't be paying attention because of the party stuff. Plus, I can bring some of my mom's makeup down to you and help you put it on if you need me to," Nina suggests.

"I'm not wearing your mama's makeup, Nina."

"Fine," Nina says, chuckling.

Nina's celebration is just what she wants. Selah makes good on her promise and makes the best chicken wings in the world. After some fun birthday games, Nina and her friends—including greedy Mister—head over to the dining room table to devour the goods. She sits at the head of the table and purposely has James sit next to her on the left, because her mother is sitting on her right. He is too preoccupied with the wings to notice that he and Selah are face-to-face. Selah has never been one to ignore the obvious, so Nina knows it's just a matter of time. Lalita on the other hand has the misfortune of getting stuck between chatty David and his mother, who also chatters way too much, but doesn't hear well enough to listen to anyone else's stories. Nina plots to save her soon.

"James, how do you like school? Have you lived in the apartment building long? I don't remember seeing you around," Selah begins to question.

"Um, not too long. I just keep to myself a lot, but yeah, I'm usually at the bus stop with Nina and Lalita."

Selah watches James barely chew his food, almost swallowing his meal whole, like he hasn't eaten in days. She smiles and says, "Don't be shy. There's plenty."

Selah shoots Nina a look, and no words are needed. Nina sees it. "You can get another plate AND pack up one for later for yourself, or maybe for your mother?" Selah halfway offers, halfway asks.

Knock ... Knock ... Knock!

Like she has heard people coming for her, James' mother is at the front door, determining her son's party time is over. Everyone in the room stops talking.

Selah suddenly grabs James' trembling hand, turns him around to look directly in his eyes, and says, "If you need any help, you run right back over, do you understand?"

"Yes ma'am."

"What are you going to do, James?"

"I'm going to run back over here," he promises.

"Good."

Selah opens the door as wide as her pretty white smile. "Hi, so glad to meet you! James is such a good kid! We're making you a plate right now to go, unless you want to stay and eat or have some cake too with us? We would love to have you." She knows it's hard to be mean when you have niceness vomited on you.

"No, we have to go. James, let's go now," his mother demands. Everyone is uncomfortable. You can almost cut the tension with a machete.

Selah lets it go and watches James walk down the hallway slowly behind his mother. She closes the door once mother and son are on the elevator. She turns to Nina and assures her. "You did good, princess. Don't worry, I'll take care of it."

Nina takes a deep breath in and exhales like when she's sitting cross-legged, feeling a great sense of relief and peace, mixed with a bit of guilt for taking so long to bring James' burden to Selah. If only she could tell her mom her own secrets.

Cleanup is over and the apartment has almost forgotten a party ever existed. Selah and David are in their bedroom with their party outfits on, passed out on the bed with two pieces of cake on the dresser uneaten. Lalita is waiting for her father in the living room with Nina, and they are talking about their latest journal entries.

"I wrote a story about the lunch lady's head turning into a potato," Lalita admits, laughing at the recent memory. "People would come up to her and try to peel the skin off her head and put butter and sour cream on her when she'd nap in the corner."

"That's crazy, Lalita!" Nina says, admiring the silly creative stories her friend writes.

"Nina, pick up the phone, baby. It's your dad," Selah yells down the hall, half asleep.

Ugh, why now? Nina thinks. She was just working up the nerve to actually brush the hair out of Lalita's face this time. But instead, she puts on her happy voice. "Hi Daddy!"

"Happy Birthday, Nina Josephine! You have a great day?"

"Yes, Mom threw me a party. And my friend Lalita is still here," Nina says, trying to keep the conversation short.

"Ok baby, well, next year we'll make sure we come and celebrate too."

"Yes Daddy, that'll be good."

"Ok love, I'll let you go and be with your friend. Oh wait, I have a question for you."

"Yes?" Nina strangles the telephone cord with her fingers, looking at Lalita's runaway strand of hair.

Mike doesn't like confrontation, so the pause is longer than usual.

"Daddy?" Nina pushes, anxiously.

"Lexa is missing some type of gold bracelet with hearts or something on it. Supposedly, it's special to her. She seems to think the last time she saw it was when we visited a couple of weeks ago. Do you think you may have picked it up by accident?"

"Oh wow, that's terrible. But no. I can't remember seeing it," Nina responds, as she admires her newfound gold bangle dangling from Lalita's wrist.

CHAPTER SIX

The walls and rugs are the color of pastures. No wonder the previous owners fled to Florida, where the water is blue and the sky is colorless.

"Mom, can we change all the walls to pretty pink?" Nina asks.

Selah compromises. "Maybe we can paint your room a pale pink like Baby Jasmine's, but everything else will be white, princess." Despite the overwhelming green, their new house looks just like their previous apartment, long and wide, except it's double the size and has a large furnished basement. It smells like old people—Ben-Gay and hot pastrami—but Selah has a detailed plan on how she'll transform this house into a home.

The only other Black family on the block lives across the street, and they give David and Selah the communal head nod as they unload the final boxes out of the moving van parked in the dead-end street they now share.

"This is a good move," David reiterates to Selah. "Jasmine will have her own room when she's old enough to get out of ours. And it's a bit more diverse here for Nina. She'll get to experience some different types of kids. And maybe now we can settle in with each other in our very new home, one you've always wanted." Selah has been experiencing a bit of postpartum, and he is struggling to find his way professionally, so there is a little weight on their union that both are eager to lift.

Nina is nervous about fifth grade. A new school, a new home, and the pain of missing Lalita and James. Lalita and her family moved to Silicon Valley, because her father got offered a lucrative tech job. Even though Nina and Lalita promise to write each other, it's not the same without the smell of spicy curry and floral incense. Selah tells Nina that James is now living with his aunt while his mom gets the help she needs, so that maybe one day when she's better, he can be reunited with her without fear. Nina still feels bad for setting up the intervention, but Selah reminds her that she might've been the one who saved his life.

Life hasn't changed much for Nina. She walks to the bus stop every morning with her guard up, keeps to herself, pretends she likes school, and avoids the bullies. She doesn't understand why kids pick on her, saying that she acts like she's "all that," when she thinks it's quite the opposite. She wishes she has the confidence of her parents to believe that and push back.

The boys are a little more aggressive this year, swarming like bees, buzzing in her ear daily. Dance class is further away now because of the move, but Selah and David make sure they get her there each week—her happy place, her calming constant. Nina's talent has elevated, and she's now performing both locally and nationally, traveling once every couple of months.

***

"Hi. My name is Calvin."

"I'm Nina."

Nina and Calvin walk up the steep hill from the bus stop in unison but not together, which they've done for months now, without a word. He's the only other young person in her immediate neighborhood, like James was in her last apartment building. Calvin is petite, with caramel-dipped skin and hay-colored eyes. He has a colony of freckles battling for space on his face and neck. And if you didn't look too close, you'd think he's a redhead. He identifies Black, but Nina's never seen anyone look like him that identifies as such. If he were a girl, he would be beautiful. He speaks with a gentle delicate tone, like a good doctor sharing bad news.

"I know you're kinda new here. You live with your mom and dad?" Calvin asks.

"Yeah, well my mom, step-dad, baby sister, and my dog Mister," Nina responds, finding it difficult to hide her delight of finally being asked about herself by someone her age.

"Oh, that's cool. Who's home now?" Calvin asks nervously.

"Nobody. My parents don't get home until six or seven, and sometimes later. It just depends," Nina says, revealing her latch-key status.

"Well, my grandmother lives with me and my mom. And she bakes good homemade bread every day as my snack before homework. I mean, you can come too if you're just home by yourself anyway."

"Oh ok, well my mom is kinda strict, so I have to ask her. And then she'll probably need to meet your mom and your grandmother. What about your dad? Does he live there too?" Nina asks, channeling her mother's interrogation tactics.

"My dad isn't around," Calvin says, looking at his feet with a frown, as if he's pulling up a painful memory.

"Oh ok, let me ask my mom and I'll let you know," Nina says, as she opens the gate to her front yard.

Calvin stands there watching Nina's long legs lunge up her walkway, skipping two steps at a time, thick brown ponytail swinging like a pendulum. She can see Mister in the window panting with excitement, and Calvin in the reflection, motionless. She turns around. "You ok?"

Calvin coughs, and responds, "Yeah, sorry. Your dog is cute."

"Thanks, see you tomorrow," Nina says, feeling warm thinking about his grandmother's bread.

It takes Selah a year to approve Nina's afterschool plan with Calvin, but it's worth the wait. The first time Nina walks into his house down the street, the aroma of fresh buttery dough rising expands the small kitchen. His grandmother slices the bread thick and spreads more sweet butter right up to the edges, accompanying it with fresh and cold apple cider for the wash down. It's everything Nina has hoped for and more. Selah warns her not to eat too much bread every day, but she doesn't care. In fact, she hopes to gain weight in all the places her dad's *Jet* magazine girls carry theirs in—booty and boobs.

"Even I have bigger boobs," the heckling girl at school had announced to Nina, when teasing her about not wearing a bra yet. "I thought Black girls are supposed to have more tits than us."

"You ready to do homework?" Calvin asks, putting their empty plates and cups in the sink. He thanks his grandmother, who is a spitting image of him, except her hair is streaked with silver strands.

"Yes," Nina responds innocently.

Calvin's grandmother likes Nina because she's polite, pretty, and of course strokes her ego by loving her homemade bread, so she doesn't question her much. Nina follows Calvin down the creaky staircase into the dark and barely furnished dungeon of a basement, which consists of one long vintage dining-room table that appears to be left behind from someone's medieval dream. There's no couch, just a random rocking chair in the corner. Therefore, they settle in on the wide Indian rug positioned far from the vision of the staircase.

"Let's play a game first," Calvin suggests.

Nina is sitting in her usual cross-legged position, oblivious to Calvin's desires. "What do you want to play?"

Calvin smiles impishly, pulling a stethoscope from his book bag, like a wizard pulling a snake from his magic basket. "Take off your shirt," he instructs, with an even softer tone than usual.

Nina hesitates and thinks of her parents. None of them would approve of this. But for the first time, she feels wanted by someone who wasn't born to love and appreciate her. She feels powerful and regal. So she does as she's told, pulling her unicorn t-shirt up over her head, apologizing for her white undershirt that clings to her young chest, instead of the fashionable training bra with a little pink bow she sees in department stores.

"It's ok, I'm going to check to see if you're growing properly," Calvin says, surprised Nina is letting him engage her at all. "Take off your undershirt."

Nina doesn't move. She thinks about Veronica and the dozens of *Jet* beauties that men can't seem to ignore. Ironically, she thinks of her mother, who stops traffic by breathing in a way that's simply enchanting, racing admirers who never have a chance against her incomparable magic. Right now, Nina feels like magic with this boy who is hypnotized by her. Without a word, she complies.

The cold metal of the stethoscope glides across Nina's bare chest, running high on each collarbone, across her small mounds, and dipping low to the edge of her valley. Her body feels calm yet tingly, like it does when she's home alone touching herself, thinking about some of her cute peers at school. The texture of her goosebumps has more grit than usual, though inside she feels nothing emotional, specifically for this boy. She doesn't want Calvin, just the feeling of knowing he wants her.

Nina's never told anyone that she knows how to pleasure herself, because it's so good and addictive it must be wrong. Just like her desire for girls. Once she thought about confessing to Grandma Rosa's pastor, when she missed the opportunity with Uncle John. But again, she doesn't want to risk God being mad at her, considering she already does everything in her power not to have her parents feel the same.

"No, you can't go there," Nina warns, grabbing her jeans button, making sure it stays closed.

"I know, I won't," Calvin says, almost annoyed that Nina questions his methods. "I'm not stupid," he says, sighing as if she has interrupted his groove. "Well, that's it. You look healthy, but I'll have to check you again next week. How you feel?" he asks, successfully shifting back to his doctor role.

"I feel good," Nina confirms, putting her layers back on to keep warm, and just in case Calvin's grandmother gets suspicious and runs down the staircase like the Flash. Calvin accepts that playtime is over and walks over to the dining room table where their homework papers are already laid out, ready to be tackled. They sit next to each other, swapping shy glances in between spelling work.

"Next time, maybe I can check your lips and kiss you, to see if they're working ok?" Calvin asks hopefully, awkwardly.

"Sure," Nina says, distracted by Calvin's struggle. She can't help but sneak a peek at his homework, deciding to help him by replacing all his wrong spelling answers with correct ones. This is the one subject Nina has begun to master. She feels beautiful and smart right now, a double win.

"Thank you, Nina," Calvin says, grinding his teeth, attempting to hide his embarrassment.

***

Nina continues to visit Calvin's house every day after school, except Fridays when she has dance class. Baked bread, dungeon checkup, homework time, repeat. No one knows of this secret life they have, not even Rae, Nina's self-proclaimed best friend, bodyguard, and all-around professor of real-life facts. The two meet when Rae comes to Nina's rescue one day at recess, when four girls are looking to jump Nina after one of their boyfriends is giving her too much time. Nina and Rae have been tight ever since. Nina wonders why girls at school are so mean, looking to fight her.

"It's because you're so pretty and quiet," Rae said. "They think you're stuck up, like you think you're better than them. What they don't know is you're just quiet 'cause you scared."

Nina wasn't sure how Rae could see right through her. "How come you know that?"

"Uh duh, 'cause I know I'm the shit. I ain't threatened by you and your pretty ass."

Nina loves how Rae's confidence allows her to see past human shields.

"Nina. Somethin' up with you. What's different? Spill it," Rae demands, coming up from behind Nina in the school lunch line, loudly whispering in her ear.

Nina smiles, and without looking back at her intuitive friend, she says, "You trippin'. I don't know what you mean."

"Oh, you don't know what I mean? Bullshit!"

Nina turns around fast. "Rae ... shhh. Stop cussing, you gonna get us detention," she warns, trying not to laugh.

Calvin walks by with the bagged lunch his grandmother packs for him, and the container of liquid diabetes that Jones Middle School calls chocolate milk. He locks eyes with Nina way too long for Rae's taste.

"Excuse me, what the hell was that?" Rae asks.

"Oh my god, nothing Rae. We're just friends. He lives down the street, give me a break," Nina quickly snaps back.

"Nah, nah, nah. What you do with troll boy?"

Nina ignores her insult. "Ok fine, we kissed, like how me and Van did last year," Nina admits, without admitting anything.

"Um, no. That disaster with Van was no kiss, girl. That was a dumb boy taking a little virgin girl in the back of the school and accidentally kissing her in the eye, and then has the nerve to blame her, saying Virgin Mary didn't kiss right," Rae reminds her.

"True. And then he lied and took his Mickey Mouse chain back when I was standing in the lunch line, like right here." Nina stomps her foot, and Rae jumps back a little. "Can you believe he said he was just gonna get it cleaned, or something dumb like that? But his cousin called me that night and broke up with me for him—stupid coward," she continues, finishing the dramatic rendition of the situation. "See, now you got me all mad again."

"Ha! Don't change the subject, Nina," Rae says, even though it amuses her when Nina gets angry. "Listen, meet me after school today. I know you can take a break from kissy face to hang out with your girl. It's been forever."

"Ok, I'll meet you at your bus," Nina says, looking forward to spending time with the only girl who gets her at school, who still likes her. Selah forbids Nina to see her, especially over in her neighborhood, but she's one of the most honest people Nina knows, and with Rae, she feels safe.

"She's just fast, Nina," Selah says once. "She and her whole family have a bad reputation. Her two sisters had babies at fourteen and sixteen, I think. And from what I observe the few times I've seen Rae, she's following in their tracks."

Nina doesn't care about all that. She knows Rae is a good-hearted girl, and Nina doesn't know any girls like her, so she will hold onto their friendship for as long as she can.

Nina beats Rae to her own bus and isn't happy about it. *Come on, Rae, hurry up.* Nina has problems on her own bus: snide comments, "accidental" bumps, overt confrontation. And those are from people who are used to her presence. She can't imagine if she's left too long with people who aren't used to feeling angry or jealous around her.

"I'm here, I'm here, girl, I'm here!" Rae exclaims, running onto the bus, knowing Nina enough to know exactly what she's feeling. "Sorry girl, that nigga Tyrone was trying to holla to me about taking me out or something."

Nina gives Rae an accusatory stare. "Take you out or get you to put out?" she asks sarcastically, laughing at her own wit.

"Well that's mean, little Virgin Mary," Rae says, masking her hurt feelings.

Nina realizes she's gone a bit overboard with the nasty comment. So, she decides to pay for Rae's cheese fries and grape soda at her neighborhood carryout.

They get off the bus and cross the street, switching worlds. Rows of identical single-family homes turn into working-class apartment housing. Specialty grocery stores and elite gyms turn into liquor stores and fast-food carryouts, one of which has Nina and Raes' mouths watering. Nina watches Rae strut into the carryout and hopes her own walk practice will result in Rae's seductive sway one day. Rae is average height with a *Jet* magazine body, coated by dark-brown skin and topped with burgundy Chaka Khan hair with loose curly bangs. Like Calvin, she has freckles, but they're mostly hidden by her chestnut skin. Her mouth is full, like someone stuffed loads of cotton in her lips, but they still can't hide the slightly bucked and crooked teeth she's hoping to get fixed one day.

Sitting on a bench, pretending not to notice the beautiful teenage Black boys playing dominos and swapping cash for dime bags, Nina and Rae devour a large order of cheese fries, drowned in ketchup and hot sauce.

"Remember that time when you rode your bike down here, with some preppy little outfit on, trying to impress Darnell, the baddest boy on the block?" Rae asks Nina with a mouthful of cheesy potatoes.

Nina laughs out loud. "Yessss! I stole my mother's broken pager and had it clipped to my shorts, trying to pretend like I was cool. I was so busy looking at him, trying to arch my back

DANCER IN THE BULLPEN

with my booty up like you showed me, and then ran right into the bus top pole at the same time he looked up at me. The pager shattered in the street and I was face down on the ground."

Rae's laughing so hard, she can barely catch her breath. "You had the biggest knot on your head for days. I think you was supposed to go to the doctor for that shit, but you were so damn stubborn hiding it from your mom, cutting your hair to give yourself bangs."

"Yeah, that shit was funny," Nina admits, emulating Rae's dirty mouth. "But Darnell is all kinds of cute. Where is he these days, anyway?"

"Hey Nina."

Nina and Rae immediately look up and stop laughing, like a game of Red Light, Green Light.

"Calvin, hey. What you doing here?" Nina asks, mostly annoyed he's killing the vibe, and just a tad worried this run-in isn't a coincidence.

"Oh, I'm meeting a friend at his house down the street, since I don't have any homework due tomorrow. Do you have any, Nina?" Calvin is purposely making a point that she hasn't given him a heads up that she isn't coming over for her buttered bread and feel up.

"Yeah, I have a little," Nina responds softly, feeling bad she's disappointed Calvin.

"Well, have fun, Calvin," Rae says, cutting the awkward moment short, happy to dismiss him.

"Are you sure you don't wanna hang out with us?" Nina questions an invitation.

"No, it's ok. I'll see you tomorrow, Nina."

Nina watches Calvin walk away and sees thin trails of smoke coming from his head.

"Rae, you see that?"

"Girl, that troll is a bit off, don't you think? Why he always say your name after each sentence, like he's an old man, or a serial killer?"

"Girl, stop," Nina says, trying not to think about how many times he does that.

"I heard his dad like murdered somebody and they never caught him," Rae reveals, as she stuffs another forkful of fries in her mouth. "He fled the country but left his family behind. I think Calvin was like five or something."

Before Nina can answer, Rae continues. "There's just something off about him. Hmmm …" she contemplates, looking at Nina suspiciously. "Just like there's been something off about you. I'm gonna find out what's going on with you two!"

Nina ignores the terrible gossip and Rae's dangerous mission.

✸✸✸

Nina has recently had a big show with her ballet group, so it has been easy to avoid confronting Calvin. She hasn't been in school consistently for the past seven days, so walking down to the bus stop almost feels like the first day of school. David warns her that she can't afford to miss the bus this morning, because he has an early meeting and Selah goes in to work even earlier.

Nina is usually the last student in the bus line. But this time, it looks like there's one person who beats her to it. She doesn't recognize the back of his head, or the jeweled red cloak draped over his back, which flows unending. His crown is slightly too big and tilts to the left, but it doesn't matter. The unidentified boy is radiating majestic sun rays, even from behind. But then he turns around, and the entire street crystalizes.

"Hi, I'm Nina." This time she takes the initiative.

"Hi," says the king that Nina has been anxiously waiting for. "I'm Phillip."

Sir Phillip, how can I help you? Nina's mind drops her to her knees in a full curtsy, wishing she has the courage to request to be his queen right now, at first sight. "Nice to meet you, Phillip," she confesses, face turning just as red as the velvet fabric he's draped in.

Phillip's hair isn't straight and stringy. It's curly, though not quite thick. His features are confusing like Calvin's, but exquisite at the same time. He is the color of sand, with a wide nose but thin lips. He has a royal metal gate entrapping his teeth that he says will one day give him a pretty smile like Nina.

"You have pretty teeth," Phillip states.

"Oh no, you must need glasses. My teeth have a lot of space in between them, especially my front teeth. I probably need braces too," Nina says, confused by Phillip's observation.

"You know in some African countries, gaps between a girl's teeth means she's really pretty," Phillip shares. "And I agree with that. It's obvious you're the prettiest."

Nina is smitten. Where did this royalty come from?

Phillip explains that his father holds a high-ranking position in the military, so the family moves around a lot, sometimes in the middle of a school year. They've just come from California, but before that, they were in Germany. Nina is impressed by Phillips' world-knowledge and understanding.

Other kids have joined Nina and Phillip in the bus line, but neither of them notices. The rays of sun are too bright, blinding them from the common folk. Nina is so engaged and in tune with Phillip, a crown sprouts from her scalp. She reaches up and runs her fingers over the pointed arches.

Phillip comes close to her and asks softly, "Do you like that?"

"Yes," she replies.

"Hey Nina!" Calvin's loud greeting flings Nina right out of the kingdom without ease or grace.

"Oh, hey Calvin. Wow, it seems like I haven't seen you in forever."

"Yeah," he says, glaring at Phillip.

"This is Phillip. He just moved here from California. Don't you have family there too?" Nina asks, feeling like she has to pee suddenly.

"Hey man, what's up?" Phillip asks with enthusiasm.

"Hey," Calvin responds dryly.

"Hay is for horses," Nina teases, attempting to break the awkwardness.

"So, do you two, like, go together? Like boyfriend and girlfriend?" Nina's new king boldly asks whoever will answer.

Calvin jumps on the opportunity to respond. "Nah, we're just friends."

Nina looks at Calvin, trying to see an expression past the stone wall he has up, but he gives her no eye contact or hint of emotion. She is not sure how that makes her feel. Sad? Relieved? Petrified? All three, perhaps. Nina loves the attention but doesn't want anyone mad at her, which makes her feel unworthy of love.

The school day is long, and the bus ride back home is too short, not enough opportunity to watch Phillip smile and laugh with classmates. Once they all get off the bus, Nina says goodbye to him quickly, grateful he lives a long walk away. She and Calvin take their normal climb up the hill, past her house, toward the scent of buttery bread. Nina can feel that her invisible friend is near because the weight of the air is heavier over her left shoulder, and she feels warm breath in her ear. Nina wants to talk to her, but doesn't want Calvin to hear.

I'm here in case you need me. You know you don't have to do it, her friend says.

"Oh, you're not going home?" Calvin asks, mood lifting as he thinks of getting his checkup tools ready.

"No, why would I?" Nina asks, seeing now that he is simply jealous of Phillip; he still wants her. She ignores her invisible friend's energy and follows Calvin into his house.

Calvin's grandmother sees Nina and begins to pull down a second bread plate from the cabinet. "Oh Nina, how nice it is to see you! It has been awhile, yes?"

"Yes ma'am. I was traveling with my dance group in Philadelphia."

"Wow, that's wonderful. Your mother shared with me and Calvin's mom that you're an angelic bird when you dance," Calvin's grandmother says. "I'm hoping one day, we all get a chance to see you fly. I'm sure Calvin would love that too, wouldn't you, Calvin?"

Calvin nods his head and manages a slight smile.

"I'll let you know when tickets come out for the summer show here," Nina promises.

"Oh, that'll be great, Nina!"

Nina and Calvin walk down the dungeon staircase with full bellies. As a habit, they put their books and assignments spread out on the dining room table, but plop down on the Indian rug, away from view. Nina crosses her legs, but this time closes her eyes and takes a deep breath in, then exhales. When she opens her eyes, Calvin is already leaning in, ready to kiss.

"Calvin, wait. Don't be mad, but I don't want to play this game anymore."

He pulls back and gives Nina the emotionless face again. "It's ok, I'm not mad. But why not, though? It's the new boy?"

"No, no. Not him. I just want to take a break from all the touching and stuff. It kinda makes me feel a little weird, or bad, I dunno. I just don't want to get caught or feel like this."

"I thought it makes you feel good?" Calvin asks with a sad tone of betrayal.

"It does, but I want to be a good girl, ok? Listen, I still wanna be friends, do homework, eat bread, hang out, you know?"

"Ok Nina. I get it." Calvin's menacing tone penetrates Nina's chest.

"Ouch!" she exclaims, extending her legs and dramatically leaning forward to clutch both calves.

"What's wrong with you?" Calvin questions, resisting the opportunity to be sympathetic during a time he's not getting his way.

"It's nothing, just my dancers' legs."

"What's that?"

"My mom says my legs are growing, and because I use them so much by dancing, they ache sometimes."

"That doesn't look like an ache to me. You look like you in crazy pain."

Calvin's concern is short-lived, and he stands up and walks slowly to the bathroom, which is dark and cold. Nina never ventures there. She either holds her bladder or goes upstairs to the fancy French-style toilette. She moves off the rug and over to the dining room table, trying to ignore Calvin's waterfall splashes in the bowl, and begins her homework. This time, she relies on his math answers to replace hers.

Nina attempts to write a series of numbers on the crisp white paper, but the table is vibrating, trembling, like the wood is afraid. Or is it her hands? "Calvin?" she calls out, not sure if he's aware of the earthquake, and not sure if she really cares. She just wants to know he's there to save her.

Nina slowly stands up and walks to the bathroom door, feeling the ache of her bladder.

"Calvin?" she whispers, this time sensing the familiar nausea, but with more intensity. She presses her ear against the dark mahogany, which is slowly turning into the beautiful bright-red that Nina remembered dripping from the magic mirrored coffee table not too long ago. She is hoping to hear anything through the door, a heartbeat at least. But all she hears is fear dripping down the seam, and the faint sound of labored breathing.

"Calvin?"

The inhale-exhale tango intensifies, releasing a foul heat from under the door, which begins to shake violently.

Nina is afraid but doesn't waver. "Calvin!"

She doesn't want to do it, but her knees bend and drop to the ground. She gets lower, stomach flat on the cold concrete, left cheek deflated on its side. She brings her eyes as close to the opening under the door as possible and decides that if she doesn't see Calvin alive in this abyss, she will go tell his grandmother.

"Calvin, please, answer me. Are you ok?" Nina pleads, suddenly feeling an intense desire to protect him.

She squints her eyes to get a better view, and discovers two oversized translucent red eyes squinting back at her, its mouth yawning blood-orange fire like she woke it from eating Hell. A giant scaly tail whips around from behind and slams into the door. Nina jumps back, startled and speechless, until she screams at the top of her lungs, but no one can hear her.

It doesn't matter, I'm going to get in this door! Nina convinces herself, overcome by a surge of bravery. "Calvin, I'm coming in! Step back." She rushes in with her frail body and blasts the door open with the force of her shoulder, releasing a monstrous backdraft. "Calvin, get down!"

"Nina! What the hell are you doing? Why are you on the floor?" Calvin questions, confused.

Calvin's grandmother runs halfway down the staircase and yells, "Is everything ok?"

"Yes Grandmother, it's fine," Calvin snaps with agitation. "Nina just saw a big bug in the bathroom, go back upstairs."

Nina is limp on the floor like she's been pushed, sweating and disoriented. "You didn't hear or see that ... dragon, Calvin? I was yelling for you. Everything was shaking and there was so much heat, like fire from behind the door," she rants, panting with confusion. Nina has never questioned any of her visions or experiences before. She usually trusts everything she encounters and questions everyone else, because people lie about what they feel and believe all the time, especially those closest to you.

"No Nina. I think you're tired from all that dancing you do, or whatever," Calvin says dismissively. He helps Nina from off the floor and reiterates, "All I did was go pee, flush the toilet, and wash my hands. Our toilets and sinks are super loud, maybe that's what you heard."

DANCER IN THE BULLPEN

Nina stares at Calvin, just now realizing his freckles are even more invasive on his face than she had realized. *He's so pretty*, she thinks, but feels nothing but exhaustion.

"I'm going to go home then," Nina announces, defeated by her own thoughts. Calvin doesn't fight her, watching her walk up the stairs. She pulls her hand back off the banister, because it's so hot.

***

The next morning, Nina isn't feeling well, but decides to go to school anyway. There's a poetry workshop she doesn't want to miss. Calvin isn't at the bus stop, but Phillip is, with Nina's crown in hand, eager to appoint her.

"I know this is kinda fast," Phillip says, "but I want you to be mine. And I know you like me 'cause you be smiling so hard with me." He brushes Nina's overgrown bangs away from her eyes, so she can see him clearly. "I want to keep you smiling," he confesses, making Nina's knees weak with desire. She is happy that Phillip has quickly realized that they're made for each other, and has wasted no time labeling them girlfriend and boyfriend. They can "go together" now, and she finally feels special—on her way to becoming queenworthy.

Sitting on the bus, holding hands, Nina is beyond excited to finally be claimed by someone who doesn't want to hide how wonderful she is, but instead be out in the open like the king and queen at the ball.

"So, I'm going to this poetry workshop in second period," she says. "Some real, live poets are coming in to share their stuff and help us write our own—even read what we already have. I don't know though. I have some stuff to share, but not sure if I want to, because it's not like I'm a poet, and what if they hate it, you know?"

"Shhh Nina. You're talking so much, and so fast. Come here. Kiss me," Phillip demands, hungry for Nina's softness on him. She leans in and closes her eyes, giving into the warmth of his probing tongue and the scent of his dad's cologne.

"Stop," Nina says, without conviction. "People are watching."

"So, who cares? You're mine. We can do whatever we want. Nobody will bully you now that you're with me."

Nina is one of the three students who show up to the workshop. It becomes evident that her peers are here to get out of second period, with little interest in the actual art form. After a brief lecture, the students are asked to read a few poetic samples and then create a piece of their own.

"Which poets do you like, Nina?" says Sarah Sullivan, the young local poet the school has brought in. She engages students in a unique way.

"I love Maya Angelou, of course, Nikki Giovanni, and Langston Hughes. My mom has all their books. So I just try to read all of them, one by one. But I also love Shel Silverstein books and Dr. Seuss. That's all poetry."

"Yes, they are," Ms. Sullivan says.

"I love singers too, like Nina Simone. I get that she's a singer, but she writes her music, and her songs are just poems with music, you know?"

"I do know. You have a smart prospective, Nina. Is that how you got your name? One of your parents likes Nina Simone?"

"No, *both* of my parents love Nina Simone. But yes, that's who I'm named after," Nina confirms proudly. "I know

DANCER IN THE BULLPEN

your poems too. Well, just one. I think it's called 'Still Standing.' Something about a tree that never dies."

"Wow Nina. I'm impressed. How do you know my work?" Ms. Sullivan says, flattered.

"I saw it at the bookstore my mom takes me to sometimes," Nina reveals, happy that she has pleased someone she admires.

Boom, boom, boom!

Phillip bangs on the classroom door, finds Nina's eyes, and motions his head toward the lunchroom. Nina is embarrassed and looks up at the poet apologetically.

"Alright kids, it looks like there's never enough time for creativity," says Ms. Sullivan. "It's lunchtime. Thank you for your participation and I hope to see you all soon."

Nina jumps up and dodges to the door.

"Nina wait, please." Ms. Sullivan asks.

Nina pivots dramatically, annoyed that this woman is keeping her away from her king.

"Do you write poetry at home?" Ms. Sullivan inquires.

"Um, not really. A little." Nina lies.

It's as if the poet knows she's lying. "Ok great, well, here's my contact information. Maybe you can show me some of your work one day. I bet they're amazing, better than you even realize."

Nina doesn't understand why she would say that. *She doesn't even know me, or if I'm any good.* "Ok, I will," she says with no intention of doing so, but she does put Ms. Sullivan's business card in the safest compartment of her book bag. Nina walks to the door again and pauses. She turns back around to the poet and take a deep breath in. "Actually, I just finished writing something yesterday, if you want to, I dunno, read it

139

and see if you like it, maybe." Nina's statement sounds more like a question.

"Yes, please!" The poet can't mask her excitement.

Nina walks over to Ms. Sullivan's desk, unable to hold back a smile, but purposely not sitting in the chair next to the poet, in case she has to snatch her journal back and escape from humiliation. She pulls out the composition book from her bag and opens it to the last page. "I don't think it's a poem really, just my thoughts," she explains in case it's not well received.

Ms. Sullivan quietly begins reading the untitled piece:

> *I'm just a superhero*
> *Only one in the world*
> *Alone in this crowded room*
>
> *Hundreds of voices fight with car horns outside*
> *Palms collide with "Hi, I'm such and such," lies, lies*
> *People die to fly with wings caught in windows*
>
> *I am just a superhero*
> *Only one in the world*
> *Alone in this crowded room*
>
> *Nina*

"Are you reading it again?" Nina happily asks. It must be the reason it's taking Ms. Sullivan so long to lift her eyes from the page.

Ms. Sullivan finally resurfaces. "Nina, this is incredible. Simply amazing that you wrote this at your age." She pauses

DANCER IN THE BULLPEN

and stares at Nina, like she's trying to figure out why her mind is so much bigger than her little body. "I love the way you implemented a repetitive format," she continues. "Why did you do that? I mean, where did you learn that?"

"Maya Angelou: 'Caged Bird.' I ask my mom to read it, even though I know it pretty well now. When poetry is read to me, it is easier for me to connect to it. Maya Angelou repeats a lot of her words in this poem and it's like a song or a dance. I love how it flows."

"I dunno," Nina continues. "Sometimes I don't really understand what I write, the words just come to me and it can take a long time for me to even get what I meant." She reaches for her journal and Ms. Sullivan lets go without hesitation, as she can tell her time with it is up.

"Well, thank you for trusting me enough to share your art with me. It means a lot," says Ms. Sullivan.

"Sure, no problem, thanks." And just like that, Nina is out the door, rushing back to her normal.

Nina walks into the lunchroom and can barely see. The lights are so dim; they might as well be off. Everyone is wearing a black cloak and has black paint covering their faces. Calvin is sitting at the corner of his usual table, but unusually, not alone. A swarm of boys and girls—including Phillip, who looks disgusted—are hovering over him and looking back at Nina.

I thought Calvin wasn't here today, Nina questions, scratching the inside of her thigh. *And why is Phillip over there?*

Nina looks around and everyone stops, frozen in mid-sentence or mid-stride. She tries to find Calvin's face, but all she sees is a dark shadow and those red piercing eyes. The cafeteria begins to shake like the floor is going to part. Calvin stands up and begins to grow high above his table, as his skin transforms into a scaly hide with a thick tail. The wings are so massive they could fan the sun cold. Frozen blood-filled veins map them, and the dragon gleefully spits fire when he tells the world: "Nina is a whore. She lets me feel her up and play doctor with her every day. I tried to get her to stop, but she always wants more. Just want to warn y'all, Nina is a whore."

The cowardly dragon finishes his evil address. The lights lift, and everyone returns to being normal elementary school kids again, except for the intensified stares and whispers.

"Nina, what the fuck! I just heard what the troll did!" Rae is furious. "What you want me to do? Want me to get him jumped, send poison cupcakes to his house? Whatever you want, tell me." She is bouncing, pacing like a boxer in front of Nina, ready for a knock-out round.

Nina struggles to lift the boulder from off her chest, overwhelmed by the pain of betrayal. She vomits her morning breakfast, along with the color of her skin, in a nearby trashcan. She is ghost white, desperately trying to lick her cracked lips, but her tongue is too dehydrated.

Phillip is showing off that same smile and laugh Nina first adored on the school bus, but they now seem cruel and treacherous. He catches Nina's stare and challenges it, dropping his wide grin into a wicked pout.

"I can't believe my king has turned into a traitor," Nina says with disappointment.

"Forget about him, and all of them, Nina. Don't worry. Everyone knows you're Virgin Mary. Besides, look at me …" Nina shifts her eyes off Calvin and looks into Rae's eyes, unable to mask her hate for him. "People think the same of me and I don't give a shit!" Rae pauses from her rant and takes a good look at Nina. "Wait girl, you don't look so good. You ok?"

Nina nods her head yes, but her body temperature is boiling and she's thinking about her death. She looks back at Calvin, probing him with her dark-brown eyes, which have now turned stone black. There is no dust invasion or trembling limbs, and she doesn't let up as his eyes widen, and his throat begins to close.

"Are you ok, man?" The boy next to him asks.

Calvin grips his freckled neck with both hands, gasping for air, looking around frantically as a plea for help. Nina clenches her teeth and squeezes her eyes, now their normal shade of brown, and retreats back to her supportive friend. Her body temperature returns back to code.

"It's ok, Rae. Let's just go to class," Nina says with a cottonmouth and emotionless face, just like Calvin taught her. All the kids at Calvin's lunch table are on their feet now, watching him cough up clots of blood.

"Oh my god, someone get a teacher!" one girl screams, her previous cackles replaced with panicked gasps.

"What the hell is going on?" Rae asks, stepping away from Nina to get a closer look at the commotion, like the rest of the cafeteria. Calvin looks like a cheetah who's just finished his first kill, mouth and neck dripping blood, barely breathing.

"There it is, that pretty red," Nina mumbles. She knows she should be afraid, but she's not, at all. She welcomes the rich brightness with open arms, entranced by it. Rae turns back around and looks at her with horror, as the gym teacher and school nurse rush to Calvin's side.

"Yo! What's going on, Nina?" Rae asks, realizing that Nina is not supposed to be able to answer that question.

"I dunno, is he ok?" Nina asks, embracing the thought of his death with her own.

Rae comes closer to her, looks her in the eyes, and asks, "Did you do this?"

"Do what? Make him choke? From all the way over here? Um, Rae, you sound crazy. I'm not a wizard," Nina responds nervously, afraid that maybe she did do it. "It's not me. You the one who said he's a serial killer. Maybe he did this to himself. And my uncle always said, 'God don't like ugly.'"

"Your uncle ain't the one who made that saying up, Nina, but yeah, I guess you right," Rae submits, taking a deep breath in and exhaling just as slow, concluding that Nina is just a regular hurt little girl. It must be that "karma is a bitch" thing, like her mama says.

Calvin doesn't die. He's taken away by the ambulance, and doctors are able to stabilize him at the hospital. There is no clear determination of the cause of his choking, but rumor has it that Nina put razors in his food. She is amazed at how stupid people can be. But she actually likes that many of her peers are frightened of her now, so she can stop being so frightened of them. Calvin's grandmother calls and tells Selah that he has a rare disease that he doesn't share with anyone, and the symptoms are triggered by anxiety, so he's being homeschooled for the rest of the year. At least Nina has that satisfaction.

"We miss Nina," Calvin's grandmother says to Selah. "Maybe when Calvin's feeling better, she can come for a visit." But the only thing Nina misses is the baked bread and the idea of trusting a boy ever again.

***

"Hey princess, how are you doing? How's school?" Selah asks.

It's 8:15 p.m. and Selah is just getting home from the hospital, after saving the children of the world that Nina is beginning to hate. She is proud that Selah is one of the best pediatricians/medical professors on the East Coast, following in Grandma Daisy's footsteps and making history, but sometimes she wishes her mom was just a mom, focused on only her.

Selah kicks off her shoes, drops her briefcase, and plops down on Nina's bedroom loveseat. She's tired but misses talking to her oldest daughter. So, she tries to catch up on her life and confirm that she's ok. But Nina doesn't have the courage to tell her mom that she carries a fear of the unknown in the pit of her stomach. Selah doesn't know that school is incredibly hard for Nina and all the lessons feel impossible, with excruciating multiple steps that don't make sense, except for her English class. She doesn't tell her mom that she wears a scarlet letter on her chest, and eats in the hallway during lunch to avoid mean girls and their hateful whore comments. Nina feels loved by her parents but she is unsure of herself, despite the beauty and talent that they brag about.

"School is fine," Nina says—the only words she can muster.

"How's science? That dumb teacher, Ms. Griffin, giving you any more problems? Is her aid helping you more now?" Selah continues to probe, now laying back, stretching out on Nina's loveseat.

"Yes Mom, I'm getting better at it now." Nina lies, frustrated she has to be subjected to these interrogations with no warning, after her armor from the day is already battered and removed.

"Ok, good. I don't want to have to go to that school again and check them white folks," Selah threatens.

At the last parent-teacher conference, Ms. Griffin, in front of Nina, told Selah not to worry about her mastering science. "Nina's a pretty girl, Mrs. Abadie. She'll marry well."

"Nina's future marriage plans should not be your concern. I need you to teach her science. And if she's struggling with it, teach her again," Selah demanded with fury.

Nina does love how her mother defends and advocates for her, even though she is also happy to hear that someone thinks she's good marriage material.

"Are you sure everything is ok, baby?" Selah asks, as Jasmine is running around screaming and drawing on the walls with a red crayon, working through the terrible twos early.

"Jazzy, oh my god, please!" Selah jumps up when she sees the smoke of Jasmine's little heels trailing down the hall. "You're ruining Mommy's walls. Jesus! Jazzy! Where's your father, and why aren't you in bed?" Sometimes Nina really believes that Selah expects answers from the baby.

"Come here, Jazzy," Nina gently summons her vivacious little sister. Even during times like this, Nina remembers how much she prayed for her. Jasmine is a reminder that God exists. So it's hard to stay mad at her and mad at herself.

Jasmine runs over to her big sister, giggling, anticipating some type of treat. Nina opens her book bag and pulls out a coloring book she bought with her chore money and gives it to the restless toddler.

"Tank you, Na Na," Jasmine says as she drops to the floor, opens the book to a random page, and violently runs the red crayon back and forth with wide strokes outside of the lines.

Nina bought this coloring book for herself. Drawing calms her, like dancing and writing. But it's obvious little Jasmine needs more calming than her right now. What are big sisters for?

"Jazzy, where's your daddy?" Selah asks again. David is downstairs, distant, as if there is a storm separating him from Selah, and there's no road that travels through or around it.

"He's downstairs, Mom. Are y'all ok?" Nina asks.

"Everything will be fine, princess. Just concentrate on school and be a good girl for me."

"Everything will be fine?" And I am a good girl, Mom. But I'm not little anymore like Jazzy. I see you, and you don't seem happy. Are you going to divorce David?" Nina asks, swallowing her own sadness.

"No one is talking divorce, baby. Don't worry about your mama."

Nina gets up from her bed and gives her mother a tight hug, because she knows that's what Selah truly wants, and what Nina desperately needs. Sometimes she feels an overwhelming desire to just sob in her mother's lap and beg for her to make the noise go away, but she doesn't want to be needy, and she worries her mother can't handle anything else on her plate. Selah's working hard, bringing in money to take care of the family.

Nina looks forward to nights. The quiet, peaceful moments before she falls asleep save her from the chaos that runs through her mind during the day. She sleeps on her top bunk, despite the risk of falling like when she was smaller. This small threat of danger makes her feel braver than she is. But the stars are closer to her, and the demons have a harder time reaching so high in the dark. Most nights, she doesn't have visitors. Although, sometimes, her bedroom is full of mysterious energy.

"Nina."

Nina believes she's dreaming, and tells the soft voice in her ear to go away.

"Nina, Nina," the voice persists.

Nina slowly opens her eyes and looks down at her exposed legs. She attempts to reach down to her feet without moving her torso too much, in search of the runaway covers. But her core isn't strong enough. She quickly gives up, and rubs her legs together like two twigs igniting a campfire, and closes her eyes again. Suddenly her body is engulfed by the missing covers, tucked warmly under her heels and around her waist and arms.

"Mom?" Nina mumbles, flashing back in time.

"Everything's gonna be alright, little one," the voice says, louder than a whisper, but not clear enough to trust.

Nina can feel soft hands holding her toes on each foot, generating heat throughout her body. Sweating, she attempts to open her eyes again, but there are weights on them keeping her vision out of focus. "Uncle?"

"Yeah?"

"How come your head is touching the ceiling?" Nina asks.

"Because I'm taller in Heaven," he responds.

"Nina! Girl, get up! I'm not gonna tell you again. You gonna miss your bus!" Selah charges in, pulling the blinds up on each window in one take, forcing the sun to slap Nina in the face, twice on each side.

"Ok Mom, dang! I'm coming," Nina yells back. She pops up to an upright position, looking straight ahead at the covers hanging from the edge of the bunkbed ladder, staring, wondering if it was real.

"Nina! Snap out of it, get up!"

"Ok, ok, I'm up."

Nina doesn't use the ladder and slides down off the bed, walking by her mom with eyes half-closed to the bathroom. Selah picks up Nina's blanket off the ground, and wonders why it's soaked in sweat.

***

Lisa: Nina's second saving grace. She is the friend who has become a safe space, outside the walls of school. Lisa reminds her that she's not weird, and definitely capable of being appreciated by a girl her age. Though they are different from each other, Lisa accepts her for the special person she is, and Nina can't imagine ever letting this kind of love go.

Tall, dark, elegant, brilliant. Lisa has gorgeous never-ending legs that are accented by matching fingers and toes with the kind of almond-shaped nails women pay a lot of money for. Her beauty is classic-meets-futuristic, not what Nina describes as current-trendy, like hers. Boys don't seem to appreciate what seems so obvious to Nina: the specialness of her friend.

Boys like what the world tells them to like. And even then, they don't know what they see, because they aren't smart, Selah once says during a "stay away from boys" chat.

It's taken Nina a short period of time to realize that boys don't bother to probe past her face and body. There's an expectation that pretty, nice, light-skinned girls are limited in their offerings. She has already been hiding her gifts for some time, so she questions their value. At the same time, she watches everyone—from a wise old man to a fine young man—hang on to every word Lisa spits by mouth or on paper. While Nina is being admired for how sweet and pretty she is by superficial boys, Lisa is going back and forth, writing poetry with the ones Nina really wants to get close to—the smart ones.

Despite the longing for what Lisa has, and vice versa, the grass being greener doesn't change the fact that Nina adores all things Lisa. She has a way of seeing past the façade, muting the roar, and cooling the dragon's fire Nina often battles simply by existing.

Nina doesn't remember much about how they met. She just has memories of a sistergirl cookout at Grandma Daisy's in Beantown—the texture of familiar cobblestones, funky sounds of Kool & the Gang and Rick James records skipping a beat—as the duo chomped down on kosher hot dogs.

Lisa is the daughter of one of Selah's best friends, and Selah allows Lisa to stay over almost every weekend, even school nights when there are blizzards. Nina and Lisa plan it out just right. When the weather forecast mentions anything over four inches, Lisa stuffs her overnight bag to accommodate at least a week's visit, just in case, and Nina includes the request for the extra treats on the family grocery list before the Armageddon run. Lisa is never a guest—she's family—which means she rides with David to take and pick Nina up from dance class, helps select the less than age-appropriate psycho-thrillers from Blockbuster with Selah, and joins Nina raking the yard with a flimsy tool in the cold, snot dripping on oversized, green leaf bags.

Lisa also finds community with Nina at the local Baptist church that Selah introduced the family to when moving into the neighborhood. "It's harder to make the wrong decisions when you're closer to God," Selah says. Everyone in the house must attend church every Sunday, which means Lisa has to practice the Baptist faith just like everyone else, and she feels as happy there as Nina does.

"What dress are you going to wear? And do you want me to do your hair?" Lisa asks.

"Yes!" Nina responds every time. She loves letting Lisa put the extra touches on her: a high ponytail with a cute set of barrettes, or a glittery belt to give something plain some pizazz. Lisa has great fashion sense, even at a young age.

After getting all dressed up like princesses, the two rush Selah, David, and Jasmine out the house to get them to church breakfast before the grits, bacon, eggs, and biscuits are gone. They climb up the steep stairs to Children's Sunday School, which they're almost too old to attend, and afterward, they head back down to the adult service, where they learn how to follow Jesus and be obedient through colorful and vibrant stories from the Bible that no one questions.

"I dunno how my mom questions the stories and fairytales I write, when there are so many beautiful but even crazier ones in the Bible," Nina whispers to Lisa sitting in the pew. She and Lisa don't care that folks say they're too old to be carrying dolls around. They enjoy the domestic roleplay with their Cabbage Patch Kids, and bring them to church perfectly swaddled, ready to hear the good word. Soon enough, the baby bottles and blankets will be replaced with sparkly purses and cherry lip gloss. They'll soon be old enough to engage with the older teens at the church youth-group functions.

Lisa always comes with a decadent artistic agenda. From the fashion shows to the choreographed performances, she facilitates it all. She is the weekend Master of Ceremonies and Nina absorbs it, feeding off of her creative energy. One could say Lisa comes over so much because she doesn't want to be alone while her mother is not home—which is often—or that Nina has her over, so she won't be so lonely despite a house full of familiar strangers. But maybe one could also say they spend so much time together because they see each other clearly, and can relate to the unwelcome solitude, outweighing the differences between their households.

But good things don't last forever. Though Nina appreciates her mother being the patron saint of protection, her need to save vulnerable family and friends is stretching the house thin; the one visible friend Nina loves the most soon doesn't have enough room to stretch her limbs in borrowed space. It's devastating for Nina, losing so much time with her dynamic sidekick, especially when she's being replaced by the presence of people Nina does not choose and who don't know her enough to love her, like Lisa does.

***

Nina's distant teenage cousin, Dani, is battling a life of addiction and bad choices. She's completed rehab and desperately needs a place to continue her recovery, heal, and figure out the next steps for her and her unborn baby. Nina just wishes there's another place she can do that in. Dani reminds her of her other cousin Lexa—nice on the surface, but another person behind closed doors, feeding her insecurities about being inexperienced and naive with boys and life on the streets. Nina is confident that if they shared the same bed at night, she'd squish her too, big belly and all. But she tries to ignore Dani and be a good girl for Selah, friendly and hospitable, despite her feeling that her cousin is hiding something.

Only a few weeks after moving into what is soon to be Jasmine's own room, Dani inadvertently reveals her secret. Nina comes home exhausted as usual from battling school, and hears the sound of liquid bubbling. She wonders who could be boiling water for tea in the bedroom. When she gently pushes Jasmine's door open, she finds her pregnant cousin freebasing crack cocaine, using homemade tools she found in the house.

"Want some?" Dani asks casually, like she's offering a bag of Nina's favorite chips.

"No thanks," Nina says coolly, closing the door in the same manner as it was opened.

Dani swings it back open just as fast. "I promise this is the last of it, then I'm done. I know I got this baby coming now, I get it. Don't tell," she says, in a tone that threatens more than pleads. Nina walks the four steps to the bathroom before feeling her legs buckle. She hugs the toilet and vomits bile, breaking out in a cold sweat. She makes the mistake of not closing the door.

"Na Na, you ok?" Jasmine asks, with her face so close to Nina's that she can simply lay her little head on the toilet seat with her.

"I'm ok, baby girl. Go to my room and get the coloring books. I'll be right there," Nina says, trying to avoid any other negative visuals.

Nina is sick to her stomach for days because of Dani's dirty habit, but doesn't tell Selah about her revelation. Quite frankly, she's scared of the girl, but also doesn't want to be the cause of preventing a family member the opportunity for something better.

Shortly after Nina's cousin settles in, a family of six who's down on their luck—and recently lost their home—

moves in. Dad, mom, and their four young children settle in the family entertainment room, which has now turned from a basement into a lower-level apartment. A few days turn into a few weeks. A few weeks turn into a few months. But the months feel like years, which feel like decades. The adjustment forces Selah, David, and their kids to be restricted mostly to the upper-level of the house, which also restricts little wild Jasmine's range of play. The dining room walls are her canvas for colorful abstract pieces. The coffee table is where she mimics big sister Nina, but journals directly onto the wood instead of the paper she's given, carving various dramatic lines and curves. But Jasmine's favorite room is the bathroom—her spa and hair salon for Mister.

"Jazzy! What are you doing in here, little monster?" Nina asks, not sure if she wants to laugh or scream.

"Doggie pretty!" Jasmine responds, as Mister looks up at Nina desperately.

"*What's she doing?*" *Mom, is that a real question?* Mister asks sarcastically. *What she's doing is killing me softly! After jumping on that there toilet and splashing water all over my paws and face, she took the Vaseline from your dresser and greased me all the way down, before shaking baby powder on me!*

Jasmine starts to giggle, like she understands what she did and understands Mister's magical ways.

"Ok, ok. Mister, I'll take care of it, like I take care of everything else for you," Nina says, scooping Jasmine into her arms and drowning her greasy face with multiple kisses, because it's hard for her to stay mad at someone so sweet and free.

All of a sudden, Selah allows Nina to have a sleepover. The decision comes when she catches Nina eating dinner in her

DANCER IN THE BULLPEN

bedroom in front of her small black-and-white TV. She has just finished complaining to her invisible friend about how she can't even have friends over anymore, like a normal kid. Now that Lisa can't come as often due to the crowd, she feels her loneliness with more intensity.

I'm sorry you feel like that. But you have me, says the invisible friend that Nina is starting to feel closer to, and miss when not around.

"You're not always here though. Where do you go?"

I'm told that I have to leave you alone to figure stuff out. But when it's important, I get to come. Nina's invisible friend drops her voice to a whisper. *But sometimes I come to you even when I'm not supposed to,* she says, closing with a childish giggle.

"Nina, why are you eating in here? You know I don't like that," interrupts Selah.

"'Cause there ain't enough room to do anything around here. Eat, play, think—nothing," Nina complains, feeling the tears well up in her eyes.

"There 'isn't,' not 'ain't,'" Selah corrects.

"Oh my god, Mom, there *isn't*!" Nina lashes out.

"What's wrong with you, Nina? Why are you so emotional today?"

Tell her, Nina's invisible friend suggests, hovering over her shoulder, still faceless and shapeless, whispering in her ear. *She'll get it.*

"Nina!" Selah yells, knowing she has gotten stuck in her other world.

"Mom, yeah, sorry. I'm just tired."

Selah walks all the way into Nina's room and places her hand lovingly on her daughter's head. "Listen baby. Why don't you invite a few friends over next weekend, and I can make

155

sure our guests downstairs have another place to be just for that night."

Nina's eyes light up. "You can do that?"

"Uh, duh," Selah responds dramatically. "This is still my house."

Nina smiles, stands up, and puts her half-eaten plate on top of the TV, which is definitely against the rules, but she knows Selah won't complain because Nina hugs her tightly. "Thanks, Mom. I'll invite a couple of girls from dance class." She's a bit sad Lisa has left early to go up north to visit her dad, and Rae just can't be invited because of Selah's opinion of her. But at least Nina's dance friends will finally see that the only Black girl of the crew does live in a nice house, with nice things. They will see she is just like them.

The night of Nina's sleepover, everything is perfect. She specifically chooses a weekend right before sixth-grade graduation and the big summer kick-off dance show, so her three favorite girls from her dance team accept the invitation to a fun girls' night with no hesitation. The weather is warm with a cool breeze, and David is nice enough to throw some hamburgers and hot dogs on the grill, and Selah makes her famous potato salad and rich chocolate brownies. The makeshift downstairs apartment has transformed into a preteen fun cave, decked out with pink sleeping bags, a tower of Blockbuster movies, flavored popcorn, sweet and sour candy, and cool arts-and-crafts kits. The girls will make beaded bracelets and giving each other punk-rock glitter makeovers. Nina is nervous but excited to host these girls at her home, now that the volume is turned down a notch. Unfortunately, not all the way down.

"Why don't you just have Aunt Selah order some pizza? A barbecue is kinda dumb," Dani says while watching Nina tease her ponytail in the bathroom mirror, waiting for her first guest to arrive. Nina can't believe Dani has the audacity to judge anything; she's lucky to even be there. Nina almost suggests to her mother that Dani go wherever the family of four goes, but knows that Selah hopes she will be kind and inclusive.

"It's fine. Everybody does pizza and I want to be different. These are rich girls. They're used to nice stuff and real food, not boring pizza that people eat after they've been drunk or high," Nina says, turning to face Dani boldly, daring her to say anything else.

Be careful, Nina's invisible friend says, her voice coming from behind Dani, but this time Nina sees the silhouette of her eyes.

"Shit, I've never seen your eyes," Nina responds quietly.

"What are you staring at?" Dani asks, thinking Nina is a bit off.

"Nothing," Nina says flatly. "But can you please be chill tonight? These are my friends and I'm ok with you being downstairs and hanging out, but can you just be chill?"

"Aight. Just don't talk shit, Nina. And I won't fuck with you and your little white friends."

The night is surprisingly going better than expected. Bellies are stuffed, and Nina and the girls finish washing up after a vibrant dance session to one of their favorite songs, Cyndi Lauper's "Girls Just Wanna Have Fun." Even Dani is caught moving her shoulders a bit from the couch. This song is special to the girls, because they once placed first in a dance competition with a routine that accompanied the popular tune, so it's been on repeat for a long time tonight.

Selah and David go to bed right after putting Jasmine down, as they're beat from all their catering and entertaining. The girls are settling into their sleeping bags with their bowls of popcorn, ready for a good movie.

"So, we got *Back to the Future*, *The Goonies*, and of course, *The NeverEnding Story*, which is one of my favorites," Nina announces proudly.

"Let's do the last one," one of Nina's friends blurts out.

"Cool!" Nina scoots over to the TV and attempts to slide the tape into the machine, but it's blocked.

"There's another movie in there, genius," Dani mumbles under her breath. Nina ignores her hate because friends are present. She presses the eject button on the VCR and a tape with a handwritten label on it that reads "WW & The Chocolate Factory" pops out.

Nina puts it down on the floor and is about to put her movie in when one of the girls asks, "Wait Nina. Is that *Willy Wonka & the Chocolate Factory?*"

"Um, I don't know," Nina responds. "This isn't mine."

"Ok, well put it back in. It's probably just a bootleg your mom got for Jasmine, or something. My brother taught me about bootleg," the girl shares with excitement. Nina looks down at the movie, and then back up at her friends, trying to ignore her cousin's eye roll. She doesn't want to share that this video is most likely owned by the family of four who got kicked out of her house for the night just so she can pretend she is like her friends. She doesn't want to be accused of snooping or taking any of the family's things. But she cares more about not looking weird or paranoid to her friends, so she submits.

"Ok, sure," Nina says with slight hesitation. She pops the tape back in and presses play.

DANCER IN THE BULLPEN

Nina and the girls learn quickly that the "WW" written on the tape label doesn't stand for *Willy Wonka*, but for *Wet Women*. The movie's opening scene consists of two voluptuous Black women in an all-white manufactured kitchen making a homemade barbecue sauce—using each other to taste test.

"Oh. My. God," the shyest girl from Nina's dance crew says out loud. "What is this?"

Another one shrieks.

"I don't think you're supposed to do that in the kitchen," another girl determines.

Nina gasps and jumps over to the VCR again to take it out.

"No!" Dani hisses in a demanding whisper. "Leave it on. This is funny. Stop being scary little girls."

Nina ignores her and reaches for the stop button, but the girls don't like being called little. "No Nina. Leave it on for a minute," says the girl with the bootleg-pro brother. Nina gives her a confused look.

Dani releases a roaring laugh, extremely pleased with herself. "See, y'all mad cool after all."

"This is gross, y'all. We don't have to watch it," Nina says. But all the girls in the basement have their eyes glued to the screen, wondering if people in real life actually do this stuff.

The barbecue chicken is now in the oven and the big Black chef enters the kitchen, so proud of his hot helpers. "Good job, sluts! Now come here and show Chef Daddy some love before I make chocolate lava cake for you both."

It's obvious this is an amateur video, the focus is inconsistent and the stability and clarity of the camera is a D-effort at best. Nina learned about cinematography from Uncle John, who was always critiquing the quality of movies and television shows. She looks around the room and is mortified that this is what her friends are probably going to remember most from her sleepover—the big Black porn movie at the one Black girl's house they've been to. *I really hope they don't tell their parents.*

"Ok, I gotta turn this off, I'm sorry. My mom and David would be furious if they knew we were watching this," Nina says as she shuts the videotape down.

The girls understand, and Nina's cousin keeps quiet for once as *The NeverEnding Story* begins. But who can really concentrate on the magical land of Fantastica when you can almost taste and smell the new nastiness of barbecue sauce?

The next morning, Selah makes an amazing breakfast of corned beef hash, eggs, and homemade biscuits with molasses. The girls show their gratitude with scraped clean plates and genuinely seem happy about their time at Nina's house.

But what will they tell their high-class families? Nina wonders. Her dancing community is one where she doesn't feel judged or bullied. But now she is anxious the chocolate porn will be another dragon waiting to breathe fire onto her confidence. Between the hidden drug lab upstairs and the porn show down below, she's had enough. *Baby Jasmine can't be around this shit.* So, she changes her mind and finds the courage to come clean about what she's seen.

"Mom, you got a minute?"

Nina tells her mother everything, even though she's worried she'll get in trouble for some reason. Selah doesn't talk much about a challenge; she instead takes action. Miraculously, shortly after the chocolate factory incident, the family of six discovers they have family nearby who has plenty of space in their home to offer up. Selah provides some significant resources for the family to go and feels good about the win-win result. Troubled cousin, however, is a more complicated situation. She doesn't accept the help she needs. She becomes weary of Selah's intervention tactics and finds a way to get back up north, in the same place Selah saved her from. Only God knows of the baby's fate.

***

Nina thinks her parents are more excited about sixth-grade graduation than she is. For the first time, Mike and Dionne take the four-hour drive down south to see her reach a significant milestone, and they experience a little of her life and passion for dance.

Rae chooses to skip the punch and cookies at the post-graduation reception, and darts straight over to Nina and nestles herself in the circle of parents and siblings, excited to engage in her community. "Hi, I'm Rae! One of Nina's best friends! Mrs. Abadie, now I know you don't like me, but I promise Nina is not like me, so don't worry!"

"No one dislikes you, Rae. It's ok," David says with a kind, almost sad tone, compensating for Selah's silence.

"It's Dr. Chase," Nina whispers to Rae, trying to keep the relationships clear.

"Yes, but who really calls her that? She still looks like a Mrs. Abadie to me," Rae whispers back, but everyone can hear her. Nina shoots a worried look at Dionne but she's all smiles.

Rae shifts her attention to the visiting parents. "Hi! Mr. Abadie, I'm Rae, just like I said. It's so nice to meet you! Wow Nina's dad, you're tall! And Mrs. Abadie Number Two, you're tall too!" She leans in for hugs and surprisingly gets a couple of warm ones. "Awww, and who is this little homie?"

Dionne is holding Nina's little brother face-forward so he can make everyone swoon from his sweet smile. Rae is caught in the trance, until Jasmine pulls on her graduation robe.

"Hey chill, munchkin," Nina says to her rambunctious little sister. "Ok, well, we have to go soon," she says, shutting down Rae's aggressive-yet-loving engagement. "I'll call you later." She gives Rae a hug for being such a good friend these last two years. Rae's parents didn't make graduation, and their daughter hides her disappointment as she walks slowly toward the front of the school, but Nina knows it hurts.

"Rae!" Selah yells. Both Nina and Rae whip their necks back in unison, shocked at the name call.

"Yes ma'am?" Rae responds.

"Nina is in a dance show tomorrow. Would you like to come with all of us to see her in it?"

"Yes, please! I've always wanted to see Nina dance. Well, not like how she dances in the hallway at school. Like real dancing, so, thank you!" Nina shoots Rae a disapproving look for the added commentary.

"Great, well we'll pick you up at 1 p.m.," Selah offers.

"Nah, it's ok. I'll meet y'all at your house so it won't be no trouble, Mrs. Abadie. Thank you." Rae practically skips out the school gym.

Nina looks at her mother lovingly with no need to say a word.

The show is sold out, and Nina and her dance group are riding high on elevated nerves. She is trying not to let the pressure suffocate her. She's lead in a tap dance number, a jazz number, and featured in a classical-ballet dance solo. She's been struggling a bit with her stamina, not compensating for her body changes.

"You need to train more, Nina. Stretch, run, lift some light weights," her dance instructor has said. Nina agrees and has made a plan to do more training. She just hopes she makes it through tonight in front of hundreds of people, including her dad, who hasn't seen her dance since she was a little girl. She desperately wants to make him proud.

Nina is always amazed at the peace and joy that takes over once she hits the stage, killing all anxiety and fear that lurks in her mind and body. And "kill it" is what she does, as she receives a standing ovation after the ballet solo. She's soaking up the love after taking her usual bow, and slowly leaves the stage, joining the other performers who are casually engaging with the audience—their family and friends. The theater is filled with animated chatter and warm energy. Nina and her family are about to head out, when she realizes she has left her pearl hair-bun net on stage, where it has fallen onto after multiple pirouettes. She finds it right away and begins to walk off, until she hears the flamenco guitar player and conga drummer tease her spirit with an impromptu jam session before packing up. She halts and looks straight ahead at the audience.

"Nina, what are you doing? You coming?" Mike yells out to her.

But Nina can't move. The Spanish guitar strings are flirting with the beat of the conga, moving together, taking turns, simmering with the decadent rhythm. They immediately soothe her soul. The sounds are calling her name and she has to answer them, not her father's questions. She takes off her shoes and looks at the musicians with a smirk, a warning. Nina's little feet feel the warmth of the wooden planks under her soles. She moves downstage left, in front of the musicians who now anticipate her movement. She closes her eyes and inhales, leans over so low the top of her bun sweeps the floor when she comes back up, fanning her arms back and forth as she goes back down. Up, down, side to side. She has no control of her body; the music is making her twist and turn like it never has before, and the fleeting audience halts with the magical vision of her. Sweat reaches the surface of her face and neck and every single crevice, as the crowd claps and screams, "Go Nina! Dance!"

Nina can feel the heat of the camera flashes on the back of her eyelids, which makes her wind faster, dropping deeper, taking over the entire stage.

"That's it—dance! Take my hand, lil one."

"Uncle John?" Nina needs confirmation as she opens her eyes, slowly, to see if he's really on stage with her.

"Yes, I'm here," he says, reaching out his hand. Nina can almost see clearly. With tears in her eyes, she takes his hand with ease, and their fluid dance shifts into a sharp pasodoble, with Uncle John leading. Nina's movement intensifies with straight lines and heavy feet. She dances blind, so she can see her uncle better.

"I'm so sorry, Uncle John. I just can't find your ring," she says while they circle the stage, stomping the wooden floor as if pain is sprouting from underneath the planks like wildfire.

"Hush now. You are the ruby," Uncle John says.

"Nina! Nina!" Selah runs up on the stage, certain Nina is experiencing something in her hidden world. She stops dancing, but sweat is still running down her body, as if she's been hosed down.

"Mom?" Nina is trying to make sure the face she's looking at is real.

"Yes, I'm here, baby. You ok? You move like an angel, but I think you went a little too hard at the end. Need some water?" Selah asks, handing her a cold bottle, trying to cool Nina's active mind.

"Yes, please," Nina says, refusing to cry in front of Rae and her dad, because unlike Selah she sometimes worries what they think of her. Selah is a definite; Nina knows no matter what she does, her mother will be there.

"Ok, let's get out of here, and get your favorite pizza," Selah suggests.

"That sounds good," Nina responds, trying to ignore her growling belly and fatigued heart.

Nina stays in the hotel with her dad, Dionne, and baby brother, so they can get an early start on the road back to her second home for the summer. Dionne is a meticulous traveler and planner. She makes sure every detail is thought of, from the separate envelopes of toll money, to all the right magazines, snacks, and mapped-out rest stops and places to eat on the way. Nina is confident her father is more like Selah, spontaneous and unstructured, but Dionne keeps him aligned, and Nina thinks that's nice. It's nice knowing when you're going to eat, being secure knowing you got a ticket to a show early, or simply doing things without the stressful rush. It creates a priceless sense of stability. And she enjoys coming to her father's house in the summers, to rest from walking on pins and needles in an environment polluted with uncertainty.

But Nina wants more than calm in a pretty box. "Daddy? Can you let me roll down the window back here?"

"No princess. We don't want the baby catching a draft and getting sick," Mike says, glancing back at Nina through the rearview mirror of his car.

"But Daddy, it's summer and it's really nice outside. The baby needs a little breeze," Nina says, reaching down in her brother's car seat to caress his chubby cheeks.

"No Nina. I'll turn up the air conditioning a little."

Where is King Boring when you need him? "Ok fine." Nina submits to watching the army of cornstalks dance on the edge of the road.

"What are we doing this summer?" she asks Mike, but confident Dionne will answer.

Dionne pulls herself from her crossword puzzle and looks at Nina in the back seat with excitement. "We're going to visit some friends who have kids that I believe you know from past summers, with big houses, pools, and other toys that will be fun for you. We also have you enrolled in a summer camp for a couple of weeks."

Nina's interest is peaked. "A writing camp?"

"No, more like an outdoor camping excursion for a week. It'll be a nice opportunity for you to learn some camping skills, how to start a fire, explore nature."

Nina is already not feeling the camp. She loves exploring nature, right before she decides to come home and use a real toilet and cook a meal on the stove. *Dad won't let me crack the window for fresh air, but will let me live in a forest with bears and raccoons for a week? Crazy.*

Outwardly, she agrees. "Sounds good. Also Dad, I may do some writing and radio stuff next summer, and in another year or two, I can be a junior counselor at the YMCA. You know how I love kids and I'm a good swimmer, so I think it will be fun and I can make some money."

"Well that all sounds good," Mike says. He's actually happy Nina is thinking of future activities. "But why can't you be a camp counselor near your papi? We have YMCAs here."

Dionne goes back to her crossword puzzle. Nina doesn't know how to tell her daddy that she needs to be close to Selah. And Selah needs to be near her too, no matter how crazy it gets. "Daddy, why do you live so far? Can't you all live closer to me? They have companies like the ones you work at in D.C."

"Princess, I have so much going on here."

Yeah, everything but me.

***

"How was the summer with your dad and family, Nina? You got a beautiful tan, and gained a little weight I see," Selah whispers, as if saying it quietly won't make Nina feel as bad.

Hearing that stabs Nina in the chest, puncturing her self-esteem. She's frustrated with the changes that are happening to her body. She has gone from stick legs to thick chick in all the unexpected places—waist, arms, even a little in her cheeks. "Dionne cooks a lot of good food, Mom. I'll try not to eat so much next time."

"Oh baby, I'm just teasing. It's not like you're eating junk," Selah says, attempting to smooth things out. "It's just the older you get, the more aware you have to be on what you put in your body," she warns. "Nina, I do want to talk to you about school, though."

Nina sits down on the couch, dropping her suitcase on the living room floor, bracing herself for another change. Selah wastes no time. She is barely in the house before her mother slaps her with reality. "You're going back to private school. I found a really good one while you were with your dad."

The truth is Selah has gotten wind of the chronic elementary school bullying, and the teachers' inconsistent value of her daughter's brain. And though Selah has made nice with Rae, she's still concerned about Nina spending so much time with a girl who's already having sex in her preteen years.

Nina understands why Selah is scared, and she agrees that it'll be safer among the privileged. The problem is the white environment Selah wants to return her to doesn't have any multicultural poetry workshops or bus stops across the street from the local carryout with the best cheesy fries. It's simply a massive Episcopal school nestled nicely in a quiet, rich neighborhood. Nina doesn't know there are schools where seventh graders share the same space as twelfth-grade seniors, or schools that don't have a dance squad because their football team is replaced by a sport called lacrosse. But the students are friendly, and the teachers seem to treat her like everyone else.

Nina is still actively dancing, but she realizes she has to create a new training routine as her body is filling out more, especially since she has started her period this year. She tries out for the track team, as it's a great opportunity to tone up and engage with some of the few Black students in school.

Janet and Jackie are a set of ninth-grade twins and most likely the fastest girls on earth, let alone the school. Meeting them is easy. Nina plans to try out as a sprinter, under the delusion that she is fast. When Janet and Jackie see her warming up and ignorantly venturing over to the fast side of the track, they politely suggest that distance running may be a better fit: "Your stride is perfect for the long game. People think sprinters are strong, but it's runners who can pace themselves slow and steady, who are powerful." And of course the twins are right, and Nina makes two new friends.

Selah overestimates junior high school. The challenges are subtle and deceptive, which are possibly worse than overt slaps in the face. Everyone smiles and is really nice. Kids don't go out of their way to be mean, but the dismissing and ignoring almost feels worse. The teachers seem fair and actually engage all of the students. But every once in a while there's an experience that just doesn't feel right.

Like the time Janet, Jackie, and Nina are invited to cook for their track coaches, as a teacher appreciation activity. The request is for the young students (who happen to all be Black) to fry chicken and make macaroni and cheese for them. When Nina returns home at 8 p.m. smelling like KFC, Selah is livid. The next day, Selah calls the headmaster and tells him that if she hears about another incident where Black students are frying chicken for their white teachers, she will report them. The headmaster takes her threat seriously and suddenly there is a math tutor available for Nina, as requested at the top of the school year. It looks like some dragons know when to retreat.

CHAPTER SEVEN

"We're going to Jamaica, Daddy?!"

"Yes, baby girl. Since I only have you for a few weeks now because of your busy summer schedule, I figure we do it up really big, finally show you the paradise your grandpa spoke so much about."

Nina is lying on what Dionne lovingly calls the "shrink" couch—a long purple velvet piece of furniture that's so comfortable, the chances someone will confess their greatest secrets while relaxed on it are high. She is flipping through the latest *Jet* magazines and almost feels the urge to tell her father some truths of her own from the magic couch.

Daddy, I let a dragon feel me up, and then he told the world after I told him I wanted to stop. He's made me feel like a bad person, much more so than when I touch myself most days. And I love God but I also love girls. So, what's for dinner?

"I'm so excited, thank you, Daddy," she says instead. "I can't wait to see where we're from."

"I'm excited too!" Mike says with sincerity. "Dionne has planned everything from start to finish, so there'll be no stress." And that's exactly what's missing until it shows up.

"Don't give the beggars money when you get off the plane or they will never stop," Dionne's local friend says, but Nina disregards the warning, and gives them what she can.

How can I not give the begging children money I don't really need? Especially when they look like me.

Dionne's friend has recently moved back to her Jamaican homeland to care for her mother, and showing Dionne and her family around Kingston for a couple of days, before they go to the resort, is a welcoming distraction from the stress of caregiving. Dionne doesn't believe in packing light. Even Nina's baby brother comes with three bags, because there's no such thing as too many things for her baby. Dionne's friend doesn't own a car big enough to hold her guests, so she hires a driver during their time with her.

"Yuh folks from New York?" the driver questions, glancing down at Mike's "I Love New York" t-shirt as he loads the pile of luggage into the back of the minivan.

"Close. We live in New Jersey, right outside the city," Mike answers.

"Well, *I* am from Washington D.C., our nation's capital," Nina interrupts with pride.

"Ahhh, suh yuh kno di president?" the young driver asks Nina playfully, with an accent slightly stronger than her grandpa's. But she has no problem understanding him. She remembers having to decelerate the pace of her listening to understand Grandpa's words when she was small. And now she's a pro.

"No, I don't know President Bush, but my mom met the first lady once at her job's charity event," Nina brags, proud of her mother.

"Oh, fancy mada," the driver responds, plopping the last piece of luggage in the van. Nina is standing close, staring at his long dreadlocks, wondering how many years it took to grow them, and what makes them smell like coconuts. Sensing Nina's curiosity, the driver asks, "Yuh have family here or dis just a vacation?"

"We're on vacation, but my grandpa is from here. He passed away but he used to talk about this place a lot. He talked about being a Maroon, a special tribe of people I've also been reading about," Nina shares, unsure if it's the warmth of the Caribbean sun or the loving memory that's making her upper lip sweat.

"Yuh Maroon?" the driver loudly asks, radiating awe and excitement.

Nina looks at her father.

"Yes," Mike says, with a comparable energy. "The Maroons are our ancestors! I heard there may be a way to go on a tour of their land, is that true?" Mike looks to Dionne for confirmation.

"Yuh mean your land," the driver corrects.

Though Dionne is listening, she's struggling with strapping the baby's car seat in the van, despite her friend's help.

"I dunno, Mike. We have a lot of things planned, and doing that would take a lot of maneuvering," Dionne yells, voice muffled from inside the van.

"But Dad, I thought we came here to see where we're from, and the people we are connected to?" Nina says, doing her best to mask her annoyance by not speaking directly to her stepmother.

"No problem man, mi gi yuh mi bizniz card an yuh cya call mi eff yuh wa di tour." The driver hands Mike his business card and they all finally get into the sardine-packed van, anxious to drop off the load and answer the water's call.

Kingston is tragically more beautiful the higher you climb up the mountain to where the privileged live, high in the sky, far away from the impoverished people they work hard to ignore.

Mike hears about a lake nestled in one of the little towns, right next to a small locals' chicken jerking business. The family eats first, not wasting time to wipe their mouths of the incomparable herbs and spices. The joy of licking their fingers almost matches the therapeutic bath from the local lake.

"Oh my, Nina! What's that bathing suit you have on?" Dionne asks with some admiration, but mostly concern.

"It's called a Brazilian," Nina says.

"Has your mom seen this?"

"I don't know," Nina answers honestly.

"Sheesh Nina, we may have to get you another bathing suit," Mike asserts. "You look like one of those *Jet* models. You're fourteen and too young to be wearing this string thing," he says, watching two teenage boys breaststroke closer to Nina in the water. "You gonna make me have to push these boys out the lake."

"You think I look like a *Jet* beauty model, Daddy?" Nina is beyond thrilled.

DANCER IN THE BULLPEN

Mike sees the satisfaction on Nina's face, as she's getting circled by sharks. "This is not a good thing, Nina. We gonna get you a new bathing suit at the resort."

The resort is beautiful and what Dionne calls "all-inclusive." You don't even have to carry cash on you—just charge anything to the room. And the resort has everything. Restaurants, bars, and clubs for both the adults and teenagers. It even has babysitting services for Nina's little brother, which Mike and Dionne take full advantage of.

"Do you like the resort, Nina?" Dionne asks, proud of the wonderful amenities she's gotten lined up for all to enjoy.

"Yes, a lot," Nina responds respectfully, but she thinks the resort kinda feels like her private school. A compound of privilege keeping the real beauty out, ironically from land they should own.

But the boy Nina meets from California is cute. He's fourteen too, and they first make eye contact at the restaurant, where he's having dinner with his family like Nina is with hers. They share their first Red Stripe together at the adult bar; no resort employee stops them partaking. Nina brags about her Jamaican Maroon lineage, and the boy is so impressed he kisses her under the lifeguard beach chair.

"You're so pretty," the boy says, in between kissing Nina on the cheeks and mouth.

"You are, too," Nina says nervously.

"You're smart too, which makes you prettier."

"Why you say that?" Nina asks as she looks down at her big knees. The Disney scars are still on them.

"'Cause of the big books you got in that beach bag. And 'cause you spent like an hour talking about your Jamaican people. That's a lot of fuckin' research."

Nina laughs out loud. "Some research and some just Grandpa."

"That's cool," the boy says. "You're real pretty though." The boy thinks that's what she'd rather be. Little does he know the smart part made her happiest.

***

Nina enjoys the attention, and the abundance of teenage activities, but can't suppress her nagging desire to get off the resort and explore beyond the walls. She realizes the best chance of getting what she wants is by going through her stepmother.

They are halfway into the vacation and everyone is a little tired of the communal buffet. So, Dionne orders room service—ackee and saltfish, paired with sweet ripe plantains. The family is eating together on the balcony of their suite. Nina is cautious not to speak with her mouth full, and uses the correct fork with her cotton napkin placed perfectly in her lap. She is confident that demonstrating the most proper etiquette will please Dionne, making her more open and agreeable.

"Good job, Nina! You're eating like such a lady. I'm so happy our lessons have stuck with you," Dionne praises.

Boom. This is the perfect time to ask, Nina determines. "Thank you. And thank you both for this amazing trip. I'm having so much fun and can't want to see the waterfalls today! I noticed on your notepad that we don't have anything planned for tomorrow. Do you think we can all do that Maroon tour your friend's driver said he would arrange for us?" Nina doesn't

DANCER IN THE BULLPEN

break for air, hoping to overwhelm Dionne just enough to extract a yes to make it stop.

"Oh princess, I dunno," Mike chimes in. "Tomorrow would be pretty last minute and I don't know if we can book a full-day excursion up in those secluded mountains without the proper coordination."

Nina glares at her father and wants to tell him to shut up. He never makes the event decisions, and now he wants to block Dionne before she even makes this most important one. "Daddy, please! Can we try?" she pleads, trying hard not to cry over her saltfish. "This resort is beautiful, but how can we leave to go back to the U.S. without seeing where we come from?"

Dionne is silent for what seems like several minutes. She takes a deep breath in and exhales out, before smiling gracefully. "You're right, Nina. Tomorrow is a "free" day. If your father is able to connect with the driver for a tour, I'm happy to accompany you two for the day." She gives her husband an encouraging look.

Before Mike can respond, Nina shouts, "Thanks Daddy! I bet he can help us." She grabs the business card from off the dresser and brings it to Mike. "Can you call him now?"

It's 7:00 a.m. the next morning, and Nina is ready to go. Her baby brother is with the resort sitter, and Dionne and Mike are waiting for the tour guide right inside the lobby glass doors to keep cool. Nina is outside with a clear view of the resort entrance gates, rubbing sunscreen into her tanned arms. She has on all-white tank top, with matching shorts, sneakers, and sporty white sunglasses. Her relaxed hair is in a high ponytail, already frizzing from the moist air.

Earlier in the hotel room, Mike had questioned Nina on her clothing. "Princess, you not going to a baptism. Why you wearing all white?"

"Dad, the Maroons are spiritual people, and white represents purity and good. So, I am wearing white out of respect for them," Nina had justified.

Now, Nina waves at Dionne and Mike to come outside, because the tour guide has arrived in a bright yellow Jeep that reads "Irie Trips" in big letters. A curvaceous brown-skinned woman with short and curly wild hair jumps out the jeep like she weighs half her size.

"Hi, I'm Josie! I'll be your guide today, and I'm excited to show you the place where my people, and your people thrive—deep in the Jamaican Blue Mountains. Jump in and belt up! We goin' for a long bumpy ride, but it'll be fun!"

Nina already loves Josie's happy energy. And she's beautiful, wearing a white t-shirt and cargo shorts in the design of the Jamaican flag. Her key physical assets are respectfully covered, but it doesn't matter. Her natural vibrancy makes her look half naked, but Mike doesn't seem to notice, thankfully.

Josie grabs a few cold bottled waters from the cooler in the back of the Jeep, and passes them out to Nina, Dionne, and Mike. When Nina's fingers inadvertently grab Josie's long ones during the exchange, both of their bodies jump, as if experiencing an electric shock.

"Woah!" Nina gasps, getting the familiar sensation of heat running throughout her body, but she doesn't feel afraid. It actually feels good … comforting.

"Are you ok?" Josie whispers, with a bewildered look on her face.

"Yes, I'm ok," Nina responds loudly. "I think I must have gotten a static shock by touching your shirt or something, sorry," Nina lies.

"It happens all the time," Josie responds with a big smile, looking deep into Nina's eyes, realizing they both felt the same thing—something special.

Dionne and Mike don't notice the interaction. They're too focused on arguing about whether not they should request the Jeep cover to come up or stay down, based on the aggressive sun and undisciplined wind.

Josie starts the car. "It's so much better if you let me keep the top open, so you can better experience all of the beauty we're about to pass through. Like I said, we're going to have some great fun! What you're about to experience is not the usual Blue Mountain tour, where you get to only pass by the area where the Maroons live. No, I tell yuh. This is a VIP exclusive Maroon tour," she reveals, looking back at Nina through the rearview mirror.

Nina tingles from the quick body temperature spike prompted by her gaze. *Why is my body reacting this way?*

Josie continues her introduction as they pull away from the resort. "We're going to actually walk through the town and explore the private farms, where we grow a variety of nutritional and medicinal plants, yams, cocoa, and so many other vital crops. I'll take you to the river and streams, where one of the elders will show you the true art of fishing. And if we're lucky, a council member will talk about our very own system of governance and economics. You'll hear about Nanny, a strong and fearless commander who freed more than a thousand slaves. There are other warrior women too, who didn't make the books I believe you read, Nina."

Mike interrupts Josie's rambling. "Wow, that all sounds wonderful. But we didn't book this exclusive tour. I don't think we have the time or money for something this detailed. Has there been a mistake?"

"No sir, no mistake. Don't worry about the money and time. I was told you all are Maroon family, and I will do my best to keep the tour educational and condensed. Does anyone have any other questions before I start running my mouth even more?" Josie says with a boisterous laugh, while they all bounce up and down on the rocky roads to a higher altitude.

Nina has lots of questions, but she decides to go slow so she can remember the answers better. But her slow is fast for the average person. "Why isn't your Jamaican accent strong like our driver's before? And why do you look young like you are in high school or something? Are you really a Maroon too, or do you just say that for tours? Do they school you in the town? Are you not allowed to go elsewhere?"

"Nina!" Dionne yells, more embarrassed than angry.

Josie lets out another wild laugh. "It's ok, ma'am. Nina, those are all good questions. Ok, so, I am a Maroon. In fact, my mother is a respected elder who sits on the council. I couldn't have access to the ground I'm about to show you unless I was in the tribe, or, of course, had special permission. You have a good ear. I was educated by my family in the early years, and continue to be educated by them. I have also completed high school in the United States, and now college, while living with my father in Michigan. I'm almost finished—just one more year in undergrad. I come back home during school breaks and help the family with the farming, but mostly give tours, because of my 'gift with people,' as the elders say. I lost some of my way with speech to fit into your culture subconsciously, I think. But mi proud of who mi be."

Nina giggles at Josie's language shift.

"That is amazing, Josie," Dionne says. "Your commitment to your education and family is commendable."

"What do you want to be when you're done with school?" Nina asks, anxious to gain some wisdom from this *Jet* beauty: Jamaican Edition.

"I'm thinking of being a lawyer, but bringing my knowledge back home, so I can help fight injustice for all of us Jamaicans, "Josie says, with great strength in her tone. "What about you, Nina? Do you know what you want to do when you grow up?"

Mike and Dionne look back at Nina in unison, anticipating her answer. *Sheesh. No pressure.* "If I could live off dancing, I would. I love to dance. But I'll probably just do something journalism related. I write ok, I guess. And I like to look things up. So, yep, I'll probably work for a newspaper or something, or maybe be on the radio or on television news."

Josie again shoots Nina a supportive look in the rearview mirror, and says, "I am sure you will find your way."

Nina smiles back, feeling an incredible sense of calm that intensifies with each mile they climb. The day is filled with nonstop discovery and community. Josie makes good on her word—guiding her guests through the sacred land of the Maroons, letting them dig their fingers in the farm soil, snacking on fresh mangos and coconut water. They receive demonstrations on how warriors camouflaged themselves with tree branches and leaves during their fight with the British, the weaponry, and Nina's favorite communication tool—the abeng.

She has enjoyed reading about it, but falls in love with the instrument when seeing it and touching it in person.

"This is more than a bull's horn!" Nina announces to Mike and Dionne, knowing they only see with their eyes.

"What do you mean?" Mike asks, even though he's not sure if he has the energy for any more answers. It's almost dusk, and he's exhausted from the day's activities and can tell by reading his wife's face, she has long been ready to go back and get Nina's baby brother.

"I can just tell this is magic!" Nina replies, feeling the power of the horn seep into her fingers, making its way into her bloodstream.

"Magic indeed, Nina," Josie says. "They used this to communicate with the troops at war, or when they needed to assemble or simply send a message or warning, creating sounds with special coding only the Maroons could understand."

"But they still use it, right?"

Before Josie can respond, a woman with a powerful aura, draped in fine ceremonial clothing approaches them.

"Mama, these are my new friends," Josie says. "Mike and Dionne Abadie, and their daughter, Nina." She leans in closer to the woman and whispers without being heard, "The girl. She has the power. That's why I brought her here."

Though Dionne is a bit agitated at the length of this special tour she didn't ask for, she can't help but be intrigued by this extraordinary woman. She can tell she's of high rank, just by the way she stands up straight as an arrow, not a hint of a slouch or lack of balance. It's evident a celebration is about to begin, as most of the town is busy preparing the campfire site for an important ceremony. "Thank you for allowing us into your town, Mrs. ...."

"Jus Mama. Yuh cya call mi Mama."

Dionne doesn't argue, and without a word Mama slowly walks up to Mike and places both of her hands on either side of his face. Nina is amazed at how someone with pure silver hair and wrinkly hands can have a blemish-free face so smooth, almost as smooth as Josie's.

Nina is surprised that her father lets a stranger touch him without a known reason.

"Abadie. Wi kno yuh lifeline well. Mi hear yuh ancestas whispering wid excitement behind mi," Mama says nonchalantly. Mike is motionless, quiet and calm.

The silence is loud. Scary to Dionne, yet soothing to Nina. She can tell Mama's touch is powerful and she can't help but want to experience it too. She's not brave enough to touch Mama directly without an invitation, so she gently holds Mike's left hand while Mama continues to hold his face, hoping she'll get another hit of what Josie gave her in the jeep.

Mike jumps back from Mama's touch and releases Nina's hand. "Shit, what was that!" he loudly whispers. "I mean, sorry. Something stung me, or bit me, I dunno," he says, refusing to believe the impossible—that Mama plus Nina created a powerful energy surge.

"Daddy, are you ok?" Nina feels hot again, but there is no tremble or fear. She scans her father's body with her eyes to make sure she doesn't see any bleeding.

"Yes baby, I'm good. And Mama, it's like I can see my ancestors through you and all around this place," Mike admits.

"Mike, we must go," Dionne warns. "It's going to take at least two hours to travel back to the hotel. And just in case whatever you just felt really has something to do with your blood pressure, your medication is back in the room. Plus, look! It's a full moon shining bright, and it's not even dark yet."

Dionne tries to mask her discomfort, but everyone sees it. She's worried that whatever is about to go down at this celebration knows no part of Jesus.

"No worries, ma'am. I can carry you back now," Josie assures.

"Abadie, ow bout yuh an Nina stay?" Mama asks, disregarding the emotional aftermath of the energy surge.

Josie explains. "We are about to start another day of celebration for one of our elders, who recently passed on to the spirit world, and I think you, and especially your daughter, will benefit from the gathering. We have a big home just up that road." She points in the distance. "It has plenty of rooms and we can have a big breakfast in the morning before I take you two back."

"No, no, we *all* must get back," Dionne insists, slowly backing away from the huddle.

"Ow bout Nina stay?" Mama pushes.

"Yes Daddy. Please! Let me stay!" Nina feels at home, and is imagining the good food and music that's waiting for her.

Mike wants no problem with Dionne, who is ready for Josie to burn rubber. He looks back and forth at his fiery wife tapping her foot next to the bright yellow Jeep, and his even brighter daughter standing under a sky that's slowly turning red, cradling a bright white moon.
"Princess, I'm sorry. But you need to give Mama the abeng and come back to the hotel with me and Dionne."

Nina feels disappointment and panic rise through her lungs, up to her face. Mama can see her fear like it's right on top of her. She makes eye contact, and motions for Nina to hold

DANCER IN THE BULLPEN

her father's hand again. She obeys, while Mama closes the circle and holds Mike and Nina's other hand. The sky immediately brightens, like it's illuminating speckled gold, piercing through the red, blinding Nina's vision of her father. There's no jolt, just a mellow vibration running through their bodies.

"Daddy, do you see that? Do you feel that? Oh my goodness, it's so pretty." Nina is almost intoxicated by the warmth and the beauty.

"See what, Nina?" Mike asks, now unsure if what his daughter sometimes sees is actually real.

"I'm going to stay Daddy. Can Josie just take you and Dionne back and then return to watch me with Mama overnight? I know she can bring me back to the hotel early, before any resort activities for the day. Right, Josie?" Nina asks, embracing the power of confidence she's sure Mama is transferring to her.

"Yes, absolutely," Josie promises.

To Nina's surprise, Mike submits with no hesitation. "Ok."

Mama abruptly releases their hands, and watches Nina realize what just happened.

Mama helped me make Daddy say yes. No, wait. Is that possible?

Mama turns to Mike and gives him a long hug. "Mi pray fi yuh Abadie. Travel well si yuh next life," she says.

Mike bends down and gives Nina a longer hug. He whispers in her ear, "Are you sure you wanna stay?"

"Yes," Nina says, holding her father tightly, taking advantage of his euphoria. Mike stands up straight, feeling at peace and certain of his decision. "Please be careful, princess.

And Mama, nothing can happen to her, or I *will* die an early two deaths—one from my pain and the other from her mother."

"No worries, shi safe wid mi dan back home," Mama says, with her first smile of the day.

Mike turns to leave, and then stops like he suddenly remembered something. He looks at Mama with a slight concern. "Why you say you'll see me in my next life? You think something is going to happen to me?"

Mama touches Mike's shoulder and says, "No son, yuh just nah return tuh Jamaica til afta mi gaan tuh di next world."

"And that's ok, I guess," Mike responds hopefully.

"Yes, it is," Josie chimes in.

Nina watches her father follow Josie down to the jeep, preparing for a battle of judgment with Dionne. But then she quickly refocuses on Mama, who she is completely in awe of, and the upcoming celebration of the dead.

Young men and women pull leaves and branches off a large fire pit, where jerk chicken and vegetables have been slowly cooking for hours. There are many fresh fruits to eat and herb-infused beverages ready for libation. Everyone begins to change into their ceremonial outfits, and Nina is concerned that her soiled white outfit isn't quite appropriate now. All of the farm play and sitting on the ground during various story times throughout the day has taken a toll on her ensemble.

"Follow mi," says Mama, "Mi find sum fancy threads fi yuh tuh wear."

Nina follows Mama with no hesitation, still with the abeng in hand. Mama leads her into the big house, into a large room filled with many women and rows of shelves of folded dresses and hair wraps—some with simple solid colors, and others more vibrant, like rainbows battling themselves. And the women. All different ages and sizes are yelling at each other with no malice, and no organized method of engagement. They're just shouting their truth out into the air, hoping someone will catch it, and respond appropriately. But the language being used is different. Nina can only make out one or two words here and there. And when Mama begins using the same tongue alongside them, Nina gets nervous because now she can't understand anyone. Mama observes Nina's fear and pulls her in close to the gathering's eye. Various garments that might fit are being pulled from the shelves and placed on a table for Nina to try on. Before she can protest changing out in the open, all the women start doing so, helping each other with hair garments, wraps, and jewelry.

"Wi all one here," Mama says, wrapping Nina's head in a blood-red fabric, bringing a pop of color to the shapeless black dress with gold trim that was chosen for her.

"Dis here represents yuh blood magic," Mama says with no expression.

Nina shakes her head affirmatively, grabs a pair of gold hoops, and follows her elder down to the celebration grounds. *Welp, I guess I went straight from kid clothes to grown old witch clothes.* Nina chuckles to herself.

But nothing is funny when Mama has Nina sit down on the ground in front of her, during official announcements, as if she is publicly claiming her as one of her own family members.

The night has fallen but the sky is stained red. Nina stares at the moon and swears it has a heart that pulsates with each beat of the drum. Men and women are dancing in between the prayers and short stories, in between the feast and libation. She gets up with some of the children and dances with them in ageless form, enjoying the shake of the Earth's chest. Nina takes it all in, closes her eyes to embrace the joy, which she hopes will heal her from the pain she evokes.

Nina?

Nina? Is that you?

Nina opens her eyes slowly, recognizing the soft voice with matching eyes and no body. It's her invisible friend, and she's hovering near the central fire pit. "What are you doing here?" she whispers.

What am I doing here? I belong here. Aren't you supposed to be at the hotel with your family?

"Oh so you *did* know I was going to be here," Nina questions, satisfied she is right.

I always know where you basically are, but sometimes, not exactly. You are in a sacred place right now, with sacred people. It doesn't make sense.

"I know. I feel like they are like me or I am like them, but good—not bad," Nina responds, confusing even herself.

Well, I can't talk to you freely here. I have to go, Nina's invisible friend abruptly announces, before disappearing into thin air.

"Nina? Are you alright?" Josie is back, catching her new friend talking to the fire, as does Mama, who is on the other side of the stage with a few of the elders.

Shit, Nina thinks. *I forgot where I am.* "Hey, hi. Yes, I just talk to myself sometimes. It helps me relax. My dad and stepmom make it back ok?" She attempts to change the focus quickly.

"It's ok, Nina. I already know you're special. That's why I brought you. You are safe here with us," Josie assures. She sits down on the ground with Nina, to share more soothing vibrations.

"You don't get it," Nina says, exhausted by the weight of her own energy. I think I can hurt people, like really hurt them if they're trying to hurt me. It could just be a series of coincidences, but because I want the hurt, I think I did it."

"You know, there's a story Mama would tell me over and over again as a young child. It's about my great grandfather, who was a courageous Maroon warrior. It's been said many times that he could kill an enemy soldier just by thinking about doing so. And with the same power, he could bring a child back to life if he requested the power of his ancestors, and focused all his heart and energy into the rebirth of a pure soul. It's easy to think this could all be a myth."

"Yes, that sounds unbelievable," Nina admits.

"But then why does Mama have the same power?"

Buzzz ... Buzzz ... Suddenly, a blue hummingbird begins singing in Nina's ear.

"Don't move," Josie commands. "A spirit is sitting on your shoulder."

The drumming stops, and the chatter quiets down. Everyone is looking at Nina, staring and pointing.

For a split second, Nina wonders if it's Uncle John. She almost calls out his name, but thinks she's shown her tribe enough of her cluttered mind. "It's just a bird, Josie. We're out in the wilderness."

"Uh huh ... and how many birds you see flying around at night? And like, that's *just* a bull horn in your hand that you won't let go of, right?" Josie probes.

Nina has no words. She sits still, with the bird on its human throne, allowing herself to succumb to the magnificence

189

of the campfire. The moment she closes her eyes and relaxes with the bird, it flies away, but she doesn't notice. Except for Mama, all the observers return to their tasks, and the drummers resume their pounding, Nina's body reacting to the increased beat. With eyes still closed, she slowly rises, swaying her hips side to side, like the wind does to the tree branches. The soles of her bare feet stomp hard into the dirt, like there are plump grapes beneath her.

Sweat, heat, and tears dispense from her body and she dances along the stone circle surrounding the fire. No one is surprised that the ancestors have made themselves known, but everyone is amazed this young girl has caught one of them on her own.

Josie scoots back to keep out of the way of Nina's wild, flaring arms and spiritually drunken footsteps. She looks past Nina at Mama, who is unwavering with her stare, singing an unrecognizable song, and rocking herself back and forth.

Nina is completely lost in her own movement. She now has no control. The abeng is slippery in her hand, but it manages to find its way to her mouth.

Blow Nina. Tell wi di news but kip dancing red gyal. Dance!

Nina, doesn't recognize the many voices that are overlapping on top of each other, giving her the same instruction. But she begins to blow, and her feet lift off the ground. The drums get louder, the song gets faster, and Nina is above everyone floating in the air. More people arrive, responding to the call. Visions of Grandpa and Uncle John spin around her. She even sees her invisible friend's eyes, though hers are closed.

"I'm too high," Nina mumbles. She doesn't yell with fear, because she's not sure if she wants to come down. Her stomach starts to quiver and is ready to drop. She looks down and at least a dozen sets of long arms are woven within each other, palms up, heads down. Nina begins to plummet and screams, "Promise you'll catch me!"

Mama is the only one who lifts her head up as Nina gets close to their hands. "Yea mi red gyal. Mi promise."

The sun finds Nina through a small hole in one of the bedroom's curtains, gently waking her to a spellbinding vision. The room is painted seafoam green, with only a touch of white in the curtains and cloud-shaped pillows filled with organic plush fibers. In the room lives two handcarved wooden chairs, and a long, brown leather Chesterfield sofa, draped with silk and lace runners, placed in the center of the room as a reminder of the Maroon's win against the British. The round oversized bed that Nina is swaddled in has a wooden frame accented by wild flowers and plants. It smells like a garden just watered, with a hint of ginger and lemon that's infusing the hot herbal tea on the end table beside her. The white teapot with matching porcelain cups is next to a silver platter of Nina's favorite breakfast pastries.

Where am I? Nina looks down at her body and discovers that she's in a long white dress. She sits up in the bed and begins to sip on the tea.

"I can't just let this get cold, now can I?" Nina asks the mirror.

Her reflection is different than a couple of days ago: calm and peaceful, with hair filled with white flower petals. Nina feels like a princess in her very own Caribbean fairytale, though she can't remember how she got here. All she knows is that the drums were pounding and she was ready to dance.

Nina jumps at the sight of Mama behind her in the mirror. "Oh Mama! You scared me!" she yells, standing up to face her.

Before Mama can part her lips to speak, Nina is running her mouth. "But thank you, though. This is all so nice. The bed felt so good. Is this your room? It's so beautiful. And this bed, oh my goodness! I wish I could take it with me. I slept so good. I can't remember dreaming," Nina spouts.

"Mi promise yuh fada mi wud tek care of yuh," Mama says.

"You didn't have to dress me in this pretty white dress … and the flowers in my hair. Mama, why?"

She steps close to Nina and holds both of her hands. The room brightens like the sun has been set on fire, then dipped in glitter. The magical pair is glowing, managing the rumble underneath their skin. "Wi Maroons, Nina, an di Maroons a spiritual people. Di white represents purity an gud like yuh seh."

Josie walks into the royal suite, and Nina lets go of Mama's hands. "Ya ready to go, red gyal?" says Mama.

Nina nodes her head affirmatively, before hugging Mama goodbye. She wishes she could bring her home. "Thank you for letting me visit," she whispers.

"Yuh neva gaan. Yuh did here yesterday. Yuh here todeh. An yuh ago bi here tomorrow."

***

It's the first day of high school, and Nina quickly realizes she is the only white girl in attendance. Not because her face is white, but because this is what her Black girl classmates are already calling her.

"Hey, white girl, where you from? White girl, why you shave your legs? And why are you wearing them fake-ass silver diamond earrings?"

Nina hasn't even made it out of homeroom, and the pounding on her spirit is relentless. Archbishop Smith Catholic High School is a college preparatory institution consisting of all upper middle-class African Americans, a couple of Latinos, and one white boy who was raised by Black parents in a Black neighborhood. But Nina doesn't hear anyone calling him "Black boy."

Right before summer break, Selah tells her that it's time to engage with more kids who look like her and share the same experience, the same culture. But Nina is confident that when Selah saw Italian Jack at the door last fall, holding a homecoming dance corsage, she got worried. It's not that Selah isn't inclusive, but she has an expectation for her to marry a specific type of man. A Black man.

Nina is queasy from the cultural whiplash and also anxious of the unknown, so she withdraws verbally. She is used to bullies and their annoyance of her silence. She is vastly aware that her quiet demeanor triggers their assumption of her being stuck up, which makes them bully her more, but she refuses to engage in their fear anymore, as Mike warns her not to.

"Don't empower their ignorance," he once says. "If they want to get to know you, they'll be nice to you. And if they don't, they aren't worth the energy of caring."

Today, it seems as though everyone is afraid, because it's the first day of a new and important chapter of life.

"Ms. Abadie, can you stay back a minute?" Father Anderson is Nina's soft-spoken English teacher, who carries a lot of wrinkles on his face but is always smiling. He's white, like all of her teachers, which is odd to her, considering 99% of the students at the school are Black. But he seems to be well-liked and confident in his lessons, despite his hesitation when he speaks.

"Yes," Nina responds softly, pivoting back toward Mr. Anderson, who is gently holding a few pieces of paper as if they are treasures. She almost laughs, as she's never known anyone who smiles so wide, especially when speaking. *How is that possible? Maybe that's why he has so many wrinkles around his mouth.*

"Nina?" Mr. Anderson interrupts her musings.

"Oh yes, sir—I mean, Father. I'm sorry, what did you say?"

"I asked if you've thought about writing for our school paper. Your entry essay was exceptional. No other student I've come across in all my twenty years has described their life and interests as you have. Your vocabulary is elevated. Have you ever engaged in a spelling bee? What type of books are you reading?" Mr. Anderson is spiraling in his own ideas of Nina's possibilities.

"I mean, I dunno. I haven't really thought about it," Nina responds half-heartedly, scratching her legs through her plaid skirt. She looks outside the classroom door, watching the popular girls yell "white girl" as they pass by giggling. She turns back to Mr. Anderson, fighting back tears. "Actually, I was thinking of being a pom-pom girl."

***

It's like every teenage movie: the lunch scene. New girl walks in with her tray of questionables, desperately searching for a table to join where the clique accepts her. Nina glances around the massive cafeteria. She's already at a disadvantage, because this used to be an all-boys school, and all the girls who are now integrated in come from their sister school, a school filled with girls that the boys have already grown to love from their dances, athletics, and academic activities. They're already family, even the ones who don't fit in the mainstream. Nina is an outsider who is shy and comes from an institution that reminds these Black girls that they don't quite fit in the outside world. And it doesn't help that she's the fresh meat all their crushes want to sink their teeth into.

The popular ones, the bullies, the jocks, the nerds—all tables full. The religion fanatics, the teachers' pets, the girls who put out—all seats taken. Nina finally finds an empty spot on the edge of a back table near the trash can by the door. She sits and attempts to eat what could be considered to be meatloaf, mashed potatoes, and diced fruit, but it's evident all of it has been made in a lab. She nibbles on the mystery meat, but there's no chance for the mashed potatoes, which have been infiltrated by lost juicy chunks of pineapple and mandarin orange pieces. Nina hates the raw texture of fruit, even when it's fresh. She attempts to hold her breath while she eats, so the aroma of trash doesn't fill her lungs. Three girls walk by and glance down at her, expressionless. They don't look like they belong to a clique other than the one they have made for themselves. Nina is curious. Where are they going? She gets up, adds more trash to the trash can, and walks out of the cafeteria in their suspected direction.

Nina passes three empty classrooms until she gets to the music room. Boom! There they are, sitting at a small back table next to the piano. She is proud for finding the unidentified girls, but quickly realizes she has exposed herself.

"Can we help you?" one asks. "You good?"

"Oh, sorry. No, I was just lookin' around. I'm new here."

"Yeah, we know."

Nina determines the one who is talking is considered their "muscle". She's quick to defend and protect herself and her friends. The other two girls say nothing, but one is observing the other, and one is observing Nina. She is sure that the one with eyes on her is the lead decision maker. Nina exits the room without another word, and is grateful for getting through the pain of lunch today, as she will the next day, and the day after that.

Many classes are anticlimactic for Nina, with a few exceptions. Math is math and history is history. However, she loves English, despite Mr. Anderson's relentless pressure to strive for editor status at a school that already hates her. She thinks the notion that they will read or trust her stories is a stretch. He finds a way to get her to showcase her writing by helping Father Jessup with the programming for mass—writing a few tributes and religious activity descriptions.

Father Jessup teaches religion and philosophy, and Nina is fascinated by them both. But it's difficult for her to get into a rhythm with her studies while dodging mean girls.

"Nina, do you mind if I ask about the faith you practice at home?" Father Jessup inquires lightly, rocking in his office chair. "It's clear you embrace your spirituality, despite your comfort in challenging all things religion."

"Honestly, when I was little I was exposed to my grandparents' religion, and I do believe that because of them I became open to know God. I'd say it has been about four years since my mom decided the house needed faith, to keep us humble, grateful, and protected I guess. I don't know how I feel about the rigid structure of many religions, but I do know where God lives and when He's close," Nina testifies.

She stands up to pace a little while schooling Father Jessup. "Two years ago, the pastor was preaching and it moved me so much, I walked up to the front of the altar to become a Christian—'saved,' as they say—and was later baptized. I'm pretty active in my church youth group now because of it."

Father Jessup stopped rocking in his chair. "Oh, so you're baptized. Wonderful. What was it about the pastor's sermon that made you give yourself to God?"

"To be real, Father Jessup, I don't think I've given myself to Him. I was moved to go to the altar just because I saw Him up in the pulpit with the preacher, and it made me want to be closer to Him."

Father Jessup looks confused. "So, you're saying you saw God?"

"Yes, I did and sometimes still do. That's why I got baptized, just to be close. I knew He would be with me under the water and be pleased. But I'm pretty sure He doesn't want me to give myself to Him."

Father Jessup now stands up, feeling the need to stretch his legs and mind a bit while listening to her. "Why do you think God doesn't want you to give yourself to Him? And don't you think that's what you've already done?"

Nina sits back down in the chair in front of Father Jessup and simply says, "Because I've done bad things, you know? I've had bad thoughts."

"That's everyone, Nina. We're all sinners. Those are the people God wants."

"Nah Father, I'm pretty sure God's not waiting for me, since there are things about me I'm sure He doesn't like and I can't promise I will change. He probably thinks I have a fucked-up ideology." Nina sees his expression. "Sorry, Father, I didn't mean to say that. But you know what I mean."

"No Nina, I think you're wrong," Father Jessup says. "I don't know why you're so hard on yourself."

Nina pauses to consider this and let it sink in, as if grappling with a new language. *I've never heard anyone say that to me before,* she thinks to herself while walking out the classroom.

✳✳✳

"Hey, white girl! I saw you grittin' on me in class today! I hope you ready to get yo ass kicked."

Nina is almost at her locker. She has a long ride out of D.C. back home to the Maryland 'burbs, and isn't in the mood for bullshit this afternoon. Before she can turn around and address the monster, she gets hit by a cowardly push from behind. Time stands still and it seems like everyone in the entire school is in the locker room, staring, watching, waiting for her to get pounded on. But no one can see Nina's temperature rise, or hear the rattling of her bones, which she's beginning to control under her flesh.

She has always known a time would come where she would need to fight one of these brutes who call her "white girl," but didn't think it would be so soon. In years past, the hostility was less overt. When too many boys took notice of her, girls would simply stare and quietly plot for a month or so before executing their rage on the playground. But these monsters are much more grown and confident with their hate.

DANCER IN THE BULLPEN

Nina turns around with fist closed and left arm cocked back, until the monster's face is front and center. *Pop!* Without even a breath of warning, she punches the bully point-blank in the face. The bully is stunned and her knees drop, forcing her backward on the floor.

"Woooaaah! Oh shit! Did you see the white girl?! Damn!"

The spectators are in shock. No one would've thought a quiet and timid young Nina would punch the heavy-set junior in her face. Little do people know she has peed on herself a little because she is petrified, but she knows she can't show it.

And it isn't over. The monster gets up and charges at Nina. She takes the tackle and pushes back, after taking a few punches to the face and neck. Her blood is boiling from within, but Nina says nothing as she gets the advantage and straddles the monster, forcing her weight on the top of her chest, demobilizing her. Nina slaps her in the face this time and the monster's nose hemorrhages at full speed. It's impossible for her hand to cause such a physical reaction, and she is stuck in an intoxicating trance. The monster immediately stops talking shit, afraid of Nina's coal-black eyes and paralyzed state. The sounds of students screaming and chanting in the locker room are muted. But the sound of blood dripping off the monster's chin breaks Nina out of her trance, and she immediately wants to knock her out, stop the bully for good.

I know she's not a good person but you have to stop, please. Don't be like her, Nina's invisible friend says, straddling the monster from the opposite side, so she's facing Nina. *Think about what your future kids will feel when they hear that their mom killed a bully in a locker room, when she could have just walked away.*

"You're not a cloud," Nina exclaims, as she's staring at the frame of a real body, with a real face, though none of the features are clear. Before she decides to throw another blow or listen to her invisible friend, a tall boy with broad shoulders runs over to stop the madness.

"Hey, hey, ok girl, you got her, damn that's enough!" he says, pulling Nina's small body off the mountain of evil. "Don't go too crazy now. You don't want to get expelled at the beginning of the school year, do you?"

"I *was* stopping. Who are you?" Nina asks, uninterested in the answer, as she looks down at the drops of blood on her uniform. *Shit, Mom is going to kill me.*

"I'm Jason Ferguson. The oldest of the four Ferguson brothers—and the best of them, I might add. I'm good looking, smart, and I play a mean trumpet. But we can talk about that later. Go on now and catch that train."

"Um, aight," Nina says, forgetting the rest of her books, and soon the conversation she just had with the weird boy. She bolts out the backdoor and runs all the way to the Metro station without breaking stride. On the train, she thinks of excuses for her red-stained uniform. *I got a bloody nose in gym class. Yeah, that's it.*

The next day, rumors of the brawl reach the administrative office and both Monster and Nina get reprimanded for violence. It doesn't matter who started what. The girls just need to be nice and learn to get along. Sometimes Nina wonders how adults can be so dumb and lazy. She doesn't know which one is worse. She is just relieved Selah is not called, which is what should have happened.

DANCER IN THE BULLPEN

***

A few weeks in and high school has become one big Groundhog Day: class, mass, lunchtime sad—with a few bullies in-between. Nina is sitting at her usual corner seat at lunch when this tall, slim Puerto Rican scoots right next to her, ignoring the personal space rule.

"'Sup, pretty Nina. I'm Marcello."

"How you know my name?" Nina asks, now curious about this Latin giant.

"Everyone knows you, girl. Even us old heads. You cute, but a little strange," Marcello explains with a smirk, as he pulls the plastic nose plugs out of Nina's nose. "Like why you got these in there?"

"Because it's hard to eat with trash fumes in my nose."

"Then why you sit here?"

"Because there's nowhere else to sit," Nina explains, lip trembling a little. *I will not cry in front of this fine El-DeBarge-looking boy.*

"Aight, I get it. I'd sit here with you, but I'ma get kicked out if I miss one more class. You gonna be good though," Marcello says, not moving from his bench across from Nina, eyes still locked on her face. "Wanna get some ice cream or something after school?"

"Sure," Nina agrees with ease. She's hungry for a little attention. Why not get it from this cutie?

As Marcello rises to leave, the three music room girls walk by and glance at Nina, again expressionless.

What's up with them?

***

Nina and Marcello have become inseparable, except for when in class. He's a senior, so he gets out early and is always waiting for her when she reaches her locker. Tongue kisses and booty rubs are his signature moves and Nina loves all of it, the warmth it gives, despite the judgment burning the back of her neck each day. Even though Marcello is aggressively passionate, he never tries to go further than what she is ready for. He gets high off her touch and presence, but she has a couple of concerns brewing in the pit of her stomach.

Why doesn't he have any friends at school, not one, and he's been here almost four years? And I know people don't like me, but why do they dig their daggers in deeper when I'm with him?

"Nina! That boy Mario or Mandingo or whatever is on the phone!" Selah yells with an annoyed tone.

"Mom! His name is Marcello! And we're just friends."

"Uh huh. I hope you're spending the same amount of time on those books!"

"Yes Mom, I am. Thank you, you can hang up now!"

Nina fixes her hair and licks her lips, as if Marcello can see her face through the phone.

"Hey you," she swoons, trying to sound seductive.

"Where was you at yesterday?"

Nina's face immediately drops. "Huh?" She is scared to probe further into Marcello's anger.

"You heard me! I was waiting for you by the locker, and you never showed."

Nina drops her voice to a whisper, in case adults are eavesdropping. "Don't you remember? I left early to go to the radio station in the city I may be doing some work at. You know, like hosting a show. Isn't that dope?" She attempts to give him a little of her excitement, but it doesn't seem to be working.

"Meet me at the school early tomorrow, I need to talk to you."

"I dunno if I can get out the house early, but I'll try."

"Just do it," he says, unwavering.

"Ok," Nina submits, certain that Marcello just threatened her life.

Click. No goodbye or anything. Nina can't understand why he's so mad. It's eating at her; she hates to disappoint. She attempts to refocus on her math homework, but it all looks like enraged angles and schizophrenic lines. She puts the assignment back into her book bag and searches for an empty journal under her bed. She finds an empty page and begins to write:

> *Quietly laid to rest*
> *In a coffin softly dressed*
> *With flowers and if-it-hadn't-beens*
>
> *Loved ones gather round*
> *Praying heads hang down*
> *Grasp strong to high heavenly winds*
>
> *When the pain overflows*
> *And the dove can't fly no more*
> *All I want to know is where the fight goes*
>
> *Nina*

***

Nina tells David she has to get to school early to get some extra help with ideas regarding her biology project. She arrives at her locker and Marcello is already there looking angry and tired.

"Hey babe, you good? Why you look so tired?" Nina asks softly.

"I dunno about you, girl. You say you here, and you there, but I see all these bammas lookin' at you, like that one there!"

Nina looks in the direction Marcello is focusing his hot gaze on, and sees that Ferguson guy. *Wait, what's his name? Jason?*

"I don't even know that guy!" Nina yells back. She's getting mad now. "This is dumb. I can't control guys looking at me. But I think he's looking at you 'cause you acting crazy for no reason!"

Marcello grabs Nina's arms. "Don't you ever talk to me like that, little girl. You hear me?"

Nina fights her nausea and tightens her pelvic muscles, and looks into Marcello's green eyes and figures it out. "Are you high?"

Nina's unsure if it's because the locker room is the same place she punished the Monster, or because the self-proclaimed "Best Ferguson" boy is watching, or the fact that Uncle John came to visit last night to give her strength, but she gets unusually bold through her fear.

"Get your hands off me. I will talk to anyone I want to and go anywhere I want to go," she says, and walks to homeroom early without a glance back.

DANCER IN THE BULLPEN

Nina forgets her nose plugs, so she needs to find another place to eat her questionables. Mirroring the three music room girls, she finds her way to the empty art room. She almost forgets her food because of all the beauty on the walls—watercolors and oil paintings, glass art, clay sculptures.

"Hey Nina."

Nina turns around and sees the three music girls in the doorway. "Hey," she responds back suspiciously.

"Want to come eat with us?"

"Ok," Nina responds quickly.

As she walks behind them to the music room, she realizes the one who invited her to come is not the leader and is not the muscle. She's something else Nina can't figure out yet. They all sit down at the small table in the back and begin to open their bagged lunches, as if they forget Nina is there.

"Y'all don't buy lunch?" Nina asks.

"Nah, we don't eat that shit," the muscle says.

Nina is dying to know their names, so she introduces herself. "Well, I'm Nina. What are your names?"

The music girls start laughing together. "You kind of are a white girl like they say—talkin' all proper like. We know your name, Nina. Everyone does," says the girl who invited Nina over to lunch, and who introduces herself first. "My name is Keisha."

"Hi Keisha," Nina greets politely.

"I'm Cat," the loud muscle says.

"Hi Cat."

"I'm Diane."

"Hi Diane." Nina says, realizing she's the leader. "How y'all know each other? I know you because I see you all in some of my classes." She has many questions.

"Keisha is my cousin and Cat we found on the street one day," Diane says with a smirk. "We all came from Lady Theresa's, the sister school of this one."

"Why did you just invite me over?" Nina asks, unable to hold back her curiosity and desire for good news.

"We wanted to check you sooner, but needed to feel you out a bit. Make sure you weren't a kind of trouble we like to stay away from. We were a little worried about you slobbering all over Psycho Marcello. Rumor has it, he put a girl in the hospital last year 'cause he crazy jealous, but no one could prove it, and that's why he still here. It was all over the halls when you told him off in the locker room. That's when we knew you was aight. We teasin' you about the white girl thing, but we see it bothers you."

Diane's focus shifts down to her plaid pleated skirt. She begins pulling on a worn thread at the root, one that needs a good pair of sharp scissors, her fingers yanking, threatening to unravel the entire skirt. Keisha puts her hand on top of hers in a maternal protective manner, and she stops torturing her uniform.

"You seem lost, I guess," Keisha continues for Diane. "And we get how that is. We don't roll with them high-class cheerleader bitches, but we not geeks. We not sluts, but we ain't part of that nun squad. And you ain't white but you not Black yet either. So, we all kinda out of place."

"'Yet?'" Nina asks.

"Yeah, *yet*," Diane stresses. "I mean, clearly you brown, but look at you. Your legs all bare like them white girls. When you start shaving? I bet with one of them blonde Barbie girls in her mansion with a gold razor."

DANCER IN THE BULLPEN

Cat tries to muffle her laughter as she gets up and walks across the room behind the instruments. She stuffs her oversized lunch bag into the small trash can meant for scrapped music sheets.

"Dang Cat. Can you wait, and put that shit with the lunchroom trash? They gonna know we be up in here when you do that," Diane complains.

"Bitch, they already know we be up in here."

Nina watches Cat bend over, forcing what looks like a boulder through the hole of a needle. She's just now discovering how muscular and toned Cat really is, and can't help but giggle at the fact that the muscle really has muscles.

"What's so funny?" Keisha asks in a suspicious tone. Cat retreats from the needle hole and looks back at Nina in unison with the others.

"Nothing. I was just thinking about something," Nina responds defensively. *Shit. I wasn't even looking at Cat like that. I was just looking at how dope her body is, not because I want her or anything. Damnit Keisha.*

Keisha doesn't follow up with additional questioning. She decides to observe this newcomer a little more, but Diane continues to probe. "You talk like you not from anywhere and you act like one of them. Maybe your mama don't like Black people. It's not your fault. You'll get Black after some time up in here. We may not be hood, some are even big-time bougie, but all of us in here Black."

Nina looks at all three girls—all so beautiful, with different shades, shapes, personalities, and probably different home lives. But they are all young Black girls trying to thrive together. "Is that why these girls in here hate me?" she asks, feeling a knot forming in her throat.

"Not really. They hate you more because you're new and shiny. The white girl part just makes it easy to kill your spirit," Keisha says.

Keisha is the intuitive one, check. "I'm used to being bullied at the white schools too. It doesn't matter where I am," Nina states nonchalantly. "My daddy says I can't feed into it, I have to ignore it."

"Your daddy is smart, but he also ain't in high school," Cat reminds.

"So, what do you all know about the dance team or pom-pom squad?" Nina questions. "Not sure what y'all call it here."

Keisha and Cat look at Diane, waiting anxiously for her to answer.

"You wanna be a part of the dance team?" Diane asks, looking Nina up and down as if she's trying to find a reason to think she deserves that opportunity. "Are you any good? And I don't mean 'white girl good' either."

"I'm better than regular 'Black girl good.' I'm country hood good," Nina boasts, almost believing her words.

"Awww shit!" The music girls scream in unison through their laughter.

"Let me find out you trying to start a riot up in here. White girl takes over the pom-poms!" Cat jokes.

The girls take some time to settle down, and then Diane gets serious. "So, here's the deal. I'm on the dance team. And the only reason I'm there is 'cause my dad went to this school and my mom to Lady Theresa. My mom was the best dancer on the team, and my dad played the saxophone better than most."

"They like legends around here," Keisha brags.

DANCER IN THE BULLPEN

"The crew who runs the dance team now knows what's up with my family rep. Plus they need me to choreograph because they don't know shit," Diane says.

"Ok great, so you can get me on the squad," replies Nina. "I mean of course, I'll audition for you."

"It's not that easy, light-skin," Diane warns. "The entire team needs to approve you, and 95% of the team are the girls who want you gone. In fact, the lead dancer, Mo, is the one who sent Latoya over to stomp on you in the locker room that day."

Nina's tights are starting to itch, and the pee she's holding is getting heavy. "How do you know that?"

"Diane makes it her business to know everything," Keisha says with pride.

"I don't remember seeing this Mo," Nina says, attempting to doubt her strength.

"You may not have seen her, but trust me, she's seen your ass, and is watching your every move," says Diane. "Mo is not the sturdiest fruit on the tree, so you better be careful with her. I hear her mother is like in a D.C. gang and her dad in jail for starting some type of drug ring. She lives with her grandmother, but that sweet old lady can't control her. The only reason why she can even go to this school is because her grandma won the lottery and kept it away from them dirty relatives she got, keeping the money clean and used for her only grandchild. You would think Mo would be grateful and be nice to bitches up in here, but nah. She enjoys torturing girls and boys alike."

"Shit." It's all Nina can muster.

"So, you still want to try out?" Cat dares.

All three music girls stop and stare at Nina, who's looking down at the table, gently stabbing the mystery meat with

209

her fork. Finally, she lifts her head up and looks Diane directly in the eyes and says, "Yeah, let me dance for the crazy bitch."

No laughter this time. Just three surprised smiles.

"Nina, you may be ok after all," Diane says.

***

It has only been a couple of weeks since Nina stopped performing with her national dance group. She has always been heavier and curvier than her counterparts, and she's missing out on roles because the anorexic girls keep snatching them up. Despite the self-esteem chats from Selah and Mike, she still sees the looks when she gets a second plate, and hears the offhand comments about her growing thickness. Sometimes it's what's being said under the breath, quietly, that stabs Nina's gut. Regardless of the shift, she is simply exhausted with the constant movement, back and forth from show to show: a constant beatdown on the body. When her knee gives out during her last *Nutcracker* performance, she is confident it's time to rest for good.

"I'm only fourteen, Mom. I don't want to have arthritis at twenty-five like some of these athletes do," Nina announces, shortly after dropping the dance group without consulting anyone first.

"But you've been dancing since you were three years old, princess," Selah whispers, as if mourning her own talent. "I think you're just not doing enough strength training and stretching. You just need to be a bit more disciplined with your diet, so you aren't straining your limbs—"

"Mom!" Nina loudly interrupts. She looks at Selah and almost allows the rawness of her mother's disappointment pull her into submission. Her face softens, and she smiles at the beautiful face that mirrors hers, understanding her mother just wants the best for her. "I'm just tired of all the shit, Mom. I won't ever get the leads like these white girls, even when I practice harder, or even if I'm better than them. I will not be the star Black ballerina you want me to be." *Not while trying to survive this new high school,* Nina thinks, successfully holding back tears.

Selah ignores her daughter's profanity and responds softly, "I just want you to be the best you can be, Nina. But really, I just want you to be happy and not have regrets."

Nina embraces her mother. "I'll replace it with something good, I promise."

The school dance team is different. Practice is only three times a week and less restrictive. Nina is hoping to have fun again, after she poisons all the bullies. Diane is right. Mo is a force, petite and mocha-brown with a wide mouth that is constantly frowning. Her eyes look sleepy as if no one lets her rest at home.

"She can't deny me if I'm good, because they want to be the best squad in the city, right?" Nina whispers to Diane, outside the gym before being called in.

"First of all, stop talking to me. I can't look like I'm your friend right now. Even though they already know I brought you in. And yeah, her ass sure can deny you just because her boyfriend checked you out yesterday!"

"He did?"

"No girl, I'm just sayin'! But probably. You don't even know who he is, do you?" Diane is ranting because she's nervous for Nina.

"I got this, Diane. Just drop the beat," Nina commands with a grin.

Diane does just that, and the bass of Public Enemy's "Fight the Power" bounces off the walls. Nina's body begins to jump and wind, leap and bend in ways the girls have never seen.

"Damn, this girl is good," Nina hears one of Mo's tribe whispers.

"Shut up, Carol," another disciple responds.

Nina doesn't stop. Her building sweat just motivates her to go harder, go longer, but Mo has had enough. She stops the tape and glares at Diane with no words.

One of her faithful crew knows how to interpret her mind well. "Thank you, Tina."

"It's Nina," Nina corrects sternly.

"Of course, right, Nina. Well, we'll take your performance under consideration and get back to you in a couple of days," the girl says with a fake proper voice.

Nina knows they are playing her, but she refuses to give them the satisfaction. She simply responds, "Thank you for your time and I hope to dance with you all real soon."

Afterward, Nina is surprised that Diane is surprised the tryout went any differently.
"You're the one who said Mo is crazy," she says.

"I know," Diane admits. "It's just that you're so good. Like *really* good, Nina. And I think her stubbornness will get in the way of us winning. Listen, I'll work on her, but in the meantime, will you just try to not flirt with nobody and stay out of her way?"

Nina laughs, even though there is nothing funny. "I'll try not to wake the monster."

DANCER IN THE BULLPEN

"Nina home! Nina home!" Jasmine is waiting at the window with her new dog, Snowflake. He's a white poodle with not much wit or charisma, but he's sweet. He's definitely no Mister, but no one could possibly replace him. Nina still feels the pain of letting Mister out into the yard last year to take a quick pee. She went into the house to answer the phone, only to return to a missing best friend. The search lasted for months, but it was as if he disappeared into thin air. It's another hard loss she hasn't quite recovered from. Selah seems to think Mister wore out the ground under the fence, making a hole big enough to run away.

"You just don't know my Mister, Mom. He would never leave me on purpose," Nina says.

David thinks someone stole him. "The thief probably cased the house, waiting for Mister to be out alone." His contemplation makes sense. Nina just prays a nice family found Mister or saved him from a terrible situation. She wonders if he shares his magic with his new family, or if it died when he left her. Snowflake is no Mister. He's not magical, and he doesn't understand how to love like Nina's dog loved her. But little Jasmine is happy, and that's what matters to Nina now.

It's like Jasmine has lived four years in only four minutes. It feels like only yesterday when Nina was at the hospital, the first person to comb her hair.

Nina walks in the front door and drops off her shoes. "Where's your daddy?"

"I dunno," Jasmine responds, shrugging her little shoulders.

But Nina knows that if Jasmine doesn't know, it means David's downstairs in the basement sleeping, tired from disappointment and missed opportunities. Selah and David moved their bedroom downstairs after the family they were sheltering left, to make more room for their kids and the periodic visitors Selah houses in Jasmine's bedroom, the one that's not quite hers yet. It's wild to Nina that at one point there was a family of six, one pregnant teenager, and a two year old running up and down the halls. Selah's heart is sometimes too big for the home in which she dwells. It's hard to say no to a family in need, yet the risk is finding the ones that will leave. Though it's quiet now, Nina feels another tidal wave coming. She is bracing for the hit.

"Are you hungry?" Nina asks her cute little firecracker of a sister.

"I dunno," Jasmine repeats.

"Ok, Chef Boyardee it is."

Nina pulls out a small pot and begins heating up the quick-fix dinner, since Selah is working late. It's been a long time since she has heard the sizzle of good food cooking on the stove, but she understands that her mom is trying to provide her family with the best by putting in so many hours at the hospital.

Nina bathes Jasmine, reads her a bedtime story, and lets her sleep in the bed with her. She tells David that Jasmine is looking to cuddle with her, but really she is looking to cuddle with her sister.

"You like school, Jazzy?" Nina asks, trying to center her mind on something simple and nice.

"Yeah, I get to draw and play with blocks," Jasmine shares.

"'Yes', you mean," corrects Nina.

"Yes," Jasmine repeats. "You like school?" She likes this question game.

DANCER IN THE BULLPEN

"It's ok. School is hard. I have a hard time paying attention sometimes in class and the numbers are a lot. Most of the girls are mean, and the boys just want to kiss me."

Jasmine starts giggling. Nina's venting has her forgetting she's in the presence of a baby. "Go to sleep, little one," she instructs. "You'll see Mommy in the morning."

***

"Nina!" Diane is running down the hall like her hair is on fire.

"What, what?"

"Carol broke her foot!" Diane announces with sheer excitement.

"Yes! Yes!" Nina responds with the same joy. She grabs Diane and lifts her up, even though the girl is bigger and taller.

"Y'all are some sick chicks," Cat accuses, walking up to the happy duo. "Straight to hell you both go. Look at y'all geekin' 'cause this girl all broken and shit."

"Oh, she'll be ok," Keisha says with a giggle, walking up behind Nina and completing the foursome in the hall. "How you know Mo gonna let Nina replace Carol?"

"Because Carol is the best on the team, besides me, and Mo knows that," says Diane. "She'd be a fool not to let Nina on after seeing how dope she is." Nina blushes, loving Diane's admiration of her. "Also, I already got a little insurance in motion," she reveals with pride. "I told the headmaster that Monica was smart to recognize Nina's talent early when she tried out, and already had her ready to go if someone got hurt. So, now we'll keep the tradition of our fly-ass homecoming show alive, no matter what, and it's all because of Mo."

The three girls laugh and look at Diane warmly, impressed at how smart and proactive she is. All of a sudden, Keisha pulls a bobby pin out of her emergency makeup pouch and slides it over Nina's stubborn curls, which have escaped the back of her high ponytail. Nina can feel them all bonding together, and it feels good.

"Then I added that maybe he should go let her know how great she's doing, because sometimes she doesn't feel appreciated," finished Diane.

"Wow, that's slick," Cat says.

"Yeah, I couldn't have done that shit better," Keisha cosigns.

✸✸✸

"Well, hello beautiful. You lookin' extra fine. No big bad bullies tryna kick yo' ass today?"

"What's up with this locker room? Why it bring out the crazies?" Nina questions back, flirtatiously.

"I don't know about all that, young lady. The only thing you need to know is my name is Ferguson. Jason Ferguson, the oldest and best of all the Fergusons," he says with confidence.

"Oh yes, now I remember you. You pulled me off a big ol' monster months ago, helping me escape from the Catholic Feds."

"Yep, so I need my payment please," Jason says.

Nina's joking tone switches quick to a defensive one. "I don't owe you nuthin," she informs adamantly.

"Nah, I know, I'm lunchin'." Jason softens, lifting his eyes from Nina's waist to her pretty dark-brown eyes. "You gonna let me buy you some pizza or sumthin though?" he asks, hoping for a yes, as he's waited all this time for her to look happy before approaching.

"I dunno. I've heard a lot about you, already," Nina warns.

"Oh yeah, like what?" he says, standing up straight with his six-foot-four frame, looking down at her, fearlessly smiling.

"I heard your family like real religious and strict, but you're one of the most popular boys in school, so you're probably bad. You're on the honor roll and play the trumpet so you're also a nerd but you be frontin'."

Jason rolls his eyes but smiles with pride, extending his long arm to brush Nina's bangs away from her face.

Nina ignores the gestures and continues, even though the goose pimples on her arms from his touch are mountainous and distracting her view of his face. "And you like to work out so that's why you look like that." She squints her eyes, a bit out of breath, trying to avoid eye contact.

"Oh, so you like my body," Jason teases, stepping in closer to Nina, forcing her to back into her locker. He retreats just as fast, nervous he's moved in too close. "Wow, you must be one of them TV psychics, or you paid someone in my family to tell my secrets," he continues, with his signature smirk. "Aight then, my turn. Can I do you?"

Nina smiles, enjoying Jason's energy. "Sure, I think," she approves reluctantly.

"You grew up in them rich and fancy cracker schools, but your mom wants you to be Black now. She threw you up in here with all of us fake Christian heathens to give you some Jesus. You're a little weird. I see you talking to yourself sometimes, like in the hall, and even when you was jumping the girl who jumped you, so I don't know who also lives in that pretty little head of yours."

Nina fidgets with her skirt, and her calves start to itch under her knee highs.

"Girls be hatin' on you 'cause they jealous as shit. You pretty and smart and all mysterious, so that pisses them off. You write secret shit in a book, and you move your body like a wild belly dancer or sumthin."

Nina steps away from her locker, closer to Jason, smiling with her head tilted up so she can look into his eyes better.

"I catch you looking at them drawings in the art room, but you never stay to draw nuthin, so I guess you can't draw but you wanna. I heard you got a whole lot of sisters and brothers you live with, but you never talk about them. I dunno. You look sad a lot and sometimes it looks like you mad. So, that's why them bammas hate you."

Nina is speechless, and is trying to fight the urge to pee, but she can't breathe. She just needs to get out of the building.

Don't be afraid, you're amazing and he sees it, her invisible friend whispers in her ear. Nina begins to cry and runs out the same way Jason taught her to escape last time.

But this time Jason runs after her. "Wait Nina, wait! Sorry girl! I'm not tryin' to make you sad. I was just fuckin' with you." He reaches for Nina's hand, and she lets him hold it, enjoying the strength of his grip and the silkiness of his skin. "You know I been checkin' you since the first day you came in here. Watching you waste time with them dumb niggas who don't deserve you. How you kicked that girl's ass with no help. You all that and a bag of chips, is all I'm sayin'." Jason gently pulls her hand, forcing her a little closer. It's cold outside but she is sweating.

"Your name be on every Jesus pamphlet that goes out, too, like you run this place. Who hiding brains now, huh?" Jason asks.

Nina is hypnotized, desire seeping from her pores. She can't stand it anymore. "Kiss me," she demands.

Jason doesn't hesitate. He's been waiting for the opportunity to devour her since they first met. He will not deny her what he's been wanting for so long. They're out in the courtyard and only see each other, not the crowd of students finding their way to their cars. They kiss long and slow, and their feet begin to elevate. Nina can feel his lips tremble underneath her full mouth. She warms them slow, probing her tongue deep in his mouth, increasing the speed of their flight, opening his mouth wider, making him more vulnerable. His mouth stops trembling and moves in rhythm with hers, pulling his body closer to hers. They're high in the sky, way above the trees.

"I love you," Jason says when he comes up for air, breathing in thick white clouds.

Nina giggles. "You don't love me. Wait, do you?" She doesn't want to dismiss what he's feeling.

Who am I to tell him that he doesn't love me? Love at first sight is real. The fairytales are real. And like he said, he's been watching me for so long and loves everything about me.

"I love you too, Jason," Nina admits.

Jason smiles and says, "Great baby. You're mine. Kiss me." And again they deep kiss, until the clouds burst and desire dampens her underwear.

"Wait, stay here a minute," Nina says. "You can't go play the trumpet like that."

"Oh, damn right, you made it stand up like that, with those magic lips. You da bomb, girl. I can't even imagine if your mouth was on it. You'd probably break it." They both laugh together and force themselves out of the sky, refusing to kiss again until the tornado passes. Jason finally pecks Nina on the corner of her mouth to keep the wind calm, and she watches him walk away, still sitting on cloud nine.

"Bitch!"

Mo has never spoken directly to Nina before, and it's no surprise she starts now by calling her something like that. She turns around and Mo pushes her up against the wall with a force she has never seen in a girl before.

"Let me tell you this," Mo says. "I don't give a fuck that you're on the squad now, or that you givin' your coochie away to the nearest dog. You'll never be good enough for us, or this place, little white girl. You better watch your back. I'm watchin' your ass."

Nina says nothing in response. She simply takes the dagger nestled in her scars and pulls it out a little, thinking about the dance that will make Mo a star. "Bitch," she says, low enough so Mo won't turn around and walk back.

***

The music girls can't wait for Nina. Lunch started fifteen minutes ago, and they're already digging in their brown bags. Finally, Nina walks in with a Washington Redskins bomber jacket on and a thin herringbone gold chain nestled above her collarbone. She sits down and opens her brown bag, joining the girls like nothing is different.

"Um hello?" Keisha questions. "You ain't gonna tell us what the hell you got on?"

"Jason," Nina simply states.

"Jason who? Jason what?" Cat interrogates.

DANCER IN THE BULLPEN

Diane has already heard but must get it from the horse's mouth, so she can believe it.

"Jason Ferguson," Nina announces proudly.

"Oh Jesus," Keisha says, dropping her sandwich and rubbing her temples.

"Go on, Jason Ferguson, what?" Diane chimes in.

"Jason Ferguson is my boyfriend! And don't y'all tell me how he's bad or whatever because he is not."

"It's not that he's bad. It's the opposite," Diane explains. "You just locked in the dopest boy in school—well, except for the ball players. He got a car and money, and he's not an asshole. He used to date a girl name Trina, but she was a year older than him and slutting all around the city. It really broke his heart, so he just stopped messin' with girls. Some people think he went gay, but anyone who really knows him, knows that's bullshit.

"Now his brothers and cousins are a different story. They just nasty. It's almost like Jason was the only one who got the good gene."

Keisha looks at Nina, shaking her head like a nosy old neighbor watching a man sneak his mistress out the house. Cat scoots her chair closer to Nina, gently lifting the herringbone off her chest to get a closer look.

"Listen, it's all good you and Jason found love in literally five minutes, but girls are gonna come for you even harder. We may have to give you some pepper spray," warns Diane.

Cat laughs, "Wow, that's crazy."

"I ain't playin', Cat. This girl over here prancing around like a queen and shit. I'm just trying to keep her alive."

Nina is scared of the potential backlash for finding love, the one she's been looking for all this time, but not enough to

221

give it up for these cowards. She listens and gets the pepper spray though, from some boy Diane knows. You can never be too careful.

***

"Nina, what do you think we should do differently for our homeless friends down at the soup kitchen this winter, in addition to giving our time and service?" Nina is half paying attention, and Father Jessup knows it.

Nina thinks of the question, and answers sincerely. "I think we need to do something less tangible."

"Interesting. Go ahead, like what?"

"We should each write a letter or a poem or some type of testament for them."

"That's easy for you to say, you're good at writing," a classmate mumbles.

"You know what, that's true," Nina says. "Ok, how about if someone like me draws or paints a picture. I have no experience in that. The point is to go out of your comfort zone and give a gift of courage that is personal, that takes time and care. There's value in giving a gift like that—a gift of discovery."

"Yes Nina, that sounds beautiful—perfect even! How about you write out the assignment and bring it back to me tomorrow for review, before I share with the class?" Father Jessup asks, infused with newfound energy.

The bell rings and Nina is ready to get to pom-pom practice.

"Nina, can you hang back, please?"

"Yes Father."

"Great work today. It's nice to see someone think outside of the box for the betterment of everyone."

"Thank you."

"You're stellar in this philosophy class. I'm proud of you. How are you doing in your other classes?"

Sometimes Nina forgets that Father Jessup is also the guidance counselor. "Um, well I have an *A* in English, obviously, but the other classes are a bit of a struggle. I had a math tutor, but it only helped for a while, so I just ask for afterschool help from the teacher. And I do the same for science and history." She feels the weight of her book bag double in pounds, so she lets it drop to the ground.

"I'm just not good at it," Nina admits, weary from always trying to be better. "And my family is all doctors and lawyers, so mastering math and science is a priority for them. But I'm just trying to get out of high school, Father."

"I think we can do more than just get you out, but you have to want to do it. You have to believe you can do it, and maybe limit some other distractions. You're in the tenth grade now, Nina. You are halfway there."

"I can't give up the dance team, Father. I've already given up too much dance already, by leaving the group I grew up with. I can't give this one up too."

"No, but you can give up writing papers for some of the football team."

Nina looks up at Father Jessup and feels the urge to pee. She begins to make excuses. "Father Jessup—"

"It's ok, Nina. You just need to stop. I figured it out based on your beautiful style of writing. I know these boys aren't writing in natural poetics," Father Jessup says with an unanticipated chuckle.

"Ok, I'll stop. I'm sorry. It makes me feel good when they ask for help, and then I realize when it's too late that I'm writing the entire paper."

"I understand. It's the nurturer in you."

"Some things don't come easy for us. And even though there is no reason to seek a career in accounting when you're a journalist, it's important not to give up just because it's hard," Father Jessup reiterates. "I'm hoping you'll reconsider Father Anderson's invitation to apply for the editor-in-chief position. We need you, and I think it'll be good for you."

"Alright, I'll reconsider the editor position. If it gets crazy though, I'm coming to you," Nina says with a smile, happy Father Jessup cares enough to stop her.

"That's fair," Father Jessup acknowledges.

"Thank you, Father," Nina says, appreciative of the candid and forgiving conversation.

"Nina, you're a wonderful student. Now go and write my assignment for the rest of these slackers, including me."

"Yes, will do," Nina says, swinging her book bag over her shoulder, which is now light as a feather.

✳✳✳

Nina and Jason have been one of the hottest couples in school for over a year now. Jason, the best of the Ferguson brothers and lead trumpet player, meets Nina Abadie, mysterious lead pom-pom girl. Their love affair has been supported and doubted by family, friends, and ratchet enemies. But when it's just the two of them, the noise is muted. Unfortunately, it's rarely just the two of them.

"Hey baby, if you're not ready, it's ok. I can wait. Shit, I can wait on you for as long as you need. 'Cause you know I love

DANCER IN THE BULLPEN

you. Your body is just icing, you know that right?" Jason has Nina in her usual position at lunchtime, up against her locker, her hands softly placed on his torso, head tilted up, lips soft and flavored his favorite fruity cherry.

Nina is scared of making love with Jason for the first time, until he says he can wait.

"Let's do it today," she suggests quietly.

"Are you sure, baby?" Jason sincerely asks, not wanting to rush his girl and jeopardize their closeness.

"Yes, I'm ready."

"Aight, meet me after school. I'll find somewhere private and chill for us," Jason instructs. Nina loves his confident assertiveness. She has finally found her king and she wants to give him all of her.

Nina steps up into Jason's Bronco and throws her book bag in the back seat, with no plans of unzipping it for homework later.

"Damn girl, what took you so long?"

"You know, I had to wash up and get all clean and pretty for you," Nina explains, as she leans in the driver seat so he can be seduced by her scent.

Jason kisses her neck like he's trying not to bite it. "Shit woman, you do smell good. Let's hurry up, hmmm." He's hungry for his sweet girlfriend.

Nina rolls down the window so she can feel the wind between her fingers, and thinks about how to be sexy for her man so he won't ever leave.

Jason pulls up to what looks like a frat house. Nina follows him through the front door and she immediately feels uncomfortable.

"Jason, where are we? There's like five guys in here."

"Don't worry, baby. This my boy's crib, and the rest of these niggas are just his roommates."

"Ok, so where we gonna go up in here?" Nina already smells a problem. This is not feeling at all romantic or sexy.

"I'll be right back. Just sit tight right here. It's all good."

Nina sits on the edge of a couch that has a sheet cover on it, hopefully for a reason that involves protection versus covering up a blood or pee station.

"Hey baby, come back here!" Jason yells from the back. Nina follows his voice and finds him in what looks like a master bathroom decorated by Grandma Rosa. She walks in the bathroom and he closes the door with a seductive grin, like he's doing something hot and tempting.

"Um, what we 'bout to do?" Nina asks with an accusatory tone.

Jason starts kissing Nina's neck and unbuttoning her Catholic school button-down shirt, and for a minute she's into it. But then a part of the sink cracks when Jason lifts her up to sit on the edge of it. She jumps off when she hears the sound.

"Oh my god, baby, did my fat ass do that?" Nina asks, feeling her insecurity fill up the sink.

"Yeah, P-H-A-T. Phat. You need to stop saying that kinda shit. You're skinny and beautiful. You been watching too much fuckin' TV or spending too much time with them skeleton dancing bitches." Jason is mad that Nina doesn't see herself as the beauty that she is, and the fact his sexy plan isn't working.

Nina regrets showing Jason how crazy she is about her body. She realizes he doesn't like girls to whine about stuff, but some things need to be addressed. "Jason, I can't have my first time be in an old lady's bathroom."

"Shit, I know, baby, my bad," he admits, racking his brain for an alternative.

Nina follows him back out of the bathroom and they make a stop to talk to his useless friend.

"Baby, wanna smoke before we go?" Jason asks.

Nina gives Jason a look. He knows she doesn't smoke, so that answer is obvious. She wonders if he needs to smoke just to get ready for her.

Jason decides to take Nina out to Virginia country, where there's an abundance of trees and green plains. He finds a secluded field with big tall trees to park in between.

Once Jason parks and pushes the back seats down, he pulls out a soft blanket and spreads it out on the floor of their makeshift hotel room. He pops in his favorite slow jams tape, and Anita Baker's "Sweet Love" spills out of the speakers. Nina joins him, crawling in the back of the truck. They slowly take off each other's clothes, exploring each and every body part.

"I promise I'll be gentle," Jason whispers in Nina's ear as he cradles her in his arms, finding her soft warmth with the strength of his pulsating muscle.

"Jason," Nina gasps as they stare into each other's eyes.

Jason is gentle, but his new lover can't help but grimace in pain. "You ok, baby?"

"Yes, don't stop … just go slow."

Jason's long arms find the opening between Nina's soft frame and the reclined seats. He cups her back and deep dives inside her, keeping his eyes locked on hers. "Nina baby, you know you're my first and only. I fuckin' love you."

"Don't say that. You don't have to say that," Nina begs, holding on to the back of Jason's neck as the sting between her legs begins to shift into a pleasurable ache.

"I'm keepin' it real, baby. This is my first time. You're my everything," Jason confesses, pulling back and diving in again, just enough to build a sensual friction.

Nina can't fight back the tears. Her heart is throbbing, at risk of completely exploding. Passionate, they kiss as one body, one heart, one soul. "I love you too, Jason."

"You got me all fucked up," Jason responds, as he grips Nina's small body and flips on his back, taking her with him, forcing her on top of him. "Don't be afraid, let me look at you. You are far from fat. Look at your amazing body. All these youngins want you, or want to be close to you. Shit, some of them even wanna be you."

Nina looks down at Jason's face, and he can tell she is unsure of what to do.

"It's ok, baby, go slow, but make love to me like you know how bomb you are," Jason says. Nina moves her hips like she's dancing, and he responds in rhythm.

"Hey niggers! Get off my property!"

Nina and Jason halt and look at each other, as if they're trying to determine if their mind are playing tricks on them.

"I see you niggers!"

"Oh my god, Jason! Where is that coming from?" asks Nina.

Jason is smart. He doesn't wait to figure it out. He releases Nina and jumps over the front seat naked, starting the truck's engine.

"Shit Jason, they're behind us! Go, go!"

Nina sees three white men with bats and sticks running toward the Bronco like Jason stole their livelihoods. They must live in the big mansion at the top of the hill, and the property Jason and Nina are on is theirs.

DANCER IN THE BULLPEN

Jason presses down on the gas with no hesitation and speeds away, with no chance for these men on foot to catch up with them. Nina gets dressed as Jason flies over bumps and rocks, crawling back up to the front passenger seat and buttoning up her uniform shirt.

"Whew, well that was some runaway slave type shit, huh?" Nina jokes, but thinks none of it is funny. In fact, her heart is beating at the speed of light.

"Are you telling a funny, Nina?" Jason teases.

Nina starts laughing to dispense the fear. "Yes, I am." She is enjoying the view of Jason driving his truck naked.

"I'm sorry, baby, for real. I'm gonna save up for a hotel room or something next time."

"Nobody gonna let you get a hotel room under eighteen, Jason," Nina rationalizes. "Plus, I'm too amazing—like you said—for you to wait that long." She smiles.

"I got friends who can get it for us. Don't worry. You shouldn't have to go through with that again," Jason says in a regretful tone.

Nina runs her fingers down Jason's arm, looking out the window, happy she's no longer a little girl. She's a queen.

Jason and Nina are famished from all the adrenaline of coming close to death. They go to a twenty-four hour pancake house and crush breakfast for dinner.

"How you feel?" Jason asks, hoping Nina feels the way she looks—stunning, with a glow.

"So good. You made it special, baby, thank you. What about you? Was that really your first time?"

"Yeah," Jason says with a calm disposition.

"But I know Trina was definitely not a virgin, so, I don't get it."

"She was off the chain, man—too busy fucking other people. I just never went there with her. I wanted to, but I didn't want to just be another nigga. I guess people assume I be rollin' hard, but who I screw or don't screw is nobody's business. I wanted it to mean sumthin too. And now it does." Jason leans over and kisses Nina on her sticky lips. "Thank you, hotness."

Nina stabs a few pieces of her syrup-soaked pancakes with her fork, and puts them in her mouth with a trembling hand. She begins to sob softly.

"Nina, don't cry. I promise you, I'm telling you the truth. I never did nuthin with Trina."

"It's not that," Nina says, lifting her head so Jason can look at her directly. "I just don't know why people are so mean, you know? The bullies, your hoochie ex, the men trying to kill us off their land, and like this whole Rodney King thing too, shit." She is overwhelmed with love and despair. So many emotions all muddled together.

"People are evil 'cause they don't have something good like this happy-forever thing we got," Jason says.

Nina touches Jason's hand with hers and manages a grin. "Forever and ever."

✳✳✳

Jason is not playing when he says Nina is all his. He has no hesitation in telling everyone who asks that she is his girlfriend and to back off. Even though they've been together for months, he doesn't hold back his public displays of affection, or his wrath when anyone engages in anything negative against either one of them because of their relationship, or any other

DANCER IN THE BULLPEN

reason. He uses his popular status at school to get Nina and her friends in on some of the best parties and activities.

The problem is Diane was right. The girls who already hate Nina now want her gone. The boys who love her are now plotting against Jason. And the Ferguson boys don't think she is worth the stress.

"I'm just saying J, this girl is not in your league," says Jason's cousin. "Sure, she's hot and all, but come on now. She doesn't have money to hook you up with anything. She doesn't have a car and she can't even stay out or her mommy and daddy will come hunt you down."

"Nigga, you just want her to have a car, so you can drive mine," Jason pushes back.

"Ok, maybe I want to drive your truck, but you know I'm right. She's just a little girl. I bet she barely knows how to give a good BJ," Jason's cousin accuses.

Nina walks into the gym for the pep rally and gives the music girls a heads up that she'll be sitting with Jason and the Ferguson boys.

"Hey baby!" Jason greets her happily and motions her over to sit next to him on the bleachers. The rest of the Ferguson brothers and cousins are on a row of bleachers above them.

"Ewww, what's that in your hair?" Jason's youngest brother asks, tapping Nina on the shoulder.

"What?" Nina turns around and looks up at Jason's cousin.

"You have dandruff or chunks of something gooey in your hair."

Nina is humiliated. "No, that's my perm. The chemical burned my scalp a little, so it's just the scabbing." She's annoyed she is even giving an explanation.

"Nah, that's something gross in your hair. Dandruff or something, I don't care what you say," the brother continues to taunt. "Hey J man, you know your girl got a dandruff head?"

Nina can't believe she is being bullied by her boyfriend's own brothers. She looks at Jason next to her, waiting for him to defend her, regardless of whether he knows what's going on with her scalp or not. But he says nothing.

"Whatever man, let's just watch this shit so we can bounce," are the only words Jason can pull together. Nina is appalled. She can't believe this guy who's been flaunting their relationship up and down the halls for months can't stand up to his bully family.

"What the fuck was that?" Nina asks Jason, as she straps herself in his Bronco for the ride home.

"Nina, I didn't know relaxers burns girls' hair, ok?"

"No, it's not ok! It doesn't matter if you know shit or not. You should know I'm your girl and protect me, even from your asshole brothers and cousins."

"Damn, you lunchin'. Why it gotta be all that?" Jason asks, feeling conflicted.

"You know what, it's fine, Jason. Just drop me off at the train station."

Jason pulls the truck over and parks on a side street. He unstraps his seatbelt and Nina does the same, following his lead without question, unsure of what the next move is. "Come here," he demands with a low husky tone.

Jason reclines his seat all the way down, while Nina flips off her Mary Janes and removes her panties. "Come here," he repeats.

DANCER IN THE BULLPEN

Nina straddles the love of her life and brings him inside her, forgiving him for all wrong doing.

"I love you, Nina. I'm sorry."

"I love you too," Nina says, letting Jason drive her all the way home.

***

"When are you going to let us meet this boy, Nina?" David asks.

"I dunno, David, I think there's a lot going on in this house. Not sure it's a good time."

"What do you mean by that?"

"You and Mom just adopted Baby Bryan, we have another cousin who has some serious mental health issues staying here, and Jasmine is running around like a wild animal with that crazy little Snowflake. And you know, Mom is still working a lot," Nina reminds her stepfather. "Also, you seem a bit distracted."

"Distracted?"

"Yes, I know you and Mom aren't the happiest you've been. I see it. I hear it."

"Relationships are hard, Nina."

"I know. That's why I don't want to bring Jason here."

David is too tired to fight Nina. "Understood," he submits.

Nina doesn't understand what happened to her magic dad, the one with so much hope and ambition, the one who would blindly lead her anywhere beautiful.

Nina changes her mind after Jason insists that he come and meet the family. He realizes that the more comfortable the family is with him, the more she will be able to see him, which right now is barely at all because of Selah's strictness, which puts a strain on their shared love.

"Hi Jason, I'm Nina's mother. Sorry I'm late, but I have a super demanding job, and somebody has to take care of this family," Selah explains, making sure everyone is reminded of her sacrifice.

"I totally understand, Mrs. Abadie."

"That's not her last name, Jason," Nina whispers.

"It's fine, Jason," Selah interjects. "You hungry?"

"No Mom. Jason is not staying long," Nina interjects.

"I mean, I could eat," Jason admits.

Nina shoots Jason a harsh look that could bring down the sky above them. He responds with a shrug, and focuses on the woman who's down to spoil him. Selah comes out of the kitchen and brings him a plate of spaghetti that Nina didn't see her make, and an ice-cold soda she never keeps in the house.

"This is good, Mrs. Abadie! You're a great cook!" Jason compliments.

"Thanks Jason. We got to get Nina in the kitchen more, so she can stop reheating those canned meals. So unhealthy," Selah says, as if she's advocating for Jason's help. "Jason, you're a senior now, right?"

"Yes ma'am," Jason answers respectfully.

"You already know what college you're going to?"

"Yes ma'am. I'm going to Princeton."

"Oh, that's wonderful! See Nina! Even your boyfriend is going to an Ivy League school"

"I know, Mom, he's smart."

"You're smart too, baby," Jason whispers. Nina rolls her eyes and regrets bringing him to her own little abode of chaos.

"Hey guy! Who are you?" Jasmine screeches, running up to Jason with a reprimanding finger in his face, shaking it violently. "Nina can't have a boyfriend!"

"Jasmine, stop, come here," Nina demands. Jasmine laughs out loud, waking up Baby Bryan, who begins wailing at the top of his lungs.

"Baby, I think there's a knock on the door," Jason whispers.

"Who is it?!" Nina yells through the door.

"Nina, no need to yell, it's your cousin. Just open it," Selah says.

"This is another one of my distant cousins, Mary, who goes to college nearby," Nina whispers to Jason when she gets back to the table. "But when she was experiencing kind of a breakdown, Selah was the only family she had close by. And Mom couldn't let her go back to the dorm scared and sad."

"Nina, I think I'm going to go," Jason whispers again, feeling overwhelmed by all the people and activity. "Thank you, Mrs. Abadie, for dinner," he says to Selah.

"Of course," replies Nina's mother. "I hope to see you again!"

Nina walks Jason out to his car and says, "Thanks for dealing with my crazy fam, my mom likes you."

Jason leans down and gives Nina a peck on the cheek, and responds, "Yeah babe, aight then, see ya Monday."

***

"'Aight then?' That's what he said when he left?" Cat questions, concerned.

"Right?" Nina mirrors Cat's feeling.

"Nina, you moved too fast with that boy," Diane says.

"He loves me, Diane. He just got a lot going on. But he's not a quitter. He wouldn't have said all those things to me about us getting married one day, having babies, ruling the world together, if he didn't mean it." The music girls are quiet, oozing doubt.

"He sees me, goddammit!" Nina bangs her fist on the music room lunch table, and then stands up and begins pacing.

"Nina, girl, it's gonna be ok," Diane says. "He's just a boy, another one will come if he starts flakin', and you'll love him too. You'll be fine. It's not like you gave him the goodies or anything."

Nina stops pacing and looks down at Diane with hurricanes in her eyes.

"Nina? Aw damn, you gave him the goodies? When?" Diane asks, feeling concerned for her naive friend.

"A few weeks ago," Nina mumbles with her head down low.

Diane gets up from her chair and hugs Nina. "We don't know if he's switched up on you, girl," she says, looking Nina in the eyes. "I talk too much. He's a boy, they act funny sometimes."

"But it is always harder to get over your first," Keisha says. "I still think about mine."

Nina's relieved to hear that she's not the only one.

"Sometimes you'll say his name for no reason in the middle of the day," Keisha continues. "Cry at a memory or when hearing a mention of stuff you used to do together. It's like a cut on your soul that takes time to heal. And nothing can speed it up, except for a lot of time with people who love you, and remembering you're still you without him."

DANCER IN THE BULLPEN

"Damn y'all. Acting like the nigga broke up with her and shit. He just said 'aight,'" Cat says. "He could have had to take a shit or something and didn't want to do it in Nina's house. Y'all going Oprah-style too fast." All the girls laugh in unison and finish their dry turkey sandwiches.

Nina is concerned about her relationship with Jason. He recently bought her a medley of gifts with the assumption she would reciprocate a little. But she can't ask her mom for money for a boy; Selah doesn't play that game. Jason says he understands, but it's obvious he's getting a great deal of pressure from his brothers to get a girlfriend who is more independent financially and socially.

"I'm fifteen, Jason," says Nina. "My mom is super strict, so I hope you get it."

"Of course, baby," Jason says, but Nina doesn't believe him. He's already acting distant, influenced by his boys who are getting weary of the weird "white girl" who can't hang out or buy her man fun gifts.

***

It's the Friday before homecoming, and everyone is hyped and ready to show some school spirit. Nina is excited she has had the opportunity to help choreograph the main dance for the homecoming show on Saturday. She's nervous but knows it will be amazing. She is breaststroking in the best, clear-blue mood she's been in for a long time, and she can't stop smiling.

Now, if only she can find Jason. It's unusual for him to be MIA in the mornings. He thrives off seeing her before the day starts.

"Sup bella. Looking for your Black string bean boyfriend?" Marcello questions, evil with pleasure.

"Shut up, Marcello," Nina shoots back.

"I would check your relationship status, sweet lips. The last time I saw him, he was rubbing Tantalizing Trina's sweet sexy face."

Nina's heart drops to her feet, and she feels a knot forming in her throat. The second time Jason and Nina kissed, it was in the gym stairwell on the side by the back parking lot, because he said that's where you get the most privacy. If what Marcello says is true, then that's where Jason and this whore are.

Nina is taking long strides down the hall, blinders on, going back and forth with her invisible friend.

Nina, I think you already know where he is. Don't fight the obvious. It's better if you accept it and let go.

"No, he wouldn't do that to me after our forever promises."

Please, stop walking. Turn around.

"No! I'm sick of you always telling me to let go, that it'll be ok if I just this or that. Leave me alone!" Nina shoots back over her shoulder. She doesn't notice the music girls yelling her name, waving at her to stop and talk to them.

"Who is she talking to?" Keisha asks her crew, genuinely worried that Nina has lost her mind.

Nina doesn't see the bullies laughing and pointing, or the nuns and priests judging and praying under their breath. All she sees is Jason being a lying coward. She busts open the double stairway doors and looks up but sees no bodies.

"Jason!" Nina yells in a trembling soprano octave. "Jason!"

"Hey, hey. I'm right here. Shhh, we all good here," Jason says, doing his best to calm Nina down. He is behind her in the doorway, so they both back out into the parking lot.

Nina takes a deep breath in, happy that she didn't see a terrible scene in the stairwell. "Where have you been? I've been looking for you," she says, trying hard not to snuggle Jason's chest and cry with relief.

"Nina, babe, we have to talk."

Babe? No more Baby? Nina looks up at Jason and sees it. The face of a boy who is going to break a girl's heart. She looks past him and sees Trina walking up to the homecoming fence that Nina helped decorate, and takes another deep breath in. Nina looks back up at Jason and lets him speak.

"Baby, you know I love you, right? It's just that I think we in two different places in our lives, keepin' it real with you. I ain't realize I still have feelings for Trina until she came back into town last week. I swear I didn't do nuthin with her, you know, like more than kiss. I wouldn't do that. I just need you to know you're amazing and I know one day when you're older and things ain't so crazy for you, you'll be the perfect wife."

Nina feels robbed and violated, even though she has been a willing participant in this lie of a relationship. She touches Jason's face lovingly and tilts her head up to be kissed. He bends down slowly, scared of the consequences, yet needy for her mouth. She kisses him deep, and notices his lips aren't trembling like they used to when excited to touch hers. Her power only gets him to her door, but he won't walk in anymore, and she feels his absence already. She pulls back from his mouth, releases her hold, turns away, and becomes a dead girl walking, feeling empty and ruined for anyone else.

It is all too much, the noise in Nina's head. And none of it is voices. No Uncle John or her invisible friend. It's all just white noise—static. She goes to the bathroom on the top floor of the school. No one goes there because the ceiling is low and the air is tight and hot, and you can barely breathe. But it's perfect for when you want to hide. Few people, if any, know it exists.

She walks in and immediately hears deep sobbing: heart-wrenching cries from the belly of a pained beast. She questions if it's herself, but calls out anyway.

"Hello, who's there?"

The sobbing wanes, but no response.

Nina bends down to look at the shoes and immediately recognizes the skull-bone shoelaces.

This crazy bitch. "Mo?"

"Come on, I hear you," Nina presses. "I know you hate me but open the door, or I'm busting it down! I ain't having you ruin my dance tomorrow because you did something stupid, and it ends up being all about you ... memorial flowers, blah blah blah."

Mo unlocks the door but doesn't open it. Nina slowly pulls it with her foot because she still doesn't trust this chick.

"What do you want?" Mo complains. "I'm up here minding my business. Shit, you always around. Don't you got a valley girl party to go to?"

Nina comes into the stall and looks at Mo's face. Her perfect makeup is bleeding black down her cheeks and her eyes are swollen and red, like a devil who smoked too much green.

"Jesus, you look like shit," Nina says, as she pulls a fresh batch of toilet paper and scrunches it up in a ball to help wipe the monster queen's face.

DANCER IN THE BULLPEN

"What you doin'?" Mo asks without fighting.

"I'm fixing your face. You can't go to your car like that. Or I'm going to have to tell people I kicked your ass, like I kicked that monster's ass you sent for me."

Mo laughs. Nina is taken aback because she has never seen her straight white teeth before. "Whatever bitch, I'll kill you in here. Don't think cause you wipin' some snot off my face we friends."

"Damn Mo, why you always so mad? What got you all fucked up? Who died?" Nina asks, truly concerned.

Mo pauses for a few seconds. "My mama died. We not really close or nuthin, but you know, she still my mama. She was into some really bad shit and it caught up with her."

"Oh damn, Mo—"

Mo interrupts Nina and keeps sharing. "These teeth I see you staring at, my grandma had to buy them after my mama knocked the original ones out my mouth. So don't get it twisted, we weren't friends, but you know, like I said, she's my mama. And now she's dead."

Even though that's not her life, Nina gets it. *Don't really matter what they do, they still our moms.*

Nina steps in closer to Mo and says, "I'm really sorry, Monica. And I pray for your healing and a peaceful heart."

Mo comes closer and gently embraces her enemy. Nina brings her nose close to Monica's collar bone and can't help but smell her floral body spray. She releases from their hold, caresses Mo's face and says, "You're too pretty to be so ugly."

"This is how you seduce them niggas, huh?" Mo questions nervously. She leans in to kiss Nina, and Nina pulls back.

"You don't want me. You just want to not feel anything. You'll just hate me again later." Nina kisses Mo on the collarbone and slowly backs out of the bathroom stall. "See you tomorrow, bitch," she says in her most loving tone.

Nina gets her things out her locker, sneaks past the pep rally, careful not to be seen, and cries all the way down to her favorite neighborhood store. Her book bag is hanging uncomfortably low on her back, forcing the friction between her wool plaid skirt and underwear tag. Her knee-highs are scrunched down around her ankles, but she doesn't have the energy to stop and fix herself. All she wants is a fresh bag of salt-and-vinegar potato chips and an ice-cold grape soda to drown the pain of Jason's abandonment.

"How was school today, little one?" asks Mr. Lee, the store owner.

"Huh?" Nina replies.

"How was school today, Nina?" Mr. Lee repeats, speaking with a firm but kind tone.

"Oh, yeah. It was ok," Nina lies, walking straight toward the refrigerated beverage section. "I really shouldn't be eating this shit," she mumbles to herself, as she pulls her crumpled dollars out of her glittery rainbow change purse. She's been noticing the recent tightness of her clothes, but often blames it on her period, when deep down she worries about getting fat. No guy will ever want her fat.

"It will get better," Mr. Lee predicts as he rings up Nina's junk food. She forces a smile, not feeling so sure.

The bell on top of the store door rings violently. Before Nina can turn to look, Marcello is in her face. "Well hello, pretty thing! Making a quick stop for a snack before you go beg for your boyfriend back?" he asks with a devilish smirk.

Nina holds her breath, attempting to avoid Marcello's hateful stench, and says nothing. She withholds eye contact, which agitates him. She turns to walk out the door, but his tall lean frame is the Great Wall of China. There's no getting around him. Her fever returns with a vengeance, creating an inferno inside her body. She's petrified but does her best to channel Grandma Daisy. She looks directly into his eyes, and sternly asks, "What do you want from me?"

"I want you to know that you ain't shit," Marcello whispers grimly.

"I think you need to leave," Mr. Lee warns.

Marcello ignores his shaky demand and lunges toward Nina, hitting his left thigh on the edge of a metal potato chip stand. He clutches both of her arms, taking her back to four-years-old in the Brooklyn apartment, when Selah's monster boyfriend locked her in a similar way. "You see, this is what happens when you dump a man and go play with a little boy."

Nina fights her fear, weathering the pain in her calves and the nausea brewing in her belly. "Ok Marcello, you win. I'm sorry. But I really gotta go home," she pleads, more for his safety than her own.

"No, you're coming with me!" Marcello demands, pulling her arm toward the door. Nina suddenly has the strength to stop this kidnapping and looks down at his legs with a calm and peaceful expression, like she's in a trance.

"Oh, it's my red ... so beautiful," she says serenely, watching a circle of blood saturate Marcello's pant leg. The blood is a river, moving fast down his denim, seeping onto the dirty white vinyl floor.

Marcello releases Nina and steps back. "What the fuck!" he yells, as she also steps back to prevent the puddle of blood from tainting her Mary Janes.

"Guess you cut your leg on that metal," Nina says with a dark tranquility.

Marcello doesn't feel any pain when he bumped into the stand. He does his best to suppress his fear and grabs Nina's arm again, stepping in the blood, worried if he lets her go something worse will happen.

Mr. Lee gasps, but doesn't want any trouble. He instead drops his head, submitting to his need to not interfere.

"How about you just let the young lady go?"

Nina whips her head toward the soft voice coming from the back of the store. She thinks he appears out of thin air, but he has been in aisle two by the granola bars, quietly witnessing everything, debating his next move. He's half Marcello's height, and has a thick trunk and broad shoulders like a Washington Redskins football player, but he's too young for that. In fact, he looks young enough to be in her grade, but she's certain he doesn't attend school anymore. She thinks he would be fine enough to model if he was taller. His chestnut-brown skin matches his eyes, and he's wearing all black, ready for a robbery—if he only had a ski mask.

Nina can hear her mother's warning like she's right there with her: *It's not good to stereotype, baby, especially your own people.*

The stranger easily slips himself between Marcello and the front door, and Nina recognizes the scent of panic.

"Nigga, get out the way," Marcello snaps back.

Nina feels the sting of his slur pulsate on the side of her face and wonders if any of this is really happening. But she looks down and the blood is still there. The stranger steps back, propping himself up against the glass door, ignoring the crimson that's now painting his feet. He uses the door as a backdrop to his nonverbal threat, lifting the corner of his layered cotton shirts, revealing, tucked in his waistband, the promise of a pain greater than what Marcello is ready to give.

Marcello retreats and the stranger drops his hand in unison, preventing Mr. Lee's 911 call. Nina stands still, but her adrenaline is running like a freight train. She wonders if there are bullets in the gun, and if he's ever had to replace them.

Why would he risk getting in trouble for me? She is not sure who she is more afraid of—Marcello or the hero stranger.

The stranger looks at Nina and motions for her to come outside, opening the front door wide, with piercing eyes locked on Marcello. She obliges and walks out to the crowded parking lot, still feeling afraid and alone. The stranger swiftly walks past her and stops at a white Mercedes. "You coming?"

Nina walks to the passenger side and gently rests her hand on the car door handle, looking at her rescuer suspiciously.

"Listen, you don't have to get in," says the stranger. "I can let you walk to wherever you're going, but I'm sure his car is faster than your legs, and he'll catch up with you all angry and shit like he is now."

Nina begins to open the car door.

"Wait," the stranger says. "Take off your shoes. I'm going to take mine off too. We gonna put them in a plastic bag I have in the trunk."

Nina gives him a confused look. *A plastic bag for the dead body later?*

"Just until I get you where you going. You got blood on them. I don't need that nigga's blood in my car," the stranger says with no hesitation.

Nina follows his lead and walks back to the trunk with him to put her shoes in a bag with his. She and the stranger get into the car. It jerks back in reverse, wheels screaming and engine roaring with laughter at Marcello standing under Mr. Lee's store sign that reads "Security Cameras in Use."

Nina has never been in an all-white car before: exterior, interior, even the floor mats are white. The contrast with the stranger's all-black threads makes him look boundless, like he's floating through the North Pole. Ironically, she is not afraid of this stranger now that they are alone, escaping a bad situation together. There's a unique protective honesty that she gravitates to.

Nina breaks the silence. "Is this your car?"

"Yes," the stranger responds simply, looking at Nina with amused curiosity.

"Why is the engine so loud?" Nina probes.

"I made some adjustments under the hood to give her more power, so that's why she sounds like that."

"Why is it—I mean, why is *she* all white?"

"Because it's the color of clean, pure, perfect."

"I think that about that color black," Nina shares, looking out the window, and then cracking it to get some fresh air to calm her nerves that are still jumping. "It absorbs every color. It's perfect and stronger than any other color. You gotta believe that a little bit. You wearing all black."

"Nah, I'm just trying to be mysterious," the stranger teases, smirking, his eyes disciplined on the road, driving right under the speed limit. "I would think red was your favorite color, though. I heard you mumbling about how beautiful the color red is while that asshole was tryin' to kidnap you, when he was bleedin' all crazy. That was wild, right? You see him get cut? Man, shit don't make no sense. Weird."

DANCER IN THE BULLPEN

"Yeah, it was weird," Nina says, knowing now that she makes these things happen, this dark magic she will never talk about. She suddenly remembers she's wearing white panties and her period is coming soon. *Damn, if I bleed in this car, I'll have to jump out before he pulls a gun on me,* she thinks, anxiety flirting with her mind.

"Hey, you ok? You're safe now, even though I know you don't know me," the stranger assures.

"I'm not afraid of you. Why would you hurt me after saving me?" Nina questions rhetorically, pretending to be secure and confident.

"My name is Bee, by the way. What's yours?"

"I'm Nina. Is it that the letter *B*, or the insect?"

"Like the insect." Bee quickly changes the subject. "Is the station ok? Or do you want me to drive you home?"

Nina thinks about not knowing Bee at all, and imagines her mother shaking her finger at her. *Don't get into cars with boys,* Selah would say.

But what if the danger is outside on the street? Nina rationalizes. "The train station is cool, thank you."

Bee and Nina ride in silence until they reach the commuter parking lot. He stops the car and gives her a stern parental look. "Listen, I be seeing you around. You gotta be careful out here and watch who you know. That crazy back there got issues, so he gonna continue being a problem. Watch your back. You got any pepper spray or something?"

"Yes," Nina responds flatly, trying not to stare at Bee's right hand, which is scarred badly and missing a thumb.

"Ok good," Bee says, a bit surprised she's already carrying pepper spray but hasn't used it.

"Maybe I need something stronger, like what you have in your pants," Nina says.

"In my pants? Maybe we should slow down, we barely know each other," Bee teases again.

Nina doesn't push. She is mentally drained and happy to be at the station, so she can stop pretending to be ok and sleep until tomorrow's homecoming. "Thank you for helping me out," she says in a quiet, melancholy tone.

"Yeah, no problem," Bee says, wondering if this girl is a witch.

Nina gets out of the car, happy not to see blood in the seat, and puts her shoes back on. She walks into the station without looking back but can feel the heat of Bee's stare on her.

Nina, wake up. It's almost time to go.

Nina's head is being held by the train's glass window, and she's deep in a dream state. Her invisible friend is in the seat angled in front of her.

Nina, wake up, your stop is coming up next, she repeats, her warning an octave higher. She scoots to the edge of her seat and gently touches Nina's leg.

"Uncle John, sorry, I still can't find it," Nina yells as she awakens abruptly, wiping the drool from her mouth.

It's not Uncle John, it's me! the invisible friend reveals playfully.

Nina opens her eyes and attempts to focus and make out her facial features. "I see. Well, kinda." She stands up to walk to the train exit doors.

Well, I just came to check on you, make sure you're ok. I know things are hard right now and you were really mad at me the last time we spoke in the hall at school. *I'm not really supposed to be here today, but I missed you.*

"Me too," Nina says, to her invisible friend's surprise.

I think you need to get more sleep, and drink more water. Nina's invisible friend feels more open to share her concern today.

Nina is taking her usual long strides through the city side-streets to avoid nosy people. "So, wait. You think the reason why my body goes crazy sometimes is because I'm not taking care of myself? Why wouldn't you say anything sooner? And I don't know ... I may eat too much junk. No, that can't be it. I don't know, you could be right and I could be wrong." She puts her key in the front door of her house, and looks down at the grayed-out human figure. "What do *you* know?" she teases to her friend. They laugh together.

"You want to come inside with me for a while?" Nina asks, hoping to find more comfort with her mysterious figure.

I probably shouldn't.

"When you gonna let me see all of you?" Nina asks. "I'm happy you're not just a cloudy thing anymore. But I don't know, it is kinda worse 'cause I can almost see your cheeks and nose and body. It's torture."

I'm sorry. I wish I could fix it. The good thing is I can see you clearly.

Nina finally unlocks the double lock and turns back around to make sure her friend doesn't want to come in, even for a little, but she has already disappeared.

✸✸✸

It's Monday and everyone is still glowing from the homecoming win. Many students stop the dance team members in the hallway, congratulating them on an incredible performance.

"The choreography was dope," one freshman girl says to Mo in the hallway.

"That was all her," Mo proclaims, motioning to Nina at her locker. "She did her thing with that one." The two exchange soft smiles from across the hall.

"What the fuck was that?" Cat asks loudly in the back of Nina's ear.

"Shit Cat! You scared me."

"Oh my god, you are soooo scary," Cat teases in her best white girl voice, giving no personal space, using her book bag to bump Nina into her locker. "When you and Mo start smiling at each other and shit? You two were kinda friendly yesterday too."

"Yeah, I noticed that" Diane chimes in, with Keisha by her side. Nina is surrounded.

"Spill it, Nina," Keisha demands.

"We ran into each other on Friday, and we was just chattin'," says Nina. "We got some things in common, I guess. It takes a lot of energy to be mean. Maybe she's just tired of being angry. No need to overthink it. Y'all should be happy, shit. Less drama."

"Hmmm, interesting, but sounds good," Keisha responds, knowing there is more, but letting her intuition rest a bit.

Jason walks through the hall with his crew and their strides are in slow motion, like they're on a New York fashion runway. He smiles back at the pretty girls and gives dap to the underclassmen who admire him. Nina feels tears awakening, but she stretches her eyebrow muscles, widening her stare to keep the flood at bay.

DANCER IN THE BULLPEN

Diane discretely reaches for Nina's hand and embraces it. Keisha mirrors the gesture with the other hand, and Cat follows Jason, aggressively yelling, "You not all that! Bitch-ass coward!"

Keisha is right. It's easy to physically recover from your first love, but the mental slavery is torture. Though Nina may not be consciously thinking of Jason, her heart won't let go. She catches herself saying his name at dinner, dancing to a random song, even when praying about people more important.

"Jason."

"Jason."

How could you do this to me?

How can any of you do this to me?

Nina needs a distraction from disappointment. She walks to the convenience store hoping to see a familiar face. "Hi, Mr. Lee," Nina says, trying to keep her tone upbeat.

"No trouble today?" Mr. Lee asks.

"No trouble today," Nina assures with a smile. She buys her typical chips and grape soda, and walks out peacefully, with no red-blood storms.

"Look who it is with her healthy diet," Bee teases.

Nina is thrilled to see him, but tries to stay cool, thinking as soon as she begins to care, she'll be abandoned. But it's difficult, because she thinks Bee is wonderful. He's fine and protective, with a bad boy edge that she loves. But most importantly, he seems honest about what he thinks of her, unlike that joker Jason.

"'Sup Bee? Are you being good?" Nina asks as she puts her chips and soda in her book bag, so she can easily roll up her knee-high socks to a comfortable height. Bee is leaning up against his ghost-colored Mercedes, looking like he's waiting on the photographer for his modeling shoot. She can't help but enjoy how fine he is, but she's more attracted to his confidence and warm attentiveness.

"I was gonna ask you the same thing, Red," he says. "I don't see Crazy Pants following you today."

"No, I have quick feet today. Well, actually, I don't think I've seen him in a few days, now that you mention it. Maybe he moved on to overstay his welcome at another high school."

"You're funny, Nina," Bee chuckles, trying to think of more to say to keep her close. "You need a ride?"

"Yes. But can you take me home this time?" Nina asks, already walking to the passenger side. "I haven't stepped in any blood today, would you still like me to take off my shoes?"

"Nah, keep your shoes on, unless you want them off," Bee says, looking happy and relaxed. They take two laps around the Beltway just to learn more about each other.

"My mother left me at six years old with my alcoholic father," Bee discloses. "And then when he died, I moved in with my grandmother who ended up needing the care from me versus the other way around."

"I'm sorry," Nina says, placing her hand on his damaged one. She now sees who Bee is. He doesn't want anyone good to feel bad like he has.

Bee is surprised by her sweet touch. "It's life, you know? I'm actually pretty smart. I got a big scholarship to study engineering, but it wasn't enough when Grandma's medical bills started piling over."

"Is that why you dropped out?" Nina asks, feeling sad for his sacrifice.

"Yes."

DANCER IN THE BULLPEN

"Is that why you sell drugs now?"

"It's just temporary. I'm gonna stop soon and Grandma will be all good. Then I'll finish my degree."

"I believe you, Bee," Nina says and means it, wishing money was free. "But I hope you go back. It seems like you could do some great things. Can I roll the down the window a bit?"

"Yes, roll it all the way down," Bee offers. And Nina does just that, pretending she's flying again in the North Pole.

✼✼✼

Nina arrives at school, and her girls are standing at her locker anxiously waiting for her.

"Hey, what's up? What's wrong?" Nina already smells the color of blood.

"Did you hear about Marcello?" Cat spits out.

"Clearly not, Cat, I just got here," Nina says with unexplainable agitation.

"I guess he hasn't been home for a few days, maybe a week or something, which is enough to make his family worry."

"That's weird," Nina says, feeling her stomach flip and twist. She contemplates telling the girls about her last interaction with Marcello, but then thinks that maybe it isn't a good idea, considering Bee threatened him. "Well, I do remember when I first started talking to Marcello, he mentioned that one day he wanted to go home to Puerto Rico and never come back. But he's a bit of a drama queen. I'm sure he's cool."

"I don't know y'all, he is not a well-liked person," Diane says.

"Let's not talk about it, ok? He's probably rubbing some whore's booty on a Puerto Rican beach," Nina suggests.

253

But it feels like there's a huge tumor growing in the pit of her stomach. *What if Bee did something to him? Did something for me?* She must do a little investigating to give herself some peace of mind.

The end of the school day doesn't come fast enough. Nina sprints down to the convenience store with her invisible friend in her ear, but this time, Nina is running the conversation. "Listen, I get it. Shit is fucked up, but I have to ask."

I think there are some things we don't have to know. You could just let me be your peace of mind.

"I can barely even see you," Nina says, as she keeps jogging down the hill.

Yes, you can. Look at me.

Nina looks next to her, the source of the voice, but still she only can see her eyes and the softness of her facial frame. "I can't deal with you right now," she says to her friend. "Maybe later."

Nina arrives in the parking lot of the convenience store but doesn't see Bee's car. "Shit, where is he?" But she's here, so she might as well get her chips and soda. Before she can step into the store, a white Mercedes screeches up beside her.

Bee rolls down the window. "Hey beautiful, looking for me?"

"Did you do something to Marcello?!" Nina screams, releasing the bottled-up panic from the day.

Bee is expressionless and tells her to get in the car. She hesitates, but for some reason her fear is muted and she jumps in. He is not wearing all black today, but all white—a complete transformation.

"Why you dressed in all white?" Nina asks, distracted by her own curiosity. "And where are we going?"

"I went to a funeral for a friend from a different culture, where they believe everyone should wear white to represent a joyous life on earth and peaceful transition to the afterlife. See, I told you, white is right."

Nina rolls her eyes, grinning, but then shifts back into serious mode. "I'm sorry about your friend."

"Thanks Red. He was in the wrong place at the wrong time, but now he's at rest. Oh, and to answer your question, we're going to my house," Bee says nonchalantly. Nina feels like she should be scared, but she's more excited.

Bee pulls up to a historic D.C. row house, fifteen minutes from the store. It looks well cared for. Nina walks in and immediately sees Bee's grandma in the living room, napping in a recliner chair.

"Come downstairs with me," Bee instructs. Nina follows him and she ends up in a beautifully furnished basement apartment with top-of-the-line electronics, exotic art, and plants by the unusually large window by the back entrance. "You like it?"

"Bee! Did you do something to Marcello?" Tell me right now, please."

Bee wants Nina so much. He grabs her waist and pulls her up against him. "What do you care? He won't be bothering you anymore."

"Shit, you hurt him?" Nina asks, as her body goes limp in Bee's grip. The thought of him hurting Marcello for her is terrifying, but the thought of him doing the extreme to protect her is intoxicating.

"Red, don't worry, everything is ok," Bee assures.

Nina likes her nickname but is still cautious of getting too comfortable. "Bee, how old are you, really?"

"That doesn't matter anymore. I need you, Nina."

"Tell me, please," Nina pleads, as Bee hugs her tightly, knowing they both just need to be held.

"Seventeen," Bee says, but Nina knows he's lying. She disregards anything evil and lets him drug her with passion.

***

Nina uses Bee as medication. He's her new baked bread, her new dance class. Every day he picks her up from school and they joyride, talk, make love, smoke. They get high: a new hobby he introduces her to at a party he shows her off at. She still carries the heavy tumor of not knowing if Marcello is dead or alive in the pit of her stomach, but it's still lighter than the rock weighing down her heart.

Bee's car is at the mechanic so he shows up in a different car with different friends in the driver and passenger seats, who Nina has never met. Bee is in the back seat waiting for her to come and curl up on his lap and take shotguns of herb from him.

"Hey, sweet Red, your day was good?" he asks, as Nina crawls in the back seat and plants a big kiss on her new man. She mumbles hi to the two friends upfront and they do the same.

"Where we going?" Nina asks Bee.

"Wherever you want to go, sexy," he says, accommodating her needs.

"Let's ride."

Bee and Nina are in the back smoking and making out with the window cracked as she likes it. In the distance she hears a siren, and it's slowly getting louder. She gets a little nervous and so does the driver and passenger. It gets louder and louder and Bee asks the driver, "Yo, is that for you?"

The driver looks at Bee through the rearview with a worried look. "Fuck man, is this hot?" He presses his foot on the gas, mumbling something about not going to jail.

"Oh my god, please stop!" Nina screams, as Bee sits up straight and says "Bro, we can't outrun these niggas!"

The passenger is silent but looks like he wants to jump out the window.

"Stop, please! I can't go to jail!" Nina screams.

The driver is flooring it and there are two police cars in a full chase. Nina closes her eyes and braces herself to die among strange criminals. All of a sudden, Bee grabs the back of the driver's neck, pulls out his gun, and presses it to a vein. And in a chilling calm tone he tells the driver to stop the car now or he'll shoot him, in a way he'll survive but suffer so terribly he will wish he were dead. The driver immediately starts slowing down and Bee looks at Nina, gripping the sides of her arms.

"Nina, you gonna need to listen to me. You don't know shit. You don't know these guys or that this car is stolen. In fact, you barely know me. I just offered you a ride, like 'pick you up 'cause you're cute' type shit. But you're a good Catholic schoolgirl. I'm sorry but you're a minor so they gonna call a parent or something."

"Ok, so you're not a minor?" Nina asks in a childlike voice, turning back into the little girl in the ballerina outfit climbing into the elevator, with someone else's secret about where she's been—waiting for instruction.

"Don't worry about all that now," Bee says. "Ok, they about to pull up, just be easy. You didn't really smoke. It was in the car, so it will be ok," he directs, digging deep into his pocket for peppermint that's broken in its frail wrapper.

"But are you gonna be ok?" Nina asks, while Bee frantically releases the candy into her mouth.

"Don't worry about me. Just say what I said, ok? Deny everything, you are clean, you will be ok."

The stolen car is cornered by three police cars now and Nina is blinded by the swirl of flashing lights. Bee kisses her like it's the last time. She starts crying and hits him in the chest. "Why? Fuck? Why you do this to me?"

"I'm sorry, Red. I'm so sorry," he says, holding her face in his hands like he's absorbing all her love and pain in his skin.

"PUT YOUR HANDS UP WHERE I CAN SEE THEM! GET OUT OF THE CAR! SLOWLY!"

Nina has never seen police officers outside of television and movie screens, parades, or helping direct traffic. And she definitely has never seen a Black police officer close-up so angry, ready to bring criminals like them down.

There are six police. All with guns drawn, but four of them are primarily focused on the driver and front-seat passenger. Those two barely make it out of the vehicle before getting forced onto the concrete face down. Nina and Bee are forced out from the back, but on separate sides. Bee is instructed to join his friends on the ground, yet Nina is kept standing. The weight of the weed is ironically comforting, as she is confident it'll be the main reason for her demise. The taste of peppermint has been replaced with a fistful of invisible cotton.

"Hey, we got a kid over here!" one of the officers yells out to his colleagues. A female officer comes over and spits a series of questions at Nina, mainly to do with what she possibly has in her possession, and on her body, before patting her down.

Where's Bee? Nina thinks, looking around, searching for a glimpse of him. *He's living up to his name—the bee that stings you and then dies, leaving you alone with a swollen face, or in this case, heart.*

"Looking for something?" the officer asks.

"No, ma'am," Nina responds, thinking about what Bee said. None of it seems real, as she watches people in cars slow down, look, and point. *"Look at that dumb Catholic schoolgirl with those thugs. I guess her mama ain't teach her right," they're probably saying.*

Nina is lost between worlds, not equipped to move in either direction, until the only Black cop comes over, wearing a kind face. She immediately feels safe. She just needs to explain.

Before the officer begins speaking, she goes in. "Hello sir, I'm so sorry but I don't know what's going on. I go to the, um, high school back there and I usually walk to the train station. But I have a bad knee from dancing, 'cause I used to dance a lot, and this guy was nice enough to offer me a ride. I usually don't, you know, get rides from strangers, but I was really tired, so I took a chance."

The officer smiles as a courtesy and asks, "What's your name, and do you have any identification?"

"My name is Nina Abadie and I don't have a license yet."

"That's ok, Nina. Do you have some form of identification with your face on it, like a school ID?"

"Yes," Nina answers, and pulls out her school ID from her purse. She hands it to the officer and jumps back into reality, the place where fear lives, and where her bladder is about to burst. "Officer, I can't go to jail. Am I going to jail? Because I really can't go to jail."

The officer takes a deep breath in, like he's sad to share the truth of the world. "Nina Abadie, I'm sorry to say, but you are going to jail today." Her knees almost buckle, but her stare is unwavering.

Oh no, deep breaths, Nina. Try to keep calm, her invisible friend warns. *You know how you get when you get scared, and you don't want to scare the cop.* Nina wants to tell her friend to stop talking, but she knows the law surrounding her won't understand. She instead keeps silent and watches the officer wipe his bloody nose as she's escorted into a cop car.

Nina does everything she can to avoid having her mother pick her up from jail, but nothing works. Selah is quiet when she arrives at the precinct; she doesn't say anything on the car ride home either. It isn't until they arrive home, that Selah asks her to sit down at the dining room table and explain why she was caught riding in a stolen car with three young adults eighteen and older.

"Mom, I was just trying to get a ride to the station, and didn't realize these guys were bad news."

"Bullshit Nina. I wasn't born yesterday. You like the bad boy, don't you? You could've done some serious time. In fact, you are lucky to even be out right now. Those badass boys will get you nowhere but to prison—not the cute little cell you were in today—or dead. Do you want to die, Nina? Are you not happy?"

"No, and yes, Mom." Nina is afraid that if she tells her mother being dead doesn't sound so bad right now, Selah will just make it about Nina has failed her. And Nina can't handle any more responsibility.

"It's like you stopped dancing and haven't replaced it with anything else, except shaking some pom-poms and scribbling in your journals. Clearly you don't like learning, because you half-ass that. I'm really curious to see what your grades are gonna look like this semester. Are we going to have another problem with that, Nina?"

"No," Nina lies again.

"Nina, soon you will be in eleventh grade, the most important year of high school. Do you even know what you want to do? Do you know who you are?"

"I mean, do you?" Nina snaps back.

"What did you say?" Selah asks, daring Nina to test her bravery.

"I feel like the only thing you are certain about is work—saving other people's children from pain and despair. But who's saving you? Who's saving me?" Nina sobs, and then runs into her room and slams the door.

Selah doesn't chase after her daughter and Nina doesn't mind. Instead, Selah washes the dishes she sees piled high in the kitchen. It's been a long time since they have been the only two home together. Even though it will be short-lived, Nina takes comfort in knowing that just for a bit, even with all the tension, it's only them.

***

Nina is back on Mike's couch, cross-legged, taking deep breaths, waiting for him to come lecture her about her final tenth-grade report card. Not only are the two *D*s a problem, but it's the attempt to change them into *B*s that is concerning.

Selah has already taken care of her verbal beatdown, so now it's Daddy's turn. It could be worse. He could have been informed about the jail visit, but Selah has left that incident out of conversation.

"Nina, what were you thinking?" asks Mike. "If you needed help, why didn't you just tell us?"

"Daddy, I've had help, tutors, counselors, I even tried to bribe my teachers."

"Nina!"

"I'm just kidding. Sorry Daddy. I was scared to tell you and Mom. I knew you would be so disappointed in me, and I do want to try and get the grades higher."

"I know you do. Your mother and I found a special summer school you are going to go to for a couple of weeks when you return home from us this summer. Look at your brothers. They are already looking up to you, even at three and one years old."

Nina looks at her sweet brothers in the playpen and agrees. "Ok, whatever you want." She has no desire to take on summer school, but she needs to be forgiven and make her family proud.

The rest of the summer is relentless. Nina is focused on finding purpose, doing more than just getting by. She's juggling work as a summer camp counselor, relearning math in a private summer-school program, and attending a collegiate journalism program at one of the top universities in the city. Selah is smart to keep her busy and out of trouble, hopefully igniting some passion for a career.

The music girls are all working or visiting family as usual this summer, and from the word on the street, Bee is still in jail. Because Nina is so busy, she thinks she will have no time to feel lonely. But loneliness finds her, just as easy in a crowded room or empty closet filled only with unsold chocolate bars.

She still has eight boxes of chocolate in her closet, which were meant to be sold for the school fundraiser last fall.

I wonder if I can still sell them? Nina asks herself. And each day she asks herself, she eats a bar.

What's one bar?

Two bars?

Three bars?

No one is home to stop her except the bathroom mirror, where Nina battles her reflection.

"Nina, open me up," her reflection instructs. "Get the bottle from the top shelf. Take them all and feel your pain go."

Chocolate borders Nina's mouth and laces her fingertips. Thirty foreign pills in the palm of her hand.

"Should I pop them one by one or do half, and then the other half?" Nina asks herself in the mirror.

Nina. Stop. Look at me, little one.

"Uncle John?" Nina looks in the mirror and sees him clearly.

"Where have you been?" she asks.

I'm here, Nina. I've never left you. Don't give up. Find yourself. Live.

The least Nina can do for Uncle John is live. She takes a shower, changes her clothes, bags up all the unsold chocolate, and throws it away, along with the unidentified expired medication. She cleans house and decides to fight for the self she doesn't know yet.

CHAPTER EIGHT

"Mom, Auntie Josie never has any parking in front of her house. Want me to drop you off first and then park, so you don't have to walk so far?" Nina likes to take advantage of any opportunity to drive now that she has a permit.

"Sounds good," Selah says. "We won't be long. I know you have math practice to finish." Nina has had a busy couple of months, but Selah knows her mental health is fragile, so she pushes her daughter to engage with the community to lift her spirits.

Aunt Josie is Selah's friend, and she makes some of the best rice and peas on the East Coast. She is a part of a big West Indian family that is close to Selah's, and they are always inviting her and her family to annual cookouts like this one.

"Murder She Wrote" is blaring on the stereo, and the red pepper and curry spices are streaking in the air, daring to be devoured. Nina is wearing her favorite floor-length sundress with a high split that stops mid-thigh. Her fresh Halle cut keeps her neck cool as she takes long strides into the backyard. She finds Selah by the DJ, already settled with a plate of Caribbean goodness. She thinks about getting a plate but is dying for a cola champagne—if she can find one.

"Hey girl. Can I help you with something?"

Nina is bending over one of the many coolers. She looks up, trying to get a clear visual of what sounds like a flirtatious kid.

"Hey wassup, can you step out the sun so I can take a good look at you?" Nina requests in her usual sweet tone. "What's your name?" she asks the bold boy.

"Alex. And yours, gorgeous?"

Nina smiles, thinking he can't be any more than thirteen. "Nina."

"What a lovely name for a lovely woman," interrupts a Michael Jordan replica, who just rolls up out of nowhere, bombarding the conversation and limelight.

Nina can't believe she is looking at the most beautiful man she has ever seen. His skin is silken onyx, like creamy black butter just poured on his bones. He is a giant tree one must climb and perch on until the branches give way.

"Hi," Nina says, having difficulty expressing her thoughts. "What's your name?" *And will you marry me?* She thinks he is different from all the others she wanted to marry.

"My name is Malcolm. I'm Auntie Josie's nephew. How do you know these fine troublemakers?"

"I'm Selah's daughter, who is friends with your aunt," Nina explains, unsure how she's ever going to pull away from him.

"Wait, you're Selah's daughter? Oh wow! I remember you when you were so much smaller," Malcolm says, looking Nina up and down, amazed by her brickhouse frame. "You have grown into a fine young lady, wow!" He is beyond smitten: completely captivated.

Alex is angry. He looks as if someone has stolen his money, and then had the audacity to charge him for the time to do so.

Malcolm is unfazed by his little brother's frustration. "Are you sure you want a cola champagne and nothing stronger?"

"Um, I can't drink yet." Nina says, purposely pretending to be a good girl, and hinting at her age to keep it real from the beginning.

"Shit, how old are you, Nina?" Malcolm asks before taking a swig of his beer.

"It'll be my sweet sixteen next month," Nina announces with pride.

Malcolm chokes on his beer.

"Are you ok?" Nina asks.

"Yes, sorry. Wow, I mean, you don't look fifteen."

"I know. And you're how old?"

"Nineteen," Malcolm states with disappointment.

"Oh," Nina says, dropping her head down. "So, I guess you can't take me out for dinner?" she questions, relentlessly flirting anyway.

"No, I cannot," Malcom says simply, a bit annoyed at Nina for looking so beautiful and grown.

"That's too bad, I'm a fun date," Nina brags.

"It really is too bad," Malcolm says, feeling the third beer he's sipping on, and discreetly interlocking his fingers with hers to feel the electricity.

Nina tries to ignore Malcolm during the cookout, but his fineness is everywhere. And his eyes are always locked on her. The attraction is magnetic. There's no escaping, and she knows he feels it too.

After partying for hours, Nina and Selah agree it's time to go home, and Nina goes to get the car. Malcolm appears at the car with a plan in mind.

"So I know it's wrong, but I don't care," Malcolm admits, looking around to see if anyone is listening. "Let me see you this summer."

"Are you sure? I don't want you to go to jail for me," Nina jokes, though she's very serious. "I'm going to be at a pre-college journalism program at a university for a couple of weeks. It's local, so maybe you can come see me there?"

"Yes, I will," Malcolm promises.

"I love it," Nina says. *But I will make sure not to love you so fast.*

***

Malcolm makes good on his word. He stays with his uncles in Maryland during the summer instead of his home in Brooklyn. Selah lets Nina hang out with him because he's not only the son of a well-respected friend, but he's a well-educated and charming young man. Every day after her pre-college journalism classes, Nina sneaks off campus for dinner and late-night excursions at local Caribbean parties—grooving and winding until the roosters sing their songs. At every restaurant, and in every house party, Malcolm shows her off by walking one step behind her, so she is the feature. He often pauses to remind her that all eyes are on the most beautiful woman in the place. She knows many folks would argue that, at barely sixteen, she is definitely not a woman.

"You are perfection," Malcom whispers in Nina's ear. She can't help but straighten her posture and put a bit more switch in her hips after each affirmation.

Finally, I am Queen. The goddamn Jet Beauty of every week! she announces to herself with pride. And as a reward for her coronation, she sneaks Malcolm back into the college dorm she is staying in for the summer program, where they make love until classes start. It's not right, so it must be perfect. Everything before him has failed.

While Nina learns how to hide bias in news reporting, Diane is back from the South, and happily planning Nina's sweet sixteen birthday party—funded and approved by Nina's mother of course. Selah is so busy and she regrets not having time to plan the party herself, so she welcomes Diane's offer to serve as an understudy. The party is the talk of the high-school rumor mill, and school is not even in session. When Nina returns from the journalism program, Diane calls her to provide just enough information, so she knows how to dress and where to be.

"Diane, please tell me everything is going to be cool," Nina asks, a bit worried about the invite list.

"Girl, stop being a worrywart. I wouldn't make this a Bully Nina party, duh," Diane teases. "Plus, more people like you now, since Mo loves you and shit."

Nina laughs at the accuracy of her statement. "Ok girl, I trust you." She means it.

Nina is perfect in a purple, sleeveless collared blouse that just covers the booty of her thigh-gripping white biker shorts. She is balancing well on a pair of purple platform sandals, which compliment her sky-high faux bun. Malcolm compliments her looks with jeans, the newest kicks, and a button-down purple silk shirt. The armory is glitzed out in sparkling lights, a plethora of balloons and flowers.

The DJ is stirring up the crowd and the folks are still arriving, ready to dance.

"Wait Diane," says Nina. "I saw Jason and his brothers walk in the door. Did you invite them?"

"Yes duh, Nina! If you don't invite them, you might as well not invite anybody," Diane says.

Nina is sitting in her birthday chair, center stage, when missing Marcello walks in with an unidentified friend. She gasps and looks over at Cat, who's already running over to her like she's ready to start a war. Malcolm is on the sidelines watching the dramatics, about to stand up and walk over to Nina to make sure everything is good. But she reassures him nonverbally, because nobody wants her king killed at her sweet sixteen.

"Girl, what you want me to do?" Cat asks, right by Nina's side, ready to defend her girl.

"You know I ain't invite him, 'cause none of us thought he was alive," Diane says. "You know, since rumor had it that you and your neighborhood thugs chopped his head off," she says to Cat, only half joking.

"Diane, shhh. I don't want y'all to do anything. Let him come to me and we'll see what happens," Nina says, like she's a mafia boss.

You think that's a good idea? Nina's invisible friend says, hovering over her back left shoulder. *He could think you tried to kill him and be here on this special occasion to get his revenge.*

Nina looks back at her friend, whose face and body are in clear view now. "Well, hello. I can see you!" she says, staring at a beautiful girl with vanilla-crème skin and dark-brown braids resting on each shoulder. Her floor-length lavender dress sparkles under the party lights.

You can?

"Yes," Nina whispers. "I wonder why that is? And why do you look so young? But wait, actually you don't look *too* young. How old are you?"

The music girls have accepted the fact that Nina talks a lot, sometimes to people they can't see, and in the end they don't mind. They accept she may just need to do what she needs to do to be secure. The alternative reason is too difficult to accept; she actually does see people that are not there.

You're busy now, we'll talk later. Happy birthday, Nina Abadie, the invisible friend says with a warm smile, before vanishing once again.

Marcello is slowly making his way toward Nina, as Keisha makes the observation: "There's a lot of niggas in here."

"Well, Nina is becoming Black after all," Cat teases.

"Nah for real, y'all," Diane says. "Most of these guys all want Nina, and for the most part hate each other."

Malcolm walks up to the girls. "What kinda security they got up in here?"

"Security?" Keisha asks.

Diane realizes that is the one thing she didn't coordinate. "Shit."

"Hey girl, wassup? Happy birthday, bella," Marcello says, reminding Nina of his charm when they first met. He respectfully gives dap to Malcolm and speaks to the music girls like he once wasn't trying to kidnap Nina from the convenience store.

"Thanks. Who's this?" Nina asks, referring to Marcello's companion, making sure they are not planning to take things down up in here.

"Oh, this my brother from Puerto Rico. He came back with me and gonna chill awhile. Ya heard I had to go back home a bit right? My family needed some help with businesses."

"Naw, we heard that someone killed yo ass," Cat says with a sting of aggression.

"I guess you'll be doing another year in high school, huh?" Nina says, remembering this past year was Marcello's fifth. She's actually happy to see him. It means Bee is not responsible for something worse than gun and drug charges. "You gonna be chill while you here though, right?" she asks, motioning her head toward the Ferguson brothers.

"Listen, I just came by to extend my olive branch to you, and I don't want no beef with them. If they cool, I'm cool," Marcello assures.

"Aight, let's clean slate it," Nina says, as she pulls Malcolm onto the dance floor.

Unfortunately, not everyone is as mature as Marcello tonight. Jason says a few words to Marcello, and he returns the gift. Jason's cousin doesn't appreciate it so much, so he decides to throw a punch. A brawl ignites, which only starts the chaos. Not having security on-site is a mistake. Two girls from the neighborhood decide to crash the party. One of them pulls a gun from under her skirt, and the other spray-paints the building. An hour in, the police arrive, the party is over, and Malcolm offers to take Nina, Selah, and David out of there before more mayhem happens. Interestingly enough, everyone loves the drama, and Cat is sure this party will be the talk of the town until the next one.

Malcolm and Nina make it to her house safely, despite it looking like a bad hip-hop video outside. They snuggle on the couch and open gifts from her music girls and boys, who have been waiting for Jason to die, not realizing Malcolm is alive and is Nina's king … for real this time.

Malcolm's presence in Nina's life this summer has rejuvenated her spirit. He provides the perfect dose of attention and affection to counteract the stress of her growing pains. She works hard during the week, knowing she'll be rewarded with romantic long weekends to New York and Philly. Selah allows her to break curfew when she knows he's the reason for the delay. Nina even feels safe because of him.

Nina knows Selah wouldn't feel so safe with some of the behavior of Malcolm's male role models. Malcolm and Alex have a sister close to Alex's age they've just discovered, and she is graciously loved and appreciated by their mother and the rest of the family. Sometimes it's hard to keep all the women straight: wives, mistresses, and girlfriends. When Nina visits Malcolm at the apartment he is staying at with his two uncles, things sometimes get confusing. The uncles both have main girlfriends and alternates. When she comes back to Malcolm's room after one of the infamous Caribbean parties, she never knows which girl will be coming to the kitchen for water. She makes a cheat sheet of all the chicks and kids and keeps it in her purse.

"Malcolm, am I written on somebody's notepad?" Nina asks. "Is someone trying to keep track of my name too?"

"Queen, consider me the black sheep of the family. I grew up watching my mother cry because of my father's indiscretions. It would ruin me to kill a woman's spirit like he's done to her. I don't cheat."

***

Selah repeatedly reminds Nina that eleventh grade is the most important year of her high school education ... no pressure. Nina is proud of how she has buckled down this past summer and gotten a *B+* in her math class, and aced the intense journalism program Selah worked hard to get her in.

Nina has been successful keeping depression at bay. She has been distracting herself with new love, exploration of purpose, and being grateful. She has come so far in such a short time, so she figures why not listen to Father Jessup and do the best she can with the editor-in-chief position?

The bell that dismisses English class rings and kids scatter to their next class, but Nina stays behind and approaches Father Anderson's desk.

"Yes, Ms. Abadie, how can I help you?"

"I'm ready," Nina announces simply.

Father Anderson doesn't need to ask what she's referring to. His smile brightens up the room and he claps his hands loudly, like he has just figured out the mystery of life. "This is great news, Nina!" He shuffles some editorial papers, happy to call the first meeting to transfer the ownership of responsibilities from him to her. "We have some good contributors for the school paper, but I'm confident you can inspire and push them to greatness."

"Thank you, Father, I'm starting to believe you." Nina heads out the door, with a little pep in her step.

"Hey Nina!" Father Anderson calls out.

Nina turns around with a smile. "Yes?"

"I think your engagement and leadership will help with the other stuff too. It's harder to bully someone who not only knows their worth and hears their own voice, but also helps others find theirs."

Nina holds back her tears. "Thank you, Father, that means a lot to me."

"Hey hoes! Y'all miss me?!" Nina walks in the music room making a scene on purpose, and gives Diane, Keisha, and Cat a group hug before they all sit down in their usual spot, with their usual brown bag lunches.

"Bitch, we just saw you at your ghetto-ass birthday party last month," Cat teases.

"Whatever Cat. That party was talked about all summer. Shit, people still hitting me up about it, asking when I'm going to throw another one. And they actually mentioned your name nicely, Nina," Diane brags.

"Oh lawd. Next thing you know you gonna be a concert promoter and rapper groupie," Nina says, continuing the roasting of Diane.

"Shit, yo ass be the first one wanting to know which celebrity niggas gonna be there. Stop playing, Nina."

Nina laughs out loud as she pulls the sandwich out of her brown bag.

"Speaking of fine asses, I see you were pretty busy during the summer," Keisha chimes in. "Where you get that fine-ass drink of chocolate milk from?"

"I know, right?" Nina admits. "He's actually the nephew of a family friend. Supposedly we've known each other since we were young, but I can't remember," she shares, gleaming.

"You can't remember because you were probably like two and he was ten," Diane says.

"Shut up, Diane! He is not that much older than me," Nina responds, still giggling.

"On the real though, shit don't even matter, Nina. You deserve to be happy, especially after dealing with these jokers up in here."

"Well, what's good? What's the gossip?" Nina probes, talking fast. "I mean, Jason didn't even say anything to me at my own party. I don't care, but what up with him? He still with that tramp Trina?"

"Ya see, this is what I'm talking about," Keisha says. "Jason's dick done trapped Nina's mind. No matter how good that Milk Jordan wannabe is laying it down, she always gonna be soft for Jason's dick. That first shit, I told you! You probably be calling his name out for no reason, *still*. A damn shame."

All four girls get up to dump their trash in the hallway, laughing at Keisha's point.

"Whatever, I was just asking, damn," Nina says, trying to downplay something she has actually struggled with. Changing the uncomfortable subject, she makes an announcement. "Soooo … you are looking at the new editor-in-chief of the school paper!"

"Awww shit, that's awesome, Nina!" Diane says, leading the pack in giving out kudos. The girls are using the last few minutes of their lunch break to freshen up in the bathroom, before swapping out books at their lockers.

"Nina, this is a big deal," Keisha determines. "As I'm sure you learned this summer at that fancy pre-college journalism class, knowledge can really help you guide what people read in here. You can make sure we get heard, so we can get more funding for band camp and our pom dance squad."

"Damn Keisha, I didn't know you were that smart," Cat jokes, but she means it.

"You should come write for the paper, Keisha," Nina says, just realizing how attuned her friend is with the pulse and culture of the school.

"Ya think so?" Keisha asks while freshening up her apple-cinnamon lip gloss, knowing Nina's answer.

"I do! I'll let you know when our first meeting is."

The girls have completed their facial refresh and walk down the hall together, in their own world as usual, until Keisha makes an observation. "Hey y'all, nobody has gritted on us or called Nina 'white girl' today."

"Again, I'm tellin' you … it's Nina's ratchet party! It has made her cool, and is keeping the bullies back!" Diane says.

"Speaking of bullies, look who it is," Cat says.

"Hey." Mo greets all the girls but is looking at Nina.

"Hey Mo!" Nina responds, genuinely happy to see her, and a little hurt she didn't come to her party when everyone else from the squad came, even the girls Mo poisoned into hating her.

"Listen, can I talk to you for a minute?" Mo asks. "I know we gotta go to class, but it'll only take a minute and I can't wait till after school because I jus' can't fuckin' wait till after school."

"Ok, ok, breathe, Mo. Let's go outside real quick," Nina says, feeling like a therapist taking an emergency call.

The girls, each at their designated locker, see the panicked interaction and are looking forward to hearing what it's all about from Nina later.

Nina and Mo go outside by the football field, away from any nosy ears. Nina's only regret is she didn't grab her coat; it's a colder than usual September morning.

"First of all, I'm sorry I couldn't make it to your party," says Mo. "Family shit, you know?"

Even though Nina doesn't believe her, she appreciates the sensitivity of even giving an excuse. "It's ok, Monica. What's wrong?"

"Ok, so, how did you know you were gay or bi or whatever?" Mo asks in such a whisper, Nina barely hears her.

Nina starts laughing nervously. "I'm sorry, is this what you brought me out in the cold for?"

"I know, I know. It's just I met this girl over the summer and I think I'm feelin' her. And you know the thing with you. I mean, that was something, right? I'm just trying to understand how you knew?"

Nina stands there for a minute looking at Mo, understanding what she's saying but not sure if she wants to take responsibility for the answer. "Mo, I don't really know what to say. Probably because I've never had to, and maybe because I'm not sure I'm ready to. I can tell you though that whatever you feeling is real and you should believe in it and be honest with it, for your sake and whoever this dumb girl is for liking you like that." She teases at the end, to lift the pressure Mo is sharing with her. The back of her calves are beginning to itch, but surprisingly she doesn't have to pee. For once, she's actually not afraid of something kinda scary.

"Why you got that silly grin on your face?" Mo asks, as she playfully locks arms with Nina, an admission that they need to hurry to class.

Nina ignores Mo's probe, and stops at the door before going into the building. "Listen Mo, the moment we had in the bathroom was real, you know? But I think it came from a place of stress. I feel like this is a time where we all just trying to find out who we are, and it's ok to not be sure yet. I've always been special, from before I knew I was, and I'm still figuring it out I guess. And it's ok if you are too."

Mo gives Nina a hug and quietly says thank you before wiping the tears from her face. Nina watches her walk away to class.

Without looking back, Mo yells out, "And don't be late for pom practice, bitch!"

Knock knock!
"Yes, come in."
"Hi, Father Jessup, I'm hoping you have a few minutes for me. I know it's off-hours."
"It's ok, Nina. What's going on?"
"I just wanted to give you a few updates about what I'm up to," Nina says, trying to be more open. Father Jessup motions her to sit in her usual chair across from his desk, where she continues to speak. "So, I'm now the new editor-in-chief and I just want to thank you for pushing me. I had my first meeting with the student writers and we have some really good talent, some who can step this paper up a notch."
"That's great, Nina!"

Nina is happy to make Father Jessup proud, as it helps rebuild her self-confidence. "Also, I've been thinking about making something good out of something bad, in regard to my writing papers for athletes. What if we create a volunteer effort where senior high school students who have great writing skills help elementary kids write better—like an elevated tutoring program—where a certain number of us will go to them maybe once a week and assist with their writing assignments or lessons as needed?"

"Again, a wonderful idea, Nina! Let's schedule a meeting with the president. In the meantime, how about you put your proposal down on paper?" Father Jessup suggests with excitement.

"Ok will do, Father, thank you," Nina says. "Lastly, I just wanted to let you know, I'm going to try to talk to God more. I can't promise where it will go, but maybe we can have some open dialogue. Though I have my church family, I'm hoping I can come to you for a chat from time to time."

"Nina, I have to tell you, this is the best of all three of your announcements. I hope you know I pray for you every day and I'm always here to talk to."

"Thank you, Father. That really means a lot."

***

Without having to sacrifice the school dance team, Nina turns her high school experience around. Nurturing her literary talent and heartfelt need to give back to the community creates a purpose-driven and structured mindset. She finds students who are experts in various subjects she struggles with, and learns how to navigate the tough content from those who have mastered it. It's also hard to bully her when she's humbly confident, and eager to share resources, space, and time. It doesn't hurt that Malcolm, her overachieving college boyfriend, offers his mind for probing and support.

"Dad, I know you were an English major like Mom, but you're also a numbers wizard like Dionne. I'm hoping you both can help me, since Mom helps with everything else," Nina requests with a giggle.

"Of course, princess!" Mike says with enthusiasm. He's happy he can finally help Nina with her academics, or anything that provides an opportunity to thrive.

The following year, Nina graduates with a solid GPA and acceptance to one of the top ten journalism schools in the country, close to home in Maryland. She successfully reigns as editor of the high school paper for two years, and supports a handful of small religious publications and not-so-small community efforts for the underserved. She is perfection in her passion for theology. In fact, classmates are surprised she is honored for her excellence in philosophy and religious studies, but that's just because she keeps her love for it quiet, because of how personal it is for her.

Malcolm is in his last year of college down south, and it's tough focusing on a future with him while Nina is busy transitioning into college and navigating the loneliness of his long-term absence.

"We will be ok, Queen. Just hang in there," Malcolm says over the phone.

"I know," Nina says, trying to convince herself. But college is not what she expects. She anticipates confusion and indecisiveness. However, her experience creates an incredible sense of clarity. Because she has created a method of conquering the tough classes, she is not so much overwhelmed by them; she's just certain she doesn't want any part of them in the future. And the classes she excels in, she also doesn't want. Nina gets accepted to write for both the mainstream college publication and the underground publication, and though it's interesting, she is not passionate about writing straight news.

"If you want to get into broadcast journalism, you're going to have to sacrifice," Nina's college counselor warns. "You are an African American woman and it's 1993. You may need to start with radio or explore the idea of moving to a small town for a bit."

No, I will not, Nina thinks.

The question is, What will Nina do instead? And what will she tell her parents?

In the first semester, Nina almost immediately checks out academically. Even when writing for the underground African-American publication, she is not passionate or connected to the content. She regrets not taking a creative writing class, which could have served as inspiration to dust off her journals. She does, however, find the campus athletic center which has a small room with a floor-length mirror in it, used for cardio classes on the weekends. Whenever Nina gets an urge to move her body, she sneaks in there—day or night—and sweats for hours to the pulse of her heart. High school ended her dance team days, but it's difficult for her to let her love for the art form go.

Socially, Nina continues to struggle. Though she and her roommate, Autumn, connect in a positive way, the other girls on her dorm floor hate Nina. It's evident the reason is territorial. The dorm floors are split, boys on one side and girls on the other. Her particular floor of students is New York/New Jersey heavy. So, her next-door neighbors resent the fact that their "Northern boys" beeline to Nina and Autumn's dorm room to hang out and flirt. It's high school all over again.

Autumn is from Delaware and breaks up with her boyfriend from back home right after homecoming weekend. It is pretty common for freshman girls to clean slate it during this time frame, so they can comfortably date or hook up with guys at school.

Though Nina has a difficult time saying no to male attention—athletes, campus party promoters, hot brothers from New York who remind her of her boyfriend—she refuses to end it with Malcom. He has proven to be the best potential king she's ever encountered, and she won't give him up just because it's what people who are damaged and flawed say you're supposed to do.

Nina is discreet. She doesn't bring the athlete to her room. Instead, she aligns visits with her classes on the other side of campus where he stays, so Autumn doesn't inquire. Better yet, if she needs more time, she often says she's going home just thirty minutes away to visit family. Sometimes she just wants to write in her journal in her athlete's room and feel a body—some mirrored heat. Guilt only comes when Malcolm visits. When he's away, she justifies her time, and that time is plentiful.

Kevin is going pro early, most likely next year. His girlfriend is back home out west and he can't remember the last time he saw her.

"Candi girl, there you are." Kevin opens the door to his shared athletic dorm, lets his secret inside, and quietly escorts her back to his room, where everything is oversized to accommodate his six-foot-eight height. He is one of four basketball players who share the space, but he is quiet and keeps to himself off the court. The only reason he met Nina is because he couldn't find a textbook he needed at the bookstore, and she helped him. A coffee turned to a drink, and a drink turned into sleepovers.

"You are one of very few women I know who looks best natural and in sweats," Kevin says, bending down low to kiss Nina on her mouth. She loves how he calls her a woman, even though he mostly calls her Candi, since she often has a cherry Blow Pop in her mouth when writing. "You brought your notebook," he observes with satisfaction. "That means you staying the night, right?"

"Yes, is that ok? Your bedroom is a nice escape."

"Of course, sweets, I like that, waking up to you writing and shit. It's super sexy. But no writing right now. Come here," Kevin says with his hand out, already lying down in his oversized bed. They make love for hours, then share a bottle of red while waiting for a pizza delivery.

"Do you have anything stronger?" Nina asks, consistently feeling the need to calm her worry and anxiety, even when she can't quite pinpoint the cause of either.

"Yeah, I got some Jameson here, but no weed. 'Cause you know, I can't get down with that and play ball."

"Of course, baby, I know, The Jamey is fine." Nina lets Kevin caress her thighs, enjoying the silence, while she sucks down two cups of whiskey. He doesn't question her, as he's gotten used to her quiet addiction.

"What are you doing for the holidays?" Kevin asks.

"I'm traveling with my boyfriend. What about you? Heading to the West Coast?"

"Yeah, you know." Kevin rolls over on top of Nina and looks deep into her eyes.

Nina smiles uncomfortably, and after what feels like ten minutes, she says, "Kevin, don't complicate it. We just keeping each other warm for now, right?"

"You're the one who's supposed to accidentally fall for me, chase me for my ball money or sumthin, but you're so loyal. I mean, not with your body obviously, but with everything else," Kevin says, showing unexpected vulnerability.

"I feel you, Kev. You're so sweet and sexy, baby. But you have a woman in California who called you twice while you were on top of me, and my man will be looking for me tomorrow. Go to sleep, so I can write and then make love to you in the morning."

"I'll take what you can give me."

And this is the last of it, Nina thinks, before she puts the journal back in her bag, and lets him engulf her body with his.

CHAPTER NINE

It's three days before Christmas 1993, and Brooklyn is suffering from hypothermia, but Nina ignores the city's frozen tears running down Malcolm's bedroom window. It's too hot under the sheets to care about the cold outside. Their combined body heat flushes her cheeks and runs through the veins of her legs, which are wrapped around his. She turns her nose slightly inward to inhale the indescribable scent she has missed so much, and the intoxication of it sends her mind awry.

Her friends warned her that long distant relationships with age differences are tough. *But look at us,* Nina thinks. *We've made it through the hard part.* Malcom's last year of college down south, while she pushes through her first semester. She knows she has made a lot of mistakes in the past, but it's different now. She's walking on a new path, disciplined, away from all the juvenile bad seeds she has had to hide from him in so many dark places. She's been a good girl these past few months. And at least now, he's only a train ride away. His working on

Wall Street while saving money living at home has its perks and benefits, which fund the time they make for each other.

I'm less distracted, so I know we'll make it, Nina lectures herself, then slides up to his height, kissing his ajar sleeping lips and hoping he'll wake to continue the seductive dance from last night.

"Malcolm!" Mrs. Thomas yells from outside the door, disrupting Nina's naughty intentions. "The drivers will be here in fifteen minutes!" It's 3:15 a.m. and Malcolm's eyes open without urgency.

"Oh shit, baby, what time is it?" Nina screeches, panicked, jumping up out of the bed wearing Malcom's flannel pajama shirt and sweating, already knowing the answer.

"It's ok, hun, we've already packed, and fifteen minutes is really fifty minutes to my mom," says Malcolm. "No time to get cute though, just throw your clothes on. Remember, layers up top, it will be hot there. And don't drink the coffee I'm sure my dad is making for you, you know how your stomach gets when traveling."

Nina loves how Malcolm always looks out for her, protects and guides her, but she is looking forward to this trip as an opportunity to showcase her maturity and independence to his traditional tight-knit and judgmental family; prove that she's not just a spoiled eighteen-year-old American girl who doesn't know how to take care of her West Indian man. Malcolm is the first of his generation born in America but spent his early years on the island raised by grandparents, while his parents got the highly sought-after prestigious education in the United States to make a better life for him and his brother Alex. This planned hiatus is Malcolm's delayed graduation present, to remind him of his cultural roots, show him where he came from, and Nina is thrilled to be invited on such an intimate journey of discovery.

***

It's unusually hot and humid for a December afternoon on the island: well above ninety degrees Fahrenheit. Nina's long, relaxed hair has transformed into a wild rebellious afro fighting to escape its restrictive hair tie. She has flown on airplanes before, but never deboarded directly onto the runway.

Earlier, the captain announced there was some sort of problem with the designated gate, and malfunction at the alternate gates. "I'm afraid to say, you will all be getting a little bit of exercise today," he joked with a thick British accent.

After a long power walk, Nina, Malcolm, and his family are now at baggage claim—a small white building with few windows—steaming hot, like a tight interrogation room but without the chairs. They are standing restlessly, waiting for what Nina suspects will be either relief or death.

"Malcolm, does this sort of thing happen often?" Nina whispers to the back of his shoulders. Despite the balance skills in her three-inch heels, she still can't reach the bottom of his ears, and immediately regrets not listening to him back in New York about choosing comfort over fashion.

"Queen, how should I know? This is the first time I've been here too, remember?" he shoots back without looking.

"So, when you were here as a kid then, that doesn't count?"

This time Malcolm does turn around, giving Nina a look that would slice steel clean. She dares not respond, quickly realizing he is just as agitated and on edge as she is. The flight was packed with a lot of turbulence, yelling babies, and unusual scents—a cocktail with all the worst ingredients. It didn't help that she projected her innate fear of flight onto him: frantic murmurs, sweat-filled hand squeezes, and nervous tremors which all kept him on anxious alert and in unison with her. Now, on the ground, they are both tired and anticipating the joy in this exotic reward.

"Don't worry, it's going to be ok," Malcolm promises Nina, as he tries to be positive. He pushes hard to produce a smile, while side-eying the accompanying group of too many cooks in the kitchen—his family—who are debating on where and when the luggage will appear. Although they are now a significant distance from the island's organic platform, Nina can almost taste the aroma of the Atlantic Ocean. She can't wait to prance around first thing tomorrow morning in her new purple Brazilian-style bikini, her body painted in thick coconut oil with the lowest SPF, pebbles of golden sand hidden between her bronzed toes. *I can be patient. This is how Jamaica teased me years ago—a rough start at the airport, just to end up in a magnificent paradise.*

While fantasizing about her beach affair, someone calls out her name with jovial conviction from the other side of the building. "Nina!"

It's hard to see who it is, but Malcolm has already given his permission, so she slowly walks through the crowd, hesitant it is someone she doesn't want to run into. But as she draws closer, she recognizes the short stocky frame with the wide grin, dark-olive skin, and shiny, full black beard. "Neal! Oh my god, hi! So good to see you! What are you doing here? Vacation? Are you going or coming?"

Nina is so excited to see her college friend; she almost forgets to hug him in between her probing questions. Neal is a

DANCER IN THE BULLPEN

senior student at her college and writes for their underground radical Black newspaper like she does. They don't engage much outside of the student union, but there is something about seeing a familiar face in this foreign country that calms her. Neal explains he is there for his favorite grandmother's funeral.

"But wait, what are you doing here?" Neal asks.

"I'm here for vacation with my boyfriend and his family."

"Yeah, but why?" Neal seams perplexed.

Nina gets a sharp pang of worry in her throat. "What do you mean?"

"Like, why here?"

"Well, this is where my boyfriend is from, and his parents thought this would be a great opportunity to enjoy his homeland."

Neal lets out a chuckle, but clearly nothing is funny. "Nina, this is not a place you come for vacation. Hell, if it wasn't for my grandmother dying, I would probably never return here. This is not Jamaica," he warns, like he can read Nina's mind.

Suddenly, Nina's gotta pee, and she can feel new sweat building under her armpits. "It can't be that bad, Neal," she responds, trying to convince him to ignore the truth of his experience, yet not brave enough to ask why he says these things. She knows he comes from a wealthy family, and has heard him brag about frolicking in some of the most exotic places around the world. *So of course, he's going to be hard on his homeland like we all are.*

"Well, it will be an experience I'm sure, girl. It's so good to see you. Let me go find my folks outside, I think they should be here now. Be safe and try to have some fun," Neal advises, with an empathetic look that makes Nina feel off balance. She watches him walk away flinging his tightly packed duffle bag across his shoulder, confirming he is here only for a quick visit, and obviously brilliant for not needing to deal with baggage claim.

Back with Malcolm and his family, Nina almost decides to step out of her high heels onto the dusty floor, but then feels a breeze that is almost cool hit her face, as airline workers open back doors she hasn't seen until now, which face the runways. After a lot of commotion and following all the other passengers from multiple flights, Malcolm grabs her hand and leads her outside, which has a view of a concrete wall that's height is parallel to the roof of the building. About ten men are strategically positioned and straddled on top of the wall looking down on the opposite side, as if they are waiting for direction.

Before Nina can panic, Malcolm explains without really explaining. "For some reason they can't get the bags through the receiving belt, so you need to keep your eye out for yours as the men drop them to us."

"Wait, what? Drop them to us?!" Nina whispers loud enough for Mrs. Thomas to look over at her.

"Queen, I know, just stay close, and look out for your bag. It's red, right?" Malcolm questions, trying to keep Nina focused. She is speechless as she witnesses young slim men catch heavy and bulky suitcases thrown up to them from men on the opposite side of the wall, then shift their cores and drop the suitcases below to other men on her side of the wall, for distribution to the correct owners. Nina can only be grateful that her bag is bright apple-red with her name in bold black letters, standing out from all the common, nameless black ones. She is impressed by the rhythm in which they move collectively, yet still hears Neal's voice in her ear questioning what she is doing here.

It takes two mini vans to carry all thirteen of them—Nina, Malcom, Malcolm's younger brother, parents, aunts, uncles, and a few rambunctious little cousins sitting on top of the suitcases.

Nina is happy to be squished between Malcolm and the window; at least she can feel the breeze again, hitting her face, but now with more of a gentle hand that lulls her to sleep briefly, until one of the cousins yells from the back. "Is that the beach?!"

Mr. Thomas proudly affirms and begins telling a story of how he fished with his dad just beyond the seawall, which looks like a fortress the ocean built, not the other way around.

"Oh my god, we can't swim in that," Alex complains. "It's so brown and murky! I thought there'd be hot beach chicks here. What was the point of bringing our swimsuits unless there is a pool where we're staying? Dad, is there a pool where we're staying?"

"No," Mr. Thomas replies simply and directly.

Alex turns back to glare at Malcolm. "What the hell, man? I thought you said this would be fun?"

Mrs. Thomas hits Alex on the head. "Stop complaining and be grateful you have the chance to see where you come from, with your brother and the rest of the family."

Nina feels Malcolm's eyes on the side of her face but pretends not to notice, and keeps chasing the cracks in the seawall with her eyes as the van speeds by.

Just outside the capitol, twenty minutes from the airport, they arrive at their destination—a two-level stone building

293

comprised of two adjacent rental homes. It is the only building on the street that looks like it may meet a standard housing code. There are two big streetlights working, spotlighting the wooden house across from theirs, which appears as though it has lost half its body in a fire. There is a solid door, but holes in the frame surrounding it allow anyone to see the missing planks on the second floor, and right through to the back of the house. The rest of the street looks the same—damaged and abandoned. Nina knows Mr. Thomas is cheap, but this is ridiculous.

Nina watches Malcolm carefully unpack his suitcase, putting his folded shirts into the broken drawer of a worn dresser, in a dim-lit room with three twin beds to be shared by two brothers and one annoyed girlfriend named Nina. "Malcolm, is this for real?"

"I know, Queen, it's going to be ok."

Nina grinds her teeth, holding her breath, doing her best not to argue. *But no, it's not going to be ok,* she lectures herself. *It's a million degrees with no air conditioning, no beach, no privacy, and no hint of anything that suggests luxury.* But she doesn't say a word. She gracefully prepares for dinner, takes a shower with her sexy purple Brazilian-style bikini on, just in case one of the undisciplined cousins runs by the bathroom with no door. She doesn't complain about the trickling shower head, or the water bucket with no handle to make up for it. *I've been camping once before; I know how to rough it. I just have to think how wonderful dinner will be back in the city.*

It's weird watching a Chinese man share the evening's special with a West Indian accent. The restaurant is tucked away at the back of an alley off a major road, but apparently it's very popular, as it's packed with what looks like both tourists and locals. Beside two women at a corner table, the Thomas family and Nina occupy the private space on the side of the restaurant—an enclosed patio with hanging Chinese lanterns and fumes of piping hot egg rolls, which help Nina forgive the island for her bamboozlement. Mrs. Thomas shares the trip's itinerary for the next few days, and things are looking up. Visits to the Tropical Botanical Gardens, historical churches, and island zoo are all ways Nina can quench her thirst for architecture, nature, and wildlife. But first, she must pee.

"Excuse me, sir, can you direct me to the bathroom?"

"Of course, one second," the waiter responds.

Nina is confused. *Why does he have to go somewhere first before telling me where the bathroom is?* But she is patient and mature on this trip, so she holds tight like a good girl.

Malcolm places his hand under the table on top of Nina's trembling thigh. "Shhh, you're ok," he whispers, as if he's talking directly to her leg. As if he's a comforting parent. But he is not even looking at her. He's focused on who all the other uncles are focused on: the hot island *Jet* beauty in a plush green dress, bending over to pick up her runaway napkin. Her tits are fighting to escape, while the side hems are sprinting in the opposite direction toward her waist.

Nina calmly leans into Malcolm. "Are you fuckin kiddin' me? Can you not do that? I'm right here!"

Before Malcolm can defend himself, the waiter returns and hands over a roll of toilet paper and a small portable lamp. "Just walk outside that screen door and into the back where you will see a curtain. Go behind there. Just be careful because it rained last night, so the dirt around the hole may be a little soft."

Nina shoots Malcolm a look, and this time dares him to say it will be ok.

Back at the house, Nina and Malcolm escape from the music of boisterous children and their drunken elders by sharing a big, cushioned chair in the corner of the balcony. With legs draped over Malcolm's thighs and head dropped heavily on his chest, Nina can't help but wish they were back in his New York bed. Despite her anger that still lingers from dinner, and the longing for the familiar, she feels peaceful at this moment. She embraces the pitch-black backdrop of midnight, showcasing the flicker of fire from the trash that young boys are burning across the street.

Malcolm breaks the silence. "Dinner was good, yeah?"

"It might have been the best Chinese food I've ever had," Nina affirms, genuinely satisfied.

"And peeing in the backyard hole doesn't change your rating?"

Nina's smile drops into the street. Malcolm immediately regrets bringing up the tense timing during dinner.

"Hmph. You're lucky I have strong thigh muscles, or you'd be washing someone else's shit off me right now," Nina jokes without a hint of laughter, lifting her body up and off Malcolm's chest. "I guess I'm not lucky though. I learned you aren't as different from your uncles as one would think."

"Nina." Malcolm can't say much else, except for her name.

"'Nina' what? You're not a cheat?" she challenges.

"You know I'm not, Queen. Her tits were literally sweeping up the dust on the ground. That piece of cloth dress was hiked up so high I saw the number of stretch marks she had on her torso. I mean, babe, it was just one big unbelievable distraction. It wasn't like, you know, I wanted that. Come on now, you're my only queen and nobody compares to you." Malcolm dishes out his defense with a honey-coated spoon.

Nina looks into Malcolm's beautiful dark-brown eyes and can't find any monsters. She lies back on his chest, inhales his fainted cologne, and quietly says, "Ok, fine."

"Ahhh! Don't let the rat get out! It's my pet!"

"No, it's mine! Open the lid!"

Nina and Malcolm's private moment is abruptly interrupted by the screaming demands of his devilish cousins. They both jump up, but only Malcolm goes inside to investigate the situation. Nina has never seen a rat in person and is not planning on doing so tonight.

"Jesus Christ, I wish I smoked," Nina mumbles to herself, sitting back in the chair she now drowns in, wondering if this situation warrants a drag off a cigarette like she sees in the movies.

After what seems like thirty minutes, Malcolm appears back on the balcony drenched in sweat and out of breath.

"Baby, are you ok?" Nina asks, but what she really means is, *Is that rat gone yet?!*

"Yes, the rats are gone."

"*Rats?*" Nina exclaims.

"Can you believe these monsters caught a couple of rats and were keeping them in two trash cans with water in them, like they were fish?"

"Malcolm, that doesn't even make sense. First of all, are rats just walking around here to be caught as pets? And secondly, why would they put water in the trashcans, do rats swim?"

"Nina, I don't know. Well actually I think they do swim, but they are gone. They're probably just lurking around because they want some of my mom's hot pepper sauce for their cheese," Malcolm says with a chuckle. Realizing Nina doesn't think that is funny, he steps in close and wraps his arms around her sweaty frame. "I know this is not ideal, but we will get through and have a good time. Let's take showers and go to bed."

Nina realizes she *is* acting a bit spoiled; she decides to try stepping outside of her comfort zone and be sensitive to her environment.

Once again in the shower in her sexy purple bikini, Nina tries to remain positive as she habitually opens her mouth to let the trickle of water run between her teeth onto her tongue.

"Shit, shit!" She curses frantically as she spits out the water she was warned not to drink.

"Everything ok in there?" Mrs. Thomas is at the side of what should be a door, seemingly concerned, though Nina thinks she is probably laughing, rubbing her palms together slowly like the Wicked Witch of the West, chanting "I got you now, my little pretty."

Maybe it's the heat that is making Nina think crazy thoughts. The ceiling fans just turn the hot air into hot air with track shoes on, and she is already soaking through her pink nightgown.

"Malcolm, oh my god, what's that?!" Nina screeches, pointing to what looks like a black rat with wings on the wall.

Amused, Alex looks up from his bed and says, "Oh I've heard about these. That's a flying cockroach."

"Alex, shut up!" Malcolm demands. "Don't worry, I'll get it." And just as he promises that, the black rat-roach flutters its wings, as if daring him to approach.

"If that thing flies off the wall, I gotta roll out, Malcolm," says Nina.

"Hey bro, turn off the fan for a minute, so you can concentrate on whacking the hell out of this thing," Alex suggests. Malcolm interestingly enough does as he is told and turns off the fan. As he draws close, the black rat-roach spreads its wings like an evil angel, nosediving directly into Nina's open suitcase.

"Oh my god!" yells Alex. "Yo, that thing is in Nina's bag!"

"Shut up, Alex!" Malcolm demands as he looks at Nina.

"We gotta go, babe," Nina declares in a calm but assertive manner.

"Queen, listen, I'm going through your bag now, I'll get it out and make sure we get rodent spray in the morning."

Without another word, Malcolm walks out of the cramped bedroom—where two brothers, one annoyed girlfriend, and now one black rat-roach dwell—and calls his Uncle George, who lives just a few miles away. Malcolm's uncle is Mr. Thomas' older brother, who has recently got divorced from his substantially younger third wife and supposedly proposed to the fourth just yesterday. A valued employee of the presidential office of the government, Uncle George enjoys certain privileges, including a home with limited rodents and consistent running water.

After a confirmed welcome from his uncle and difficult talk with his parents, Malcolm finds Nina back on the balcony, the only place she feels safe.

"Alright Nina, we're going to my Uncle George's house. I don't know him well, but I do know I'm his favorite nephew from my days here when I was young. And on the phone he bragged about his cool air conditioning and comfortable clean rooms, which I'm confident is true. I also told my parents that it's nothing against them, we are grateful for this trip, but we can't stay with rats and flying roaches and shit."

Nina chuckles through more tears. She almost feels bad about the talk with his parents, but not bad enough to push through.

✳✳✳

Though it's 12:30 a.m., Uncle George agrees to send a driver to transport Nina, Malcolm, and Alex to his home. There was no way Alex would let Malcolm leave him there. They are two peas in a pod and Nina loves how their personalities balance each other, making for such a warm and entertaining environment.

"Thank god, right Nina?" Alex teases with a wink, as they pull up in the personal driveway of Uncle George's beautiful home. It isn't any more elegant than a typical single-family home in the States, but at the moment it's as grand as the White House to Nina.

"Yes, now this is much better," Nina says.

There is no need to knock on the door; an older heavy-set woman with kind eyes is standing in the open doorway, yelling "Welcome children!" as if they all just came back from school, and she is their mama greeting them.

She introduces herself. "My name is Ms. Mary, and I will make sure you cutie-pies are well taken care of. Your Uncle George is an old man and is already off to bed, but you will see him in the morning at breakfast. He probably dreamin' about ya all right now, so don't ya fret. There will be some fun times tomorrow."

Nina usually doesn't like being spoken to in such a juvenile manner, but this is different. Ms. Mary feels safe and warm, and smells like Indian curry (her favorite). Suddenly, she is famished.

"Drop your bags off right here and someone will make sure they get to your rooms soon. But right now, come with me. Do you want a little something to eat? I have some shrimp and beef patties I just baked for your uncle's dinner meeting tomorrow, but I think you three can be my taste testers, yeah?" asks Ms. Mary.

"Oh yeah," Malcolm agrees, immediately turning five years old.

Nina giggles. She loves that he can't turn good food down, or anything palate pleasing for that matter—like herself. *Look at him. So tall and fine, smart and attentive. Taking charge and making it happen for us, a more appropriate place for us to stay. Mmm, I wish I was the beef in his patty.*

Malcolm squeezes Nina's hand under the kitchen counter and mouths *Stop* half-committedly. He knows this look on her face and how she is when coddled. She is hungry to reciprocate. She is gluttonous, basking in the West Indian spices of this decadent cuisine and companionship. But then, a sudden twinge of anxiety stabs her neck. *What the hell am I thinking? Getting Malcolm to bring us here like this, in the middle of the night, like we've escaped some inhumane slave quarters? His mom must think I'm a spoiled brat. Dammit! How am I supposed to show my independent womanhood when my man—her son—must rescue me from an environment she is clearly enduring?*

Nina doesn't say anything to Malcolm. The two plump shrimp patties in her belly, married with the fatigue of the longest night in history, barely allow her lead feet to trudge up the stairs to their room. She loves the sound of Alex saying good night and walking down the hall to his. She wonders if his room is comparable to her and Malcolm's, which is equipped with a regal canopy bed, armoire, and a simple vanity set angled at the corner by the window. They have a view of the background garden Mary referenced as a "breathtaking amenity best seen in daylight." Everything is white—the walls, every piece of furniture, and every piece of fabric—which creates an intentional contrast to the polished African mahogany floor.

"I could live here," Nina confesses as she plops down on the bed, completely exhausted.

"Queen, get up and get into the shower," Malcolm lazily instructs as he struggles with unpacking for them both.

Nina stands up and comes up behind him, eyes closed to prevent the burning redness. "Hey, listen you control freak, how about you let me do this, while you take a shower first, because you always get mad when I pass out before you, which is crazy but accepted by now."

Malcolm looks at Nina, then at the clothes drawer, then back at her.

"Don't worry, I'll keep them folded and in straight lines in each drawer, for God's sake," Nina chides. She knows better than to be so stern with Malcolm in public, but during these quiet times, when his guard is down, she is confident he loves to be handled a bit.

"How about this, put the clothes down and come with me," Malcolm whispers tantalizingly.

Nina does as she is told without a word and follows Malcolm into the next-door bathroom. Again, every element is white—from the walls to the toilet roll holder—but the only attraction that captures her eye is a Black, naked body turning the shower on, its wide shower head at full-force. The contrast is too divine not to submit and be part of. Nina and Malcolm wash the day away, then return to the bed and make love in the light of sunrise.

It's high noon, and the sound of drums playing down the street is muffled, yet rhythmic enough to stir Nina awake. With eyes shut, she stretches her limbs as if being pulled by tightropes in opposite directions. She feels rested and relaxed, ignoring the piercing light from the sun beaming down onto her eyelids. Suddenly she sits up, casing the space around her, and exhales slowly, accepting she's not back in her college dorm room, late for class. It's a blended feeling of relief and anticipation, as the faint smell of curry entices her nose once again.

Laughter roars from the downstairs parlor, led by an unrecognizable voice that must be Uncle George. Nina hears Malcolm and Alex dangle from every whispered word about his incomparable career of importance, his ungrateful family, and his obsession with young women with big melons, schooling his nephews on the steps of maintaining power and discretion in a relationship.

Men are such frauds among each other, stroking their insecurities, hoping they'll turn into gold. Or maybe this is who they really are without the audience of women and children.

Nina has always been intrigued by human behavior, yet focusing more on others' than her own. However, today her hunger to explore this unfamiliar country leaves these thoughts behind as she gets cleaned up and dressed, ready to be discovered when the men stop bantering

"Well, don't you look beautiful," says Malcolm, gleaming as Nina walks down the stairs in her habitual slow, dramatic fashion, letting the wide hem of her peach sundress sway, enjoying the admiring eyes on her hourglass body. Her hair is trapped high into a waterfall-style ponytail, still warm from the flat iron; her skin is bronzed by the invasion of the sun, which has already found moments to kiss her face. Even Ms. Mary can't resist staring at how effortlessly stunning she is.

"Nina!" exclaims Uncle George. "Your ears must be burning, my dear. I was just telling Malcolm how excited I am to meet the goddess that has stolen his heart."

Nina can't help but blush a little, and the earlier whispers are forgiven, though she knows Uncle George is lying. She has been eavesdropping all morning and recalls no memory of her name mentioned, but the amenities of his home outweigh any minor offense. "Oh thank you, Uncle. I see where Malcolm gets his fine looks and magnetic charm. I appreciate you for graciously allowing me here, and I'm thrilled to be able to get to know Malcolm's favorite uncle." She knows this game all too well, and plays it all the better.

"What would you like to eat, dear?" Ms. Mary asks, interrupting the charm play and walking over to Nina with a cold bottle of water, anticipating her thirst after seeing her down four of them back-to-back late last night.

"Thank you, Ms. Mary, but I'm too excited to eat, just ready to get the day started." Nina pauses. "Wait. Please. Um, maybe just a piece of fruit?" She feels guilty for being indecisive, as she focuses on a delicious-looking orange bursting out of a basket on the kitchen island.

"Of course, dear" Ms. Mary responds, quickly navigating her way back between Malcolm and Alex, who are now standing, abiding by Nina's cue that it's time to head out now.

"Well, I'm ready!" Alex shouts, pulling out his strawberry-scented lip balm from his back pocket, rolling the almost completely worn wax over his wide mouth more than enough times. "There's gotta be a lot of fine hunnies out there who don't even know they lookin' for me!" he exclaims with confidence.

"Easy brother," Malcolm warns. "Mom and Dad will be watching your little stinger like a hawk, so let's not cause any trouble with the local innocence."

Uncle George chuckles with an almost inappropriate pride. "It's ok, young man, listen to your big brother and soon you will be surrounded by beautiful young women at the annual New Year's Day party I host here at my home."

"Sounds great, Uncle!" Alex seemed satisfied with the future opportunities to execute his plan of American seduction.

Like a cat, Ms. Mary magically appears in the foyer again with a bag of two oranges and a piping hot shrimp patty wrapped tightly in aluminum foil. Before Nina can protest, she whispered in Nina's ear. "Shhh child, I know you'll be hungry an hour." Nina smiles, wondering if Ms. Mary would be willing to come back to the States and live on campus with her.

The idea to take a walk by the seawall is Nina's. She knows the Thomas family, including the little ones, won't be able to resist the calming and peaceful effect of the ocean's breath on their faces, which she hopes will whisk away any resentment or blame toward her for separating the princes from their royal clan.

Mrs. Thomas finds the perfect opportunity to create a quiet moment with Nina, despite the presence of a crowd. "How did you sleep?" Malcolm has walked ahead, keeping watch on Alex's wandering eyes, while the others stop to listen to a musician play a song on a string of old cowbells.

"I slept like a rock," Nina responds, with the slip of a nervous tremble in her voice. "Didn't realize how strenuous our journey here would be."

Visually, Mrs. Thomas is a striking contrast to the rest of her dark, tall, and boisterous kinfolk. She is petite, soft-spoken, with skin the hue of an eggshell. Her full mouth and round, high Caribbean cheekbones are the only reasons she can't pass for white. When Nina first met her, she was baffled at how neither of her sons inherited the slightest touch of her tone, or any resemblance of her personality—as if she were simply an observer of the family. She was once pretty, but the vodka and pain have continued to quietly punish the clarity in her eyes and deepen the cracked lines in her face. She is brilliant, and Nina is afraid of her. She is afraid of how much Malcolm adores a woman she can never compete with. Despite her submissive cloak, Mrs. Thomas is absolutely the most powerful person in the room, even when outdoors, walking alongside the ocean.

"I can tell you like the water. Have you had many experiences at the beach?" Mrs. Thomas inquires.

"Yes ma'am. I'm a water baby. Both my parents are strong swimmers, and my dad was even a lifeguard for many years."

"That makes sense," Mrs. Thomas flatly states, relaxing the smile lines mapped on her face into a stern restricted position. "You know, Nina, speaking of lifeguards, when Malcolm was just a young teen back home, working as a summer camp counselor, he had an intense crush on a young lifeguard he worked with, and they engaged in quite the romance—"

"Oh, nice," Nina interrupts, ignoring the mention of the young crush. "I was a summer camp counselor growing up as well. Malcolm never mentioned he was one too."

With an impatient sigh, Mrs. Thomas continues her story telling. "Well yes, it was only for one summer. He would come home every day sharing his admiration of her confidence in her job—constantly checking the pool for kids in distress, proactively voicing warnings, helping to minimize danger." Nina is silent, unsure where this is going, but believes it's nowhere she wants to be.

Mrs. Thomas continues. "But then, one day a kid pushed another into the deep end of the pool, not realizing he couldn't swim. The young boy was drowning, and Malcolm's beloved lifeguard didn't move. Not even an inch. It was like she was frozen with fear, stuck in a lifeguard chair. A real lifesaver had to be alerted to come and do her job. Yes, the boy was saved, but not before taking in too much water in his lungs, which Malcolm found out later resulted in some significant damage."

"That is terrible, Mrs. Thomas."

"Yes, it is. What I believe to be most tragic is how my son, being the caring person he is, tried to understand the "stage fright" which prevented his girl's follow-through. But slowly, Malcolm began to lose interest. He said it was because of their daily schedule conflict, and he just didn't have enough time to see her. But in the end, I believe he simply couldn't accept her lack of courage. You want to make sure you're not the lifeguard without courage, Nina."

"You see me as the frozen lifeguard, Mrs. Thomas?"

"I see you as a young lady who needs to show she is more than just a pretty face, capable of jumping in the water and demonstrating endurance, stamina, and value."

Nina's blood boils as she unconsciously makes two tight fists at the side of her thighs, and digs her nails into her palms to prevent her from saying something she is sure to regret. She winces at the pain in her calves, but refuses to give into her power and punish Mrs. Thomas in a physical way. For the first time in a long while, she feels her invisible friend's presence, though she does not make herself known. *Where are you?* Nina wonders.

"Nina!" Alex yells, walking back to where he sees trouble brewing. He can tell a distraction is needed. "You want a piece of milk chocolate? I know it's your fav!" Though he's like a brother to Nina, it's moments like these where she remembers he was the one who noticed her first so many years ago, telling his big brother about a girl he just had to marry one day.

"Oh god no, Alex," says Nina. "Look at the wrapper. It is so old, and the chocolate is seeping out the edges because of the heat. Where did you get that?"

"From the man with the cart over there." Alex points to something that may have moved once in a year but hasn't seen oil or a repair in decades.

"I wouldn't eat that, Alex. Seriously."

"I agree with Nina, son. That wouldn't be smart." Mrs. Thomas' cosigning carries her usual soft voice, a distinct switch from the scratchy witch-bitch sounds from just a moment earlier.

Nina doesn't tell Malcolm about the added tension with his mama, and neither does Alex. After a full day of exploring architecture and historic gardens, the ride back to Uncle

George's home is quiet, with an air of fatigue and unspoken relief that they are going back to the white house.

Malcolm's uncle has left the tour hours ago, in preparation for his dinner party with some important political colleagues, so it is no surprise Ms. Mary has the house sparkling when they arrive just in time to get out the way upstairs. Nina takes a quick peek at the crystal glassware and vintage silver displayed perfectly in the formal dining room, as the cherrywood den is being prepared for a nightcap of cigars and rum. Ms. Mary promises they will be able to come down and eat with her in the kitchen once Uncle George and his guests are happily full in the den.

"Today was good, right, Queen?" Malcolm asks while Nina air-dries naked on the bed after a long shower, rubbing aloe on her mosquito bites, eyeing the closet, contemplating what sundress to wear.

"Yes King. There's a lot of beauty here, you just need to know where to find it." This is the best response Nina can muster. What Malcolm doesn't know is she is mentally drained from replaying the conversation with his mother repeatedly, after strategically avoiding any eye contact with her all day. *Clearly, she doesn't think I'm good enough and that's fine, but what does she expect me to do? Endure just to say I did? Should I be expected to accept someone's rampant infidelity and all that comes with it, clutching my bottle of numbness hidden in the closet, as the rice and peas get cold on the days my husband doesn't even come home? I wonder if she knows what I know. It's more than just wanting a comfortable physical space, it's about having peace of mind. Also, we aren't even engaged.*

Nina slips on a black sundress and tells Malcolm she's having some premenstrual cramps, and thinks a short walk to the water and back may help.

"You want me to come with, or you want a little me-time?" asks Malcolm. Nina scrunches her nose, which gives him his answer. "Ok, just stay on the main road, and don't talk to anyone," he warns, like a father before his daughter's first night out.

Little does Malcolm know that Nina wants to be alone to talk to her invisible friend, who she can now feel so easily. Nina's feet are dusty from the sandy sidewalk, but she keeps shuffling along the seawall, summoning her friend.

I'm here, she announces, gently holding Nina's hand as they walk side by side.

"Finally, thank you! Where have you been?" Nina asks, happy she can still see her invisible friend's face and body.

You haven't needed me much, I guess. It feels like something is blocking me from getting to you, too. I'm trying to figure out what it is.

"Well, I need you now," Nina says with certainty.

I know, that's why I found my way back here. Don't be scared of this place. You're here for a reason. And Mrs. Thomas is more scared of you than you of her. She can tell Malcolm wants you forever, and what does that mean for her?

"I wanted to make her mouth bleed when she was being such an eloquent bitch to me. And I almost did."

I know, but look how you controlled yourself. You didn't even need me to help you.

Nina stops walking and turns to look at her invisible friend. "Yeah, but I felt you. You were close, and that gave me power too."

I didn't know you could feel me when I'm watching you. I think that's new. I like that.

Nina squints and then opens her eyes wide. "You're really pretty, and look familiar. You remind me of someone. I just can't put my finger on it."

You better get back to the house, Nina's invisible friend warns. *Malcolm will start to worry.*

"Ok, as long as you walk me back, and hold my hand," Nina says softly.

Nina is back in the bedroom with Malcolm, both of them ignoring their hungry bellies by making out in between reading. They are passing the time while Uncle George entertains, until a fierce knock on the bedroom door vibrates the floor. Malcolm opens the door and Alex is slumped over a bit, one hand holding on to the doorframe like if he doesn't, he will drop fast to the floor.

"Hey guys, I don't feel so good."

"Oh bro, you're flushed," says Malcolm. "What's wrong, your stomach hurts?"

"Yes," Alex whispers. "And my head. I think I need some water."

"Ok, let's get you to the kitchen with Ms. Mary. She may be able to help. I think Uncle George and his guests are in the den now anyway."

Nina watches Malcolm help Alex down the stairs and immediately loses her appetite. Ms. Mary's eyes widen as they walk into the kitchen.

"Can we please get some water for Alex?" Malcolm asks anxiously.

"What's wrong wit ya, child? You eat sumthin funny out there today?" Ms. Mary probes.

"Oh my god, Alex, did you eat that chocolate bar I warned you about?" Nina asks, cracking the mystery. Malcolm shoots Alex a panicked look.

"Um yeah, well not all of it, but shit, yeah most of it."

"Alex!" exclaims Malcom. "You don't know how long that chocolate has been sitting out—days, months, years. Dear Jesus." When Malcolm starts calling Jesus' name, Nina knows he's worried.

Uncle George appears in the kitchen and sees Alex slumped over the counter. "It's interesting when folks whisper loudly, as if the whisper is not heard. What's wrong with you, boy?"

"I'm sorry, Uncle," Alex apologizes. "I may have eaten something spoiled. I feel pains in my stomach and my head hurts so bad. I think I need to go to the bathroom." Just as fast as Alex stands up and attempts to walk, he wobbles and faints, dropping down onto the hard wooden floor.

Everyone is in the kitchen now, including Uncle George's five political guests.

"Alex!" Nina screams, watching Malcolm hovering over his brother, smacking his face, attempting to get a response.

Alex is conscious, mumbling he wants to go to the hospital. "Don't let me die, I can't die in this place." He is not one to omit any dramatics. It would be funny if it wasn't so scary.

"You're not going to die," replies Malcolm. "Uncle, where is the nearest hospital?"

"Hospital?" Uncle George questions back. Nina watches everyone shake their heads, almost chuckling at the ludicrous idea of taking Alex to a hospital. "Oh no, son, you don't want to go to the hospital here. I'm sure it would be worse than death right here on this floor."

Nina feels her knees buckle, but she finds a chair in time, and lets her body drop, allowing the fear to muffle her. The last thing she needs to do is draw attention to herself.

Alex begins hyperventilating. "Malcolm, I can't breathe, am I going to die? Save me!"

"What can we do?" Malcolm pleads with Uncle George.

"Mary, call Samara and tell her what's happening. She must bring her medicine bag. Malcolm, get up," Uncle George instructs. He begins to coach Alex on taking deep breaths and keeping calm. It's working for now, but Alex is sweating profusely.

It amazes Nina how calm everyone is, like unless Alex's heart has stopped, there is nothing to worry about. Though his stomach seems to still be griping, he can drink a little water and his breathing is stable. Now they just wait for Samara.

"Ms. Mary, who is Samara—a neighborhood doctor?" Nina asks, as Uncle George shows his guests out after their unexpected entertainment.

"Samara is my cousin, a well-respected medicine woman."

"Oh ok." Nina tries to wrap her head around what that means exactly. The only medicine women she is familiar with are those in movies, who know voodoo or questionable spells. She has only been exposed to traditional western medicine by her physician grandmother, physician mother, and possibly soon-to-be physician sister, who already at nine wants to follow the family tradition and save all the children of the world.

Within fifteen minutes, Samara is in Uncle George's kitchen, with two pots of water simmering, dispensing powerful fumes of clove, ginger, and a medley of unknown earthy herbs. She is calm and fluid in her preparation. Nina is in awe of her aura and hypnotic energy.

"My cousin is magic, Nina," Ms. Mary whispers. "Our family is from a local indigenous tribe, and Samara is one of the few born with a gift of healing. Don't worry about Alex, he is in good hands."

Nina believes her and is entranced by Samara's dramatic blue eyes and coal-black skin that can't hide her thick veins and soft wrinkles of eighty-plus years. "She is like a couple of topaz gems at the root of a big tree," Nina determines, not realizing she has said it just loud enough for Ms. Mary to hear.

Nina has so many questions but doesn't dare ask. She simply watches Samara pour the custom tea she has made in an oversized porcelain cup and encourage Alex to drink slowly. It's as if the first sip exorcises the bacteria immediately. After an hour, Nina is still trembling from the adrenaline of the night but trying to take comfort in Alex and Malcolm's relieved laughter as Samara repacks her bag of organic medicine.

Nina can't let her leave without saying something. "Ms. Samara, hi. Um, thank you for taking care of Alex. It got pretty scary before you came. This tea you made is amazing."

Without looking up from her bag, Samara places her hand on Nina's forearm. Her fingers are cold and strong in their grip, but Nina is not afraid. "I know you still talk to your uncle John. And there is another spirit I can't seem to recognize, who you also talk to. You have your own magic, Nina. Blood magic."

Nina's knees buckle again, but she grabs the countertop to brace herself. "What?" she asks, needing this medicine woman to confirm she's not going crazy.

"Your uncle, dear. And the other spirit you talk to. I can feel them here with us now, watching and protecting you," Ms. Samara explains without the slightest tilt of her head, still looking down at her bag, loud enough only for Nina to hear. "Your uncle in particular knows, as I know, that what you are looking for is not here."

"What I'm looking for? What do you mean?" Nina questions, now a bit nervous to hear the answer.

Samara looks directly into Nina's eyes, and squeezes her forearm just shy of it hurting. "What you seek is not here, but inside here," she clarifies, releasing Nina's forearm and tapping her forefinger on Nina's chest. "The power you possess is beyond even my gifts. You are a force, sweet girl. You simply must believe in it to summon it, control it, and nurture it. You must believe in yourself, like when you were a young girl in Jamaica. Don't you remember?"

Chills run down Nina's back and she can feel the goosebumps forming all over her skin. She feels her power idling, like when she was with Mrs. Thomas by the seawall. She takes the lesson and says nothing. *There is so much to absorb but not enough places to store it,* she thinks, feeling overwhelmed with confusion and uncertainty.

"I'm going to bed," Nina announces suddenly, revealing no emotion. She isn't sure who she is talking to, but she goes upstairs and does just that.

Each of the next five days seems to be Groundhog Day; Nina, Malcolm, and Alex spend long hours in the heat with the rest of the Thomas family, explore tourist attractions that are like the ones the day before, with the flirt of an ocean no one can swim in, teasing behind the seawall. Uncle George's white house is the safe haven of uneventful comfort. No one complains because nothing is wrong, even though nothing is right.

***

Nina misses home and is happy waking up on the eve of their departure back to the States. It's the first of a new year, and though the world is still hung over from the celebration last night, the Thomas family is excited about coming to Uncle George's house to enjoy his famous New Year's party and get a glimpse of how the royal princes and one commoner have lived for the past week.

"Malcolm, I don't feel good," says Nina. "I don't know how good I am today."

Malcolm panics. "Oh no, Queen, what did you eat yesterday?!"

"No, baby, it's my period. My cramps are really bad. Will you be angry if I sit this day out? I know it's our final day here, but I just don't think I can."

Malcolm looks disappointed but knows how Nina gets on the first day of her cycle and understands that she's fatigued from all the communal family activities. "Of course, maybe you'll feel better by party time this evening."

I hope not, Nina thinks.

The bass of the music down under the back patio is thumping, and despite the heavy rain, all of Uncle George's friends and family are charging through the outside gate, laughing and clinking bottles, singing to famous dancehall tunes.

Nina asks Malcolm to tell everyone—especially the Thomas family—that she is sleeping, because she knows each woman would otherwise come upstairs to the room, one by one, and attempt to convince her to be strong and come join the dance party. She just doesn't care anymore, even about how it will make Malcolm look to his male idols, or how she will look to his gaslighting mother.

"Samara, hi, what are you doing here?" Nina is thrilled to see her in the bedroom doorway with a big porcelain cup.

"Mary mentioned that you are not well, and I was in the area so thought I'd come make you some of my special berry tea, which will help soothe your womanhood."

Nina already feels better with Samara's presence and drinks the tea slow, not remembering when or how she falls asleep.

Again it's 3:00 a.m., and Nina, Malcolm, and Alex just make it back to the Thomas family house rental before the vans arrive to carry them to the airport. Nina thinks it probably wasn't smart for them to attend a party knowing they all have an early flight to catch. She suspects most of the family didn't bother to sleep and just stayed up to push through, yet you can't tell with all the chaos of parents screaming, passports missing, and bags being tossed in and out of the back of vans for the best fit.

"We're almost out of here, Queen, just hang tight," Malcolm assures. But Nina will believe it when she sees it.

It's déjà vu as Nina is squished between the van window and Malcolm's broad shoulder. The only difference is the van they are in is following the one which holds Malcolm's parents this time, which is a relief that allows her to close her eyes in peace.

BOOM! Their van hits the median in the road and takes flight.

Nina opens her eyes to Malcolm yelling at the driver to "Wake up, Wake up!" and it is all happening too fast!

"I got it, I got it!" The driver yells back, at the same moment the front wheels land on solid ground.

"Oh my god." Nina is afraid, but after interacting with Samara the medicine woman, she is not so anxiety-ridden.

"Do I need to drive?!" Malcolm questions as Nina closes her eyes and meditates.

"No, no sir, I am ok, we're almost there," the driver promises.

Back on the plane, Nina decides to not torture Malcolm's hand. It's time to weather whatever storm comes with the clouds above, but he finds her hand under the blanket that's wrapped around her.

He doesn't say it out loud, but he's right, Nina thinks. How would she have survived this trip without him? Or maybe it's all a lie and Samara is right. *Everything I am looking for is in me? But what the hell is that?* For now, all she is searching for is home. And just like that, as the plane evens out at the proper altitude, she forgets all about her fear of flying and sleeps the entire flight through, head and hands free.

CHAPTER TEN

Dropping out of college in freshman year is terrifying. Selah and Mike are devastated that Nina has cast off an opportunity to conquer higher learning, but Nina knows deep in her heart she has to find another way.

No one in Nina's circle, including Malcolm, knows what to say regarding her future, because what good can she do without a degree? She believes them, so she simply applies to jobs she is confident she can make a significant impact in.

Nina doesn't know a thing about coffee when she accepts the position as a barista in a D.C. café, but she loves people, so why not? Whipping handles of espresso machine portafilters isn't exactly what she expected to be doing after dropping out of college, but she needs to make some cash while figuring out where the path to the rest of her life is hidden. Moving back home after spending part of the second semester on campus not attending classes is embarrassing enough, so she feels it inappropriate to keep accepting gifts of luxurious train rides and lobster dinners from Malcolm in the Big Apple on his company's dime, without being able to afford a latte she will soon learn to make for strangers.

    It isn't a bad gig. In addition to drugs and alcohol in the city, coffee is a stable commodity. Nina is offered the weekday shift of 11 a.m. to close, which is at 6 p.m. Most customers leave the business district by then to head home. It's 1994, and in the D.C. metropolitan area there is a distinction between where you work, live, and play. Many folks live in Maryland or Northern Virginia and cross over into one part of D.C. to work, and another not-so-acceptable part to play. Nina likes keeping all parts of her life in separate boxes, hoping to keep them safe.

    Mia, from Trinidad, is Nina's right-hand espresso slinger. She's high every shift and sometimes bangs the used coffee grounds out of the metal frame onto the counter instead of the designated trashcan. It's frustrating at times, a slowing of the flow, but there is no question that she makes the best cappuccino. Travis is the café manager, a four-foot-something Black man with a six-foot-high laugh and an even higher alcohol tolerance. Nina enjoys working for him because of his clear directions, mellow mannerisms, and exuberant joy for life. After only a few months, he pushes for her promotion to assistant manager and finds his way into her safe space. Though openly gay, he is just as vocal about loving her body. He compliments it consistently, and she is never offended.

    "Girl, you better wear that dress, with them long legs and figure-eight curves," he affirms, watching Nina resurface from his condo's bathroom. She transforms from her coffee-stained black jeans and oversized button-down to a formfitting anything, ready to find a little trouble, or submit and stay with him, to drink and listen to old Motown and new house music.

During the lonely weekends, Travis is a great distraction when Malcolm can't escape down I-95 to visit, or sometimes even call, because of his constant drowning in mergers and acquisitions. Travis' husband is a physician, and his hours are just as demanding. So, he is always willing to nurse his lonely heart with a fun empathic woman who understands doctor life. He keeps her at the register most shifts because of the way she manipulates her magnetic personality to capture the upsell or turn a grumpy customer's frown upside down, kneading their loyalty, frequently creating repeat café patrons.

Nina enjoys giving customers solutions to challenges they haven't discovered yet. "Ma'am, I can tell by that power suit you're rocking, you have some big things to conquer today. Well, this protein-packed egg and spinach wrap won't let you down. I'll heat it while Mia works on your tall cup of Joe, yeah?"

The grateful customer, in turn, will respond with something like: "Thank you so much. I didn't realize I was hungry until you said something."

Nina also never misses an opportunity to flirt without shame, especially when it's too easy. "Would you like a smile with that Americano, soldier? What happened—did you get lost getting to the base this morning, or could you not resist the aroma of what I got brewing over here?"

Boom! What was initially just a random trip to the closest café near an office building the marine had a meeting in, becomes his Wednesday Americano, sprinkled with a bit of Nina spice, even if she never dishes up the seven digits.

Nina has the pleasure of painting her charm on quite a few well-known personalities, including politicians, basketball players from the formerly known Washington Bullets, and the star actress from the '70s *Wonder Woman* TV show. But often, just regular friends, acquaintances, and even ex-something-or-others will come in and get a quick drip without knowing Nina works there—like Javier.

Javier is a clumsy, skinny El Salvadoran young man who took sophomore Nina to his junior prom. Their short-lived romance wasn't too dramatic or memorable, except for the fact that he would have done anything for her, and still would, if asked nicely.

"Welcome sir, what can I get for you today?" Nina asks in her methodically polite way.

Javier looks past Nina's face, squinting through thick, black-rimmed eyeglasses at the chalkboard menu. She takes one look at him and begins to smile, happy to see his familiar face after a long lunch rush. She could never forget that indecisive "ummm, lemme see, hmmm" pattern of speech.

"Javier?" Nina asks.

Immediately, Javier takes his eyes off the blurred chalk smudge, thrilled to hear his own name so softly. "Yes," he responds, almost like a question. Still doubting this woman is speaking like someone he knows.

"Javier, oh my god, silly. I can't believe you don't recognize me. It's me, Nina!" She almost yells through her whisper, as if she's someone else in line.

Javier's eyes balloon. "Oh shit, Nina! I didn't recognize you."

"My hair is different, and I'm all grown-up now. But damn, you haven't changed a bit."

"Well, let's please have a drink or dinner soon."

"Of course, hit me up!"

CHAPTER ELEVEN

It's been two years since Javier walked into Nina's coffee shop, so she is surprised when he actually hits her up. She feels no burning desire to catch up with him, but loneliness is a bit heavier than usual, and she isn't ready to carry it home yet.

He picks a neighborhood bar on the edge of Georgetown, where the pulse of loud conversation drowns out the sound of sticky soles on a warped wooden floor; just another dive where midlife-crisis businessmen lie to impressionable young hopefuls to feel indispensable. It's a Friday night after happy hour, but before the DJ pulls his records out to spin.

Nina can feel the heat of anticipation circling her, but she's still cold. She buttons up her blue jean jacket, foolishly thinking air won't creep in the gaps between the metal rounds to massage her sheer white tube top. At least she's wearing black leather pants and thick motorcycle boots to keep her base warm. She throws back the last swallow of cheap merlot from her plastic cup and cases the bar for anyone who could serve her something more aggressive. Her mind drifts to Malcolm, who has reneged on his trip to come south to see her again.

"Work has me on lockdown, Queen. I promise to make it up soon. I'll call you to check-in before the client dinner tonight," he had assured. It's 7 p.m. and no call, but Nina tells herself his insane hours will pay off.

Nina isn't sure if she is more annoyed that Javier is late to his own suggested meetup, or that a Little Orphan Annie look-a-like is invading her personal space, raining spit on her arm, drunkenly yelling across the bar, "I need another drink!"

A fat dollop of blow is nestled in the crease above Annie's upper lip. For a moment, Nina watches the white powder battle with the fire-engine-red lipstick smeared on her mouth for attention. Discreetly, she taps Annie's shoulder and motions to wipe under her nose.

"Oh my god, thank you! I'm such an idiot. It's my twenty-first birthday, so you know it's like, go hard or go home," Annie slurs, excusing her reckless behavior to a stranger who doesn't give a fuck.

"Oh wow, happy birthday," Nina says without an ounce of enthusiasm.

"How about a water break, birthday girl?" the bartender abruptly interrupts, strutting through the "Employees Only" door. She quickly drops a cup of tap water in front of Annie before the birthday girl has time to reject it. The bartender's eyes quickly shift to Nina. "What can I get you, beautiful?"

Blushing, Nina says, "Can I get a hit of Crown, neat, with a ginger back?"

With a smirk of surprise, the bartender responds, "Ok, double-o-eight, a shot of Crown Royal with a second cup of ginger ale coming right up." She playfully winks and turns around to prepare Nina's poison.

"Whatever. You understand what I want," Nina declares with confidence. The bartender has dark-olive skin, a dirty-blond Mohawk, tatted sleeves, and a slight lisp that softens her biker chick edges.

"You order a drink like a suit, or maybe like your old man boyfriend when you're at the country club or something. This is a shit college bar, sweetie."

Nina is impressed and a little embarrassed that she almost gets it right; Malcolm isn't a member of a country club.

"Hey girl, sorry I'm late," Javier exclaims, rushing to the bar and panting, awkwardly reaching out to hug Nina. "Work was torture today."

"It's ok," Nina says flatly, half-heartedly hugging back, feeling his bony frame press up against her curves. She is ready to go home, but needs him to pay for the drinks she can't afford.

"What ya drinking?" Javier asks, soliciting forgiveness and eager to get the party started.

"Hard shit," Nina warns, shooting the bartender a look, who's smirking again. Nina knows Javier to be a lightweight, constantly standing outside of the heavyweight ring, knowing he will never have the strength to separate the ropes to enter.

"Should I get what you're having, and go strong?" Javier dares.

Nina laughs, amused at his faux courage. "Can you get him a margarita?" she requests of the bartender.

"Sure thing, beautiful." This time the bartender oozes her words provocatively before shifting to Javier and tightening her tone. "You want salt on the rim, or no?"

"Uh, no salt, please," Javier confirms, eyes darting back and forth from Nina to the bartender and back again.

"What?" Nina responds defensively.

"I saw that," Javier whispers

"Saw what?" Nina asks, challenging Javier's audacity to go *there*.

"You and your dyke bartender flirting with each other," Javier mumbles.

"Shhh, shut up. What is wrong with you? You see those guns on her? Clearly, she can kick your ass, so be careful." Nina leans in, not realizing she is seducing Javier with her voluptuous mounds, warmly scented by Chanel No. 5. "Are you homophobic, Javier?"

Attempting to maintain composure, Javier says, "You're so combative, reina. I'm just kidding. I mean, hell, it's 1996. I'm down with my girl having a girl."

"'Your girl'?" Nina questions.

"I'm just speaking in general, sheesh." Nina watches Javier snatch the lime wedge from the rim of his glass and apologize to his neighbor after clumsily squirting juice in her face. He takes a swig of his pre-mixed margarita and coughs like the alcohol is potent enough to burn his throat.

Nina giggles. *What a clown.* Unexpectedly she is enjoying his company, as the dark liquor warms her chest.

"You remind me of Charlie," Javier blurts out after a long silence.

"Charlie?" Nina questions.

"Yeah, Charlie. You don't remember her?"

"No, I don't think so," Nina says, trying to remember the other girls he used to obsess over.

"You should lay off the weed, Nina. Charlie! Shortly after we met, I took both of you to a reggae concert at Wolf Trap. You both were like fifteen, and your mom interrogated me for an hour before letting you in my car. I picked you up first, and then Charlie. You wore some scrumptious white booty shorts and an 'I love Jamaica' t-shirt with Bob Marley smoking a joint on the back, but you didn't have it on right away. You brought it with you in a bag, so your mom wouldn't tell you to take it off before leaving." Javier is frantically spitting out the details, reliving each delightful scene of entertaining two hot girls.

"Oh, right. The disturbed girl you introduced me to as your friend. And when I say friend, I mean your friend that 'put out,'" Nina responds accusingly, rolling her eyes, and nodding yes to the bartender who silently asks if she wants another.

Javier roars. "Girl, you crazy! She was—I mean *is*—just a friend who lives in my neighborhood."

"Mhmmm," Nina says, enjoying making Javier uncomfortable. "Ok, but seriously, I remember her being withdrawn and sad, and she had fresh cut marks on her arms I think she did herself."

"Yeah, she had a tough time growing up," Javier says, looking down at the bar top, like he wishes he can still save her from past demons.

"So, she reminds you of me. Why?" Nina probes.

"Because you both are mysterious and secretly attracted to women," Javier whispers, not wanting the bartender to discover she has a chance with Nina.

"What?!" Nina looks at Javier directly in the eye for the first time all night and says, "You are ridiculous. I'm just charismatic, and ok, maybe a flirt … but I'm not gay. I have a long-term boyfriend, remember?"

"I didn't say you were gay, Nina. But there is something with you." Javier is tipsy and finds some bold language hiding in between his bones. Nina is flying high despite her feet resting in the groove of his barstool. He continues. "Come on, reina, I've seen it since I've known you. And I've seen it in Charlie. I mean, I think it's cool. Maybe she should just meetup with us tonight, and you two can talk about it. She can shed some light on the feelings you both share," Javier proposes with a devilish grin, not realizing pulps of lime are trapped in his braces.

"Mhmmm, I bet she can," Nina shoots back, completely aware that Javier's dick has just jumped in response to the thought of a dirty reunion.

The intro to "Murder She Wrote" begins blaring through the speakers. Nina jumps off her barstool. "This is my shit! Javi, did you request this?"

"No," he responds, wishing he had. Already grooving to the beat, going deep with the wind of her hips, Nina can't care less that she isn't on the dance floor. She takes off her jean jacket as Javier asks the bartender for another margarita, with salt this time. Nina suddenly feels a gust of darkness, remembering she hasn't heard from Malcolm and pulls out her phone again. No missed calls.

"What time is it?" Nina asks no one in particular.

"It's 9 p.m.," the bartender responds. "Why don't you go out there and stretch those legs," she says, coaxing Nina.

But Nina has lost her desire. Instead, she convinces Javier to just sit with her and sober up. They sit in silence, watching Annie vomit in the corner of the room. The faint smell of her guts and Malcolm's absence makes Nina nauseous. She orders a train of waters. After relentlessly sucking them down, she looks at Javier and says, "So, we gonna pick Charlie up or what?"

"Yeah?!" Javier yells, like a kid whose dad just bought him the latest monster truck.

"Jesus, calm down. It's just a drink. Nobody is talking about nuthin or doing nuthin."

Javier motions the zipping of his lips and then asks for the check. They're only charged for his drinks, so Nina leaves a tip that makes up for it.

"Are you really gonna tip her that much?" Javier whispers.

"Hospitality is a thankless job. She took care of me … us," Nina explains, slipping the damp napkin with the bartender's number into her clutches, before following Javier out of the bar and not looking back.

To Nina, Charlie looks like the same troubled teenage girl who bounced into Javier's car six years ago, except she's traded in her long dark-brown curls for a fire-red pixie cut. She is still petite, with a few added curves and the same wire-rimmed glasses that mask her wild spirit. She jumps in the back seat, but her vanilla-scented body spray makes its way to the front, sitting on the dashboard and fanning its sweetness up Nina's nostrils.

"Hi," Charlie mumbles.

"Hey," Nina responds, looking back, wondering now what she was thinking coming here with these two.

"Ok ladies! What's the plan?" asks Javier. "Do you want to hit a bar, or maybe a club to shake those booties? Or … should we just go back to my crib? I know I have enough shit to make some spiced Cuba Libres."

"Let's just go to your house," Charlie suggests with a certain clarity that makes Nina nervous. Javier shoots Nina a look with a cocky grin, but she ignores it and instead looks out of the window, debating on pulling out her phone one last time for the night.

Why bother, she thinks, exhausted from the wondering. She instead counts the number of questionable noises Javier's vintage Mercedes makes before getting to his destination.

Javier still lives with his mother in the basement of her townhouse, with no separate entrance. Therefore, they have to walk through the living room and kitchen to get down to his bachelor's lair. The house reminds Nina of Javier's car—once a trophy but now old and tired, groaning creaks with each step, wrinkled cracked designs on the walls, and an intrusive smell of rusted metal. His mother stands at the kitchen sink with her back turned, cleaning chicken parts, when all three of them walk in. She is wearing the same drab bathrobe and exuding the same hostile energy Nina distinctly remembers.

"¿Es la hora de las putas?" she jabs with a dark husky tone. Javier ignores the rhetorical question and leads his dream girls down the narrow basement stairs.

"I know what she said," Nina whispers in Javier's ear. His face flushes red; he has forgotten that she understands a little Spanish, and is embarrassed that his mother accused him of behavior he only dreams of participating in.

"Watch your step, ladies," Javier warns, regretting he didn't clean this morning. The entertainment room is so dark you can barely see the oversized picture of Jesus and his virgin mother Mary on the wall above the black leather couch. Nina and Charlie have to dodge a couple of ashtrays with half-smoked joints resting on their edges, several *Super Mario* video games, and an empty bottle of spiced rum that attempts to camouflage a few splats of blood on a large, handmade rug at the back of the room. The room is decorated with a medley of rosaries and delicate gold bowls filled with exotic herbs and infused oils.

"Your sister still comes home to perform voodoo on her baby daddy?" Nina asks Javier, smirking, allowing forgotten memories to surface. She plops down on one side of the black couch that smells like hot skin, and watches the quietly observant Charlie sit next to her, neglecting the rest of the hide on the other side.

"Shit yeah, sorry for the mess. I didn't know I would have company tonight."

"I don't think you answered Nina's question, Javi," Charlie teases, showing her bright white teeth for the first time all night. "Why don't you make us those Cuba Libres."

Javier follows direction, happy his mother has gone off to bed, so he can snatch more spiced rum from her liquor cabinet. While he is upstairs prepping cocktails, downstairs the silence is deafening.

"So, I hear you make the best cappuccino in town?" Charlie asks, attempting to soften the volume.

Nina turns to defend her barista status but can't find the words with Charlie's full, wide mouth so close to hers. "Yeah, I do. What about you? Javier said something about you being in school?" she probes nervously.

"I'm studying cartography," Charlie replies, moving her mouth a little closer.

"What's that, the study of maps? Is that a thing?"

"Are you a thing, Nina?"

Shit. What did this goofball tell her? And where are the fucking drinks? Nina panics, jumps up, and yells upstairs to Javier. "You ok up there? Need any help with those glasses?"

"Shhh!" he shoots back. "Nina, you gonna wake up my mom goddammit." Charlie and Nina bust out laughing in unison and the room brightens a little.

"Hey, how about you come back here. Don't be afraid," Charlie insists. Nina is more afraid of what she is feeling and her inability to resist the request. She returns to her exact spot on the couch and watches Charlie lean across her chest and gently rub from the bottom of her knee to the middle of her thigh. "Do you like that?" Charlie asks, with a voice dipped in sweet butter.

"Yes," Nina says without hesitation.

"Look at me," Charlie demands, smelling the yearning. Nina looks at her and can't remember her being this stunning. Charlie's mouth hovers over hers, sharing the same inhale and exhale, in the exact same rhythm. "Now close your eyes and open your mouth," she orders, with a little more weight she pulls from a place unknown.

It's dark again, but Nina can hear the ocean in the distance, the sound of waves coming in slow, but building speed with the smell of the sun's heat mixed with sea salt. She nose-dives and Charlie catches her with kisses far out in the deep.

"Oh shit! Do we even need this liquid courage, ladies?! Papi is here!" Javier is at the bottom of the stairs holding way too much confidence and three glasses of mood killers, as the ocean's dance settles. "Y'all got room for me?!" Without waiting for an answer, he puts the cocktails down on top of the TV and darts over to the couch. Charlie barely has to make room for his small hips, and he squeezes in between them.

At first, Nina is overwhelmed by her senses; it's difficult distinguishing lips and tongues. Her mouth feels wet and warm, lost in a realm of pleasurable chaos. However, Charlie is on a

DANCER IN THE BULLPEN

mission to navigate the storm, and quickly dominates foreplay. Javier doesn't seem offended; he happily watches the two beauties learn each other's bodies.

"I'm just gonna get my bedroom ready for us. Don't stop. You two are amazing," Javier announces, knowing they aren't listening. Nina pulls back a little from Charlie's embrace.

"Don't worry, angel, it will be fun," Charlie assures in between kisses. Nina is baffled at how someone so small can be so heavy with seductive confidence.

Javier is changing the sheets when Nina and Charlie enter the bedroom, which is more like a large closet. Nina takes the room in. The full-size bed is the star, next to a single tall dresser, which displays another Virgin Mary surrounded by white candles and a small army of drinking glasses, draped with yet more rosaries, each containing various quantities of water not intended for consumption. Above the dresser lives a prison window, too small and low to the ground to have purpose. Directly opposite the bed is a TV older than the ancient model in the entertainment room. Next to it is a brand-new camcorder sitting on a stand, and the room is illuminated by a single fluorescent purple light lying on the floor by the door.

A poor man's porn set, that's what this is, Nina thinks, but says nothing. Her desire for Charlie is unwavering and she wants more of her. Javier's fingers are shaking as he tucks the last piece of cotton under the mattress' edge. She suddenly feels bad for him and sits at the foot of the bed, close enough for his hands to reach her thighs. He hungrily grabs them, leaning her back with his chest, tasting the sweetness of her neck.

It's not that Nina considers Javier unattractive. He has nice, soft and round facial features with caramel-colored skin, dark-brown eyes, and a matching fade haircut. Besides his thick unibrow, his long broad nose and soft gentle hands are what's most memorable about him. His slim build makes him look taller than he is. Javier is like when Al B. first came onto the music scene, without his confidence and an extra twenty pounds. Nina is simply more attracted to Javier's humor and character than his sex appeal. But tonight, she will let him explore her if it results in her having the gem he's brought home as her prize.

Charlie stands in the middle of the room admiring Nina's sexiness, and then begins to undress, watching her and Javier. Nina returns the stare, captivated by every inch of her.

Fuck that, she's better than a Jet beauty. "Mmmph." Nina catches herself releasing the same expression she's witnessed for so long—a surprising inheritance. Charlie's petite frame easily carries the weight of her voluptuous curves. And with her glasses off, you can appreciate the battle for attention between her green eyes and short red hair. She has a delicate nose and sharp jawline, bringing a strong boldness to her feminine vibrancy. Pastel painted butterflies and long green vines are tattooed on her back, arms, and thighs, strategically forcing your eyes to dance all over her like a tourist at a new museum. She's a contemporary modeling agency's wet dream, if she just had more height.

Charlie slowly rolls down her blue jeans, and then turns around and removes her red blouse and matching bra, timing it perfectly so only a glimpse of the arch of her breasts catches Nina's eyes. "Such a tease," she mumbles.

"I'm sorry, you want more?" Javier whispers in Nina's ear. "Lift your ass up a little, let me get these pants off." She obliges but he struggles to peel the warm leather down from the top of her calves. "Why do girls wear painted-on shit anyway?"

he complains, acting as if he's forgotten Charlie is there until she gets on the bed with nothing on but a red thong, removing Nina's pants effortlessly.

Javier's embarrassment is muted by the sound of the ocean tides coming in close again. "Shit, you are beautiful," Nina swoons, as Charlie crawls on top of her and dives back into the deep end, deep kissing, biting, drinking the sweetened salt from every angled surface. Javier is doing his own exploring down under, tickling Nina's entrance to heaven, trying to keep in rhythm with Charlie's fluid dance. But his two left feet can't swim, so he retreats and turns the camera on.

"Wait no, Javi," Nina protests, as the red flashing light glares in her eye.

"Don't worry about that, angel, I got you," Charlie promises. Nina isn't sure what that means but doesn't care, as Charlie happily takes Javier's place and drowns herself in the eddy he can't reach. Charlie comes up for air, only to dare her new muse with new pleasures. They ride the currents all night until they collapse with exhaustion.

Morning is still dark, and the sheets Javier perfectly tucked in are disheveled and draped to the floor like a waterfall. Nina and Charlie's naked bodies are entangled like seaweed on a high rock after a monstrous hurricane. "We may need to scrub our coochies extra hard after pulling 'em off this bare mattress, Nina," Charlie jokingly warns.

"Yuck," Nina laughs, not wanting to ever move her body from the softness of Charlie's limbs. "Oh shit, where's Javier?" She jumps up and wraps the damp sheet around her body, waiting for Charlie to lazily get up and slowly walk to the entertainment room. There Javier is, lying on the couch with his pants down, limp dick in hand. "Fuck, this is terrible. What happened, Charlie?" she asks, knowing the answer.

"What happened was he was in the way," Charlie whispers, pulling Nina close, looking up to kiss her, not intimidated by her height or curves. Nina is putty in her hands.

"Should we wake him up?"

"Hell no."

They quietly call a cab, get dressed, and take the sex tape and two half-smoked joints. They also take a rosary, because why not? They may need it, walking out at 8 a.m. and not knowing where Javier's wicked mother is. The two almost make it until they take some time figuring out how to unlock the two extra bolts.

"You better not have stolen anything," Javier's mother warns as she watches them finally unlock the voodoo haven doors.

"No, we just stole his virginity," Charlie shoots back, pushing Nina out of the door laughing.

In the cab, Nina checks her phone and scrolls through the thirteen missed calls from Malcolm. "Damnit!" she screeches, annoyed that she feels guilty.

"Just tell him you were with a girlfriend, you will be ok," Charlie responds, holding Nina's hand and looking straight-ahead.

What's up with this girl? She doesn't seem phased by anything. It makes Nina a little suspicious, but mostly curious about what is underneath the armor. "So, Charlie ... is that your real name?"

"Yeah, it's real, what ya mean?"

"I mean is that the name you were born with?"

"Oh, no. My born name is Charlotte, but do I look like a Charlotte?" Charlie asks with a quiver in her tone.

"Charlotte is a delicate, sophisticated, deceptive, gorgeous name. So yes, I think you look like a Charlotte, so I hope it's ok that I call you that."

Charlotte scoots close to Nina, directly in sight of the rearview mirror view, and engulfs her with the little frame she carries, devouring Nina's face.

"Damn girl, stop," Nina demands, but not meaning it. "What are we going to do today?"

"I'm going to do what I wanted to do when we were fifteen."

"Oh yeah, what's that?" Nina asks, giggling like a schoolgirl, watching the taxi driver get uncomfortable.

"Simply be yours," Charlotte says. This is the first time Nina has ever heard someone focus on giving her their love instead of taking hers. They spend the next three days together with no distraction from the outside world, and she can't imagine ever leaving.

***

Whenever Nina is not home, she is with Charlotte. Sometimes they are at the latest art exhibit, or shopping for new shoes and dresses, or painting the town red, two coats thick. Friends with benefits is an understatement, but even though neither of them flaunts it until it's unavoidable, their connection is undeniable. Where one being ends, the other one starts. They can spend a full day at a coffee shop talking, or in bed with no words at all.

Charlotte lives at home with her parents, who used to have to push heavy furniture in front of the door to keep her from sneaking out. Now they're just happy she's still alive and learning something meaningful in college. She doesn't bring men home, but she brings Nina over often, not at all concerned that her parents know she is someone special.

"I feel like dancing tonight," Nina announces out of the blue.

"Haven't you danced enough for three lifetimes, hot thing?" Charlotte teases.

"There is no such thing as dancing too much," Nina shoots back with a smirk.

"Ok, let's do it."

After a quick shower together, they slip on matching black lingerie but choose different outer layers. Black stiletto heels in one hand and a clutch purse in the other, they both skip to Nina's car barefoot, heading to the corner liquor store to get a pre-party going. Cheap whiskey warms the back of their throats as they recline the car seats and let the sound of Method Man and Mary J. Blige's "You're All I Need to Get By" thump through the radio.

Nina and Charlotte walk into the swanky new club and all eyes are piercing their skin. Holding hands, they walk to the bar and order more poison. Nina compliments Charlotte. "You look good, beauty."

"Not as good as you," Charlotte says, returning the appreciation and nibbling Nina's ear, forgetting for a split second where they are.

A couple of delusional men approach the bar. "Heeey, ladies! Y'all save a few kisses for us?"

"Sorry, we only have enough kisses left for each other," Charlotte warns.

Nina can already sense Charlotte is getting agitated, so she redirects focus. "Come on, baby, help me find a platform to crawl up on."

Charlotte finds a high ledge for Nina. Nina caresses the metal pole in the middle like a lover who's just returned after a long journey. She sways back and forth until the DJ plays the right song for her to dig deep in. Everyone is watching, including the two delusional men from the bar.

Nina lets the music take over, seducing with her limbs like a snake charmer. Her red wrap dress waves behind her, revealing the muscles in her thighs and intricate lacing in her black panties. The lights are low, but she can still see glimpses of yearning. A celebrity slowly approaches the platform Nina is intoxicated by. His entourage is close, but they don't dare approach alongside their famous friend. Charlotte loves the attention Nina receives and steps closer to smell his desire. He accepts her company and whispers in her ear as they watch Nina's performance. Greed is all that is being served tonight, and everyone is famished.

"I don't know if I should pull out my wallet, or pull you down and cover you up," the celebrity says to Nina.

"Maybe you should do both," Nina coyly answers, as her pelvis winds down in her signature circular motion, not losing eye contact with her admirer. She immediately realizes who this man is—one of her favorite soulful R&B singers—but she doesn't let on.

After a sexy game of cat and mouse and too many bottles of bubbly popped, Nina and Charlotte are invited to come back to the hotel room for a night cap.

"You two can ride with me," the celebrity says.

"I'm not leaving my car here," Nina states flatly.

"Give me your keys. Boris will drive it over for you," the celebrity persists, head motioning toward a big Black man whose neck is as thick as one of Nina's thighs.

"He can fit in my car?" Nina questions. Charlotte leads the chorus of laughter.

"Yeah, he's a lot more flexible than you think. Ain't that right, Bo?" the celebrity reassures.

"Yep, I got you girl. Nobody gonna hurt your little 'vette," Boris promises.

Nina's car is special to her because it's the spitting image of Selah's old car. She found a deal on this refurbished model and considers it her baby. Charlotte gives a nod of approval.

"Ok," Nina says with a lack of certainty.

"Here angel, take this." Charlotte pulls a freshly wrapped joint from out of her cigarette box and passes it up to Nina in the front seat of the celebrity's rental. She helps herself to the lighter in the console, letting the fire feed off the white paper, before inhaling slowly. She cracks the window, flips down the sun visor, and captures Charlotte's stare through the mirror.

"Thank you, beauty," Nina says, smiling at her mischievous influence. She looks over at the celebrity, takes in a couple of more hits, then offers him a turn.

"Not yet, baby girl. Let's wait until we get to my room. They just dying to catch a nigga like me out here, ya understand?"

"Yeah, I do," Nina responds honestly, pulling out the ashtray.

DANCER IN THE BULLPEN

"No, you don't have to stop, it's ok. Or pass it to your girl," the celebrity suggests, taking a calculated risk, but not wanting to halt the energy.

"Nina, pass that thing back here," Charlotte whispers.

"Let's wait. I don't want you to burn yourself. I saw your eyes closing back there," Nina says. Charlotte doesn't fight her, leaning back and closing her eyes.

Nina leans her head back as well, beginning to feel the green paint her insides, massaging her shoulders and chest from within. She looks over at the celebrity, analyzing his dark-brown chiseled profile, noticing a small scar running along the bottom of his jawline. She can't recall seeing him with this scar during his music videos. *Then again, he did have a beard then.*

"What you looking at?" the celebrity asks with a smile, catching Nina in a trance.

"I'm just surprised you drive yourself around alone, would think you'd be in a limo or have a driver or something."

"I'm not alone."

"You know what I mean," Nina shoots back, kind of regretting she brought up his status.

"I'm not Michael Jackson, and I'm here a lot. I have a house a couple of hours away. People are used to seeing me around, I think. Plus, my boys are behind us, staying in the same hotel. You're safe."

"I'm not worried about me. I was just curious. It must get lonely is all, being around a lot of people."

The celebrity parks in the hotel lot instead of pulling up to the valet, turns off the engine, and turns to look at Nina with his beautiful brown eyes. "Why would you think I'm lonely if I'm around my people?"

"I dunno," Nina says. "I feel like when you're around a lot of people it's hard to really be close to all of them. When you have one or two friends, you have the time and energy to know them, really see them, and have them see you. They're not too busy fighting for your attention, ya know?"

Without warning, the celebrity leans in, grabs Nina's face, and deep-kisses her aggressively, like his life depends on it.

Charlotte wakes up. "Oh ok, we're starting the party already."

"You two hotties are the party," the celebrity says.

Nina sits in the uncomfortable hotel suite chair, long legs dangling from one side, with just her stilettos and black lace panties on, like she sees sexy women in the movies do. She's sipping Crown Royal naked with no ice, watching the celebrity make love to Charlotte with the force of a tornado. Her petite frame is hidden by his broad, toned shoulders, but Nina still sees the beauty of her eyes and her wide mouth agape with pleasure. Nina avoids distraction by not touching herself. She keeps her eyes on Charlotte to keep her hot for the celebrity, because she is aware that Charlotte entertains men mostly because of her. It turns Charlotte on to please her. Ironically, she prefers only Charlotte ... outside of Malcolm.

The celebrity puts Charlotte to sleep. He even gently tucks her in on one side of the king-size bed. "I'm going to clean up a bit," he whispers to Nina, before leaning down to kiss her on the forehead, like she's a young girl. Just like Malcolm does.

Nina can usually suppress how much she misses Malcolm, but she's beginning to forget how he smells. A cold gust of loneliness raises goosebumps on her arms. She hears the shower turn on and quietly crawls into the bed, gets under the covers, spoons Charlotte's warm naked frame (perfectly puzzled into hers), and falls fast asleep.

Nina is awakened by birds chirping outside the hotel window, but it's still dark outside. She sits up in the bed looking for her bra. She finds a white wifebeater that is clearly the celebrity's and puts it on. When she stands up to go pee, she hears a familiar voice in her ear.

Nina, are you ready to talk to me? Or do you need more time? asks Nina's invisible friend.

"Ready for what? I'm always here for you, but I haven't felt you since you let that island medicine woman Samara scare the shit outta me. I thought you left me for good this time," Nina complains. "Is my uncle there with you?"

"What?" the celebrity questions, suddenly appearing from the dark.

"Oh shit! Damn, you scared me!" Nina gasps, hoping the celebrity will let it go.

"Whose uncle? Am I your uncle? I've had women call me daddy before, but never uncle. That's a bit weird," the celebrity teases.

"Really?" Nina questions. She's amazed how guys are so quick to claim what is not theirs. She ignores the celebrity's interrogation, turning the desk lamp on, curious to see what he's been up to in the middle of the night all alone in the dark. Her mini notepad of random thoughts and poetry is open at page twenty-one.

He is a nomad traveling with a parade of memory, a herd of elephants. Looking for love in a faraway ocean of flesh and expectation. Deception is communal. They say I should yearn to be a groupie and he should want to leave me in the morning, but he dares me to stay, so we can be alone together, though it's too tight to love here.

"Hey, what the fuck?! This is mine. Private shit. You don't have a right to go through it," Nina aggressively states, furious more so because the celebrity has read her personal thoughts about him.

"So, that's what you were writing in the car earlier?" the celebrity asks. "I saw you pull that notepad out from your purse, scribbling something, looking at me, and then scribbling something again. I needed to know what you were saying. Sorry if you feel violated."

"I do," Nina says, not at all forgiving him.

"You have a beautiful mind, Nina. You share your work? Are you writing something—a book?"

"No," Nina snaps nervously. She looks at Charlotte, who has not stirred at all, wishing she would get up and demand to go home.

"Why not?" The celebrity probes. "What you afraid of? I looked through the rest of the forty-something pages, some really good stuff, poems, little anecdotes. You're good. You work at a coffee shop or something, right?" The celebrity walks over to the desk and grabs a joint. He lights it, walks back over to Nina, and sprawls out on the couch in front of her. "I think you're better than that coffee shop."

"You don't know me," Nina snaps again, thinking about the shame she carries for not making it through a state school when all her family are Ivy Leaguers.

The celebrity reaches and grabs Nina's hands to gently bring her close to him. "I don't know you, you're right. But I know you're in a hotel room with a girl you hide and a guy who you don't really want, sneaking around and writing poetry."

Nina begins to cry, plopping down on his lap. He holds her without a word for what seems like an hour, before softly asking, "Wanna write something with me?" He pushes her hair back away from her face. "It'll be fun."

"Ok," Nina submits, looking down at him, with her arms around his neck.

"I can tell you're special, Nina."

"Kiss me," Nina demands.

The celebrity obliges without a word. Long, deep kisses, devouring Nina's pain and insecurity, before moving her down to the five-star rug. They make love fast and write slow together. Though this encounter is meant to ignite the fire in her body, her creative energy is blazing high.

Fled my jungle
And found refuge in his thick forest.
The restlessness of pleasure's chorus
Hid patiently in the bedroom closet.
On the nightstand freshly picked aloe
Gripped the base of an iced whiskey glass
In case his bad behavior warranted swift healing.

He adapted to the absence of a smoked-out chimney
Lit the earth and I inhaled the secondhand smoke green.
My heat made sure he would never ever come clean
So I let the choir sing their high screams.
Nina

The silent alarm of the sun wakes Nina an hour before check-out, and she's right back in the bed, spooning Charlotte. She sits up and looks over the room, questioning if her love-making and lyric writing are all a dream. What's real is that all evidence of the celebrity is gone, except for Nina's car keys and a note written on an empty page of her notepad, still vulnerable on the desk.

> *She is a ballerina with broken toes wrapped tightly in pink satin, running leaps and bounds with no legs. Contradiction is confusing, like me leaving because I'm a coward when I want her to come save me and fly. They say I should be an honest man and stay to lie, be the nice guy, so she won't be alone together with her secrets, but it's too tight to love here.*
>
> *P.S. I will find you at your first book signing. Be brave, Nina.*

***

Work. Write. Charlotte. But in the opposite order. These are the elements dominant in Nina's life, even though Malcolm is still pushing to get up from under his highly demanding job, to become the priority again.

"I'm going to see you in a couple of weeks, Queen, and then stay for seven days or so."

"I know, but then once you leave, you won't be back for another month," replies Nina, reminding Malcolm of his business trip to London.

"Oh shit, right. You just got to hang in there for me."

"I'm trying, baby."

"Just trying?"

"No, I'm hanging in there, baby. You're right, it's going to be ok. We'll finally be together for the long run soon," Nina says, fighting to believe it, but more so to appease Malcolm.

Malcolm recognizes the sadness in Nina's tone. "Isn't your friend Charlotte keeping you company? I know you two go out a lot. Aren't you enjoying your time with her—a good distraction, right?"

Yes, she is. In fact, I could be in love with her, and I hope she loves me too. But she's a wild child who drinks a little too much (maybe like I do), and goes a little heavy on the drugs for my taste. Most importantly she hates you. But if I didn't have her here, I would go crazy.

"Nina, Queen. You hear me?" Malcolm snaps Nina out of her private rant.

"Yes, yes. Charlotte is a good friend, and she's been great." *And that is the truth.*

***

"Angel."

"Yeah?" Nina answers.

"You mean, 'yes,'" Charlotte teases, enjoying knowing almost everything about Nina's life and family, which makes her feel close to her friend.

"Ok Mother," Nina jokes.

"So, listen. I was thinking we do something a little different. Can you come pick me up?" Charlotte asks.

"Sure. What time tonight—seven?"

"No, how about like in an hour?"

"Oh ok, a day date. There's a festival in town?" It's rare that Charlotte randomly wants to do something in the day so last minute. The duo always keep their eyes glued to the weekend section of the newspaper, and plan in advance when they stop everything and spend the day doing something artistic.

"No, just come get me, and wear a sundress or something, you know, one of your girly looks."

"Um, ok, we having a summer wedding?" Nina teases.

Charlotte immediately shifts to a serious tone and calls Nina's bluff. "Shit, we can. I'd marry your gorgeous ass today, don't play with me."

"Shut up, girl. Ain't nobody letting two girls get married here. Well, at least anytime soon," Nina says, wondering if Charlotte is serious, or just talking bold because she knows they can't.

Charlotte drops the subject. "Ok angel. See ya soon."

Nina doesn't get a chance to respond before hearing the phone cut off. *What's going on with this girl?* Charlotte has her mind doing back flips. *She just talking. She wouldn't marry me if she could. She just trying to fuck me up.*

"You shouldn't do that," Jasmine warns. Nina jumps at the sound of her little sister's voice in her bedroom doorway, nervous her thoughts are heard. But she's only been caught chewing on her cellphone antenna, standing in front of her closet.

"I know, Jazzy, you're right. Your big sister needs to quit chewing on stuff," Nina admits, putting the new battered phone down to reach out and hug her. She can't believe how big Jasmine's gotten. Even though she sees her sister a lot now that she's back home, this is the first time in a while she's taken a really good look at her.

DANCER IN THE BULLPEN

"You good? Crushing sixth grade? Nobody being mean to you?" Nina tries to get all the reassuring answers she needs from her favorite little person before she starts her "different" day.

"Yes, I'm good," Jasmine says while looking through her big sister's closet, as if she's the one heading out. "Yeah, this! This is my favorite!" she announces with a big smile, placing it against her chest, modeling it in front of Nina's mirror.

"Oh, I forgot about that one. I love it!" Nina cosigns. Jasmine's favorite is long and sky blue, with mini yellow and white daisies all over it, and a plunging v-neckline held up by two spaghetti straps. Nina slips it on as Jasmine sees what else is in the closet she can explore.

Jasmine grabs a white cardigan. "Here, take this. In case you get cold, or one of your boobs pops out." She laughs loudly at her own comedy.

Nina grabs her little sister and starts tickling her. "Oh we got jokes, huh? Are you too old to be attacked by the tickle monster?"

"Mom, help me!" Jasmine begs playfully. Selah appears in Nina's bedroom doorway, enjoying the vision of her two baby girls.

"So sorry, Jazzy honey, your mama can't help you this time," Selah says, mirroring the same jovial energy. "What y'all doing, playin' dress up?"

"Oh no, Mom, I'm going out to a garden party." Nina learned a long time ago, the less mystery for her parents, the less questions for their daughter … sometimes.

"Oh that's nice. Malcolm is back in town?"

"No, I'm going with Charlotte."

349

"Oh, you've been hanging out with her a lot this last year or so. Did you meet her when you were in college for that short time?" Selah begins her interrogation with a sprinkle of disappointment, but Nina wants no part of it.

"Mom, I really can't talk right now. I gotta bounce," Nina says, kissing her on the cheek. She turns to Jasmine. "You can borrow anything in there, just bring it back, ok?"

"Ok, I will!" Jasmine promises, excited for full access, wishing she could fit into the grown-up dress her big sister is wearing right now.

Nina is waiting outside of Charlotte's house, watching her struggle to lock the front door while carrying a picnic basket, lawn blanket, and purse. She drops her keys, picks them up, and drops them again.

"Hey beauty!" Nina yells out the car window. "You sure you don't need any help?"

"Nah, I'm good, stay there, I got it!" Charlotte yells, laced with stubbornness.

Nina lets her be in control and manage whatever day this will be. She pulls the flask of whiskey from her purse, looking at Charlotte strut to the car in a simple maize babydoll dress and emerald-green gladiator sandals that accent her infamous eyes. She has swapped out her traditional smoky shadow and red lip for a bronze palette with a pale pink mouth.

Charlotte puts all the things in the back seat. She jumps in the front, snatching Nina's flask from her hand—the engraved one she gave Nina that reads: "Angel, sip slow. Let me fly with you."

"I'm thinking we actually go dry today," Charlotte announces, twisting the flask top back on tightly.

"Aw shit, really?" Nina is now incredibly curious, and a bit annoyed. She's never known this girl to say no to any type of toxin. *Why is today the day she lets go of her addictive ways and restricts my casual indulgence?*

"Yep, and no herb too," Charlotte says with certainty.

Nina starts laughing. "Wow ok, pretty lady. Whatever you want. This is *your* day." She can't help but stare. "By the way, you're looking really nice. Do you have a stylist on payroll? You look like a model. And where you get them laced-up sandals from, they're dope!"

"They're my mom's. I found them in her closet and had to borrow them, 'cause I knew you'd like them." Charlotte rests her feet on the dashboard, giving Nina an enticing first-row view of her creamy thighs.

"Charlotte, you're glowing like the sun in that yellow." Nina leans in. "You're so sexy. You sure you don't wanna go back in the house for just a few minutes to show me what's under that?" she asks in a seductive tone.

Charlotte drops her legs and sits up straight in the passenger seat, like she's ready for serious business. "No, we're going to be good, angel. Let's go!"

Nina is impressed by this girl's discipline and completely turned on by it.

Charlotte directs Nina to a perfect spot right by the Potomac River at Hains Point. It's a beautiful March day. Cherry blossoms aren't quite in bloom yet, but the grass is green. They lay out the large blanket and open up the picnic basket filled with meats, fruits, cheeses, a French baguette, and Grandma Daisy-style tea sandwiches. There are also chocolate truffles perfectly wrapped, which are Nina's favorite. The only beverages to choose from are sparkling water with lime and sweet iced tea.

"Dang girl, this is like a movie. How you know about all these fancy cheeses? Oh wait, your dad is European, duh." Nina is a bit nervous, mostly because this is the most romantic thing anyone has done for her. "I don't know if we're allowed to have food out here like this without a permit or sumthin," she warns, having a difficult time hiding her anxiety.

"Do you think I care about that? Stop worrying about shit for no reason yet," Charlotte demands with her usual confidence. "Just relax, angel, and let me prepare your fancy snack on this here fancy Dixie plate," she says in her best royal British voice.

Nina giggles. "Please do, my lady."

The two lovebirds take their time enjoying the homemade charcuterie board, and what Nina considers to be a million dollar view of the water. The peaceful scene has brought her guard down. She contemplates telling Charlotte about her blood magic. *She of all people will accept me and not tell anyone. Maybe she will even understand. Do I really want to risk that today though? She's made this so amazing.*

"Hey daydreamer! Where'd you go?"

"Sorry, I'm right here," Nina responds, placing her hand on the creamy thigh she's craving.

"I know you got a journal with you, like Linus always has that damn blue blanket."

Nina chuckles, and pulls out her latest journal from her oversized purse.

"I knew it!" Charlotte exclaims. "Read something about me. I know you got something in there. Well, you better."

Nina hasn't written a lot about Charlotte since feeling secure in their special friendship. She's been too busy living the poetry in real time. "I think I have something from awhile back," she says.

Nina flips a few pages back from the end and reads it out loud to Charlotte:

> *Seasons battle outside my window*
> *But I'm afraid to intervene*
>
> *I watch her dance and*
> *make me breakfast I no longer eat*
>
> *And wonder*
>
> *Will she leave me with the green*
> *Or copper leaves*
>
> *Nina*

"Shit, that's fucking beautiful!" Charlotte's warmth for Nina is bursting out of her seams. After talking for hours, the girls lay down on their sides facing each other.

Nina gently brushes a strand of hair out of Charlotte's face and says, "Your hair is growing out. You gonna let it get long?"

"I dunno. Should I? Would you like it if I had long hair?" Charlotte asks softly.

"You could look like Mr. T or Mr. Clean for all I care, and still be perfect."

Charlotte scoots her body closer to Nina. "I got us out here like this 'cause I wanted you to see we still feel each other even when we not drunk or high. I hope you know I can be soft like you too, if that's what you want," she says, bravely opening up.

"I see that. I see all of you now. This day with you makes me happy. You make me feel special, not weird or crazy, or not good enough. Just another reason why I ... I mean, it just makes me ..."

"Love me?" Charlotte finishes what Nina can't seem to say.

"Yeah, love you." Nina exhales, lying in a sense of relief for telling the truth. "I'm sorry things are so complicated. Listen, I actually want to tell you something," she says, not sure if she's about to explain why she can't leave Malcolm, or how most times when afraid she makes people bleed.

But Charlotte wants no part of any negative energy right now. "Shhh, let's talk about him and whatever else another day."

Nina submits and keeps quiet. They hold each other and kiss deep without a care in the world, oblivious to anyone watching.

"Now take me home, and stay with me tonight. I don't care what your poem says, I am not leaving you for any season or reason," Charlotte promises.

✳✳✳

Nina is at Charlotte's house in the kitchen, on her mother's phone talking to Malcolm, and no one seems to care. She hurries to get off before the breakfast Charlotte's mother has made gets cold. It's been a couple of weeks since the picnic on the Point, and Nina has barely been in her own bed since. If she were asked to start paying some of the mortgage, it wouldn't be an odd request.

"Let's go to the piercing shop," Charlotte says, as she takes the last bite of her pancakes.

"What?" Nina asks, to make sure she's hearing correctly.

"I'm going to get a tongue ring."

"Oh wow. That sounds crazy as shit. But great, I'll watch."

"You should do more than just watch," Charlotte says, as she gently strokes Nina's arm in front of her mother.

"Hey," Nina warns with a whisper.

"Whatever," Charlotte responds. "I am who I am and I'm a girl who loves me some you."

Nina waits for the anxiety and fear to surface, but it's nowhere to be found. Still, she knows she can't say it back again, or she'll be accountable for her part in this relationship.

Charlotte sees Nina's wheels turning and ignores her mental battle. "Let's get ready. I have to make a stop first."

"Ok cool, where?" Nina asks, hoping it's nowhere shady.

"Just to visit my friend in the hospital. He's recovering from surgery and I need to bring him some magazines and sweets."

"Unless you're his sister, I don't think they gonna let you up in there."

"Girl, you don't know me! I can sneak in any hospital. I've been peoples' wife, kid, sister … hell, even impersonated a brother once."

Nina laughs out loud, "You're crazy, girl."

"Ok, let's go do that and then get them tongue rings."

"Ok, fine," Nina submits.

The dynamic duo leave the piercing shop laughing at how swollen their tongues are. They have been warned not to drink alcohol until the swelling goes down, but Charlotte is itching to party and celebrate their new jewelry. Evidently, the special day of sobriety has come and gone.

"Let's just go for a couple of hours, angel, please," Charlotte whines. "We don't have to drink. We'll just hit a joint in the car before we surface."

But all Nina wants to do is drink. Her craving for any type of liquor has intensified. She is also tired and needs to beautify herself for Malcolm early tomorrow, and she knows it will be awhile before she sees Charlotte again. "Ok, but not too long. I'm rolling super casual and not wearing anything sexy underneath. We not taking no bitches home."

"Ok, ok," Charlotte promises, kissing Nina all over her face like a new puppy.

Nina hates going to Charlotte's college frat parties, which used to also be her college frat parties. The only difference is she gravitated toward the Black community during her brief stay there, unlike Charlotte who embraces her white peers. Yet Charlotte clings to her Black community outside of school—from the businesses she patronizes, to the clubs, men, women, and friends. Maybe it's Charlotte's way of playing out her mixed race—honoring both her white and Black culture—or maybe it's something else. Nina doesn't mind the whiteness, though she doesn't work hard to impress any of them, as she is sure they don't give a shit about impressing her, unless they want something. She believes it's just dangerous to be in an environment where Black is minimal. If something goes down, color stands out.

It's the usual scene. Big frat house with multiple small rooms, each designated with a specific poison. Alcohol. Pussy. Weed. Mushrooms. Nina and Charlotte are already buzzing from the green in the car and don't need anything else, but Charlotte is restless.

"Angel, want a shroom?"

"Nah, I'm good. You be easy though, ok?"

"Ok, just one," Charlotte says, as she prances over into the corner with three girls who look like they need no more.

Nina steps out of the room, heavily craving a drink, but instead asks one of the frat boys for a cigarette. She takes a drag and immediately puts it out, remembering her swollen tongue. She strolls past the various rooms, seeing all of what she expected, except for one packed room in the back-right corner. Her curiosity leads her into the room, and she's greeted by a medley of white lines on glass. Nina has only seen a room like this in the movies, and it makes her have to pee. She turns to leave to go find Charlotte, but there's no need. She's right there at the door.

"Oh, you found the powder room," Charlotte says. "I'm gonna do a line."

"No Charlotte. The shrooms were enough. Coke is too much," Nina warns, as her calves immediately cramp up and her body temperature peaks.

"It's just one line, Nina," Charlotte dismisses, as she leans down to take the hit. Nina focuses her eyes on the preppy boy providing the poison. "Are you sure you don't want to try this with me?" Charlotte asks, looking back up at Nina, who does not take her eyes off the prep. He chases his line hit with puffs of weed.

"No. I think of Len Bias, or the risk of me liking it too much. I'm pretty sure I have an addictive personality," Nina rationalizes, feeling her magic rise.

Charlotte takes a line, rises up from the glass plate, and sniffs and wipes her red nose. "Yeah, clearly you're addicted. You can't seem to stay away from me," she snaps, letting the medley of drugs she's taken run her mouth.

"Enjoy, Charlotte. I'm leaving in ten minutes," Nina says, as she walks over to Prep Boy and leans in close to his ear. "Don't you think this table is a bit heavy? Maybe ease up on the amount of lines you got going."

"What? I can't hear you," Prep Boy says. Nina repeats herself. "My bad, sweet thing, I still can't hear you. Maybe you should just do a line and chill the fuck out," he suggests in a hostile tone.

Nina steps back and simply says, "Ok." She walks past Charlotte doing a second line and says nothing to her. At the powder room door, she turns around and looks back at Prep Boy who has a finger in his right ear, and then his left, like he's trying to figure out what is invading his ear canal. She smiles as she walks outside to cool her body. *Do you hear me now?*

Nina wants to get in her car and speed away, but she's worried Charlotte will never make it out without her. Her invisible friend is leaning up against her car. *Hi Nina, are you ok?*

"Not really," Nina responds, and walks over to the passenger side to get her flask from the glove compartment.

Do you really need that? I think what's in that is why you aren't seeing me so much lately.

"What does me drinking here and there have to do with you being allowed by God, or the stars, or my uncle to see me?" Nina questions, with tears welling up in her eyes.

I am here when you believe in me, and that's when you see me more clearly. The things you use to make you numb, make me distant. You are hard on Charlotte, maybe because you two are more alike than you want to admit?

"STOP!" Nina screams, throwing her flask on the ground, and stomping back into the frat house. She walks by fragments of commotion around a closed bathroom door.

"Someone should call a doctor!"

"Are you kidding me? With all this shit we have in here? Someone needs to drive him to the hospital and just drop him off."

"I can't drive, can you drive?"

"Looks like some alien shit. Whose ears bleed like that?"

Nina doesn't miss a beat, and goes directly to the powder room to find her trouble. Charlotte is setting up to hit another line.

"No!" Nina yells from the doorway. "Please Charlotte, come with me," she pleads.

Charlotte looks up at Nina and sees that she's serious, and that she's scared. Charlotte puts the straw down and slurs, "Thanks party friends, but mama says it's time to come home." She stumbles behind Nina and gets into the car without a word, so Nina also responds with nothing, but eventually she needs to speak to get information.

"It's 2 a.m., should we not go back to your house?" Nina asks. "I don't want to wake your parents."

"Well, we can't go to yours, or your mother will find out that you're a sometimes lesbian," Charlotte says with a malicious tone.

"What's going on with you? You're being impulsive and dangerous. And if you had cut your hair back down to when I met you again, you'd have been Scarface in there. All you would need is a fucking machine gun," Nina digs.

"I'm sorry, Nina. That was too much, I know."

Nina pulls up to Charlotte's house with every intention of making sure she gets in safely and then driving right off, but she's struggling to leave her.

"I just think I'm anxious about Malcolm coming back to visit and then later staying for good. I mean, you and I have gotten really close lately, you know?" Charlotte's voice sounds like her mouth is full of cotton. She smells like stale cigarettes and her eyes are glossed over, but she's still the most beautiful woman Nina has ever wanted. "I know we said we wouldn't do this, but I guess I'm only human," she admits.

Nina reaches for Charlotte's hand and says, "I feel the same. I hope you know you're amazing, Charlotte. I've never known someone who got their GED and then worked their way into tackling a double major at a great school, all while paying their way, making time to play bingo with old people, and taking such gorgeous photos with that good eye of yours. Plus, your pussy is like golden, so … you know, there's also that." She laughs.

Charlotte doesn't take compliments well. So, she simply kisses Nina goodbye and runs to the door. Nina waits for her to get all the way in before she begins to drive off. But she reappears right away and waves Nina into the house.

"Shit, shit." Nina says, as she puts the car in park and turns off the engine.

"Charlotte, baby, wake up. I gotta go. You seen my car keys?"

"Why, what's wrong?" Charlotte asks, with her eyes still closed.

"I told you last night I needed to leave early. Malcolm is taking the train down to look at apartments with me."

"Oh right. You sure you still want to do that?"

"Don't do that, Charlie."

"Oh, now I'm Charlie!"

"I know this is hard for you, but Malcolm is moving in a few months. And one day, you know, we *are* going to get married."

"Calm down, angel. Don't get excited. I'm just fucking with you. I know my place." But they both know she doesn't. Charlotte is devastated. She retreats and hands over Nina's keys from under the bed. "I'm just saying, living with a romantic partner is a lot. But I'm sure you will be ok, and we'll still be friends. Everything will work out," she assures.

"Thank you," Nina says, kissing her secret lover on the forehead, feeling like she wants to pee and vomit at the same time.

"Call me when he's gone ... again," Charlotte yells, as Nina walks out the front door. But they both have a feeling they may never see each other again.

CHANA SHINEGBA

CHAPTER TWELVE

"Do you love this, Queen?" Malcolm asks.

"Yes, it's perfect," Nina responds.

"Finally!" Malcolm shouts, lifting Nina up off her feet and twirling her around in the air.

Nina and Malcolm find the perfect apartment on the second look, and he signs the lease shortly thereafter, even though it will be several months before he is back in town for good. He has the money to start renting early, and to slowly furnish it with everything they desire.

"You know, you can move in on your own before me. Get used to the space, begin to slowly decorate how you like it. How does that sound?" Malcolm asks. Nina circles the perimeter of the living room slowly, as if she's taunting a bull in the middle, but nothing is there. "Nina?"

Nina resurfaces from her thoughts, stops, and looks at Malcolm. "Yeah I dunno, baby. I think I'd rather wait for you. I know my mom's house is active to say the least, but I'm gonna miss them when I move out, and I'd rather be with them than be in this new apartment all alone, wishing I had them to keep me company until you come."

"I don't really get how you wouldn't jump at the chance for your own space, but whatever you want," Malcolm says with some hesitation.

"It will be fine. I can bring Jasmine along to slowly get the little things that will bring this space to life!" Nina does her best to financially contribute to their future, but her and Malcolm both know the barista pay can only afford but so much. "Now, all I have to do is tell my mom and dad," she says, opening her eyes wide in mock fear that is actually real.

"I think it will be ok. You're grown now, and we've been together for almost seven years. Everyone loves you, everyone loves me. We are perfect."

But it's not ok. Mike believes Nina and Malcolm are walking into a life of sin; unmarried cohabitation is unacceptable. "I don't understand why you can't just get married? Y'all love each other, right? Princess, don't let him have the milk without buying the cow."

Nina is happy that she's talking to her father over the phone, so he can't see her mortified facial expression. "I don't think that's exactly the saying, Dad," she reacts, trying to hold back laughter.

Nina's father has followed Dionne's lead and now embraces a life in the Baptist faith. He's even going to theology school to one day be a minister. Therefore, Nina accepts the fact she won't be sharing most details of her lifestyle. She complains about his religious focus sometimes, but in reality, she loves that he is passionate about all things religion, philosophy, and spirit. They have something strong in common now, even though she hasn't seen God in a long time. She's a bit envious that the man who was once so easily distracted is incredibly disciplined and sure of himself.

"Nina, I love you. I just feel you do things the hard way a lot of the time. This is the hard way. Trust your papi, I know a thing or two."

Nina recognizes that Mike's found his purpose, and it's beautiful to finally see it, even though it battles with the discovery of her own. "I know, and I hear you, Daddy. But this is a good thing for me, and once you get to know him better, I know you will love him. We will get married soon, I promise."

Nina knows Mike is thrilled that Malcolm is of a high-class caliber, prime-grade respectful man, but she thinks Mike would rather hear news of a pregnancy that warrants a gunshot wedding. Doing "the right thing" matters most when the accepted result is the traditional one.

"Cha," is the sound Grandpa used to make, and the only response Mike can muster. But at least it's better than nothing.

Selah is in denial. Nina talked to her months ago about a ballpark move-out date, but when the moving truck comes three months later, she is shocked, distraught, and reacts as if Nina is uncommunicative and impulsive.

"Mom, you've known about this for a while. Why are you being so combative now? I thought you liked Malcolm."

"I don't remember you telling me this was happening so soon. You're barely an adult. I don't think it's smart to move in with him, when you haven't had enough time to explore life without him."

"Haven't had time to explore life without him"? I've explored plenty of life without him and it's been quite exhausting and confusing. Take me back to the ballet when it was just you and me, and let's start over.

"David, help me out here," Selah pleads. Nina's stepfather is sitting on the couch by the door. She can't tell if he's there to defend her, or to just be a passive witness.

"We hate to see you go, Nina. Have you thought this through? Maybe take a little more time," David responds, walking on the safe balance beam; one that's low to the ground, so if you fall off it's not gonna hurt, but damn sure won't impress anyone if you stay on.

Nina is hurt, but mostly angry. She's angry that she feels guilty, and actually thinks about not disappointing her mother again. But no one stopped Nina from loving this man for all these years. So now, at twenty-two years old, when it's time to move forward with her king, there's an air of delay and cautiousness.

Too late to warn me now, Nina thinks as she kisses Selah on the cheek and hugs David without a word. She has already said goodbye to Jasmine and her two baby cousins—who are now staying at the house. But she looks back at them anyway with tears in her eyes. "Be a good girl, Jazzy," she instructs, and then reneges. "Just be you, Jazzy. I love you. I love all of you guys."

Nina grabs her childhood night lamp and walks out the door.

✳✳✳

Malcolm is right. Everything is perfect. Nina is micro-focused on him, once again distancing herself from all distraction. Most especially Charlotte, who she has only spoken to a couple times, pretending they will one day catch up and have a drink, as if that wouldn't be excruciating for them. It's 1998, a year since Nina and Malcolm began sharing the same space every single day. They are in a new rhythm. After a few years slinging coffee drinks, she is recommended by her boss Travis to move upstairs to the corporate office, as the receptionist.

"Girl, you need to get better compensated for them bomb people-skills you spoil our clients with," Travis says, after writing a letter to corporate explaining that Nina is overqualified for managing the cash register and espresso machine. They agree, promoting her again to salesperson before her hand gets warm answering the phones.

Malcolm leaves Wall Street, because the insane hours and overwhelming demands have taken their toll on the Suma Cum Laude overachiever. His excuse is that his brother, Alex, is going through some health challenges, and he has to be there for him—family first, of course. But Alex is safely back in New York while Malcolm has alternate entrepreneur plans that involve real estate. However, in the meantime he needs cash, and a local friend shares with him that bartending is the way to go.

"Hey Queen, I'm thinking of going to this bartending school. Once I get certified, it will be easier for me to land a good gig. You want to do it with me?" Malcolm is on the living room couch of their small yet swanky apartment, flipping through brochures he picked up recently. "I know you have a job already, but it could be fun, and you can even make it your side hustle if you like it."

"You think I'll be any good?" Nina questions.

"Of course! You used to be the best at slinging coffee. It's not that much harder. Besides, you know how to pull water from a dried-up well. You will be great."

"Ok, I'm down," Nina agrees, and moves onto Malcolm's lap with her arms around him. "Thanks for taking care of me, King," she swoons. There isn't much he suggests that she doesn't do, so this is no different.

Nina and Malcolm pass bartending school with flying colors. She immediately gets private party jobs. When potential clients call the school, asking for a pretty female bartender, her phone rings. Grad school, bachelor, and even bachelorette parties are big money. But the gigs that she finds the most lucrative are those hosted by rich old white people—backyard garden parties and business dinners with cigars and spirits.

"They tip me with a check, Malcolm, it's crazy!" Nina gleams. "Mrs. Monroe gave me a two-hundred dollar check just for simple highballs for a couple of hours."

"Good job, Queen. Save it for something special."

Malcolm starts slow but ends up having great success too. He begins working at a hotel, making crap dollars, but then gets lucky with a local dive that brings in big business and high tips to match. The downfall is his schedule slowly develops into hours similar to Wall Street. Every night but Monday and Wednesday, Malcolm is grinding at the bar from 9 p.m. to 3 a.m., sometimes starting earlier and other times ending later. When he's not working, he's sleeping, which is prime Nina time.

"I know it's a lot, Nina, but don't worry. This is short-term, a year tops, just for me to get my dollars up to start these businesses that will have us in a big house in no time." Malcolm is in the kitchen, hovering behind Nina as she attempts her hand at a paella recipe Travis shared with her. "Mmm, this looks good, Queen. Let me taste."

Nina playfully slaps Malcolm's hand. "Ok, we'll make it work," she says, suspecting the only difference between his job in New York and this hustle now in D.C. is that he gets to sleep in the same bed as her, and he's never "on call." His boss is flexible with the time off, so they get to enjoy some wonderful long weekend trips to Philly and down south in Florida, and have some incredible midweek date nights when the restaurants aren't so packed.

Malcolm's mother has been trying to extend some kindness to Nina by also sharing a few recipes Malcolm calls his favorites. "Follow the instructions as best you can. It's hard for me to tell you how much of what seasoning to put. My ancestors guide me. You may have to fail a couple of times before you get it right. Malcolm will tell you if it's good or not," Mrs. Thomas says with her usual regal tone. But Nina masters it, even exploring additional dishes he is accustomed to and loves. She begins to love the culinary arts and finds herself in the kitchen most days when he is sleeping.

***

"Actually, it's been seven years, girl," Lisa says.

"I can't believe that's how long it's been since we've seen each other. Are you sure? That can't be," Nina questions in disbelief.

"Yes, seven years," Lisa confirms. "That's how long you've been dating Malcolm, even though you've only lived together for one."

"I ran into your mother the other day, who was chillin' with mine, and she mentioned not seeing you so much since you moved out of her house—a bit sad you don't really come by the house or call and check in."

"I know, I really should check in with her, little Jasmine, and those other two rambunctious cousins she's collected in the house," Nina says, missing the chaos she ran from. "I will call them."

"But you're good though, right, Nina?" Lisa asks, with genuine concern in her voice.

"I'm good, girl! Everything is perfect," Nina lies, strangling her fingers with the kitchen phone telephone cord. "Malcolm and I get along so well. We never argue and he's fine and so sweet. I've also been learning so much from him. I know how to cook, smoke a cigar, play golf, and I'm even starting to take martial arts lessons."

"Oh ok, that's good. Wow, that's a lot. But what do *you* like to do?" Lisa probes.

"What do you mean?"

"What are the interests you are exploring? Your interests. Not his."

"Oh," Nina responds simply, trying to find the best answer. But it's lost.

"Nina. What's up with your writing? Your drawing? Do you dance anymore, even just for fun?"

"How do you know about my drawing?" Nina asks, unable to deal with the loss of her dancing.

"I find out things," Lisa says with a smile in her voice.

"I only dance around in the living room these days … and I don't even do that too much. And writing? Well, I haven't been, to be honest," Nina admits, with a heavy regret she's been avoiding. She redirects. "What about you, Lisa? The last time I spoke to Mom, I remember hearing her mention that you've elevated your unique talent—writing, teaching, and even producing shows. Is that right?"

"Yes Nina, it's all been so amazing!" Lisa's exuberant energy pierces Nina's ear. "I've been performing and producing shows and poetry slams. And I'm super proud of creating and running professional writing programs for kids."

"Shit, girl, that's fucking incredible!" Nina yells, sincerely proud and happy for her favorite oldest friend. "I knew you would get to this place," she affirms softly. "It's so funny, you are to kids now what Ms. Sullivan was to me—facilitating cool poetry workshops."

"Sarah Sullivan?"

"Yes, do you know her?" Nina asks, feeling creative energy rumble in her belly.

"Not personally, but I've been in the same space as her, and we definitely run in the same circles," Lisa confirms. "You want me to see if I can connect you two?"

"Oh nah. I mean, I'm good for now. I have her card somewhere. Maybe you know, when I have more time to dedicate to writing, we'll see."

Lisa doesn't push, as she knows Nina needs to be ready to fly. Pushing her too hard will just force a nosedive. "Listen, I'm not going to hold you to taking the time to see me. But what I ask of you is to find yourself, please," she pleads with love.

Nina feels the rivers in her eyes swell, but she's been learning to keep them back. "I will, Lisa. I promise."

Nina attempts to make good on that promise. She pulls out all the journals she has collected for so many years, so she can keep them in her sight. She buys twenty more composition books to motivate her to begin writing again with a fury, not just randomly here and there. She knows this will help her loneliness.

Most mornings, Nina writes a poem, a thought, a memory. And when she returns to the apartment at night, she returns to her journal, like a long-distance lover reunited with her soulmate. These are the times she breathes freely and forgets her fears, even if short-lived.

***

Malcolm's temporary "quick cash" hustle has turned into three years. The bar is understaffed, and he's covering extra shifts on Wednesdays. Nina has to visit the bar just to see her boyfriend, because that's where he is most nights (and now days). Everyone knows and loves her there, as all of Malcolm's coworkers and friends adore her. But it's all taking a toll on her heart, and her liver.

"Hey, are you drunk?" Malcolm asks.

Nina comes in the bar right before closing, barely able to walk up to the stool. "Yes, I am," she admits, wearing a micro-mini black tube dress with emerald-green gladiator sandals.

"How did you get here?" Malcom asks for two reasons. First, it's life-threatening for Nina to be behind the wheel in this condition. And secondly, he owns the car she drives, so he is liable. He is nice enough to let her use his Accord after her beautiful Corvette died recently.

"A friend you don't know, baby, don't worry," Nina says, incorporating Malcolm's favorite motto. *Don't worry.*

"Ok, well drink some water. I'll be closing up soon," Malcolm directs with a twinge of agitation.

Malcolm has noticed that lately, Nina is a bit restless and inconsistent with her normal routine. She's not cooking, working out with him, or even awake sometimes during the specific hours he's available to spend with her. All he sees is her in some journal, or not at all when she is supposed to be around. He figures it's the stress of her fast climb up the corporate ladder. Nina has gone from salesperson to a key executive team member in record time, and she loves her new challenge, ironically experiencing no stress with her profession. No matter how much she drinks and parties, she is always on point at work, not a minute late or a task missed. Malcolm's assumption is misplaced but understandable, since he is so disconnected from his girlfriend.

Malcolm practically has to carry Nina out of the bar once he finishes closing. He's embarrassed and fatigued. They go home and he helps her reach the bathroom to pee. After he showers and discovers her passed out on the bathroom floor with vomit everywhere, he knows he must confront her once she awakens from her blackout.

"Nina, I'm worried about you. You seem to be drinking and partying a lot with people I don't know. You colored your hair bright red after I told you to just do that thing you call a rinse, and you don't care and seem withdrawn when I'm home, or you're tired. Is everything alright?"

Nina stares at Malcolm, sitting on the edge of the bed with just his briefs on. She's sitting cross-legged on the floor, because the thought of standing up makes her want to run to the bathroom. She remembers a time when he was enough, simply looking like this, long before she had to contemplate a confession. The truth is on the tip of her tongue. The weight of her lies is feeding from her inside, but she's too afraid to recognize the bottom is near.

"Baby, I'm sorry. Your long work hours are a lot. They're terrible actually, and I miss my family," Nina says. "But look at me." She has moved on her knees in front of Malcolm, holding the sides of his face. "I will be fine. I just need to set a limit on myself when it comes to the drinking, I know that. This tough time is temporary. I will hang in better."

"Queen." Malcolm inhales and exhales slowly, as if he's fighting the oxygen in the room. "You just have to talk to me. And also, go see your family if you need to. You know I'm not stopping you."

"Ok," Nina says. *But how am I supposed to talk when I'm so confused; how am I supposed to see my family when I'm so ashamed of where I am in my life? I should feel grateful. This is what I wanted.*

Malcolm senses Nina's sadness and he doesn't know what to do, other than kiss her like it's the first time. And though she has a throbbing headache and so much is left unsaid, she makes love with her king for the first time in months.

✳✳✳

Cat looks exactly the same, except her muscles are a bit more chiseled than when in high school. The fact Nina can see their definition through her winter-white pantsuit is impressive. In classic Cat style, she teases with a clingy white lace camisole.

"Jesus girl, are you weightlifting now, or what? I can bounce a quarter off your ass and thighs," Nina teases, but means it. "Wait, are those real?" She grabs Cat's breasts and gives them a little squeeze. She could care less that passersby are staring. The reunited friends are standing outside Nina's favorite Brazilian café, nestled in D.C.'s infamous Adams Morgan neighborhood.

"Girl, shut the hell up and come here!" Cat demands, grabbing Nina like a ragdoll and holding her so tight, that breathing is not an option.

Cat loves the change in Nina, how bold she is in her adult life, and thinks nothing of the breast fondling. And Nina loves Cat for not thinking anything of it. They haven't seen each other since high school graduation, but they caught up over the phone a couple of years ago when Nina and Malcolm had been in the apartment for a year.

There's no outside seating because winter is definitely singing her song. The young women find a perfect spot indoors at a back-corner table, giddy about catching up.

"Cat, tell me! How's life as a concert promoter? I'm so proud of you, even though you stay so busy with your traveling high-life self, I can barely catch you to tell you. That industry is totally you. Do you love it?"

"Yes I was born to boss these entertainer and venue bitches around," Cat gleams.

"You really were, girl." Nina looks at Cat with such admiration and warmth; she was someone in high school only known for her aggression—"the muscle" of the girls. Most people didn't see her talent for logistics and management. "I'm just happy you kept your home base here in D.C., so I can find your ass sometimes. What about the other girls—Diane and Keisha? I really need to call them."

"Well you know, Diane is in marketing or advertising, which, shit, ain't that the same thing? She in New York, probably bossing some other girls like us around. Still not married, no kids."

"That doesn't surprise me. She's so particular," Nina reminisces, trying to motion the waiter over with her eyes.

"Keisha is a shrink up in Philly, can you believe that?" Cat screams.

"Um, I sure can! She always trying to diagnose or psychoanalyze some damn body. She probably having a rack of babies with that fine husband of hers, just to diagnose some more people."

"Shit! You got it, girl. She got three damn babies! And that man still modeling, so he is in New York a lot."

"Wow, I think the last time I spoke to Keisha, she was pregnant with the first." Nina wonders if she'll ever have babies.

"So … talk to me! How are you, girl? The last time I spoke to you about two years ago, things were hard. You were feeling kinda lonely because Malcolm's ass was thinkin' he Tom Cruise in that movie, *Cocktail*."

"Oh no, he's still Tom Cruisin'," Nina returns the sarcasm.

"Waiter!" Nina yells out, because she has no patience to talk about this without liquor. The waiter approaches their table. "Yes, can you please get me a Crown neat. Um, actually … make that a double. Cat, get what you want," she offers, but in a demanding tone.

"Dang girl, you drinking like a fat old man over here. What happened to a glass of champagne?"

"Can you get her a glass of champagne too, please?" Nina asks the waiter. She's nervous, but she has to talk to somebody about what's going on with her. And it seems appropriate she does that with the person who she feels helped get her into the mess she's in.

DANCER IN THE BULLPEN

"I joined that chat site like you suggested after we last spoke on the phone, to make friends. That's it," Nina admits, cutting to the chase.

"Ok, ok, that's good! I knew you were lonely, and those chat rooms are just for mental stimulation, girl, fun play or whatever. Did you make some friends? And it's ok if it's a boy, 'cause it's not like you gonna see them," Cat justifies, as she scans the happy hour menu.

Nina leans in and whispers, "Yeah, well I saw one."

"Here you go," the waiter interrupts. "One Crown neat and one glass of bubbly."

"What you mean, bitch?" Cat whispers back to Nina, gulping down her glass in one push.

Nina is laughing so she won't cry at her intense situation. She takes a big swig of her whiskey and gives Cat the cliff notes. "His name is Jessie. Special Ops Army on the West Coast. We chatted every time I was lonely—so, all the time. He mailed me an eight-by-eleven picture of his face. I know what you thinking. How bold is that, right? But Malcolm is never home to check any kind of mail, so I wasn't even worried. Jessie's face is so perfect, so kind and sad, mysterious and fine. Of course, I mailed him one of me, too.

"I kept him company when he was stationed in Germany by writing letters every week, to calm his anxiety. He would tell me these crazy exciting stories about his military life while I was standing for hours cooking Malcolm's meals. That shit inspired me to write more, ya know? Harmless though, right? It's not like we was fuckin'.

"But … then he moved to D.C. for me without warning, and instead of coming clean about my live-in king, I felt the need to maintain my double life, saying I'm single but just wanted to take it slow. I think he fell in love with me during a hard time in his life. I gave him the impression of love and happiness because he was on another coast for God's sake, and then in another country. Who makes a move like this without telling anybody? A crazy person, I think. This is bad, I know."

"Wait Nina, wait. Shit. Let me get this straight. This nigga is living here now 'cause of you? And you told him you wanted to take it slow?" Cat can't believe what this girl is telling her. Her eyes are now frantically looking for the waiter too.

"Yes."

"So, what? You been sneaking around dating him, and now he thinks, what? That you gonna one day move in with him, and get married?"

"Well, no, not now," Nina says, defending her irresponsibility. "I cut it off."

"Ok good!" Cat exclaims, feeling relieved for her friend.

"But …"

"Damn Nina, 'but' what?"

"I don't see him, but I still talk to him sometimes," Nina confesses. "It's hard just to completely cut off someone you've been talking to for two years. That's kinda impossible."

"NINA! STOP!"

Cat doesn't realize how loud she is, until she sees the restaurant has come to a complete halt. "Sorry, sorry, I don't mean to yell."

Nina looks down in her lap, suddenly feeling like she has to pee.

Cat softens. "Look at me, give me your hands." Nina complies. "I need you to listen to me very carefully. You have to stop talking to this Jessie. He's going to be a problem for you.

You probably got him all fucked up, and a man fucked up by a woman like you is dangerous, do ya hear me?"

"You're right," Nina admits, as she anxiously swirls her third whiskey in its rocks glass. She appreciates the color, the aroma, and the taste of the poison, but resents the power it has to keep her invisible friend away.

I could just give up the whiskey. Why don't I do that? Can I do that? I think I can do that. I need my friend with me.

Cat snaps her fingers. "Nina! Where'd you go, girl? Are you ok? It's going to be ok."

"You're right." Nina resurfaces, focused. "It'll be ok. I am going to take your advice and really cut him off—no contact. And I'm gonna stop whining and give my relationship with the king I've always wanted a goddamn chance!" she says with confidence.

"There you go, girl! That's the spirit. Maybe he hasn't been doing it for you 'cause you haven't kept it real with him. Bitches be thinking men are smart. But they dumb, girl. Take charge! I say give it one more honest try, and then if Malcolm's not the one, then that's cool, move on. But this sneaky bullshit never ends well."

Nina scans the crowded restaurant as if she's looking for someone, or something, and then settles back on Cat's stern face and raises her rocks glass. "Cheers. To a good honest try." The two women clink glasses, like they've just made a verbal contract.

"Before I forget, let me write down Diane and Keisha's numbers in case you don't have them," Cat says, digging into her Louis Vuitton for a pen.

Nina can't help but stare at Cat's chest. The contrast of the white lace on her oiled, dark brown skin is captivating. She determines that she needs to get one of these camisoles.

"And no, by the way" Cat says nonchalantly, feeling her friend's eyes on her.

"Huh? 'No' what?" Nina asks, confused.

"No, these boobs aren't real. Just a treat paid for by my boy-band bonus."

"Ha!" Nina laughs out loud. "I'd say that's toastworthy. Cheers to boy bands!"

Jessie doesn't take Nina's "end-it-all" call well.

"I don't understand why we can't at least be friends, like we've been doing!" He's frantic. "Ok, so you chose to go back to your old boyfriend, but we also built history here too, damn Nina! Why you tryin' to play me like this? I changed my entire life to be here for you!"

Nina is standing on her apartment balcony even though it's a bit cold. It's the quiet place she retreats to when Malcolm is at work. She's biting her nail cuticles listening to Jessie reiterate her lie. There was never a boyfriend to go back to. Malcolm has always been the end game. Her lies have been a runaway train from the beginning of their relationship. One has turned into another, and then combined with another—a snowball rolling down a steep snow-capped mountain.

"I'm really sorry, Jessie," Nina says. "But I never told you to move here. I wish you had talked to me about you plans first."

"That's not the fuckin' point, and you know it!" Jessie's frustration peaks with anger.

Nina realizes this is a situation where her body should be transitioning to dispense her powerful magic, but her body is cold, stomach calm. She reaches for her flask from the balcony café table, running her fingers across its engraved words. *Angel, sip slow. Let me fly with you.* She tilts her head back to digest the comforting burn. She takes Jessie's verbal punishment and feels nothing, which means the whiskey has kicked in fast.

If I jump, will my wings extend and take me to you, Uncle John?

Jessie can tell his pain is not being felt, so he hangs up with no warning. Nina puts the phone down unfazed, and watches the sun get tired, while the moon awakens on the other side of the sky.

"God, you're so beautiful," Nina mumbles. She suddenly feels an urge to go back inside, feeling it's not smart to be tipsy on an open high-rise level. She turns around and feels a familiar hand on her shoulder, while the other is bracing the back of her neck, just like what she saw happen to Grandma Rosa in church as a little girl. Nina is guided back through the sliding glass doors to the living room. She stops once she reaches her bedroom and whispers, "God, is that you?"

The only response is Nina's thumping heart, and the crisp white sheets she pulls back to embrace her fatigue body for a long night's rest. But before she closes her eyes, she sees God sitting on the floor in the corner of the room, at eye level. "There you are. Please stay until I fall asleep," she murmurs.

✳✳✳

Nina knows something is up because Malcolm is feeling extra sentimental lately. He has been proactively trying to be better for her, be more present, and attempting to consider her need to feel valued, like she's the one that matters.

"Can you believe it's been almost ten years since we first connected at Auntie's cookout?" Malcolm swoons, proud of himself that he accomplished something so big.

"No, I can't," Nina says, doing her best to match Malcolm's energy, despite being hungover.

"I was thinking I give you a little extra cash to get a manicure and pedicure this week. Sunday is the Thomas family reunion and I know how you like your hands nice for special functions."

"Oh, ok babe, sure. Whatever you want," Nina says, thinking the Thomas family reunion is the last place she wants to be: an afternoon of judging the spoiled American girlfriend who still needs to master ten more meals and the art of being barefoot and pregnant.

"Maybe you can go with like a cream or eggshell color on your hands, something neutral."

"Um ok, you're my stylist now? You're being a little weird, Malcolm."

"Sorry Queen, I'm just in a good mood."

"It's ok, baby, I love it," Nina says, beginning to feed off his energy.

"Also, I'm taking off Saturday, and we're going to a place by the water I think you will like."

"Really? Oh wow, Saturday is your busiest night at the bar! Are you sure?" Nina asks, with not one care about the bar. She's just trying to be nice.

Before Malcolm can even answer, Nina says, "Awww, thanks baby!" and jumps over on his side of the bed, smothering him with her body. "We need this date night," she whispers.

The proposal is perfect. Malcolm takes Nina as promised to the fanciest Italian restaurant by the water, where the chefs hand-make Nina's favorite type of pasta, smothered in a spicy arrabbiata sauce, accompanied by the perfect Cabernet Sauvignon. The violinist serenades her as Malcolm drops to one knee and opens the black velvet box, weighted by a perfectly pure two-and-a-half carat diamond nestled in a custom platinum band—a diamond twice as big as her boss' ring.

I hope I don't get fired when she sees it, Nina thinks.

"Jesus Malcolm, it's amazing!" Nina exclaims as she tries to calm her breathing, trying not to bust a seam in the way-too-tight Calvin Klein ivory dress that matches her eggshell nails. She looks down at Malcolm kneeling in such pride of his accomplishment. His face gets a little blurry, so she looks up to refocus and sees a dark shadowy figure standing next to the bar holding a glass of champagne. Her eyes start to burn and water. The ruthless dust is back, and she wipes her eyes with the embroidered cotton napkin on her lap. She squints and widens her eyes, making sure they aren't playing tricks on her. It's Uncle John, but she dares not yell his name. She's too close to the promised land, but she can't keep her eyes off him. His glass is raised, and he's mouthing words.

What's he saying? Nina refocuses again and sees him clearly.

What you are looking for is not here, Uncle John says.

Nina gasps.

"Nina! Are you ok?" Malcolm asks, motioning the violinists to go away with the swat of his hand.

Nina is sweating, and prays to God that when she gets up there's no sweaty pussy print. She believes Uncle John can hear her, because she knows he's close, since she recently saw him on the balcony. "Oh baby, um, I'm sorry. I think it's just heartburn. I love the tomatoes but sometimes they don't love me." Her skin is itching, but she's able to mentally block the fever that's trying to grip her body. Her heart is beating hard and fast, as if she's about to have a panic attack, but she uses it to channel happiness.

"Yes, Malcolm Thomas, of course I will marry you," Nina answers, bringing up as much joy as she possesses to her mouth, but still dying to scratch the inside of her thighs and find a bottle of Pepto-Bismol she can mix with whiskey.

Malcolm takes Nina's hand and slips the blinding rock on her perfect finger. "I got them to bring us tiramisu too. You ready for dessert?"

"Oh no, no. I can't fit another thing in my stomach, or I will be walking around in a ripped dress," Nina confesses.

"It's ok, Queen. We'll save it for later."

"Did you ask my dad for his blessing?" Nina inquires, wondering who else knows about this proposal.

"Yes, of course. I figured that would be important based on all that you've told me about him," Malcolm says with satisfaction.

"That's nice. I'm sure he appreciated it. Did you ask my mom?" Nina probes, afraid to hear the answer.

"Uh, no. I didn't think I needed to," Malcolm says defensively.

"Why wouldn't you think that? Because she's a woman?" Nina asks, annoyed because she is confident that's mostly the reason why.

"I just didn't think your mom cared about traditional rituals like that."

You clearly don't know that Selah needs to feel considered and valued, just like her daughter.

"It's ok, Queen," Malcolm assures. "I'm sure she'll be happy when she hears the news from us. How can she not?"

Nina and Malcolm enjoy the rest of the day by the water, getting compliments from strangers who discover their new status, before spending the rest of the following day telling family and friends, who are thrilled that finally Nina's king has committed.

But all Nina keeps thinking about is Uncle John repeating the medicine woman Samara's message: *What you are looking for is not here.*

Then where is it? And most importantly, if I've been wrong, what is it?

***

The wedding is a little more than ninety days out and everything is on schedule. All the vendors are locked in, and the bridal party is on point. Cat's help with reconnecting Nina to Diane and Keisha proves to be perfect timing. Otherwise, Nina would've had to convince Malcolm to elope, since she's unknowingly disassociated herself from any female friend she's had since hooking up with him.

It has been hard asking family members for money to help pay for the wedding of the decade, but Nina and Malcolm do, and everyone says yes, happy that this king and queen are finally uniting. Sure, there are some hiccups during this last stretch of coordination. Nina throws up in the bridal shop when getting measured for some additional alterations, and she has a small panic attack at the venue when Malcolm and Selah disagree on the final color palette. But all in all, everything is running smoothly. At least this is what Nina tells herself.

The pressure of making sure everything is perfect for Malcolm and herself is overwhelming Nina, and she continues to find ways to self-soothe. She begins to party with acquaintances at work, after work, and almost every weekend, while Malcolm is still hustling at the bar. The problem with drinking and smoking weed with people who don't love you, is they don't think to protect you. Though Travis her ex-boss is technically still a work friend, he cares for her and worries she is plummeting down a rugged path.

"Hey girl, come outside with me for a minute," Travis requests. He is in the corporate office, just finished a meeting with the operations manager, and sees Nina with her head down in her new executive office.

Nina pops her head up and smiles at Travis, embarrassed for getting caught sleeping. She jumps up and says, "Ok, here I come." She follows him outside and looks at him like she honestly doesn't know what he wants to discuss.

"Boo, are you ok?" asks Travis. "I just caught you sleeping at your desk, and I've seen you these last couple of days downstairs at the shop, bags under your eyes, asking for three extra espresso shots in your coffee. What's going on with you, can you talk to me? That engagement ring got some evil serum that's seeping into your skin?" He hopes it to be a light-hearted joke, but Nina immediately starts to cry and initiates a hug that she desperately needs.

"I'm just so tired, T. I don't know what's wrong with me. This is the happiest time of my life. I got this perfect guy and I live good, you know," Nina rants on Travis' shoulder, saturating his shirt with her tears and snot.

"Girl, first of all, you gonna go in the bathroom and wash your face and fix your hair—which by the way, looks fabulous. I see you switched from that red to midnight-black mmmph, chile. But anyways, you gonna go in that bathroom and get yourself together, so these white folks don't see the only Black girl in the company having a breakdown. And then you gotta stop partying with them fools, honey."

Nina wipes her face and stands up straight, intently listening to her friend.

"Here, take these." Travis puts a couple of aspirin in Nina's hands. "I can tell your head is pounding like a whore on a Sunday morning, out here squinting and shit, and there ain't no sun," he teases.

Nina loves Travis for the aspirin and lecture, even though she mostly feels bad about getting caught at the job in such a vulnerable state. *I have to get it together.*

***

"Nina, please sit down for a second, the duck can wait. And why are you making a duck right now?" Malcolm asks.

"Your mother says you love duck, Malcolm. What's the problem? Do you not love duck?" Nina snaps, allowing her anxiety to surface.

"Baby, duck is for special occasions, not a random Monday," Malcolm says nonchalantly.

"Well, our Mondays aren't random. They are the only fucking time I can make a Sunday dinner because you work Sundays. And your mother said duck is what you love every day. Sometimes I think she's poisoning my mind."

"Queen, please stop. Sit down for a second," Malcolm repeats.

Nina sits down, avoiding eye contact. She is exhausted by the invisible juggle of emotions Malcolm is not even aware of.

"You don't look me directly in the eye anymore, Nina. Do you notice that?"

"No," Nina shoots back defensively. "That can't be true." She struggles to hold eye contact, as if someone is pulling her eyeballs down to the ground and she's fighting them with all her strength. She knows he's telling the truth and she knows why she can't look at him.

"Nina, you're scaring me," Malcolm admits.

Nina resents the comment, and boldly admits that she is scared all the time.

"Why Nina? Why are you scared?"

"I don't know. But it's fine. Everything will be fine."

Malcolm reaches his hand across the table and puts his hand over Nina's, takes a deep breath in, and asks, "You don't want to get married, do you?"

"What?!" Nina shouts, pulling her hand back like it's under hot coals.

Malcolm repeats. "You don't want to get married, do you?"

"I can't believe you're asking me this right now, like are you kidding me? Are you trying to break me right now?"

"Nina baby, it's ok. You don't want to get married, do you?"

"No, I don't!" Nina finally admits, and begins sobbing in her duck.

Malcolm comes over to Nina's side of the table, stands her up, and hugs her. She tries to find that feeling she once had in the beginning, and she thinks it's there somewhere, just hiding.

"You see, this is good," Malcolm assures. "We're confronting the problem. You're hesitant to get married because you're afraid. And you're afraid because I have been so busy, and you're a little lonely. This is good, I can fix this!"

Nina feels a little better but still unclear on how Malcolm is going to fix anything. "How Malcolm?"

"I hope you noticed that I've already been trying to spend more time with you, and you know, be there for you when I can. I know I've said it a lot in the past, but this time, I really mean it. I'm going to quit the bar and get a regular job. I've saved enough, and we can get you out of this apartment and maybe get you in some writing class thing. I see you still like to write. Maybe that will make you happy?"

"Yes, it will," Nina says, feeling the knot in her throat break into pieces.

"Ok good, baby, so we don't have to do anything drastic like call the wedding off. We just need to adjust, so you're happy again."

Nina is still wet, but the sweat is cooler now. She looks down at her ring, looks up at Malcolm still holding on to her, and simply says, "Ok, fine."

✳✳✳

Time not only flies, but it sometimes beams up to outer space.

It's been four years since Nina and Malcolm have moved in together. The world outside of their union moves along through triumph and challenge. 9/11 devastates the world and D.C. struggles to recover. Nina and Malcolm are lucky. Mrs.

Thomas is only lost underground in a NY subway for a few hours, and Nina's family miraculously has no personal connection to the losses. But is anyone really lucky? The good news is that the coffee and alcohol business tends to weather the economy's worst storms. So, even though Nina and Malcolm feel the strain of the times, they are still thriving at work.

Since Malcolm proposed to Nina the past summer, he's begun investing the money he's been making at the bar into real estate, as he's always wanted. However, with the investment of money comes the investment of time. In order to drop more funds into their future, he has to work longer hours at the bar, with more of his free time spent on his new investment. Nina feels guilty complaining. This is all for them. She's given up on the idea of Malcolm being a husband who's present and engaged with his queen.

One day, Malcolm comes through the door like a raging bull, excited about his real estate efforts. "Nina! I did it! I got approved to buy that six-unit apartment I've been telling you about in Southeast. I'm going to finally be a property owner!" He has just spent his day off meeting with the bank and advisors.

Nina is in the kitchen trying out a new chicken cacciatore recipe. "Wow, that's great, Malcolm! I'm so proud of you!" She means it, but also knows what it means for her.

CHAPTER THIRTEEN

D.C. isn't typically this humid before the cusp of summer, but there's clearly something trapped in the air other than water. Nelly's "Hot in Herre" blasts through every speaker in the club. The DJ announces last call, but the dance floor is still vibrating, packed with an undisciplined military formation of slick, sweaty brown bodies of various shades, shapes, and sizes, stomping and grinding. Young beautiful women overpower the stare of piercing strobe lights with the swift movement of their thick hips, squeezed into painted-on metallic dresses and low-riding pants, rubbing up against eager men in oversized denim without inhibition.

Nina is drenched in sweat, but she doesn't want to stop dancing. She enjoys watching Walter watch her move seductively slow to the fast rhythm. But she can't find her spit, even deep in the corners of her mouth. She giggles to herself, remembering an older girlfriend at her last birthday party tease her by saying, "The ability to create moisture from all crevices is one of the first things to go when getting old." Nina is far from old, though. She's twenty-seven and proud of the fact she looks barely of age to legally drink the bourbon that is drying her out.

Not even bothering to compete with the volume of Mr. DJ's hype, Nina lifts her empty, clear plastic cup with one hand and points to the double bar in the back with the other. With an affirmative nod, Walter smiles mischievously and watches her walk away with her signature long strides, not taking his eyes off her until he gets distracted by a temporary dance partner requesting his moves closer to the stage.

Nina heads for a small opening in the middle of the bar, basking in the warmth of hungry eyes. Her curves are showcased in a fitted black tank dress, which she refuses to pull down when it creeps up to a dangerous line. What they don't know is her slow roll is also the result of swollen toes choked by her blood-red stiletto heels. Strategically grabbing a handful of the middle of her dress, she yanks a couple of inches down to allow her cleavage room to get the attention needed to move to the front of the line. The bartender spots her assets immediately, but has the class to look her in the eye when he quickly snaps "Hey baby, whatcha got?"

"Um, Crown neat with a ginger back," Nina responds slowly, like she has to think about it, when she knows exactly what she wants. "Oh yeah, and some water please." *At least I'm not drinking it straight these days.*

Nina is burnt vanilla cream with a full, natural pink mouth and almond eyes. Her hair is coal black, and she keeps her Afro-Caribbean curls straightened into a shoulder-length Asian bob. She is striking and she knows it.

The lights come up and Nina is reminded to check her phone. Only one missed call and voicemail, but it's not from Malcolm. It's from Jessie. She is surprised and her bladder is

DANCER IN THE BULLPEN

weak. She hasn't heard from him since she ended their affair for good several weeks ago.

Nina isn't able to hear the voicemail, as everyone is loudly pushing out of the club to decide on what's next.

Walter walks up to the bar. "Where's mine, girl? How you not gonna get me a drink?"

"Sorry Walt, I was really thirsty," Nina half-apologizes.

"That's ok, baby girl, you can make it up to me later," Walter suggests, with nasty plans in mind. But Nina has a bad feeling and knows it's important to get out of here and head home in her own car by her own self.

Walter has just turned twenty-one but lies and tells Nina he's twenty-three. He's definitely finer than he is smart—like a male version of her father's old weather girl, Veronica. He looks almost white because his dad is, but he clings to his Black culture. With thick, dark-brown cornrows that run down his back and tats of wrenches and ankhs on his arm, he screams Conscious Bad Boy Mechanic. Nina met him at work and finally said sure to meeting up and hanging out, breaking the "don't shit where you eat" rule. It's been a tough week and she wants a distraction.

"I have to cut this party short. It's Mother's Day and I have a big day planned for mine." Nina neglects to share that it's also just a couple of months away from her wedding day and she shouldn't be out here at all. "I really have to get home and get some rest."

Walter is disappointed but doesn't want to push it. He knows he and Nina have fun, so he has to play his cards right for an opportunity to see her naked.

Nina lets her admirer escort her out of the club holding her hand, and even lets him kiss her on the mouth with a little tongue when they get to her car. "I had a really good time, Walt," she whispers honestly.

"Great, baby girl. See you Monday? But hit me before then if you want."

Nina almost feels sorry for his delusional optimism, but she doesn't have time for him now. She crawls into her car and immediately releases her cramped feet from the fiery hell they have endured all night. She tosses her half-broken-in heels on the passenger side floor and fetches her cell phone from her clutch, but this time takes a moment to enjoy the calm before the storm as she wipes her neck with a white blouse she finds in the back seat. On speaker, she plays Jessie's voice mail.

"Nina, I told him everything," Jessie says, before abruptly hanging up like he was slamming a door in a solicitor's face, just like the last time they spoke. His deep voice is weighted and morbid, like he's finally told the detective where the body is.

"Shit." Nina tries to justify possible meanings embedded in these words that won't result in her demise, but she can't think of any. She starts the engine but doesn't shift gears. Her heart races, and the pace quickens each breath she takes. "Fuck, fuck, fuck!" she screams, banging her fist on the steering wheel. "Jessie, what have you done?"

Nina pulls up to the only tower of concrete centrally located on a hill, in a neighborhood of cookie-cutter single-family homes and perfectly manicured trees. She parks in an unreserved space next to Malcolm's designated one, which usually holds his beautiful black Mercedes Benz that most people dare not park next to. When they moved in together, the agreement was that he would be the one to take advantage of this parking amenity because of his unusual bartending hours.

DANCER IN THE BULLPEN

"Do you really think a six-foot-three dark-skinned Black man should be walking from his car parked in front of a white suburban home at four in the morning?" Malcolm had asked. It hadn't taken much effort for him to convince Nina. And yet, ironically, now it's her who typically finds herself digging deep into her long strides uphill, to their apartment door from a narrow side street below.

Malcolm's car is not in its spot, and Nina immediately looks up to their nineteenth-floor balcony, squinting, as if that will help determine if he's at home hiding, waiting patiently in the foyer closet with a butcher knife. She doesn't think he's capable of that, but all the lazy Sundays of Lifetime marathons with Selah, mixed with deep-rooted guilt, are a toxic cocktail which opens the mind to wild possibilities.

Nina walks past Old Man Gregory at the security desk and attempts to pull down the rising hem of her dress with one hand, wiping the smeared mascara under her eyes with the other, and drops her cell phone she hasn't used yet to call Jessie. She knows Old Man Gregory loves seeing Malcolm and her pumping iron in the communal gym together, making out in the pool alone past closing time, or even just holding hands as they strut through the lobby to the parking lot. Gregory doesn't see a lot of couples that look like them in the building, let alone in this exclusive town of Northern Virginia, across the bridge from his historically chocolate quadrant of Southeast D.C. But he never enjoys seeing Nina stumble in alone at early morning hours like this. And though she can no longer find judgment in his eyes, she knows he worries like a grandfather worries about his rambunctious niece.

"Are you ok, Mrs. Thomas?" asks Old Man Gregory. He's been using Malcolm's last name when greeting Nina for almost five years now, even though they both know she and Malcolm aren't married.

"Yes sir, I'm just fine," Nina lies, purposefully not making eye contact.

Once in the elevator, Nina flips off her heels and doesn't bother to bend down and pick them up. She watches the floor numbers climb and she feels the heavy urge to pee. The back of her legs are itching uncontrollably, but she stops scratching them when they start to sting from her long nails. She's standing in the middle of what feels like a bullpen, trapped without her cape.

Nina is suddenly the four-year-old girl in her ballerina costume, standing in the elevator, carrying her mother's lie that has festered into her own. *No, we didn't see Walter. No, we didn't see Jessie. No, we didn't see Kevin, or my dear Charlotte. We didn't see any of them.* She hopes nothing will slip when Malcolm grips her arms.

A soft hand appears, and takes hold of Nina's left one. *I'm here, Nina. I know it's been a long time. Please don't be afraid,* her invisible friend says.

Nina is not angry for the length of her absence. She starts crying tears of joy that her magical friend has returned, and squeezes her hand, not wanting to let go. Nina turns to look at her and take comfort in the familiarity of her invisible friend's face. "I feel like I know you, or maybe knew you in a past life or something."

I know.

"That mole you have, right by your right eye, I have the same one," Nina observes suspiciously. "What's your name?"

Nina's invisible friend pauses for a long while, then finally responds, *Maya. My name is Maya.*

Nina's palm is getting hot in Maya's hand, as if the introduction has increased both of their temperatures. "I don't think I know anyone named Maya. So strange, I definitely feel like I know you." The elevator feels like it is suspended in the shaft while the two talk.

Be brave, Nina. I will see you soon, if you let me. I am only here now because you've asked for me to come, even if you don't realize it. The long time I've been away is because you turned the thought of me away. I told God what was happening and she made you see her. I will be back though. Just remember, what you are looking for is not here. And just like that, Maya is gone at the same moment the elevator dings open at Nina's floor.

Nina walks through the apartment door with her heels in hand, not wanting to make noise, even though all the rented floors are covered with plush caramel carpet—a neutral template for the light cedar wood furniture, tan armless chairs, and off-white blinds that came with the apartment. Here is where they spend most of their days apart, in a standard one-bedroom apartment, with one bathroom and one image that looks the same from every angle. She believes that the only visual nourishment one can savor is the red frame detailed with handmade tribal markings, which circles the thick mirror in the foyer—the single unique piece she captured at a Brooklyn flea market.

Everything is perfectly in place, like a model home ready to be shown. The only hints of life come from the top-of-the-line golf club bag standing regally in the corner by the television, and first and second place kung fu trophies lined up like soldiers in the only window in the living room. Nina is proud of the two trophies engraved with her name, though she doesn't have an interest in the art form. Stacks of self-help books, such as *How to Get Rich Quick* and *How to Be a Better Listener*, are fanned across the glass coffee table, among the wedding magazines that only Malcolm reads. She still gets a little queasy when thinking about their "book club" sessions, as she tries not to side-eye the latest book she hasn't read yet lying underneath the coffee table, calling her name.

This is the shit Lisa is talking about. Who the hell lives here? You wouldn't know I did, based on all this. But what do I like to do? Lisa's words are still ringing in Nina's mind.

The faint scent of Drakkar Noir slow-dances in the air, and Nina is certain Malcolm must have come home after closing the bar, no more than an hour or so ago. *Was he waiting for me? Why hasn't he called?* But she knows the real question to ask herself is: *Why haven't I called ... anyone?*

Out of habit, Nina beelines to the bedroom and takes off her gold hoops and matching bangles, placing them neatly on the end table. Malcolm hates when she just dumps her things everywhere, not accepting her excuse of unavoidable entropy: a concept she learned while researching ways to justify why it's appropriate and natural to be messy. As she spoons in the warmth of that memory, she caresses the top of her obese diamond.

Something is wrong. The ring is slipping, the clarity is fogging. Nina can feel eyes piercing the skin of her forehead. She looks up and over to the other side of the room and sees herself in her matte-white Vera Wang wedding dress, hanging from the noose of her veil looped and twisted perfectly over the door.

Their eyes meet and with restricted air, the noosed Nina gasps. *What you are looking for is not here.*

Nina screams with her eyes shut, before opening them again to discover her own death has left the room. "Oh my god,

I'm going crazy!" she determines, trying to calm her breathing. She glances at her stack of composition books neatly organized in no particular order by a man who doesn't write.

Nina slowly walks over, with the blur and sting of fresh tears. She runs two fingers down the spine of each journal, trying to determine by the virginity of their fabric which one may have empty pages. Finding no opportunity for release, she loses patience and pushes them all on the floor at the side of the bed, spreading them out and frantically picking them up one by one, flipping through them, feeling betrayed by the congestion of past thoughts, and then throwing them across the room. *Can I just get an empty page goddammit*, she now fumes through her sobs. Finally she finds one. She grabs a pencil from under the bed and begins to write:

> *Ripped off my Black porcelain face*
> *And left me in Cinderella's gown*
> *Loneliness found me in the crowd*
> *Called me magical*
> *Then hid the clock at midnight*

Nina doesn't even know what it means, but the pressure from her chest is gone and she can breathe in rhythm again. She stands up, strips down naked, and walks to the kitchen, leaving the clutter of tear-soaked composition paper and broken lead tips all over the rug. Her throat is sandpaper, so she opens an Argentinian red she finds on the counter (since Malcolm doesn't keep whiskey in the house), and fills a wine glass with a double pour without letting it breathe. *It's seven in the morning now, and if you can see clearly, it's ok to drink.*

Nina's cell phone rings from her purse on the floor in the foyer. Selah's name glows on the screen and without thinking, she answers. "Yeah Mom?"

"'Yeah'?! Nina! Malcolm just left here," Selah fumes.

"Oh, he did? Why would he come to your house so early in the morning? That's rude, sorry. Were you even awake?"

"Nina!" Selah is frustrated at Nina's lack of urgency. "According to him, you have been cheating on him for a while now with a long list of culprits—including a woman, my god! What have you done?"

"Well, to be fair, the woman thing ended a long while ago. No, sorry, I know, Mom. I've ruined everything."

"This is Mother's Day, Nina. And you've ruined mine forever!"

But secretly, Nina is incredibly relieved. At this very moment, the entire world of secrets shifts off her broken back and embeds itself back into its proper place in the galaxy. She pours another glass of wine, takes it to the bathroom, and pees while she listens to Selah cry.

***

Nina is surprised at how little she has to pack. Malcolm owns everything, except for her precious abeng and ancestral shrine, which sit pretty and tall on the highest shelf. She knows they are the most valuable items in the apartment. Everything else—the frames of the candid photos she has taken of Malcolm, the exquisite landscape captured during their travel adventures—is his.

Does he even want these memories now? What about the top-of-the-line crockpot he bought me? Does a cheater get to keep gifts?

DANCER IN THE BULLPEN

Nina leaves her possessed wedding dress hanging in the bedroom closet, and her flawless engagement ring on the edge of the dining room table. But not the car keys. She needs a way to get to Selah's house and work the next day. *Maybe we can make some sort of arrangement with the car?* She starts crying, but not because she is sad. She is angry and embarrassed. Angry that she still needs him, and embarrassed that she needs to pass Old Man Gregory to say goodbye, proving him right.

Returning to live in her childhood home again is difficult. Selah has finally made Nina's bedroom a guest room, and it seems smaller to her than when she left it five years ago. That's how long it has been since she devastated Selah by moving out to cohabitate with Malcolm. She still remembers the conversation, and she can still see the look of sadness and worry on her mother's face, and hear her own rebellious response.

"He WILL propose to me, and I thought you loved him and his family," Nina had said. "What's your problem? Why can't you just be happy for me?"

Nina lies back on the bed, wishing her mother was wrong, but wishing more that the bed still remembered and loved her. *The comforter and pillows are cold now and the mattress doesn't mold to my frame like it used to. It could even be new.* Everything has changed now.

"Nina!" Selah screams from the kitchen, but is too anxious to wait for her daughter's response, scurrying back to announce, "Get up, girl, Malcolm is here!"

It's obvious to Nina that her mother is hopeful for a reunion, confident the only thing needed is an open and honest conversation: a kiss and make up session. She rises from the bed and walks slowly to the door, but with another plan.

Nina finds Malcolm on the front porch, sitting on the middle step with his head down between his knees. "Malcolm."

Nina doesn't expect that simply stating his name will rip open his soul. He begins to sob, soaking the concrete walkway, creating almost a puddle of pain for the yard's flowers to bathe in. She knows an "I'm sorry" is not enough, but sorry is sincerely what she is feeling. She sits down next to him and slowly begins to rub the back of his broad shoulders. Even though she's the enemy, he lets her, needing the warmth of her soft but determined fingers, the healing comfort of each stroke of her fingertips back and forth in a melodic motion.

Abruptly, Malcolm looks up, swollen bloodshot eyes filled with confusion, yet laced with his usual calm dominance. "Did I not give you enough attention? Did I not see you?" he asks with intense urgency. "I know you were afraid a couple of months ago, but I thought we worked that out. I mean, I know I'm still at the bar, but I'm going to leave."

Nina opens her mouth but chokes on her usual appeasement. Silence.

"Nina?"

"No. You didn't."

Malcolm looks at her intently. Nina continues to explain, not just to him, but to herself.

"You are never there, well, when it matters. Most of the time, I went to work when you were coming in. When we did have free time together, I was loving on your family, your friends, learning the sport of basketball, of business, how to take caffeine pills at just the right time before working out so your evil aunties would stop saying I was getting too thick. I did everything you wanted—cook, clean, martial arts, learning how to perfectly cut and smoke a cigar. Hell, I'd even mastered swinging a golf club for you. I made love to you, fucked you, supported you when you dropped the high-paying demanding job to sling drinks all night long. You took on projects that kept you away from me. I did fucking everything! I am exhausted."

Nina's voice is trembling. She doesn't know where this fire is coming from.

"You've done everything but be faithful. So this is my fault?!" Malcolm yells.

Nina is taken aback. She has never heard him raise his voice like this to her, ever. It isn't scary. It's exhilarating. Finally, he is alive.

Nina lowers her voice to a whisper, remembering that her attentive mother is surely "accidentally" hearing everything through an open window. "Malcolm listen. My issues in this relationship are not an excuse for my hurting you—my hiding and choosing not to tell you what has been happening to me."

"Happening to you?! You act like fucking and leading a secret life with other people victimizes you. Come on, Nina," Malcolm explodes.

Nina ignores Malcolm's outburst. "But you must understand, I was—well, am—scared and lonely, and unsure of so many things in my life, including the one thing I've always wanted: a true prince charming, a beautiful husband like you. I longed for you before we met, and now that I've ruined my dream of you, I am struggling with telling you why."

Nina stands up and begins to pace, letting the blood move through her limbs, hoping the flow will keep the truth coming. Malcolm drops his head back down, like he is looking for a response in the makeshift puddle he has created. "Did you, or do you love them?" he asks.

Again, silence. But this time, it's short-lived. Not so sure who Malcom is referring to specifically, Nina answers truthfully. "Yes. There has been love there. But many of the interactions have been distractions. The love is irrelevant, you know. I do love you."

"Do you, Nina?" Malcolm asks, needing some sign that this relationship had some truth to it.

"Yes," Nina gently assures.

"But …?" Malcolm asks, with a twinge of anger. "You want to say 'but,' right? Goddammit Nina, talk to me!"

"But we need to end this completely," Nina determines honestly.

"End this?" Malcolm is beyond frustrated. "Nina, how can we end this?! My god, we're getting married in less than seven weeks, you might as well leave me at the altar. We are not girlfriend and boyfriend anymore. We're not in high school."

Malcolm stands up and Nina stops pacing. He towers over her and sternly grabs her arms. "We have to work this out. What are we supposed to tell people? Maybe we should go to therapy together, I'm sure there's a therapist that can see us in an emergency, right?"

"We're going to go to emergency speed therapy, Malcolm?"

"Yes! Don't you want to save us? Let's save us."

Nina is fighting conflicted feelings, because this is the first time Malcolm has expressed such desperate aggression and passion about their relationship. It's a turn-on, which is frustrating to her.

"Hey kids, are we all ok out here?" Selah can't resist. She has to check the pulse of the situation in front of her house, wondering if Nina is going to sabotage this life-saving opportunity. Malcolm releases Nina's arms.

"Yes Mom, we're fine. Privacy, please."

Selah gives Nina the "eye" and reluctantly walks back into the house.

Malcolm gently takes Nina's hand and says, "Let's take a drive."

"But I don't have my purse," Nina protests, as she slowly walks behind Malcolm to his car.

"It's ok, we won't be long."

Oh my god, he's gonna kill me.

"Don't be scared. I just know your mom makes you crazy, so I'm thinking we get away from the house a bit," Malcolm assures.

Malcolm drives only a few streets away and pulls into an empty neighborhood parking lot. He exits the driver seat and opens the passenger side door. "Get out," he demands, with a dark tone.

Great, here it comes. But Nina complies, following him into the back seat, watching his head scrape the car ceiling.

Immediately, Nina feels his uncontrollable yearning. "Are you seriously trying to fuck me right now?" she asks, contemplating if she's going to submit.

"Shut up," he demands, and pulls Nina on top in a face-to-face straddling position. "You do everything for me, do you? Make love, maybe? But I can't remember you ever really fucking me."

Oh, he's going to punish me.

Malcom unzips his jeans and Nina lifts her pelvis a little to give him the space to release his manhood. She knows this is not smart, but she needs the release too.

Malcolm hungrily finds her wet softness and grabs her hips to pull her down on him.

"Is this what you want?" asks Nina.

"Yes," Malcolm responds, enslaved by her warmth. "Is this how you do it?" he asks angrily.

Nina knows where this is going so she refuses to go slow, look at his face, or verbally share. She holds on to the back of his neck, mouth open, rubbing against the back window as she gyrates her hips like a locomotive train trying to feverishly make up time to meet schedule.

Explosion.

Malcolm and Nina are limp from the exorcism, and don't bother to wipe up the pain from the ivory leather sheets.

"How do you feel?" Malcolm asks, knowing this will be the last time he touches her.

***

Telling everyone that she and Malcolm are not only calling off the wedding but calling off the relationship is like an emotional massacre to all those who love them. No one understands and no one really wants to, either. They just want to hear that this is a joke, a mistake, a misunderstanding. Some people attempt to be kind, and others are truly mean. The only person with a truly comforting reaction is Nina's dear friend, Lisa.

"Malcolm is a beautiful man, but that doesn't mean he is THE man. I am so proud of you," Lisa says, once again over the phone.

"You are?" Nina asks, taken aback by the strength of Lisa's support.

"Hell yeah I am. You stood up for *Nina*. I didn't think you had it in you, but so happy you did."

Malcolm's family begins to knit the permanent scarlet letter for Nina's coat, and her family swears they always knew there was something he wasn't doing to make her happy.

"Maybe he's gay? Or just clueless? How hard is it to keep sweet Nina happy?"

None of it matters—the questions, the answers, the reasons. Everything is dark and hurts, and Nina just wants it to go away. Living in her childhood home with an attentive mother watching makes it hard for her to hide her spiral into a toxic depression. But she does her best to conceal it and to ignore Uncle John, who now visits every night, repeating the mysterious lesson.

What you are looking for is not here.

"I'm not looking for anything!" Nina yells at Uncle John's shadow at the foot of the bed. "Why are you torturing me, Uncle? Please just take me with you or go away."

Desperate and longing for the one person who she feels most comfortable with, Nina reaches out to Charlotte. She agrees to see Nina, though she is different. She seems even more damaged from their disconnection than Nina. Nina attempts to be patient and give her grace through the pain, to get back to where they used to be before the years of lies and distance, but it's excruciating.

"Charlotte, let's leave, they just announced last call," Nina suggests, trying to be the responsible one even though she's drunk and high too. They are at one of their favorites, a neighborhood bar that has fed many of their bad habits. "I'll be back, I gotta pee," she slurs. "Stay here and don't do anything crazy, you promise?"

"Ok angel" Charlotte agrees, not quite present.

Nina returns from the bathroom and Charlotte is getting pushed by a man three times her size at the bar, because she's cussing him out about an accidental drink spill. Despite the toxins in her body that numb most of her thoughts and physical sensations, Nina's temperature rises to its usual magical level. She wipes the dust from her eyes and clenches her teeth through the leg pain. She stares intensely at the man's large hands from across the bar, and within seconds he's bleeding from them, at the core of his palms.

Charlotte's white tank top is soiled with bloody hand prints, and she's scared, wondering how she made this happen. "Oh shit," she panics.

The threatening man's friend sees the blood and assumes Charlotte has a knife. He begins charging after her too, creating a double-team attack. Nina instinctively breaks a beer bottle on the counter and runs up to threaten both villains. Charlotte mirrors her, finding another bottle to break in the exact same way. Before they can do any damage, two bouncers looking like Andre the Giant rush through the crowd like linebackers, lifting the girls and carrying them out of the bar.

Nina and Charlotte stand outside of the bar, higher off the adrenaline than the liquor tainting their blood.

"Did you see that guy's hands? What the fuck, I didn't cut him!" Charlotte tries to make sense of what she saw.

"I know you didn't," Nina responds. "I did it."

"What you mean, you did it?" Charlotte questions, not taking Nina seriously, believing she must be high on something other than her usual green.

"I have this power to make people bleed who are trying to hurt me or people I care about. Most of the time it works, except if I'm distracted or if my body is off in some way, I guess, which is why it's weird that I was able to hurt that man because I've had more than a few drinks tonight. I didn't have time to do it on his friend, though," Nina explains, feeling open and free, loose-tongued because of the alcohol. She's not worried about how she will be accepted by Charlotte.

"So, you telling me you're a witch?" Charlotte laughs out loud. "You hung out tonight to tell me you've lost your mind?" she questions, dismissing any truth to what Nina is saying. A guy that she was flirting with before the drama comes outside, and Nina quickly realizes Charlotte has been simply waiting on him.

"Charlotte! Where are you going?" Nina yells down the street, as Charlotte starts quickly walking with him to his car.

Nina runs up to them both, and jumps in between them. "No! Charlotte, you are not going with him! What the hell is wrong with you?" she yells, crying, trying to let the cold air sober her up.

Charlotte looks up at Nina and starts crying, staggering toward her. "I love you!" she says. "And you accused me of being a junkie the last time I saw you, but your ass is a liar! Lying to yourself, Malcolm, and all these other jokers you used to soothe you, shit! So, who's the junkie?"

Nina gets it now. Charlotte let Nina take her out to punish her. And she could care less about the magic, or that Nina just saved her. She is still hurt and has no intention of letting Nina get off easily, just because Nina's relationship with Malcolm—which she chose over theirs—has died.

"Charlotte," Nina says softly.

"'Charlotte,' what?!" the girl screams at the top of her lungs, while the stranger who is just looking for a good time starts to get uncomfortable.

"I love you too," Nina admits.

Charlotte is speechless, not realizing how good it would be to hear these words. Nina is looking at her in her worst state, and she's still the most beautiful woman she's ever seen.

The stranger bounces, wanting no part of the craziness. Cars whiz by, with random male voices yelling out the windows, "Y'all girls still wanna party?"

"If you love me, be with me," Charlotte demands.

Nina hesitates, and then says, "Go to rehab first, and I'll support you through it."

"Fuck you, Nina! You go to rehab! You act like you're not a drunk. You just hide it better. 'Cause that's what you do—hide," Charlotte accuses, digging the invisible knife deep in Nina's chest. She runs away like Nina just started a fire.

"Wait Charlotte, please! Come back! Let me at least drive you home! Charlotte, don't do this," Nina calls out sobbing. "Don't leave me!" she screams, spitting a small amount of blood from her mouth onto the pavement.

Nina, please don't cry. It's going to be ok. I'll be here with you soon, Maya says, now holding onto Nina at the waist.

"You are here with me now, what do you mean?" Nina whimpers. She doesn't care that there's no answer. She's just happy to feel Maya's small hands. Nina accepts the hold and quietly cries on the sidewalk until there are no more tears left.

CHAPTER FOURTEEN

It's just past sunrise when Craig bangs on Eli's door, as if he was leading a drug bust. Ironically, Craig's personal poison of choice has already destroyed the lining of his nose, yet the drugs he continues to take keep him making bad decisions.

"What the fuck, man?! You know what time it is? You better be at my door this early because you got my money." Eli can't fake a happy greeting. He's tired of giving his questionable friend gifts disguised as loans.

"Bruh, I got you. Just need to move some green around and I'll pay you back. So, while I do that, can you let me and my girl crash here tonight?" Craig whines.

"Damn nigga, ain't ya mama right down the street?"

"Man, my mama got my four sisters living there and all their kids. Plus, you know how she be. She not gonna let me have this cutie pie up in there." Craig turns to Nina and plants a sloppy Heineken-stained kiss on the side of her mouth. She barely feels it. She is still basking in the effects of the malt liquor and weed she blazed a state back, while he drove the only thing left of Malcolm's—the black Accord.

Nina knows Craig's been driving dirty. *But fuck it. If he gets pulled over, maybe it'll quiet these demons I ride with.*

"This your girl?" Eli asks almost accusatorially, while staring Nina down.

Nina is still stunning, despite the brown circles under her eyes, saggy jeans, and bright-red split ends, caused from continuously switching her hair from black, to red, to blond, to red again. She's wearing a black t-shirt that reads, "Still a Bad Bitch" with the sleeves torn off. She could use an extra twenty pounds and a month of detox, but no one has said as such.

"Hey, what's your name?" Eli questions, with a tone that implies if he likes the name, he will let them both stay.

"Whatever you want it to be," Nina responds, oozing sweet toxicity.

"Are you for real right now?"

"What? You never watched *Pretty Woman*?" Nina slurs.

"You mean the one about the prostitute?" Eli asks with a breath of sinister laughter.

"Yes!" Nina answers with conviction, trying hard to demonstrate fearlessness of his swift judgment. "It's a fucking joke, damn."

But Nina isn't too convincing. She can't even convince herself, precariously standing next to a broken man who pays for her sex, money, and time with nothing of value—a human void temporarily filling her constant emptiness. Even when she first met Craig running a local butcher shop in her client's neighborhood, he made her cough up her phone number in exchange for the emergency use of his store phone. At first sight, he made her a prostitute for help, and the relationship has only plummeted from there.

Eli takes a long look at Nina's sad eyes, and then suddenly steps back and opens the front door wide.

"Thanks man. For real though, I got you," Craig repeats like a used car salesman, grabbing Nina's hand and walking into the beautiful single-family home that Eli's mother left behind when she died. However, she's still present in the vintage furniture and handful of Caribbean-inspired china she brought from Jamaica for her son's future family. She originally thought she would retire in South Carolina, to be closer to her children who migrated there for a better opportunity, or in Eli's case, to keep out of island trouble, but she couldn't resist the pull to return home. So, Eli learned fast how to be on his own at seventeen, forcing his twenty-three to appear more like thirty.

"Y'all got one day," Eli warns. "Meaning y'all leaving by tomorrow morning. I got company coming into town, and she don't need to be around no bullshit."

"Yeah, it's cool. I just need to get my license renewed today and you know, see some family."

"I thought all your family up in Baltimore with you now?"

"Yeah, yeah, most of them. But one of my sisters is still here."

Eli disregards the fact he catches Craig in a lie. "And she has the money you owe me?"

"Bruh, don't worry. I'm gonna get your money today."

It's clear to Nina that Eli despises Craig now, despite whatever friendship they once had. The daggers in Eli's voice scrape the back of her neck. She feels his pain but doesn't want to be alone this weekend.

Eli directs Craig to drop their bags off in the guest room, but all Craig wants to do is peak his high in between Nina's thighs. "Baby, come here!" he demands, too lazy to pretend there's an honorable reason.

Nina knows what Craig wants, and she's just high enough to let him make her feel good temporarily, but not enough to stop from crying afterward and regretting it completely. She doesn't want to make too much of a mess so early in the day, so she suggests that he take her from behind in front of the bathroom sink. At least she'll be able to turn herself on by looking at her reflection. She's quiet on purpose, to counteract the wails he uses as a bragging tool. *Hurry up*, she thinks, while he quickly climaxes and releases.

Nina exits the back room looking the same as before she gave herself to Craig: tired. "Got anything stronger than water?" she probes, head lowered into the bare fridge.

"Babe, it's 7 a.m. Maybe lay off the booze until at least lunchtime?" Craig teases, looking disheveled, ten years older than his youthful age of twenty-one.

Nina shoots back immediately. "But 5 a.m. in the car is ok?"

Craig says nothing, but Eli comes into the kitchen and directs Nina to a case of warm Corona on the back counter of the kitchen. After pouring hot beer over a mountain of ice, she plops down on the living room couch and looks up. "Wow, I love the architecture of your high ceilings. These intricate angles are dope," she observes without any expectation of a response. She sucks down the warm beer, not allowing time for the ice to do its job.

"You're fucking weird," Eli diagnoses, intrigued by Nina's conflicted behavior.

DANCER IN THE BULLPEN

"Why, because I like architecture, or because you know my pussy tastes like strawberries?"

"Oh my god, you're crazy," Eli determines with amusement.

Nina laughs out load for the first time since before her and Malcolm's split. Oddly enough, she feels comfortable in Eli's home, despite his hostile frame. She's intrigued that he's not fazed by her shock commentary—the shield she keeps up these days.

Oblivious to the energy building around him, Craig is restless and ready to go take care of business. "Babe, where are your keys?"

"On the table in front of you," Nina responds, channeling some of Eli's irritation. A twinge of anxiety shoots up her spine between the daggers still scratching the back of her neck. "Please be careful, ok?" she warns.

"It's all good. I'm about to get my license taken care of now. I won't be too long."

Eli and Nina listens to Craig speed out of the driveway.

"Can you roll another one for me?" Nina asks, eyeballing the raw weed and white papers on the coffee table in between them.

"You can't roll your own weed?" Eli challenges, beginning to roll a healthy joint for his new and unexpected guest.

"I mean, I can. I just don't do it well. You don't drink or smoke?"

"Nope, not anymore. I just keep beer here for my boys."

"Why you don't party?" Nina pushes

"I just don't, ok?"

"Ok ok, well good for you," Nina replies nervously. "I guess I should probably chill a little too."

"Hey, so, what is your name?" Eli probes again.

Nina chuckles. "Oh sorry, yeah. My name is Nina."

"See, was that so hard, Nina?"

"No," Nina responds plainly, smiling and feeling more relaxed.

"Ms. Nina, let me ask you a question." Eli takes a long pause, watching Nina light her joint, take a deep drag, and exhale slowly. "What are you doing here?"

The daggers teasing the back of Nina's neck are now painfully lodged under each shoulder blade. "What do you mean?"

"You know what I mean. Why are you in this small shit town in South Carolina with a shit person, staying with a stranger? You seem lost. Like you don't belong here."

Nina pretends to be confused, stands up, and pulls her rugged red mane up in a disheveled top knot, like she's about to dance or go to battle with something or someone. She begins pacing in Eli's living room, looking at him through accusatory eyes. She feels the urge to pee, but tries hard to suppress it. "My Grandma Daisy is from a town not too far from here, where she learned how to be a warrior on some white man's plantation. This may be a shit town, but I feel some good energy from her here," she shares, not caring if Eli understands her or not.

He understands her and says nothing, just looks past her pain and sees how beautiful she actually is.

"And why you talking trash on your boy, especially to his girlfriend?" asks Nina.

"Because I don't believe you're his girlfriend, or that he's headed to get his license renewed, or that he will have my money tomorrow. He's a fuckin fraud. And the only reason why I let his punk ass in is because of you—to save you."

Eli proceeds to spill all that he knows from his experiences with Craig—the addiction, the womanizing, the pathological lying. The more he talks, the hungrier he is to share, including the rumor that Craig caught syphilis recently. "It was in the early stages, I think," he says, motioning Nina to sit back down, as her pacing makes him nervous.

Eli continues. "Supposedly the meds took care of it, but I don't know if I'd trust that, if I were you. I heard he had to call all the girls he fucked, and that's simply impossible, because there's a lot he probably doesn't remember." His mouth is moving like a freight train, but the sound of his voice descends into the pit of Nina's stomach, where her own muted voice hides. She sinks deep into the '70s camel-colored velvet couch, almost camouflaged with the color of her skin. The weed is taking over and she submits, letting her eyelids close, trying to ignore the rumblings in her belly.

"Hey, you ok?" Eli asks, realizing he may have hit her with way too much.

Nina struggles to sit up, glancing at her lukewarm Corona and burning joint in front of her on the coffee table, resentful they both have failed at numbing her fear. Eli watches her eyes squint and widen, attempting to focus on his face.

"So, let me get this straight. Craig has a bitch here, and that's who you think he's with right now?" Nina questions.

"Yeah," Eli mumbles.

"And he's still doing coke and may have syphilis?"

"Listen, this isn't your fault. He does this shit—cheat, lie, steal, seduce chicks. I mean, usually they're dumb street girls, you know, not like you. That's why I had to say something."

Not like me? Look at me. I'm dirty, frail, delusional, and now probably have an STD.

Eli leans in and whispers, like there's someone else in the room. "Haven't you noticed something is off with him?"

Nina avoids Eli's truth, and instead sinks back into the velvet, closing her eyes again. But this time he gets up to make her some sobering coffee from the stale grounds his mom left in the cupboard.

Nina's nostrils are aroused by the aroma. But when she opens her eyes, the house she's thawing out in is gone, and she's back in her old apartment hanging from her wedding gown veil, wildly kicking her legs. Malcolm is in the entry of the bedroom door with a pair of sharp scissors. She doesn't know if he's thinking of using them to cut the strangling veil, or finish her off by stabbing her heart. Uncle John and Maya are inside the mirror above the bedroom dresser, staring at her with blurred faces and no words—no repetitive message this time.

"Say it, say it!" Nina demands.

"Say what?" Eli asks. "Hey Nina, wake up!"

"Huh?" Nina wipes the drool from her mouth and pops up, like she's late for school. "I need to get my journal," she mumbles to herself.

"Girl, you ok? Journal? You were mumbling and sweating, and just now screaming after dozing off." Eli is directly in front of Nina, shoulders almost close enough to graze her damp forehead.

Nina inhales his natural scent; it smells like comfort. She didn't realize at first how tall and broad Eli is, carrying a softness behind his resting frown. He shares her complexion, with her same wide mouth and dark-brown eyes, yet his lips are fuller, his eyes richer, more piercing.

"I think you should rest. You're out of it," Eli gently suggests, trying to ignore the electricity between them. Nina doesn't argue. She walks slowly to the guest room and gets in the bed without taking her slippers off. She forgets where she is, and is awakened by the sound of Craig slithering into bed right before dawn break. He smells like pussy and liquor, and has the audacity to rub his manhood at the bottom of her backbone.

"I just started bleeding," Nina coldly whispers.

"Oh, ok baby, you want to just kiss it?" Craig asks hopefully.

Nina begins to explain that the pains in her stomach will prevent her from pleasuring his selfish ass, but his snores cut her off. *What AM I doing here?* she asks herself, wondering if Eli is awake and if he really wants to save her. The loneliness is overwhelming, so she cries herself back to sleep, to release and feel some peace.

***

It's noon the next day, and Nina rises to voices raised. Eli's patience has grows thin, and he demands that Craig cough up the one thousand dollars he owes him. Nina calculates the amount of money she "lent" Craig, and that sounds about right. *I wonder how many thousands of dollars this dude owes other people,* she thinks, feeling a wave of confidence flow through her. She gets up, takes a long hot shower, and slips into the short yellow dress with pink flowers that Craig loves her in. She hides her pain with some makeup and sweeps her ragged red strands into a demure bun.

The arguing hasn't wavered when Nina struts into the living room. "Hey, hey, let's all calm down," she instructs, followed by her infamous bright smile. The men immediately stop their quarreling in awe of her glow. "Eli, I'm sure Craig is stepping out soon to get that money for you. Right babe?" she referees, gently touching both of their arms simultaneously.

"Yeah. I got you man, for real. I'm about to go get it now," Craig promises. Eli squints at Nina with a look of sincere anger, and she responds with a gentle squeeze of his arm, widening her smile.

"Babe, can I talk to you for a moment?" Nina asks.

Craig agrees with no hesitation, clueless of what's in store for him.

Nina invites her target to sit on the edge of the guest bed and begin to confess all her sins against him. "Remember that time I said I was at dinner with my mom last week?"

"Yeah." Craig responds with hesitation, though he doesn't really remember.

"I was really with my ex. I must be honest, baby, there's one other time I was with him too. Like a couple of days before we came here. The guilt has been killing me, so I just needed to tell you before we go back home, you know?"

"Wait, so you've been cheating on me?" Craig asks, standing up, looking at Nina as if she has shit on her face.

"Yes baby. I'm so sorry."

"Wow," Craig mumbles, trying to process the surprising news, pacing the bedroom floor. "Damn, so like you still love him or something?"

"No, it was just a couple moments of weakness. You know how I get—lonely and all."

"Yeah, I do," Craig responds, softening his tone. "You won't do it again?"

"No, I won't. I hope you can forgive me. I know you would never do that to me, so I wanted to keep it clean and honest with you."

Craig stops pacing and stares at Nina. Everything stops—the cars outside, the click of the clock on the nightstand, even his labored breath.

"You ok, baby?" Nina asks gently, feeling the blood in her veins simmer just short of a boil. *Do it, asshole. Say it.*

"Nina, it's ok, I forgive you. In fact, I must tell you. I haven't been completely honest or faithful either. There may have been a couple of times I dipped out a bit on you too. But they were just whores, didn't mean anything. You know sometimes the drink and powder gets me a little crazy, and you be busy sometimes, so …"

"So you cheated a little," Nina says, finishing his explanation for him. "And sometimes you do coke still, I get it." She continues to probe. "What about your license, babe, you get that yesterday? You came in late. What happened?"

"Yeah babe, shit got all messed up. I guess I didn't have the right paperwork and all, so I'm gonna need you to bring me back. Then I tried to, you know, get Eli's money, but things fell through. I'm about to go get it now. You seen your keys?"

"Yeah, I've seen them. But you can't have them. Just like you can't have me anymore."

"What? What you mean?" Craig asks frantically.

"I mean you're worthless. I never cheated on you. I just knew you couldn't help but tell the truth when talking too much. Thank you for confirming just enough of your lies for me to stop feeding you my fucking time and money. Get out."

"What?! Nina, you trippin'. I knew you were playing me so I played you back," Craig nervously tries to reason.

"Get out!" Nina repeats, escalating her tone loud enough for Eli to step into the bedroom doorway.

"Babe, calm down, ok. I'm sorry. I promise not to mess up again, ok? But yo, I *need* your keys to get this money and we gotta go home together. Tell her bro." Craig looks to Eli in the doorway, hoping his desire for money will be incentive enough for his support. Eli is silent, a smile growing on his face.

"Get your things and get the fuck out! Now!" Nina screams. "I don't want to have to hurt you."

"You can't kick me out," Craig yells. "This is not your house, bitch!"

Nina and Eli make eye contact, and the electricity between them intensifies. Without budging, Eli reiterates her demand. "You heard her. Get out."

"Are you serious, man? So, it's like that?" Craig says with an angry dark tone.

"It's like that."

"You don't want your money?" Craig asks in a threatening tone.

"Yes, I want my money, but I doubt you'll be able to pay, and if you do, it will be from the house of some other sucker."

Craig knows what Eli is capable of when it comes to defending himself, so he doesn't push. He slowly packs his duffel bag of clothes, drugs, and alcohol, and doesn't turn to look back when he walks out the door.

Eli lets out a monstrous laugh when the door slams. "Wow, strawberry girl. You got a little fire. Good for you!"

"You *don't* care about your money?" Nina questions.

"I knew his ass was never gonna give me my money back when y'all both stepped to my door yesterday, just like I knew he would never love you." Eli brushes the strands of red out of Nina's face, gently touching her cheek, the only fullness that remains on her body.

Nina blushes but quickly refocuses on the reality of her situation. "I better get on the road. I got a long six-hour drive by myself up north. You got any snacks I can take?" She hasn't smoked or drank since last afternoon, which is a new record of sobriety. Her body suddenly reminds her that it's missing some key nutrients.

"How 'bout I treat you to a little breakfast on the way out? You can follow me. I know a place right before the highway that has the best pancakes. You need some starch on those bones," Eli teases.

Nina packs her things and feels some sense of relief, despite the doctor's appointment she's going to have to make when she returns home.

"I'm ready," Nina announces, packed and at the door, waiting on Eli to surface from his bedroom. He's taking too long, so she finds her way to him and discovers him on the phone looking out the window.

"Nah babe, I just got a lot of things to do this week, so maybe you come another time," Eli says to whomever he's disappointing on the other end. He quickly turns around and tells the person he has to go.

"Sorry, I didn't mean to interrupt. I'm just ready when you are," Nina says softly, feeling a twinge of jealousy.

"Ok cool, let's ride."

"Hey, so listen …" Nina says, stopping Eli's stride, trying to find her words.

"Yeah?" Eli responds, almost daring her to spill some truth.

"You know if I wasn't so jacked up, I would chill with you, you know? Of course, as like friends."

"Oh, did I ask you to be my friend? I was just trying to be a good dude and save you. No one should be with him. But we aren't friends. I just need you to eat," Eli clarifies, showcasing his resting frown.

"Right. Duh. Makes sense. Well, thank you."

"Yep, let's ride," Eli instructs with a smirk.

***

"Is there a specific reason you want me to run these tests on you, Ms. Abadie?" Dr. Slate asks, concerned at the urgent nature of Nina's request. "Have you engaged in any high-risk behavior recently?" she continues, as the nurse checks Nina's blood pressure again.

"I am responsible, doctor. I use condoms, of course. But this particular person has had some serious shit," Nina explains.

"I understand," Dr. Slate responds, unfazed by Nina's profanity. "It's better to be safe."

After filling out a ton of questions about her sexual history, the nurse returns to the examination room with a tray of needles. Dr. Slate notices Nina's body tense, and assures her that everything's going to be ok. "Nina, the reason why I had your blood pressure checked twice is because the first result was a bit high, and unfortunately, so is the second result."

Nina looks at her doctor, staring at her thick black eyebrows at a loss for words. She reminds Nina of Brooke Shields.

"Are you experiencing a lot of stress lately, or have you changed your diet drastically recently?" Dr. Slate questions softly, paying close attention to the details of Nina's face.

"Um, yeah, you know ... life. I'm trying to figure mine out," Nina snaps back, feeling a bit queasy.

"I'm thinking we do a full blood panel on you, so we can rule some stuff out, simply make sure fatigue and the stress from your partner is what's got you a little out of whack. How does that sound?"

'Simply'? And he damn sure ain't my partner. Nina's glad the doctor is not checking her pressure a third time, because it's definitely higher than a kite now. *I wonder if she thinks I'm pregnant. I'm definitely not pregnant.*

"Ok," Nina says, as she watches the nurse rub alcohol on her thin arms.

"You look a little dehydrated, sweetie. When's the last time you had a big glass of water?"

Ok, I get it, I am not looking so good! "I think yesterday," Nina lies. It's definitely been a few days. The nurse takes Nina's blood, gives her a beverage known to hydrate athletes, then tells her to get dressed and meet Dr. Slate in her office.

"How do you feel otherwise, Nina?" Dr. Slate asks. "Other than physically? Besides this stressful situation, are you experiencing any anxiety or depression, any negative thoughts?"

"Um, I dunno, maybe sometimes. But I manage," Nina responds.

Dr. Slate writes something down in her little doctor's folder, looks back up at Nina, and asks, "So, what does managing look like for you?"

Shit. I see what she's doing. She's trying to see if I'm suicidal or a drug addict or something. Oh my god, what if my blood work shows her the reason why I can make people bleed? What if they have some special blood magic detector and I'm going be kidnapped by the government and tested?

Nina stands up with tears pooling in her eyes, then sits down, realizing she looks unstable for standing up like that. "Sorry Dr. Slate. Um, I write and drink a little just to calm my nerves." *Damn, she's gonna see the weed in my blood too.* "Every once in a while, I may puff a little marijuana."

"Ok Nina, I'm not here to make you feel bad, and I am definitely not judging you. I just know a highly respected therapist that I think anyone who struggles from time to time can benefit from. I have her card if you're willing to chat with her. I would, of course, check your insurance. You never know, they may offer you a discounted rate."

Nina takes the card from Dr. Slate, relieved she doesn't have to run out the office. "Thank you, Dr. Slate, I appreciate this."

"We will call you about your blood test if there's a concern, or if additional testing is needed."

"Can you just call me, regardless of the results?"

"Of course, I will note that on the chart. In the meantime, try not to worry."

Don't worry? Easier said than done.

***

It's been six months since Nina's been back from South Carolina. Six months since Dr. Slate shares with her that she has low iron and needs to pump up her vitamin D. "It's easy to get more of what you need. I will help you figure out what works best for you," Dr. Slate says at her follow-up appointment.

Nina also takes her up on seeing the therapist she recommends.

"Hi Ms. Abadie, I'm Ms. Jones!"

Ms. Jones is a small African-American woman with big hair and a bigger personality. She's so vibrant; she looks as if she was born with neon colors painted on her naked skin.

"Hello. Please, call me Nina."

"Ok, will do!" Ms. Jones complies with the energy of an entertainer at the circus.

Is she for real? Nina wonders, trying to suppress her laughter.

"So, I've read the information you provided about why you are here. Is it true that you're looking for ways to sleep better, preferably sleeping pills?" Dr. Jones asks, with no decline of her exuberant energy level.

Nina thoughtfully explains her self-diagnosis. "Well I know you can't give me sleeping pills 'cause you're not a psych, but I feel once we talk, you'll be able to understand I just have a lot on my plate, and in my mind. I get a little overwhelmed and tired, and really just need to sleep. I'm thinking you can write some type of referral to my doctor for sleeping pills, if that is something you usually do."

"How about we talk for awhile?" Dr. Jones asks, as if she's heard absolutely nothing Nina has said.

Nina looks around the therapist's small office. There's just enough room for the long orange leather couch, where she uncomfortably sits, and the wide-armed royal-blue cotton chair that looks like Ms. Jones sleeps in it when no patients are around. There's a museum of African art crowding the therapist's walls, so much so that she can't imagine it's easy to find the light switch.

Like a good therapist, Ms. Jones observes Nina's observations. "Do you like African art, Nina?"

"I don't know. My mother has become a big fan of it though, and has begun decorating her walls like you have here. I'm wondering if this is what her house—I mean, our house … well no, her house—will look like soon."

"Is there some confusion where you live?" Dr. Jones asks, thinking this can be an opening.

Nina sits up as best she can on the leather couch and chuckles at the question. "I used to live with my fiancé, then I moved out and back into the home I grew up in with my mom, but it's temporary. I'm just saving up for my own place. So, I'm kinda in limbo," she carefully shares, voice cracking at the end of her explanation.

"Is that how you feel, Nina? Like you are in limbo?"

Nina suddenly has to pee and immediately regrets coming. *What was I thinking? I don't need to relive this shit.* "No, I feel fine overall. I have a good job, a place to stay, good friends, and family. I make a mean spaghetti and meatball. I just am tired sometimes," she says, tightening up her armor.

Buzz! Buzz!

"Nina, I'm so sorry, it looks like my colleague has stepped out. Let me open up the door for his next appointment. Can you give me a minute? And while I'm gone, can you think about why you are here, if you feel so fine?" Ms. Jones instructs, giving a big dose of Selah energy.

"Sure," Nina says, grinding her teeth at the thought of being honest, but happy to have a moment alone, because she's craving a taste of her whiskey.

Nina quickly leans over and digs in her big purse for her small silver flask. Now, with it in her hand, she pauses to listen for Dr. Jones' voice, hoping to determine how many seconds she has to take a hit. *Just to take the edge off.*

No words are coming through, just some sounds at the front door of the building. Nina risks it, unscrewing the cap and tilting her head back to feel the heat flow down her throat.

"Nina." Ms. Jones is just inside her office doorway, looking at an alcoholic in denial. "I have a no tolerance drugs and alcohol policy, as noted on the paperwork you signed."

Nina screws the cap back on her flask and shamefully puts it back in her bag, without a fight or an apology.

"You can't have alcohol in your bag and continue your appointment. I can throw it away for you, if you want to continue," Ms. Jones says, her exuberance now replaced with sternness.

Nina contemplates her next move for a few seconds, slowly gets up, and leaves Ms. Jones' office and building with her usual long strides. Ms. Jones is not surprised. Many newcomers quit on the first day, but she had hoped Nina would try a little harder.

Nina stands outside the therapist's building, feeling grateful that the session got cut short. She digs back in her bag, ready to finish the flask and move on. She grips the metal in her hand, and the words of all her magicians begin to ring in her ears.

What you're looking for is not here.
What you're looking for is not here.
What you're looking for is not here.

"Maya, what does that mean? Where is 'here'? My flask? This therapist's office, the world?" Nina asks out loud, not caring who hears her. She begins to unscrew the top of the flask, and then twists it back tightly. *Fuck it. She wants me sober, and wants the truth? Fine, I'll give it to her, and see who will be running out onto the street.*

Nina goes to her car and puts the flask in her glove compartment, turns around, and walks back up to the front door of the therapist's building.

Buzz! Buzz!

Ms. Jones opens the door for Nina, smiling. "Well hello, you are back!" she announces in her original happy voice.

"Yes, if that's ok," Nina says humbly, almost as an apology.

"Of course! I assume you won't mind if I check your bag, right?" Ms. Jones is not playing with the rules.

Nina rolls her eyes but agrees. "Yes, right."

Ms. Jones does a quick search and offers Nina a seat back on the orange leather. "Should we start over? Why are you here, Nina?"

"Can I write it for you? I'm better at expressing myself that way."

"Of course! Whatever makes you feel most comfortable."

Nina asks for a piece of paper and begins to write:

All I ever wanted was to be a dancer and a queen, like in fairytales. Join a dance group and marry the king of my dreams. But dreams aren't the same when awake. And my king's cloak doesn't fit. I've been bullied all my life for being pretty, so I don't want to show anyone how smart I am, thinking they will kill me for the double threat. I sabotaged my relationship with the king I finally found, mostly because I can't seem to find my way, and partly because there's a girl I don't reveal. My body aches and quakes when the monsters come,

DANCER IN THE BULLPEN

*and I punish them with a blood magic I keep
secret. I drink to die and write to live. I guess you
can say I'm in limbo.*

"Thank you, Nina!" Ms. Jones is thrilled. "First of all, you're a wonderful writer. And secondly, this is very helpful—a first step to getting to know you. I feel honored you are brave enough to open up to me. I think our time is close to being up today. Do you have any questions for me?"

"That's all?" Nina asks. "You don't have any questions for *me* about the blood magic at least?"

Ms. Jones puts her notepad down and takes her reading glasses off. "I have lots of questions, Nina. But we have time. Are you concerned about what I feel, hearing about your blood magic?"

"Um, yes," Nina responds, craving some type of shocked reaction.

"Nina, I have a couple of folks in my family who possess magic too. One can see the future—not like the fake TV fortune tellers. The *real* future. And the other one can read minds. I know that sounds crazy, but it's the truth. My great aunt, she's pure power. I'm not sure what level yours is on, but you don't spook me."

Nina is the one in shock now. "Oh, ok, well cool. Thank you!" She suddenly feels free as a bird.

Therapy time is over. Nina stands up and stretches her legs, preparing to leave. "Ms Jones, truthfully, I absolutely love African art. I first fell in love with the beautiful people of the Masai tribe. When I was a little girl, my mom kept a large picture book of their people, and I actually did my best to recreate some of their beaded jewelry as an art project."

431

Ms. Jones realizes Nina telling her this is a big deal for her, and she doesn't take the honesty for granted.

***

Almost a year passes, and during that time Nina quietly completes a thirty-day outpatient rehabilitation program while continuing therapy with Ms. Jones.

Eli calls to check on her, ironically right when she first gets out. "Hey, strawberry girl. It's been a minute. What you up to?"

"Oh, you know. Looking for a new place, just finished a rehab program, trying to keep it together," Nina replies.

"No shit, for real?" Eli exclaims, quietly proud of her. "What made you go?"

"Interestingly enough, it was the way my doctor looked at me when I got checked out, making sure your boy didn't give me cooties," Nina says teasingly. "She just gave me this scared look like she knew where I was headed, and I didn't like it at all."

"I can get that," Eli cosigns.

"It's not a game, that rehab. Self-work stuff. But I feel better, I feel healthier," Nina reports with confidence. She's in the kitchen, cutting up lime to put in her citrus sparkling mocktail.

"That's good. You got some meat then on them there bones now? I thought you was gonna fly … no wait, better yet, wilt away when I met you," Eli jokes.

"Not really. I'm still skinny 'cause I'm eating all these fruit and veggies, but in time I'm sure I'll curve back out. But if I don't, it's all good. I don't need to be some Jessica Rabbit chick. I'm really ok with how I am."

DANCER IN THE BULLPEN

"Yeah, so confession. I had a problem like you. That's why I don't drink or smoke no more. I almost got myself killed driving on a highway fucked up."

"Damn babe, that's crazy. Glad you lived to tell the tale. So, we two sober-ass friends."

"I guess, we are."

"Well, that's good, because I don't have any but you."

Nina and Eli are consistent with their long conversations, which evolve into multiple visits by both, traveling up and down the 95. Their unique friendship begins to turn into a different kind of romance, one that's more fueled by honesty, rather than unrealistic expectations. She doesn't hide him, but doesn't flaunt him as her new king either. She is in a healing process and he is a friend with firsthand relatable experience, ready for some good, spontaneous dry fun.

"Hey you, let's go for a ride," Eli suggests one early morning in bed.

"Yeah? I'm down. Miami?" Nina suggests with great excitement

"Oh yeah, let's hit Miami. Can you handle that sixteen-hour drive with me?"

"Yes, let's do it!"

Little do they know, this trip to Miami will change their lives forever.

South Beach is exactly what Nina expects—a Caribbean-style playground of decadent indulgence, seductive music, gorgeous women, and Cuban-influenced cuisine dressed in vibrant colors and flavors. It's feverishly hot, but surprisingly not humid when they arrive at their motel a few streets off the

433

main strip. A generic brand hotel is the cheapest lodging Eli can find that includes parking and still has that upscale ambiance. Everything is snow white: the walls, comforters, and pillows, even the microwave and coffee maker displayed on the white marble countertop.

Nina knows it's crazy to drive over thirty hours back and forth for only one day and night in paradise, but life is short. Eli offers to pay and drive half the way, more than any other man has ever extended to her. Plus, she yearns for the sun full of that vitamin D she needs so much. She has always imagined the stars are brighter and more beautiful in places of warmth and passion. And she is right. Everything in Miami is elevated, including the energy between her and Eli, like a force bigger than them is making all things around them glow. They dance and make love with no barriers for the night, like their lives depend on it.

Nina and Eli are lying in the bed, limp from the intensity of their union. Batches of empanadas are baking and bongos are being beaten in the distance, accompanied by screeching ladies and salsa dancing. The streetlights beam onto Nina's face.

"Damn, I wish I had a camera," Eli says. "It looks like God is touching you or something."

Nina looks up at the golden rays, and even though they are superficial, she knows God is here.

"Before we left, I noticed your tires were a bit worn. So, they'll need to be replaced when you get home," Eli warns, regretting not convincing Nina to choose a flight over a vehicle from South Beach to D.C.

Nina takes a sip of her mocktail and stretches her tan legs on top of the hotel balcony's edge. "I can't keep this car anymore. It's not mine and I need a fresh start."

"That sounds good, Nina," Eli says. "I can help you look for a new car around your way."

"Thank you!" Nina beams. Eli has been such a positive force, and she's happy that he's present.

Eli gets out of bed and walks over to the hotel room kitchenette to get them both chilled bottled waters.

Damn, this brutha is fine though, Nina fantasizes, even though he's standing a few feet away.

"What about your writing?" Eli asks. "I know you got that great coffee gig, but maybe you should try to turn some of them journals into a book, right?"

Nina smiles at Eli's efforts to help grow her. "Yes, you right, Eli. Don't think I'm delusional," she continues, "but I'm contemplating calling this poet that I once had a great conversation with in like fifth or sixth grade. I can't remember. But I always kept her card. Her name is Sarah Sullivan."

"Damn, that's a lot of years. You think she still has the same contact information?"

"I doubt it," Nina says with ease. "But I know my girl, Lisa, can find a way to connect us. She's in the same world. Plus, I can be persistent when I want to be. Sarah told me to look her up when I have a poem or two to share. And I'm thinking I'm ready to open my journals up, reveal what I've always been looking for ... myself."

"Shit girl, get it."

"Thank you, Eli" Nina says, and truly means it. "Now come here and give me a reason to drink that water," she seductively demands.

✳✳✳

"Are you really coming to church with us today, Nina?" Jasmine asks her big sister.

"Yes Jazzy, I'm coming," Nina responds, trying to ignore how grown her sister has gotten. The fact that Jazzy will be starting college in just a couple of months is incredible. She's a straight-A student who is the best version of both Selah and David. Smart, beautiful, witty, and silly.

"Where's your mama and the rest of them at?" Nina asks.

"I dunno, sis, they be all over the place up in here," Jasmine complains. Nina chuckles, remembering the good ol' days.

Selah comes out of her bedroom like a fighter pilot ready for takeoff, flying to the front door, revving up to threaten the family that the ship is rolling out.

"CHILDREN!" Jasmine yells, so every hiding place is reached. She doesn't even have to wait for Selah's lead. She is an old pro, like Nina was in her day.

"Is David coming?" Nina whispers to Jasmine.

"Yes, that's what he said." And just like that, the entire crew is by the front door—David, Jasmine, two cousins, Selah, and Nina.

Selah is relieved to see her firstborn getting better and re-engaging with family. Everyone arrives on time and sits in their usual pews. The choir opens up with a beautiful rendition of "God Moves in a Mysterious Way" by William Cowper. Everyone is standing and singing along, feeling the spirit. The music ends and everyone is asked to sit down. When Nina does, she finds Maya sitting next to her on her right, smiling wide, quick to grab her hand.

Hi! You look a lot better, Maya says.

DANCER IN THE BULLPEN

"Thank you," Nina whispers, not too worried about if someone hears her. Everyone talks out loud in church.

How do you feel, are you feeling like you look? Maya probes.

"Um, yeah. I feel great Maya," Nina responds, curious about why Maya was acting a bit strange. "Are *you* ok?" She squeezes Maya's hand, a hand that's grown bigger now.

I don't really have too much to say today, except that I'm happy you're feeling better and you have to make sure you keep taking care of yourself. It's important.

"Ok, I will. Now shhh, the pastor is about to preach."

I'm shushing, Maya says, not breaking her smile.

Nina looks over, noticing Maya's beautiful green dress and matching green bow wrapped around her high ponytail. Her legs are longer, and her feet easily touch the floor. Nina notices the shape of her knees, which are a little too big for her joints. "Maya, why do your knees look big like mine?"

I don't know, but shhh, the pastor is here.

The pastor begins preaching his sermon on overcoming obstacles, "You can't do it alone. You must communicate with God to get through. Talk to him, lean on him."

After a few minutes, Nina can tell the pastor feels God. And the more he preaches, the closer God gets. "Oh, he's coming," she whispers. "Or, she? I'm not sure which one, I've seen her different ways."

I know, Maya says. *God is both and sometimes neither.*

God is up in the pulpit, standing close to the podium, with his hand on the pastor's shoulder. Nina and God make eye contact and he walks down to her pew and sits next her on the left, but now she looks like a woman, like when on the floor of Nina's apartment bedroom.

"Why do you look like a woman now?" Nina bravely asks.

"Because this is how you must want to see me today," God says.

Nina puts her hand on God's hand, just to see if she can feel her. God responds by putting her other hand on top of Nina's. Nina's body temperature skyrockets, but she's not afraid.

"When you don't see me, it's not because I'm not here. It's just because your faith has weakened. But look at you now." God smiles and Nina is overwhelmed with love.

Jasmine looks back from the pew in front of Nina, confused. "Nina, who you talking to?"

"God," Nina says, and she's not lying.

***

Nina is not feeling so great, but she must do a big training at the coffee shop, downstairs from the corporate office. The coffee company is introducing a brand-new fresh juicing program, which she is a big factor in the development and implementation of. She is excited, as always, to be working with Travis on this project.

But after three hours of straining wheatgrass and beet juice, Nina can't take it anymore, and runs to the restroom to throw up.

"Girl, what's wrong with you?" Travis asks, noticing that Nina has a colorless face. "You not back on that shit, are you?"

Nina tries not to laugh. "No Travis, I'm not," she says with a confident and stern tone.

"Well damn, chile, what you eat?"

"I've had nothing. I don't get it. All I know is all these fuckin' aromas smell like death to me. Maybe I ate something funny yesterday."

"Nina! Girl, when the last time you was bleedin'? You have your period lately?"

Nina starts counting dates in her head. *Wait, what's today? Did I miss my period last month?*

Travis looks at Nina carefully, trying to get a pulse of how she's feeling. "Nina? You ok, darlin'?"

"Oh my god, Travis. I'm having a baby," Nina says, in a bit of a trance. But then she repeats herself. "Oh my god, I'm having a freakin' baby!" She starts jumping up and down with Travis, but then quickly stops. She doesn't want to announce it since she's not certain, and it's way too early to tell people.

You happy, boo, that's good! We having a baby!" Travis sings, sharing in Nina's delight.

Nina halts. "Shit, wait."

"What boo? You ain't taking off no time soon. Ain't gonna be no milking this baby thing starting on damn day one now."

"No stop, for real though. What am I gonna say to Eli? I really like him but, you know, we not quite hot and heavy."

"First of all, you gonna confirm you really pregnant. You could have the damn flu. But if you are, you gonna tell that fine light-skinned giant you having his baby, and he can be a good dad or one of them dudes in the courthouse paying a whole rack of money. Which one he wanna be? A good baby daddy or a deadbeat one?" Travis preaches, with all the head rollin' included.

"Travis, I was just asking how should I tell him, over the phone or in person? You such a drama queen," Nina teases.

"Takes one to know one, bitch," Travis whispers

"Hey Nina! What's up?"
"Hey Javi!" Nina responds, genuinely happy to see him.
"What are you doing down here? I thought you moved way up the ladder to executive corporate."
"I did, I'm just down here training these good folks. What are you doing around these parts? Another meeting? You want your usual, I can make it for you," Nina spits, a bit nervous at the thought he keeps up with Charlotte, and maybe even still goes out with her.
"Yeah, I'll have my usual, thanks," Javier responds, still unable to resist Nina's charms.
"Maybe we can go get a drink sometime soon."
Nina hesitates. It's been awhile since someone has asked her out for a drink. Mostly because she keeps away from bars altogether. "How about a smoothie or a coffee? I'm not really drinking these days."
Nina finishes making Javier's soy milk latte with extra foam and gives it to him in a fancy cup, so he can sit with her a minute for a quick catch up. She leads him to a corner table by the front window of the store.
"So, you not smoking either?" Javier asks, like Nina's fun meter has dropped down to a zero.
"I'm not."
"Shit, wow. Good for you," Javier congratulates.
A wave of nausea is coming back around, but Nina doesn't know if it's her new baby, or her old friend Fear. But she can't take it anymore. "Have you spoken to Charlotte, or seen her? Know where she is?" she asks, aching with curiosity. "I tried to call her recently, but she doesn't answer or return my calls."

"I haven't seen her lately. But I have spoken to her. Maybe a few weeks ago?"

"Ok, so what's up with her?" *What the fuck? It's like pulling teeth from this man today.*

"She graduated college miraculously, not only because it was tough getting her GED, as you know, but because she really got hooked on that H."

"Damn, she was on that coke strong when we disconnected, but I would never think she'd be on that H craziness. So then what?" Nina pushes. She wants to know everything.

"Then her parents dragged her kicking and screaming to rehab. She of course got out without completing the program, but from what she told me three weeks ago, she completed the second run."

"Ok, that's good."

"She did say something interesting though, when we spoke last."

"What?" Nina is literally sitting on the edge of her seat, and Javier knows it. Her break has been long over.

"You must have left a small stack of those black-and-white books in her house. I guess she's been reading them. Some of them have a lot about some blood magic, which she seems fascinated by. Are you writing like a sci-fi book or something?"

"Why, is that what she said she thought my journal entries were?" Travis is watching Nina interrogate Javier and motions her to stop the obsession, knowing corporate will be looking for her soon. "Javier, I have to go. Let's try to do that smoothie date, and if you see or talk to Charlotte …"

Nina stops and looks at her friendly ex-lover, and says, "Just tell her I wish her the best." She doesn't deny she still feels a sting of loss with Charlotte, but she knows that like herself, everyone needs the space to move on and grow into who you're meant to be.

But fuck that, I need my journals back. After I find out if I'm really having a baby, I'll go find her, Nina promises herself. Subconsciously, she is in no rush. Though there's sensitive material in those composition books, she is aware that if she rushes to retrieve them, she's rushing the last reason to see Charlotte again.

***

Nina tells Eli over the phone because, after taking four pregnancy tests, she can't wait to let him know in person. "I understand this is not in the plans, but I am open to try to love this baby together if your heart so moves you," she requests.

"Ahhh shit, I'm gonna be a dad!" Eli is thrilled that Nina is pregnant, despite the complicated circumstances of not knowing each other well, the distance, the potential disappointed parents, and lack of money to raise a child. "I can't believe you gave me that 'You can do whatever you feel comfortable with' speech. Of course I'm going to take care of my strawberry girl—I mean, Queen and our baby. I'm gonna make sure y'all happy," he says with pride, and she believes him, though she's not needy for it.

"I'm going to be a grandmother?" Selah asks, as she almost drives Nina and herself off the road because of her pure excitement and joy.

"Besides actually raising the munchkin, we've got the hard part out of the way—telling my parents. I'm getting a nice apartment close by so you can babysit one day," Nina says, giggling at her mother's reaction.

Mike, despite his strict ideology and religious ways, feels a newborn is a blessing from God and Nina is still simply his daughter who is going to have a baby. "I love you, princess, and I know this baby is a miracle. But please think about marriage. You have a child now, and you want to do the right thing."

"Slow down, Daddy. Let's embrace one surprise without creating another for now. Eli and I are building a base. That needs to stick first." Nina pauses, and then speaks with conviction. "I no longer need to have a king, or be someone's queen as the end-all be-all. My priority now is my heir."

The baby news spreads to the rest of the family and friends like wildfire, and there's not one person who's not anticipating the arrival of the firstborn of the firstborn. Even Malcolm calls Nina to congratulate her, when he hears of her bundle of joy on the way.

"I'm really happy for you, Nina, really," Malcolm says. "I know we went through a tough time, but I think about what would have happened if we actually got married and had a bunch of babies."

"It may have been worse, right?" Nina questions.

"I think so. There would have been more people onboard that drama train," Malcolm jokes.

"Love is sometimes not what we want it to be, but what it just is," Nina says softly.

"Hey, while I have you, you still writing in those journals of yours?"

"Yeah, I am. I really need to do something with them. I have so many at this point, I can't even keep track. I'm trying to find this woman. I think I told you about her, Sarah Sullivan.

She's a big deal these days, racking in a shit ton of awards, so I'm just hoping she can get me a job in the industry. A published book will just be a bonus."

"Well, I'll be crossing my fingers for you. I'm sure you'll make great moves."

"Thanks Malcolm. And thank you for loving me. I pray you find all the happiness in the world."

Nina hangs up the phone and lets out a big exhale. *Closure feels good.*

***

Nina's belly is ballooning fast, so Eli's move to D.C. in her sixth month is almost pushing it. Though he has a job locked in, with plans of going to school at night, renting his house out in South Carolina has been a small bonus of income. Eli and Nina could have never imagined it serving as a double blessing, as one of her great cousins—who Grandma Daisy has been trying to locate in South Carolina for some time now—has rented the house. Because Eli seems to know everyone in most neighboring towns, he is able to be a great resource to Grandma Daisy.

"How crazy is it we found him and his daughter at a time they needed a place to stay, at a low rate?" Nina gleams, happy she's able to pay some of Grandma Daisy's love back to the tribe who strengthened her.

Transitioning to a foreign place, sacrificing being close to his family to build a new one—Eli has done it all. Nina has known him for a little over a year, but in this short period of time, she feels safer than she ever has before. Ms. Jones says that's not all Eli's doing; it's the work Nina has put in.

"Let me take care of those swollen feet," Eli offers. Nina is lying back on the arm of the living room couch, watching him unpack everything into their new apartment. But he can tell her feet are throbbing, and the doctor has said in addition to less salt in Nina's diet, good old-fashioned foot rubs will work wonders.

"Thanks babe," Nina whines with gratitude, and allows Eli to swing her body around so her feet are elevated on the couch's arm. "I'm a fucking whale," she complains.

"But you're a sexy, beautiful, creative whale," Eli says, grinning at his own funny.

Nina is not offended; she loves how Eli plays, keeping it sweet while keeping it real.

Eli walks over to the phone mounted on the kitchen wall. "Who's calling our house phone already?" Nina questions.

"Hey baby, it's a woman named Sarah Sullivan on the phone." Eli mouths the words, *This that famous poet right?*

And Nina mouths back, *Yes!* She wobbles over to the phone, and answers it like she's not struggling to catch her breath. "This is Nina."

"Hi, this is Nina Abadie?" Ms. Sullivan questions, to make sure she is talking to the brilliant little girl she met over a decade ago.

"Yes, this is she," Nina responds in her most sophisticated voice, watching Eli roll his eyes at her "white girl" voice.

"Nina, it's taken me some time to find you. But I'm so glad I did. I hope you don't mind. Your mother, Selah, gave me your new home number when I called for you at her house."

"Hi Ms. Sullivan, and no it's not a problem," Nina says, feeling a little excited and nervous.

"Please, call me Sarah."

"Ok Sarah."

"The reason I'm calling you, Nina, is I know you have been trying to reach me, and I've been so busy with a book tour, which I'm sure you're aware of. But when you sent me those four journals and allowed me into your mind, I had to stop everything and call you. We must meet so we can talk about your future as an author."

Eli pulls up a chair for Nina, so she can rest her back and feet while trying to understand what the hell this woman is talking about. "I'm sorry, Sarah, I think I may be confused, or there may be a mistake. I haven't sent you any of my journals." She is racking her brain. A*m I trippin'? Was my first trimester so nauseating I just lost track, what the hell?*

"Well, I'm pretty confident this is your work, as it's the same handwriting and signature. You think someone sent them for you? Your husband, or mom, maybe? It really doesn't matter though, because they are all amazing. You dance on the paper."

Sarah's affirmation has Nina sweating and heart racing.

Buzzz … Buzzz …

Nina tries to focus on Sarah's words, but gets distracted when a blue hummingbird flies up to the window, perching itself outside on the ledge. She doesn't hear herself talking. She's on autopilot, captivated by the familiar vision outside the window. "Shit, ok! I mean—sorry—yes, I will meet you! And thank you!"

"No, you're right, 'shit' is an appropriate response," Sarah chuckles. "Do you think you can meet me this week or the next? If not, it will have to wait until I'm back from Spain."

Nina glances up at her abeng, which she still keeps on the highest shelf in her apartment, regal and elevated on a handcrafted iron display stand. Surrounding it is a medley of photos

DANCER IN THE BULLPEN

of her ancestors, hurricane candles, and marble incense burners. The abeng begins to tremble.

"Oh, what's in Spain?" Nina questions, sitting straight up in the chair and cradling her belly, trying to ignore the chaos in her apartment and Eli's confusion about it.

Sara replies, "I'm working on a story about the run of the bulls."

"Ouch! Good Lord, child ..." Nina winces and clutches her belly. She watches the abeng unlock itself from the wire hooks that usually keep it secure, and it drops to her feet.

What the fuck?

"Are you ok?" Sarah responds with concern.

"Oh yes, sorry. This little one I'm carrying just kicked me for the first time—hard!" Nina looks down at her belly and caresses it lovingly. She laughs. "Well, bring out the red cape.

The matador is in the ring!"

EPILOGUE

Nina

Summer was flirting with spring, trying to convince him to let her in, with flowers and sunbeams on her back. I removed my welcome mat, clinging to heavy rain clouds and cool breezes that kept my limbs from swelling to obesity. My ankles were those of elephants, missing only the wrinkles at the base and the light-gray tone. You were calm, nestled happily in the cup of my pelvis, moving only to let me know when you were famished, until the last seven days before your due date.

"Dr. Slate, please can we bring him out a few days early?" I pleaded. "You say his heart and lungs are developed and he's now just cooking to plump. Well, I think he's fattened enough, because his feet don't fit in my body properly. I'm holding his toes with the palms of my hands, making sure he doesn't break anything."

"Oh Ms. Abadie, I'm sorry, but I think we need to wait until the baby is scheduled to come, just in case there are a few days of growing we are unaware of."

"You're right, Dr. Slate. He's just a heavy little thing."

"Not much longer now."

Your father laughs. "Oh my drama mama, our sweet baby girl is just making sure you know she's there, since she's so calm and quiet like her daddy. Aren't you a dancer? I thought that entire core and pelvis of yours is made of steel."

"Why you keep saying 'baby girl'? I think it's obvious we're having a baby boy," I said.

"No, I sense girl energy," Eli responded. "She only moves when she wants to, but when she does, it looks like she's dancing in your stomach. She can't resist the beats I thump in the car for her."

"If you keep that up, she'll turn out to be a female rapper."

"What's wrong with female rappers? Aren't they just poets, like you always say?" I couldn't fight your father on that point. He was right, so I had to give credit where credit was due. "Maybe she'll get a book deal after sharing her writing with the world, like you just did, beautiful."

I leaned over and kissed your father's bald head and said, "Thank you for loving me while I'm big as a whale."

"Whales are gorgeous creatures," he said, rubbing your feet through my belly, to get them to higher position for me.

***

It was a bright sunny morning when I arrived at the hospital to bring you into this world. Your father and I made the mistake of coaching you back off my pelvis days before, because suddenly it seemed you were not quite ready to join us. I could feel you snuggled between my flesh and internal ocean, warm and content. "Why would anyone want to leave this?" I challenged.

Dr. Slate welcomed us happily, but felt I was too calm to be preparing for the birth of a miracle. "Nina, on a scale of 1–10, what is your pain level?" she asked.

While fiddling with my hospital room television remote, I said, "Um, maybe a 3."

"Ok, I'll be back in a bit." Dr. Slate scurried away to talk to a nurse.

"Babe, you should go ahead and get something to eat while you can," I suggested to your father.

"Ok baby, you need anything?"

"No, I can't eat, remember? But I'm going to need some of those donuts from Krispy Kreme across the street after this baby comes, that's for sure."

Dr. Slate came back faster than I expected.

"Is everything ok?" I asked.

"Yes, of course!" she responded with certainty. "We just need to help the process along. It looks like this baby doesn't want to join us."

Dr. Slate had swept her hair up in a top knot since the last time I'd seen her. She'd never done that before. It must have been a long night of challenging births.

"I am going to take a look, and then you'll feel some pressure, but it's ok," said Dr. Slate.

"Alright," I said, having no idea exactly what she was doing.

Dr. Slate put her head almost under my gown and put her hand inside me, to feel where you were. I could feel you dodging her, using those little feet to kick her fingers, unknowingly giving your mama pain.

When Dr. Slate came up from down under, I asked, "What did you do?"

"I broke your water. Now, things will move along much faster."

"What's that on your neck—a bruise?" I asked.

"What? Where?" Dr. Slate asked, rolling her stool in closer next to me. "This right here?" She tilted her neck to provide a better view.

I gasped.

"What's wrong, Nina?" Dr. Slate asked with concern.

"I'm sorry, the baby kicked me. But wow, that's a beautiful hummingbird tattoo. Do you like hummingbirds?" I asked, squinting at the bird that had followed me for years.

"No, not really. It's strange. Almost a year ago, I had this incredible urge to get another tattoo, and a drawing of this hummingbird was calling my name. So, I just had to get it. I typically hide her under my hair. But I felt like letting her breathe today. I'm glad you like it." She promised to come back soon and then walked out the door.

Dr. Slate was barely out of the room when I felt you gripping the walls of my uterus with your fingers, squeezing and releasing and then squeezing again.

I panicked. "Why did I send Eli to get food?" I immediately called your father and told him to hurry; I was having his baby.

"Mama, don't rush Daddy, I'm not ready yet."

"What?" I asked, even though I knew it was you.

"It's me, Mommy."

"You're a girl?" I questioned.

"Yes, of course I am, silly. I'm not sure why you thought I was a boy. Daddy knew the truth."

"Wait, talk to me some more. I know your voice," I said, trying to figure out where I had heard it before. I had my hospital gown rolled up to reveal my belly, so I could hear and feel you better. I was holding you through my flesh, feeling the vibration of your sweet familiar voice. "Baby, are you ok, are you happy?"

"Yes Mommy. I love you, and I've always loved you. I can tell you love me, because it's nice in here. I don't want to come out right now though, Mama. It's so warm and quiet, I just need more time."

DANCER IN THE BULLPEN

I rubbed my belly, responding, "I can't wait to see you, don't be afraid. We can't hide forever, sweetie. We can't grow where it's always warm. We need to experience different seasons to grow, and Mommy's belly is only one season. I promise though, your daddy and I will protect you."

"I don't know, Mommy, the world seems pretty loud and scary out there. I'm not a dancer like you. When you were little you danced a lot, but sometimes people didn't see you no matter how much you moved. Or they were mean to you, charging at you like a big bull, huffing and puffing, digging their hoofs into the dirt, making your eyes burn from the dust. You'd jump out of the way, but sometimes you'd get trapped in the bullpen. When it got really scary, you had your own magic, and made the most beautiful blood appear in the darkest places."

"How do you know that? How did you know about my magic?" I was shocked.

"Because I was there, Mama. I was there the entire time. When you was getting bullied, and when you wrote all those amazing poems and stories. I was there when you found yourself in Jamaica, even if you lost your way a bit afterwards. I was there when you were looking for a king in all those wild and crazy guys. I was there with you every step of the way, because I chose you. And I love you no matter what. What you have been looking for has been here all of the time."

I started sobbing, realizing you had been with me for so long. But I quickly sucked up the tears, realizing you were more scared than me now.

"Mommy, I still don't want to come out. It's different to be really out there. Why can't I just stay where I've been for you?" Maya asked.

Realizing I had to be strong for you, I said, "I'm going to sing to you, baby girl. Come to your mama. You must know I will always be what you are looking for too."

So, in the midst of my pain, I sang the sweet song your Grandma Selah sang to me in her belly:

*"Baby Poo, Baby Poo, Baby Poo, I love you!
Baby Poo, Baby Poo, Baby Poo, I love you!"*

"Ahhh!" I screamed. It's as if the song opened the gate to the bullpen, inviting you out to dance. As soon as I finished the song, you made good on your promise and prepared your journey out. "Ahhh, oh baby girl, please, be easy, not so much."

I wasn't as brave as your grandma Selah, and I needed some help for the pain. By the time the anesthesiologist gave me the medication, your father and grandmother returned just in time for the waiting game.

"Nina, I thought you were about to have the baby, why are you so calm and almost high?" your father questioned.

"They're keeping my pain bearable until my body is ready to push. I have a way to go before I'm completely dilated."

"Ok, well. I heard you now believe we having a girl," your father said with pride. "So what should we name her?"

"Well, we're going to give her your last name ... Love."

"I like that."

"Also, the word 'grace' refers to the peace of God given to the restless. Our baby is that gift," I said, picking out your middle name. Your dad agreed.

Before we could decide on your first name, you were pushing your way out of me. Grandma Selah had one of my legs high by my ear, breathing in rhythmic unison with me. Your father's hands were light as feathers, so overwhelmed by the awareness of your leaps out into the open that he could barely hold my leg up.

You were determined, and fierce, allowing me only ten minutes to push you out, like Grandma Selah did with me. Your swift power put my body in shock, and I began to shake and quake, rattling from head to toe. The nurse gave me some medication to balance me, while they took you to clean all the blood you were soaked in.

"Oh my god, Nina, there is just so much blood," your dad said.

"What do you mean?" I asked your father, panicking because I looked down and saw that I was sitting in the Red Sea.

"Is this from me or my baby?" I asked Dr. Slate. You could tell she was in awe of the scene herself.

"I believe it's actually from the both of you. It looks like she made you hemorrhage profusely, and maybe the placenta or umbilical cord ruptured? But I honestly don't see the source of any of it. And this shade of red is alarming, but both of your levels are good. She is getting cleaned up now and will be brought to you."

"I am not in any pain."

"That's a good thing, Ms. Abadie. We'll run some tests on both of you once you both recover a bit."

Your dad was still woozy from the sight of the power, but he was working his way back to strength.

Finally, they finished cleaning me up and your nurse placed you in my arms. My heart almost exploded from the joy. "Oh baby, what should we call you, now that we have your second and third names set?" I dropped my face down close to yours, so I could smell the scent of your innocence and baby powder. I gasped when I looked at your face.

Maya? Your face was the spitting image of my invisible friend, who I'd journeyed with all my life, battling the bull together. The bull you had just killed, without explanation. You're a genius. My sweet baby girl. I caressed the mole on your right temple that mirrored mine, then touched mine so you could see I recognized who you were. You smiled in my arms, *gurgling with joy. I unwrapped your swaddle just a little, to rub your knees that I touched at church not so long before. Maya, my invisible friend, preparing to be my sweet baby girl.*

Because of you and me, the bull was defeated.

"Eli, I think we have it now." *I whispered your name into his ear.* "What do you think?"

"Yes, it's perfect."

"Can you please go out to the waiting room and announce our daughter's full name to our family and friends?" I asked Eli. Everyone was there: Selah, David, Dionne, Jasmine, even extended family and friends I didn't think would be able to make it.

Eli walked out to a crowd of eager people and smiled with pure joy. "Tonight, our baby girl, Maya Grace Love, was born ready to conquer the world."

Postscript

Nina and Maya stare into each other's eyes, basking in mother and daughter love. There is no one else in the room, even if there really is.

"Oh, my sweetheart, you are glowing," Nina whispers, snuggling with her new bundle, blinded by bright love. She is now certain that she has always been Queen, and the seat beside her was not meant for a king, but for the princess, who now illuminates the room.

The nurse raises her voice to regrettably interrupt the two. "Ms. Abadie, I'm so sorry to bother you, but your sister Charlotte has just arrived. She's asking to see you. Should I send her back?"

Acknowledgements

Thank you, Lisa Pegram, for your incomparable talent and professionalism. I am in awe of how you saw past the words on every page, recognized my story's purpose, and found ways to make it shine brighter. You are my literary ambassador, and I am proud to call you my editor and friend.

Thank you to all the Jaded Ibis Press members for your expertise in bringing my work to life, and helping it shine. I don't take the opportunity for granted.

Thank you, Mariona Lloreta, for creating such a magical cover, fully capturing my vision in epic art form. When I met you during a poetry forum that showcased your vibrant art, I could have never imagined you would one day elevate my work, and perfectly interpret my story's heart.

I am grateful to my beta readers—Laura, Imani, St. Clair, and Mari. Thank you for taking the time to read my manuscript and providing valuable feedback and support, which forced me to use my vulnerability in the best way.

Thank you to my literary church family—my luminous Sunday writing inspiration. Words can't express how appreciative I am for the weekly affirmation, lessons learned, and personal growth in our safe space community.

Thank you to many of my school teachers, counselors, writers, and advisors for seeing my potential and pushing me toward it. I will never forget the constant stream of "Why not?"

Thank you to all my dear friends and persistent cheerleaders, who eagerly listened to all my endless tales and anecdotes. "Girl, you should write a book," many of you said. The confidence feed was priceless.

Thank you to my ancestors for your guidance and love from the spiritual realm, especially my two beautiful grandmothers, Grandad, Grandpa, Uncle Steve, and my brother Scott. I feel you with me every day.

I am grateful to my blended family throughout the U.S. and West Africa for your unwavering love and encouragement. Dad, thank you for your warm spirit and heartfelt prayers. Mom, you are forever my hero. Thank you for loving me.

Saviour, I know it would have been easier if I had just made a book of poetry from one of my journals, but you know I had to do this project first, and you supported me every step. Thank you for all your sacrifices and patience during the many late nights of writing.

Your high fives and strong shoulders to cry on kept me steadfast in my journey. I am blessed to have you as my husband.

Thank you to my daughter, Jada Milan, for being proud of me, and being one of the catalysts of my self-discovery. I'm happy you watched me strive for something, overcome challenges, and triumph in this way. Watching you walk and grow in your path has helped me walk in mine. Thank you for choosing me as your mom. I love you.

To the Divine, thank you for all the beauty in the universe and for protecting me in peace and in chaos.

Thank you to all my readers for taking the time to experience my magical story, which I hope helped you recognize yours. I value your interest and support.

And finally, to my younger self. Thank you for your courage and determination. You did it!

Printed in the USA
CPSIA information can be obtained
at www.ICGtesting.com
LVHW010029220724
786129LV00029B/316

9 781938 841279